Critical acclaim for Robert Inman's *Home Fires Burning*

"This is an old-fashioned novel—dramatic, teeming with incidents and epiphanies, not ideas and abstractions . . . full of the juice of life. Inman is very much a southern writer. As in William Faulkner and Flannery O'Connor, Reynolds Price and Peter Taylor, place is conjured with precision and poetry. I'd wager it's one of the best American novels of 1987."

The Philadelphia Inquirer

"Here is a novel that stands head and shoulders above the crowd. *Home Fires Burning* has a quiet power that grows out of its people. Inman has written a wonderfully readable novel. In fact it is the best small-town southern novel since *To Kill a Mockingbird*."

Atlanta Journal-Constitution

"Liberally leavened with irony and humor . . . Inman has produced a deeply felt, authentic work of art. The characters of *Home Fires Burning* will keep the coals of our memories aglow for a long time."

The Charlotte Observer

HOME FIRES BURNING

ROBERT INMAN

BALLANTINE BOOKS • NEW YORK

Library of Congress Catalog Card Number: 86-20149

ISBN 0-345-34076-6

This edition published by arrangement with Little, Brown and Company, Inc.

Manufactured in the United States of America

First Ballantine Books Edition: February 1988

To Paulette, Larkin, and Lee

Though leaves are many, the root is one:
Through all the lying days of my youth
I swayed my leaves and flowers in the sun;
Now I may wither into the truth.

—YEATS

BOOK
ONE

ONE

T_{HE} black horse was first to know. It came to him across the frost of the open field, the smell of unfamiliar men. The horse nudged the air and the sinews of his neck ridged like steel cables. He snorted almost without sound and twin vapors of breath hung for a moment like ghosts in the sharp air. A tremor rippled down the muscles of his flanks. He took a half-step backward before the gray-clad rider dug his knees into the horse's side and rubbed the long smooth neck with a gloved hand.

The horseman was a powerfully built stump of a man. Though a superb rider, he seemed to sit precariously on the black horse, riding high in the saddle with its stirrups made short for his runty legs.

There was nothing of the dandy in Captain Finley Tibbetts. He was simply dressed in light gray britches and tunic, the twin bars of his rank embossed in gold on his shoulders, a brief curl of yellow braid at the cuffs of his sleeves. The plain leather cavalryman's boots came almost to his knees, and he wore a dark gray campaign hat cocked low over his intense bushy eyebrows. The only adornment to his uniform was the great curving saber at his side. It was encased in a plain, issue scabbard, but the blade itself was a marvel of silver radiance, intricately engraved with scrollwork and the name of its maker, E. Duddingham of London. In the hands of Captain Finley Tibbetts, it was an instrument of judgment.

He sat cockily in the saddle, reining in the nervous movement of the horse, head turning this way and that as he listened for a wayward noise from the copse of sycamores across the field. The shredding stump of a cigar was clamped in one corner of his mouth, an exclamation point to his sumptuous, curving black moustache.

To his left, and half a horse-length to the rear, sat his adjutant, the huge red-faced Irishman Muldoon, whose saber stroke could decapitate a man in the flick of a wrist. Muldoon was utterly dedicated, awesomely fearless. Once, in an attack on a Federal position atop a small rise, when Captain Finley had been dehorsed by a ball in his side, Muldoon had leaped from his own mount, grabbed up the fallen captain, and carried him pickaback the rest of the way up the hill with Captain Finley cursing and waving his saber. At the summit, when Muldoon had dumped him atop a pile of bluecoated bodies in the midst of the conquered Federal position, Captain Finley had doffed the battered gray campaign hat and said, "Lieutenant Muldoon, you make an admirable steed!" and fainted.

To Captain Finley's right was the boy they called Young Scout, mounted on his own chestnut, thin shoulders hunched against the cold of dawn.

And to their rear, deep in the pine thicket, hidden in the half-light and mist, were the hundred men of Captain Finley's Lighthorse Cavaliers—handpicked for horsemanship, keen eye, steady hand, and fearless spirit; dispatched upon only the most critical of missions. They and their captain reported only to General Lee.

This morning, they were the vanguard of Lee's grand assault on McClellan's right flank. For days, the two great armies had been poised like beasts, eyeing each other warily, each waiting for a precious moment of vulnerability to spring and kill. Captain Finley's mission: to lure the Federals into a false step; to create, with the chaos and confusion of a lightning feint, the illusion of a thrust against the flank of McClellan's forces near Gaines Mill. When McClellan responded with a counter-thrust, Lee would strike, snipping off the Federal advance as if pruning a tree limb, pouring through the breach in the bluecoat lines to divide the right flank and roll McClellan back along a wide front. Lee might, with speed and daring, drive the Federals clear back across the Rappahannock, perhaps even put them to such rout that they would leave the city of Washington, the Great Jewel, open to capture.

The Lighthorse Cavaliers were the linchpin of the entire enterprise. Now they must discern the enemy, mark him, draw him out. And thus they waited in their saddles under the pines, anonymous in the gray cocoon of beginning day. At first light there was no wind, only the dry marrow-chilling cold that seemed to grow more bitter with dawn. The day would be clear and blood would freeze on the ground. They waited, disciplined and patient, for sound to confirm what the black horse had already told them.

It came, finally. A clink of metal—perhaps the tap of saber against belt buckle or bayonet against rifle barrel. A careless sound, made by undisciplined troops. (The trappings of Captain Finley's own men and mounts were wrapped with cloth to muffle noise.) The sound would have gone unnoticed among the men in the copse of sycamores three hundred yards across the white field, but it carried like a shot on the brittle air to the pines where the Lighthorse Cavaliers waited. The black horse between Captain Finley's legs was quiet. There were no more of his kind among the sycamores across the way; the smells were all man-smells.

Captain Finley heard the sound. He studied the horse, and then he leaned far to his left and whispered to Muldoon, "Infantry." He smiled, the great slash of his moustache lifting as he showed large, even teeth yellowed by cigar juice. Muldoon turned to stare at the captain, and Young Scout could see the thought pass between them.

Infantry: saber against bayonet. Spread the troop and strike in a rush along the broad blue front of the enemy. Ride howling like demons to be among them quickly in a frenzy of steel and pounding horse, slashing their ranks and opening their bodies. Then wheel and roll up their flanks. Strike until they are panicked and fleeing and then give chase to put them to rout with the terror of whistling steel at their backs and the conviction that an entire corps of madmen is at their heels. That done, withdraw at a canter, stepping around the bodies.

Thus, the trap is set. Smarting from the wound, McClellan will strike back in force. And Lee will be waiting.

Captain Finley leaned and spoke again, his voice soft. "The damfools will sound us out first. McClellan's boys are in the mold of their master. He's like a goddamned old woman who tests the water with her big toe before she steps in. He wastes his artillery, probing and poking and letting every damned soul in the country know where he is. So we'll get a little shot and shell, Muldoon, because whoever is across the field yonder will want to know if there's anything lurking here in the pine thicket before they tiptoe out. But we must hold fast and not give ourselves away. No matter what."

Muldoon nodded. "If a man bolts, I'll shoot the bastard."

"If a man bolts, I'll shoot you, you Irish jackal."

Muldoon grinned. "They'll hold, Captain." And he turned and signaled with a broad wave of his arm for the troop to disperse among the pines. They moved away from each other, and it was their most disciplined act, for men abhor dying alone. They were all upright in their saddles now, sensing danger, testing the stiffness in their limbs, shifting their sore rumps, watching Captain Finley, broad-shouldered and erect on the black horse.

Presently, it came. The first shell passed over their heads with a high moan and burst a hundred yards to their rear, shredding pine trees, and the men of the Lighthorse Cavaliers reined in hard on their mounts and felt the cold knot of fear in their own guts. The single round was followed by another, then another, walking like a man with a cracking whip—first left, then right, then slowly forward toward Captain Finley's troop. The shells came faster now, one every four or five seconds, one explosion spawning the next. The horses began to dance and shy in terror, and their riders dug in their knees, still watching Captain Finley. He gave them his back and stared out at the open field.

Muldoon and the boy held fast at Captain Finley's side. Young Scout glanced at the adjutant and saw the faint glint of perspiration on his broad forehead. The noise of the shells mushroomed and the boy could feel the concussions pushing at his back and the bile rising in his throat. He had the sudden urge to dismount and shield himself with the chestnut, but he fought it. He heard a piercing scream to his rear, swallowed immediately by the roar of an explosion as a round erupted in the midst of the troopers. Smoke and dust were swirling about them now, so thick he could barely see the two other riders to his front. And then Captain Finley turned to him and shouted over the din, "Tighten your bowels, Young Scout! The Federals are sending us a purgative!" He laughed, throwing his head back and baring his teeth. He spoke again, but the words were lost in the terrible noise. The shells were upon them.

———

In the clear cold morning air above, Billy Benefield listened to the roar of the finely tuned Pratt and Whitney engine throbbing at the nose of his bi-winged Curtiss Stearman and thought of the smooth freckled thighs of Alsatia Renfroe.

Billy admitted to himself again, unashamedly, that he would renounce all—family honor, birthright, pilot's wings, the chance to glory himself in battle—for one more deliciously sinful moment between Alsatia's thighs, as he had had under the banana tree by the courthouse with summer midnight breathing on his bare bottom. Why else would he have finagled and connived for six months for the opportunity to make his cross-country flight over the sacred spot where Alsatia lay warm and tousled abed? Just beyond the blur of the propeller, Billy could see the smooth freckled thighs of Alsatia Renfroe opening, opening. He moaned. Oh, Alsatia. Oh, rapture.

Billy flew on past the open field and the woods beyond, then banked to the left and made a broad sweep around the perimeter of the town, pointing his left wing at the slate roof of the courthouse on its neat brown square of frosted lawn. From the open cockpit of the Stearman he could see the pecan tree at the corner of the courthouse lawn where the pinochle players gathered, the storefronts along the courthouse square with their awnings beetle-browed over the sidewalks, a lighted window at the radio station upstairs over the Farmers Mercantile Bank where Ollie Whittle would be giving the early morning market report and the weather forecast, another at Biscuit Brunson's cafe where the breakfast crowd would be gathering. He could see the streets marching off smartly at right angles, making other squares beyond the business district, the stubby brick steeple of the Methodist Church and the slim spire of the Baptist, squat frame and brick houses huddling under the bare winter branches of elms and oaks and maples.

The sun was beginning to nudge over the horizon now and it sent pinpricks of orange and pink through the limbs of the trees and inflamed the wings of the Stearman. Billy breathed deeply and felt the icy air sear his lungs, even through the wool scarf he had wrapped around his face and over his leather flight helmet. He reached deep into his clothing—under the fur-lined flight jacket and the wool shirt and three undershirts and union suit—and felt again, for reassurance, the silk handkerchief next to his breast. Again, the hot vision of Alsatia made him flush.

He looked down and saw far below him his own home, three blocks from the courthouse, the forbidding brown brick with green canvas awnings over the windows and a towering magnolia in the front yard—the house where his father, Mayor Rosh Benefield, would still be sleeping the sleep of a fat man this Saturday morning in the canopied bed next to his wife, Ideal.

The Stearman came full circle over the town and Billy banked to the right and set the nose toward the horizon, following Partridge Road to where the houses began to thin out and the pavement ended. The road snaked on past the copse of sycamores, the frost-covered field, the pine thicket, and then past Jake Tibbetts's house with the huge spreading oak tree in the front yard. It ended finally just beyond Tunstall Renfroe's house, where Alsatia slept now in the upstairs back left-corner bedroom. It was time.

Billy reached again deep into his clothing and plucked the silk handkerchief from its warm spot next to his breast. He removed the leather flight glove from his right hand and placed the glove on the floor of the cockpit. Then, holding the Stearman on course with the control stick between his knees, the handkerchief open in the gloved palm of his left hand, Billy unbuttoned the fly of his trousers and opened himself to the morning. With the throb of the Pratt and Whitney loud in his ears and the vision of Alsatia Renfroe swimming before him, he stroked and gave birth with a bellow. Oh, Alsatia! Oh, Rapture!

He was now several miles past Alsatia's house. He composed himself, then turned the plane sharply on its wing and throttled forward, bearing down on the house like a glide bomber. The white frame siding, the galvanized tin roof, the wisp of smoke curling out of the chimney from Tunstall Renfroe's early morning coal fire, the Packard parked in the side yard, grew large over the fat nose of the Stearman. He leveled off at five hundred feet, and as he roared over the house he dropped the handkerchief far out over the side and pulled the nose of the plane up sharply. He banked and saw the handkerchief fluttering toward the Renfroes' side yard. He waggled the wings of the Stearman, then headed east, into the sun.

In the pines, the morning was in pieces. Young Scout gasped for breath, the air sucked from his lungs, his head dizzied by the awful roar of the shellbursts and the choking smell of the acrid smoke. To his right a riderless horse bolted toward the open field at the edge of the pines, and Captain Finley whipped out his pistol and shot the animal dead with a single bullet to the brain. The horse dropped soundlessly. Captain Finley holstered the pistol and grabbed the reins of Young Scout's chestnut, pulling boy and horse to him. "Take a message to our battery," he shouted in Young Scout's ear. "They are yonder in enfilade." The captain pointed back through the blasted pines where their own artillery, five small field pieces, had been dug in beyond a low rise. "Tell the gunners we have not revealed ourselves to the enemy. The Federals will advance when the barrage is lifted, thinking the woods are undefended. They are to wait until the Federals are fifty yards from our front and then give their britches the grapeshot. We'll strike on the heels of their thunder!" He pushed the horse away and Young Scout wheeled and dug his heels into the chestnut. "Ride hard, Young Scout. Godspeed!" he heard Captain Finley shout at his back.

Horse and boy pounded through the scattering ranks of the Lighthorse Cavaliers with shrapnel whistling through the tops of the trees near their heads, lopping off pine branches with a wicked snapping sound. The ground trembled with the impact of the shells. The noise was deafening. Young Scout gagged on the bitter stench of burning powder. He leaned forward in the saddle and wrapped his arms around the chestnut's neck, trusting the horse to keep a steady course. On either side he could see the blur of horseflesh, hear the curses of men and the agonized whine of their mounts—tatters of sound shredded by the roar of cannon shot.

Then suddenly he was out of it, bursting into the open at the rear of the pine thicket beyond the barrage, galloping breakneck toward the rise where the battery of field howitzers awaited Captain Finley's orders.

A fleck of white caught his eye and he looked to see a handkerchief floating to earth near the farmhouse two hundred yards away. His throat caught. An enemy signal? Federal treachery? He hauled hard on the reins and the chestnut reared on its hind legs, pawing the air viciously. What to do? Take the message to the artillery or warn Captain Finley?

Lonnie! Hoooooooooooo, Lonnnneeeeeeeeeeee! The clear voice of Mama Pastine trumpeting across the frozen morning, calling him to breakfast, ended Young Scout's dilemma.

"Oh, shit," said Young Scout.

———————

"What we need to do is let the churches organize the wars," Jake was saying. "It would make everything a good deal more civilized."

He speared a four-inch-thick stack of hotcakes from the steaming platter in the middle of the kitchen table and dropped it on his plate.

"Take the Germans in the Middle Ages. They had the right notion. Start a war, and they'd send out a bunch of prelates to oversee the business. They had a thing called the Peace of God where the prelates would decide things had got hot enough and they'd just say, 'Okay, boys, time to knock off.' And most times, the combatants would just stop right there and then. But that didn't always work."

Jake poured a puddle of syrup on top of the hotcakes and slivers of brown trickled over the sides of the pile.

"So they had another trick they called the Truce of God. That's where the prelates would say, 'Okay, boys, no fighting between Thursday and Monday.' And sure enough, the aggrieved parties would cease the hostilities at sundown on Thursday and clean up and go to town and recharge their batteries and take in a sermon on Sunday and then go back to it hot and heavy come sunrise on Monday. Now that's . . ."

Jake forked a hunk of the hotcake pile into his mouth and chewed methodically. Twenty times. Chew every bite twenty times and you'd never have gastric distress, Daddy Jake always said. He rolled his eyes toward the ceiling, impatient to get on with his story. His cheeks puffed like a chipmunk's. Then he swallowed and the great bony lump of his Adam's apple bobbed like a head nodding.

". . . the way to run your wars." He nodded for emphasis.

"Pastine"—he held up his coffee cup and waggled it—"could I have another round, my beauty?" Mama Pastine gave the three hotcakes sizzling on the griddle a flip and brought the coffeepot to the table. The coffee was boiling hot and it bubbled in Jake's cup as she poured it. "What do you think, my darlin', on the subject? Could we get the churches to take over the supervision of the lists?"

Pastine speared him with a warning glance. She had small bright eyes that danced when she was in one of her no-nonsense moods. "You blaspheme, Jake Tibbetts. You haven't darkened the doors of a church in forty years, and you sit there and babble on about churches running wars. The Lord listens and takes note." She took the coffeepot back to the stove.

Jake glanced at Lonnie and cocked his head to the side like a small dog.

"You'd have to take turns, of course. Spread the responsibility around. Give everybody a piece of the business. You could have your Baptist war and your Methodist war and your Catholic war and your Reformed Agnostics and your High Episcopals and your Low Episcopals. And then your Presbyterians would want a piece of the action. Get a good thing going and your Presbyterians will always find a way to get in on it. Then when they do, they sit around and argue with each other."

Jake was waving his fork now, the color high in his cheeks, his ears twitching the way they did when he got on a tear.

"Your Baptist wars would be sort of grim kinds of affairs. No cussing or that sort of thing. Strictly business. The Methodists, now, they would run a loose kind of game, if you know what I mean. Bingo at night, covered-dish suppers, dancing, the like. It would give the hors-de-combat a little spice."

Jake chopped off another bite of hotcakes and chewed twenty times, drumming his fingers on the table while he rolled his eyes. The Adam's apple bobbed.

"It would give a fellow a choice of wars, too. Take for instance you had a Baptist war coming up. A fellow who enjoyed a little fun along with his combat might say, 'Well, now, I think

I'll just sit this one out and wait until a good Reformed Agnostic war comes along.' ''

"For goodness' sake, Jake!" Pastine turned from the stove and brandished the spatula she was using to flip the hotcakes. "Hush and let the boy eat his breakfast. And you," she pointed the spatula at Lonnie, "get busy. I'd think you'd be starved half to death, running around in the woods before daybreak on a freezing morning, doing Lord knows what. And then you sit here with your mouth open listening to that old goat"—she waved the spatula at Jake again—"blaspheming and talking nonsense while a good pile of hotcakes gets cold right before your nose. What *were* you doing out in the woods, anyway?"

Lonnie ignored the question. He held up his coffee cup and waggled it. "Could I have another round, my beauty?" he mimicked Jake's raspy voice. Jake guffawed, then ducked his head. Pastine hung fire for a moment, then put the spatula down with a snort and poured a small puddle of coffee in the bottom of Lonnie's cup, filled it the rest of the way with milk until it lapped at the brim, and dumped in a heaping teaspoon of sugar.

The kitchen was a warm cocoon against the morning. The Atwater-Kent radio murmured Ollie Whittle's market and weather reports from its mahogany cabinet on the counter next to the pantry. At the window beyond Pastine's head the thin edge of frost around the panes glittered with new sun, and the way it fractured the light made her face seem more angular than usual. With the glistening window at her back she seemed to hover somewhere between the table and the frostbitten morning where Captain Finley Tibbetts, Lonnie's great-great-grandfather, would just now be carving up the Federal infantry in the open field beyond the pine thicket with his glistening saber. In counterpoint to the raging battle, Mama Pastine smelled deliciously of coffee and hotcake batter and the faint aroma of lilac water.

She gave Lonnie's coffee a vigorous swish with the spoon, then turned back to the stove, picked up the spatula, shoveled the three hotcakes on the griddle onto her own plate, and placed it on the table at the empty seat. She took a glass from the cabinet and held it under the sink faucet. The water came out with a splat.

"Jake, get those pipes wrapped today."

"Ummmm," Jake said, his mouth full of hotcake, as she sat down at the table.

"I mean it."

"Ummmmm."

"One of these nights, I'll be lying upstairs on my deathbed with it freezing cold outside and neither one of you outlaws will have sense enough to come in here and turn on the faucet so it will drip, and then the pipes will burst, and come morning, you'll have a worn-out old dead woman lying upstairs and the pipes spewing all over the backyard." Pastine poured a thin stream of syrup over the top of her hotcake stack, then cut off a small bite.

Lonnie thought about the pipes. They had taken out the hand pump beside the kitchen sink and put in running water during the summer six years before, when Lonnie was six years old. Daddy Jake should have done it right. He should have had the plumbers rip out the old sink and put in a new one with faucets built in and the pipes run up through the floor. But no, he told them to just run the pipes under the house and out through the bricks of the foundation and up the backside of the house and into the kitchen just below the window. Lonnie remembered Mama Pastine fussing about it, Daddy Jake saying it was all right, he'd wrap the pipes so that they didn't freeze. Now the pipes were still bare, and Mama Pastine had to turn on the faucet and let it drip on cold nights so the pipes wouldn't freeze. Lonnie imagined the pipes busting while Mama Pastine lay on her deathbed upstairs, rupturing just at the point where the straight pipe connected to the elbow just below the window, spewing a fine spray of water that glittered in the dawn and froze as it hit the nandina bush under the window, turning the bush into a spectacular ice monster like the kind that lurked in the High Himalayas.

Jake looked up from his plate, now empty. "Well, Pastine, which do you want us to call first—the plumber or the mortician? Are you fading fast, my beauty, or will you last another winter?"

"Plumber? Who said anything about a plumber?" She pointed her fork at Jake. "You said when you had the plumbers out here to put in the pipes that you could wrap them yourself. If you weren't going to do it, why didn't you have the plumbers wrap the pipes, Jake? Or better, why didn't you have the plumbers run the pipes up through the floor and put in a new sink like you should have?"

"I'm a newspaperman, not a laborer," Jake protested. "I deal in words, not monkey wrenches."

"Then why . . ." she began, then tossed her head in disgust.

Jake took a sip of his coffee. "I have good intentions, m'dear. I simply sin and fall short. My feet are made of clay, I confess it. I'll get the pipes wrapped today, plumber though I am not. Lonnie and I will stop at the hardware while we're in town and pick up whatever it is you wrap pipes with."

Mama Pastine glared at him and kept eating. She took small bites, chewed them precisely. Lonnie watched, studying her even, deliberate movements as she worked through the stack of hotcakes, washing them down with small sips of water. She was no coffee drinker. She fixed Jake's coffee every morning, and she would allow Lonnie two cups of mostly-milk on Saturday, because she said if they wanted to rust away their insides, they would have to pay the consequences.

Jake drained his coffee cup, set it down with a clatter on the saucer, wiped his mouth with the cloth napkin in his lap, and laid it in a heap on his plate. "I wonder who that damn fool was in the airplane?"

Lonnie's ears perked. "What airplane?"

"My Lord," Pastine said, "you must have been asleep out there in the woods if you missed it. He passed right over the house just before I called you in. Almost scared me to death. Do you suppose they're having maneuvers?"

Jake shook his head. "Lost, probably, and looking for landmarks."

"You reckon he crashed?" Lonnie asked eagerly.

"Well, I ain't seen any debris in the backyard," Jake said.

Lonnie thought about it, imagined the plane clipping the chimney with a wheel as it roared over the house, tilting crazily, digging a wing into the big pecan tree in the side yard, spinning and devouring itself as it came to pieces in the limbs of the tree, scattering flaming pieces of struts and propeller and fabric over the backyard as the chickens ran cackling in terror, skittering along with their feet skimming the ground.

"Godawmighty," he said softly.

Mama Pastine looked up at him sharply. "What did you say?"

"Nothing," he mumbled.

"I heard you," she insisted, "I heard what you said."

Lonnie cut his eyes over at Jake, who gave him a don't-look-at-me-buster look. "I'm sorry," Lonnie said.

"You should be. And on the day before Christmas. Santa Claus has no truck with blasphemers."

Daddy Jake snorted. "Hogwash."

"I beg your pardon?" Mama Pastine said.

"You are confusing Santa Claus with Father Coughlin. Santa Claus makes no moral judgments. His sole responsibility is to make young folks happy. Even bad ones. Even TERRIBLE ones."

"Then why," Lonnie broke in, "does he bring switches to some kids?"

"Exactly," Mama Pastine affirmed.

"Whose side are you on, anyway?" Jake demanded.

"I'm just tryin' to get it all straight," Lonnie said. "I'm all for Santa Claus."

Jake tapped his plate with his fork. "This business about switches is pure folklore. Did you ever know anybody who *really* got switches for Christmas? Even one?"

Lonnie thought about it. "I guess not. Even Little Bugger, after he set fire to the woods down by the creek, he got a Western Flyer coaster for Christmas."

"Right," Daddy Jake nodded. "I have been on this earth for sixty-four years, and I have encountered some of the meanest, vilest, smelliest, most undeserving creatures the Good Lord ever allowed to creep and crawl. And not one of them, not *one*, mind you, ever got switches for Christmas. Lots of 'em were *told* they'd get switches. Lots of 'em laid in their beds trembling through Christmas Eve, just knowing they'd find a stocking full of hickory branches come morning. But you know what they all found?"

"What?"

"Goodies. Even the worst of 'em got some kind of goodies. And for one small instant, every child who lives and breathes is happy and good, even if he is as mean as a snake every other instant. That's what Santa Claus is for, anyhow."

"Jake," Mama Pastine said, "one of these days you are going to talk yourself into a corner you can't get out of. I just hope I live long enough to see it."

"So you can gloat?"

"No, I'll probably keel over from amazement."

"One of these days, I'll do it just for your edification, m'dear."

She looked at him for a long moment. "Sometimes I wonder if you know the difference between good and evil."

Daddy Jake grinned. "I do, but Santa Claus doesn't."

Lonnie savored it, his grandparents' warm kitchen and the ice-rimmed window, the *drip-drip* of the faucet keeping time with Ollie Whittle's soft mutter on the Atwater-Kent, the rich aroma of coffee and hotcakes, Mama Pastine's lilac water and Daddy Jake's cigar smell. And secrets. There was the secret knowledge of the Daisy Red Ryder BB gun and the two Tom Swift mysteries and the pair of brown corduroy pants and the soft black leather gloves with rabbit-fur lining he had already found stashed away in Mama Pastine's closet. And that other secret—Captain Finley's Lighthorse Cavaliers covering themselves with glory out there in the frost-encrusted field.

The moment hung suspended in Lonnie Tibbetts's imagination, and then it ended when Lonnie thought, as he so often did, of his father.

Where, on this fine morning, was First Lieutenant Henry Finley Tibbetts, U.S. Army Infantry? Somewhere in Europe, that's all Lonnie knew. Mama Pastine told him that—a nugget of knowledge gleaned from some mysterious source she had. She shared only that with Lonnie, and only with him, because Daddy Jake would not allow the mention of his son in his presence.

This morning, the thought of Henry Tibbetts bubbled unbidden to the surface of Lonnie's mind—an impression, a *feel* of Henry more than any specific memory. Lonnie, in fact, could not really remember what his father looked like. He remembered, instead, Daddy Jake's reaction to Henry, the naked anger, the disgust. Henry Tibbetts was a pariah in his own home. It was the very word Jake had used to describe his son—a pariah. A man who had disgraced the memory of his wife and deserted his son and was now off fighting a damn fool's war. He was a drunkard, a profligate, a fool. But worst of all, he had violated the basic rule of civilized behavior that says a man cleaves first to his family and forsakes all else in their behalf, no matter what the cost. In Jake's book, you stood and fought, especially when the enemy was inside yourself. But Henry had cut and run. A quitter. That's what Daddy Jake had said.

Lonnie understood all these things, understood that Henry was absolutely taboo in Daddy Jake's house. But nonetheless he lurked in every corner, a sad, fascinating shadow of a figure just beyond touching. Lonnie felt his presence, but he kept that to himself. As far as Mama Pastine was concerned, Henry was somewhere in Europe. How could you tell her that he was both there and here, that a living man could have a ghost who haunted the house and the person he had left behind? No, you couldn't tell. It was something you kept in your own heart even though it sometimes made you feverish with wondering.

"You gonna stare at it or drink it?" Daddy Jake interrupted his thoughts.

"Huh?" He looked up and blinked at them.

Jake laughed. "Where do you go when you wander off like that, boy?"

Lonnie flushed. "I was just thinking," he mumbled.

"Well, finish up. We got things to see and folks to do."

"And pipes to wrap," Mama Pastine said.

Lonnie picked up his coffee cup and took a final gulp. On the radio, Ollie Whittle was talking about a little town in Belgium. Bastogne, he called it.

T W O

*H*ENRY woke at first light and heard the wind moaning through the tops of the great fir trees and thought for a moment that the wind and light had wakened him. But then he realized how cold he was, much colder than before, and he knew Bobby Ashcraft had died sometime in the night. It had been done quietly. The warmth had simply gone out of him, the warmth Henry had been depending on for . . . how long?

Bobby Ashcraft had been the last of them except for Henry, the last of the four wounded men who had crawled under the ravaged tank, its rear end tilted up against a huge rock and its gun muzzle jammed into the snow. They had huddled there for . . . how long? Living on each other's warmth and dying one by one until now there was only Henry. It might have been a couple of days, it might have been a week. Probably not that long, though, because they all, except for Henry, had been badly wounded, and it had been awesomely, achingly cold. Men could not live long under such conditions.

They had all died quietly except for Mazzutti, who whimpered and moaned a lot until Henry stuffed his mouth with rags, crazy with panic that the Germans might hear. Then Mazzutti had shut up and when he finally died, it was with great tears streaming down his cheeks, tears of frustration because they had gagged him and he couldn't tell anybody what a sonofabitching lousy break it was to die shivering under a bombed-out tank in the Ardennes at Christmastime.

It had snowed heavily at first, just after the attack, and the drifts had nearly covered the tank and the big rock, blocking the ends and leaving them a den under the tank's belly with a narrow opening at one corner, next to the rock, for air. Henry remembered the first night, the snow, the terrible cold, the pitiful warmth they shared with each other, Mazzutti moaning and crying until Henry stopped him, but since then time had folded back on itself and he had lost track of days and nights. He marked the passing of time only by the deaths of the others—first Mazzutti, then the one with half a face whose name they didn't know (a refugee from another shattered unit), now Bobby Ashcraft. Henry was the last of the string. He would die soon without Bobby Ashcraft's warmth.

He was already beginning to feel the numbness creeping through his body, spreading from his leg, which had long since ceased to hurt. When he touched his leg he could feel only crust, a great scab formed by torn flesh and congealed blood and cloth midway between his left knee and hip. It was a clean wound, he thought. The bullet had entered the front of his leg and creased the bone and exited the back and there hadn't even been a lot of bleeding, as if the blood vessels had been fused by the impact. A man could live for days with a wound like that. But he couldn't run. He could crawl, but you didn't crawl in snow like that piled up outside, as he had found the one time he ventured out. A clean wound. Nothing like the deep slash across Mazzutti's chest that had sucked and wheezed, or the blasted mass of pulp and gristle that was left of half the nameless man's face, or the big hole in Bobby Ashcraft's gut. A million-dollar wound, that's what Henry had. If you could cash it in. But he was freezing to death because all the warmth was gone and he was the end of the string. It was an easy way to die, though, and Henry was thankful for that. He had seen how badly a man could die and he was frightened by the thought of going with the agony of unbearable pain squeezing the life out of him. This would be like drifting off to sleep. The numbness would simply take more and more of him until there was only numbness and no Henry.

But it was for keeps, and a man ought to make preparations for something this final, get his affairs in order. He was still rational enough, calm enough, to do that.

He decided first there would be no amends, no groveling and begging forgiveness. No more guilt for Old Henry, thank you. Old Henry had had his bait of guilt. He had worn it like a dead chicken around his neck for a lifetime, and it had made him, at thirty-four, old and stoop-shouldered. Folks had dumped guilt on Old Henry for a long, long time. Guilt was a way folks had of making you pay for being different. And he had paid enough. So you could take Old Henry, all thirty-four years of him, his tired bag of flesh and bones with the hole through his leg—you could take him as he was, damaged goods and all—but you wouldn't get any more guilt out of Old Henry, by God.

Still, there was a lot of garbage, a lot of rancid rot festering down there in Old Henry's gut, some of it the fear and shame of the past few days, but most of it ancient stuff, a graveyard of garbage, the burying place of all he had done and failed to do.

So. If there weren't going to be any amends, what else? A man couldn't pass out of this life having existed as a graveyard run riot with weed. What then? Well, you could dig it all up and then just forget it, he decided after a while. So he set about forgetting. He did it methodically, one step at a time, working his way back as far as possible before his time ran out, closing out the books before shutting down the store. It might be, he thought, the only neat thing he had ever done in his life.

Last things first, and first was the battle. It was unfair. Old Henry knew a lot about unfairness; it was a second cousin to guilt. Green troops, unbloodied, four months out of the States, moved into position along a quiet sector of the front to get eased into the business of killing and being killed. The big action was up north, where Montgomery edged grandly into position for another set-piece battle, or to the south, where Patton, the wild sonofabitch, was revving his engines and straining to leap across the border into Germany. And it was winter. Just before Christmas. It was quiet in the Ardennes, almost civilized. There was hot food in the kitchen, girls in St. Vith if you were randy and bold enough. They patrolled, there were a few brief firefights. But the Krauts were battered, hunkered down behind the Siegfried Line, waiting for spring and the inevitable end.

Then suddenly there were Krauts all over the place, raging through the forest of towering firs, shredding the snow with their Tigers, flailing madly with a vicious, fanatical force they weren't supposed to have anymore. Ike and the others had made an incredibly stupid miscalculation, and it was unfair. Some ran like crazy—like the 14th Cav over on the left. Cut and ran, they did, and left the whole flank of the division bare as a baby's ass, and the Krauts went storming through the hole. Then while the rest of the division should have been pulling back, regrouping and reforming its lines, some brass hat scratched his fanny and hemmed and hawed until it was too late, and then they had Krauts on all sides and there was the devil to pay. The Germans had launched the assault before dawn, and by nightfall Old Henry and his boys were doomed men. They fought because they had absolutely no place to run. They began to hear during the day, as other units fell back upon their position, how the 14th Cav had collapsed and how the brass hat had scratched his ass and how the Germans were taking no prisoners. They fought then because they believed it was the only way they could stay alive, and it turned out they were wrong about that.

It had ended for them, finally, on this little flat place on the side of a hill, a thirty-four-year-old lieutenant and perhaps thirty men, exhausted and terrified.

Henry could feel their eyes on him as they crouched and waited, all these kids who looked to him simply because he was older. Older, hell. He was ancient. They could curse like grizzled men because they had learned to curse to cover their youth, but some of them didn't even shave yet. All right, old man, they said with their eyes, what now? Up to now, they had liked him because he didn't hassle them, because he listened to them out of the ancient tiredness of his age and they took that for wisdom. No sweat, he tells them. It's his favorite expression: no sweat. Get the job done, then take it easy. No sweat. Until now. Now, there is plenty of by-God sweat. Now, in their agony, they want him to tell them what to do, and he can't. Die? He can tell them that, but he won't. No, he had no answers. Never had, really. And in that he was as guilty as Ike and the ass-scratching brass hats.

The Germans came boring in on them from all sides and cut them to pieces. They were very efficient about it. A few of Henry's men tried to throw down their guns at first, but they were shot where they stood, and then the rest of them stopped trying to surrender and backed up against the hillside and fought.

There was one brief moment when Henry had a flash of hope, when the American tank came rumbling around the hillside with its gun whumping away at the Germans. But then one *Panzerfaust* ripped away its left tread and the tank slewed sideways up on the big rock and jammed its gun muzzle in the snow, and at the same time another round pierced the armor plate on the front and blew everything inside to a searing hell, and the tank died there on the rock.

The Germans swept through them then, killing and wounding and then killing the wounded, and went on, leaving heaps of crumpled men in the deep snow. Henry was the only officer, but he was not in command. There was no command, only pitiful little clumps of men crouching in the snow and popping away with their carbines and cursing because there was nothing else to be done. He had been kneeling behind a fallen tree with two other men when a grenade, a mortar round, an artillery shell—he couldn't tell what it was—landed almost on top of them. There was a great, blinding, roaring flash and Henry felt himself lifted up and then slammed back on the ground. It had knocked the wind out of him and dazed him, but otherwise, he realized, he wasn't hurt. Then he looked and saw that the others had been torn to shreds, pulverized into shapeless lumps. He bellowed in terror and jumped up to run, to escape. The next moment he was sitting on his butt again, staring at the neat hole in the front of his left pants leg halfway between knee and hip. It calmed him. There was something almost comfortably familiar about it, this feeling that he had blown it again. "Shit," he said to himself. He was filled with pity and self-loathing because he was about to die on a worthless snow-covered hillside near St. Vith, Belgium, because he had gotten drunk in 1941 and joined the National Guard. He was sick at his own stupidity, his own weakness and helplessness—not just now, but always. His great encompassing capacity for screwing up.

There it was, as he thought back on it, trying to remember it so he could forget it and put it to rest. Guilt. Had Old Henry by the balls, it did, it did. Try to shut it out of your mind and it would sneak in through your ass like ringworms.

Now, remembering again, he saw himself sitting there on his butt in the snow, bleeding, a tremendous roaring in his ears from the concussion, watching Jerry storming in on their position. He didn't even look for his rifle. He just flopped over on his belly and buried his face deep in the cold snow and tried to shut it all out. At the end, he thought, he had cut and run. Through the roaring noise he could hear an occasional *pop-pop* that was the Krauts walking among the Americans, shooting the wounded. But they hadn't touched him. Maybe he looked dead. Maybe they were in too much of a hurry to be thorough about it.

The Germans moved off around the edge of the hill and after a while the roaring in Henry's head went away and left only the awesome silence of the snow and the towering firs and the death all around him. He waited a long time to make sure they were gone and then he crawled around the position, checking the shapeless heaps turning the snow red with their blood, and found the other three men still alive and dragged them up under the tank, where he had covered the snow with ponchos. After that they hugged each other unashamedly and died one by one while the passing of time became a glaze of pain and cold in Henry's mind.

There were long hours of delirium that Henry lost, hours when fever made him crazy and his dreams and reality ran together.

Once, he found himself kneeling in the snow outside, trembling violently with chills, holding a handful of dogtags from the dead and dying and his silver lieutenant's bars. Something powerful had driven him out in the cold, something terribly insistent that told him it was a matter of life and death to collect the dogtags. When he came to his senses he could remember nothing except the feeling of great urgency. He dropped the dogtags and the silver bars in a pile in the snow and crawled back under the tank, wondering why he did it.

Bobby Ashcraft lasted a long time and Henry lived like a parasite, sucking the warmth out of Bobby's young body. There was incredible strength in the slim frame, like a steel rod bent to the breaking point, and a quiet dignity in the smooth-cheeked face that made Henry ashamed of his own weakness. Bobby didn't talk much. He didn't want to talk. He was from some little hick town in Illinois, and Henry supposed there was a family back there, a mother and father and some other kids, maybe a doe-eyed girlfriend. But Bobby didn't talk about them.

If he had things to forget, if there were scores to settle, he kept them to himself. Bobby just quietly held on long after he should have given up and then he, too, drained out of himself into the snow and left Old Henry shivering and dying. The end of the string.

So, that was the battle. And having remembered it and catalogued it, Henry forgot it.

He could feel the numbness growing in him now and so he hurried back through the corridor of his mind, leaping over the gulf of time since they had left the States, back to the camp where they had trained—the sea of eight-man tents sprouting like drab mushrooms in what had been farm fields, the roiling clouds of dust always hovering in the air, kicked up by the swarming-about of men and machines in mock anger, learning the posturings of war. In the summer the land had been parched and brown, lifeless, choked on its own dust, fevered. Texas in agony. A miserable town nearby, slack-jawed in the heat, red-eyed from summer and soldiers. Ivie Anderson and Duke Ellington moaning from the jukebox:

> . . . like a lonely weeping willow, lost in the wood,
> I got it bad, and that ain't good . . .

and the rancid tang of spilled beer on an earthen floor. Sweat-stained khaki. The oldest lieutenant in the whole damned Army, the fool who got drunk and joined the National Guard in 1941. But he didn't fight it, because it was the first time he could remember when he was anywhere near coming to grips with himself. There were times when the heat and the dust and the swarming-about left him spent, emptied, and he sank back into the sweet soft luxury of not caring at all. He did what he was told, but he was not a very good lieutenant because he didn't really give a damn one way or the other and there was really not much they could do to him. No sweat, he told the kids. Get the job done and don't get your ass all puckered up about it. No sweat.

Henry stands before the company commander's desk, looking down at the man—another kid, really, eager and full of himself, starched and correct, a straight arrow, Jack Armstrong with captain's bars. What drives him? Henry wonders. He's not a West

Pointer. You can figure them okay. But this one—Henry can picture him one day as an overly earnest young business executive, clawing his way up somebody's ladder with whatever it is inside him clawing at his gut. For now, spoiling to get to war. He makes Old Henry feel very tired. And this young captain is no respecter of age. War has made it irrelevant.

"Lieutenant, how is it that your platoon finishes dead last in everything? Tell me that."

Henry shrugs.

"I'll tell you what it is." The captain smacks his fist into his palm. It's not an angry gesture, just earnestness. God, this man is earnest. "You're not pushing the men. You've got to stay on their butts, Tibbetts. Push, push, push. My God, man, they're winding up the war over there." It sounds like a personal affront.

"There's always Japan," Henry says.

"Japan, hell. Europe is the cradle of modern civilization, Tibbetts. Alter Europe and you alter the course of history. Ten years from now, nobody will give a damn about some piddlyass islands in the Pacific. Japan has nothing but fanaticism, Tibbetts. Europe has destiny. Hitler's a maniac, but Christ, you have to be impressed with the man's sense of history. Japan could never produce a Hitler." The captain is agitated, his face all screwed up with earnestness. He senses that Henry is not with him, not at all. "How did you get to be an officer, Tibbetts?" There is despair in his voice.

"I think I am what you would call a failure of the system," Henry says. He feels sorry for the captain. Henry thinks the man will probably never have close friendships. People will always stand back just beyond the edge of his earnestness. He will probably never get drunk with the boys.

There was the captain, and there was the woman. Henry didn't really know what to think about that, remembering it now so that he could forget it. He wondered about her. She would be okay, he thought. She was a survivor. You could see it in her eyes. She had hard eyes, a street fighter's eyes, unbecoming to a woman. She was tough and she traveled light. No, Old Henry had no amends to make for the woman. She had extracted no guilt from him, demanded no amends. No sweat on her part.

She is Colquitt's woman, everybody knows that. But Colquitt is dead now, killed in a jeep accident out there in the Texas misery, and Henry has been sent to tell her—a bit of perversity on the part of the company commander, the earnest young captain for whom Henry feels sorry.

She and Colquitt aren't married, but she is Colquitt's woman and she has to be told. Henry has seen her with Colquitt at the Quonset hut they call an officers' club, dancing listlessly by the jukebox. They cling together in the heat, she and Colquitt, swaying like broomstraw in a fetid breeze. Henry associates her somehow with Artie Shaw's clarinet, the smooth lilt of "Moonlight on the Ganges." She is Colquitt's woman, not Colquitt's wife, and therefore unapproachable. You can ask a man's wife to dance with you, but not his woman, not unless the man offers her, and Colquitt doesn't. It is not something you talk about with Colquitt, either, and so nobody really knows who the hell she is or where she came from, only that she has followed Colquitt to this heat-blasted armpit of Texas. That tells you something about both of them. Now Colquitt is dead in his jeep and here is Old Henry come to make amends and feeling his asshole puckering up with the uncomfortableness of it.

It is a single room upstairs over a dry goods store, reached by an outside stair. When he raps on the door she says, "It's open," and he steps inside and blinks in the dimness. As his eyes adjust, he sees her sitting in a straight-backed chair by the single window that looks out over the tin awning of the store to the parched dirt street. She is smoking, ashtray on windowsill, arm cocked to the side with the cigarette dangling between two fingers. It is a spare room—double bed with paint flaking from the metal frame, chest of drawers with plain wooden knobs, table with hotplate on top and beside it a few cans of food. And the single chair, in which she sits. Henry feels a sudden rush of despair, seeing the awful crushing boredom of it. At least out there in the dust and heat there is something to do, even if they move like automatons. But here . . . It is midafternoon and the day seems leaden, mugged by the stifling heat. And she sits by the window with an ashtray full of butts waiting for Colquitt. Henry looks at the bed, imagines them on it, their bodies slick with sweat. Beyond that, his imagination stops. He can't hear their conversation, their small movings-about in the tiny room, the way they spend the long hours between sundown and sunup. He can't imagine the routine, the million tiny details, of living with a woman. It has been too long. Is it different with a woman who is not your wife? In the ways of unmarried women he is untutored. Wives, he knows about. Wives, he knows in spades. But it has been a long, long time—long enough to forget what it's like to cohabit with one.

She stares at him, eyes glazed with the heat, waiting for him to say something, and Old Henry is uncomfortable as hell, boy. His undershorts are creeping up the crack of his butt. See how he shuffles his feet and scratches his ass, half expecting to say, "Yassuh, Mistah Colquitt he done tuk and died." And then blurting, "Colquitt's dead." Old Henry, appalled at himself, cringes inwardly, ashamed, wondering what amends he can make. And he sees her flinch, as if he had raised his hand to strike her. But that is all. A flinch. And then she turns back to the window and leaves him standing there in agony, shuffling and scratching.

"I'm sorry," Henry says. But he is as sorry for himself as he is for her.

She mumbles something and Henry steps toward her, trying to pick it up. "Pardon?"

She takes a long drag from the cigarette and stubs it in the ashtray and turns toward him, exhaling a stream of smoke. "I said, get the fuck out of here," she says quietly.

He does, but he returns at night. He finds her calm, composed, ungrieving. He brings a bottle of whiskey and marvels how she can toss it off neatly. He is fascinated by how strong she is, how tough and self-sufficient, and then later, after they have drunk half the bottle, how young and vulnerable, how afraid of the unknown. Henry knows a bit about that himself, and finds himself, strangely, in the role of comforter—he who craves comfort. Henry comes perhaps wanting to be flayed by her hardness (the way Hazel used to do) but finds, before morning, how wiry-soft she is and how good it is to be with a woman again. He wakes in the night and thinks of them as orphans, huddling.

Henry remembers the woman with fascination, and having remembered, reluctantly forgets and rushes on because the numbness has wiped out everything but his mind and he can feel it nibbling at the back of his skull like a small night animal. He has to pick carefully now because there is not much time.

There is the broad ribbon of highway, silver under a full moon, and Henry thinks suddenly of the old tale: A man can go crazy if he stays out in the moonlight too long. Henry is driving very fast and the car is gulping long stretches of road. It is Rosh Benefield's Packard, a powerful car that glides low against the pavement like an animal. He is driving Rosh Benefield's car because he is married to Rosh Benefield's daughter and between them (he and Hazel) they don't have a pot to pee in, much less an automobile of their own. But Rosh Benefield is a generous man with his Packard, and Rosh and his wife, Ideal, don't mind keeping the baby while the young folks go have a little fun.

Next to him in the front seat, Hazel's voice is rising and falling and beating against his ears like waves. Practice, long practice, has made him accustomed to the way she flails at him with her voice. He can block out long stretches of words, but he can't escape the rhythm of it, the rising and falling. They have both had a lot to drink. They have been to a dance in the city where Glen Gray and the Casa Loma Orchestra played sweet and mellow. Do-WAH, do-WAH. They danced a lot, their young bodies sweating against each other on the crowded floor, and drank a great deal with the other gay young couples, and then Hazel became abusive so he took her and left, driving very fast and trying to concentrate on the silver ribbon of highway and shut out the words, leaving only the rhythm. She mocks him, she taunts him. He has already begun to think of himself as Old Henry, wizened by the knowledge that in his marriage, as in all else, he has screwed up and that his balls will always be in somebody else's pocket.

It is true, he thinks, what they say about the full moon. He can feel it pulling at him the way the moon pulls at the sea and spawns tides, rising and falling. They are in a long curve now, and he holds the car to the inside of the curve, fighting the force that tugs at the wheels and makes the car want to slip sideways into the other lane and then off the shoulder into the woods where the moonlight doesn't go.

Just past this curve the road will drop sharply down a long hill and then cross the river and they will be into the town, home. Henry doesn't know what he will do then. He just doesn't know. When he stops the car and turns the engine off, there will be nothing to block out the words and he'll have to face them. But he tries not to think about it and concentrates on keeping the car on the inside of the curve while Hazel's voice rises and falls and beats against his ears.

Suddenly, she is on him. He isn't paying attention and it has stirred up the rage in her. She explodes against him, flailing with her fists, hammering at his chest and shoulders and then at his head. So for once, just once, he lets go. "Enough!" he cries, and lashes out at her. It is the first time he has ever, ever struck back. It is a powerful blow. He swings his arm in a broad circle and the back of his fist lands squarely in her face and snaps her head back. Blood spurts from her nose, a gushing of blood, and Henry senses that he has done a great deal of damage. He panics as she slumps against the far door and her hands fly to her face. She screams and he thinks, Oh God, oh God, oh God. But there is no God out there, only the moon, and all the moon has done is make him crazy. So crazy that he realizes his hands have left the wheel completely and the car is its own master now, is defying the curve, the yellow sweep of its headlights inflaming the woods where the moonlight cannot go.

That is as much as he knows about it, or is willing to remember. Here now, in the numbing snow of the Ardennes, he is grateful that he can remember it one last time and put it away. It has been with him since Creation.

Finally, quickly fixing it in his mind because there is not much time left, Henry remembers perching in the limbs of the huge spreading elm tree that hangs out over the street in front of Bugger Brunson's house, he and Bugger dropping cowshit on the passing cars.

They have built a little platform up there and they have been to the pasture behind Tunstall Renfroe's house and gathered up a bucketful of cow turds, wet them down, and stirred them up to make a thick pungent goo, and now they are sitting on the edge of the platform with the bucket between them, scooping out handfuls of cowshit and letting them drop through an opening in the lush green foliage onto the tops of the cars that sporadically pass below. They have been at it for maybe an hour now and their timing has become quite good. The trick is to avoid windshields, releasing the gobs of manure so that they land squarely on the roofs of the cars. It makes a little splat as it hits the metal, not loud enough to make the driver think it was anything too unusual. But when he gets where he's going and

parks the car and gets out and sees the blob, he must think, My
God, I've been dive-bombed by a condor. The thought of it
makes Henry and Bugger laugh until they hurt, and each time
they land a hit, the spasms start again. The aroma of the cowshit
is powerful, almost sweet. That, and the laughter, makes the
tears roll down their cheeks. They are scraping the bottom of
the bucket now. There will be enough for one more car and they
can hear it turning the corner at the end of the street. One more
and they will get the hell out of here, run like rabbits back behind
Bugger's house to the creek bank, where they will collapse and
scream with laughter until they are weak and aching. This one
last car is approaching slowly and it will be an easy mark. Bugger grins. The car rolls by under the tree and Henry and Bugger
let the cowshit drop at precisely the right moment—a bomb from
each of them. These last two handfuls are pretty well dried out
and they make a thump instead of a splat as they hit the car. The
car rolls on. Then it stops and backs up. Henry Tibbetts blanches
with sudden terror. The car stops again directly under the tree,
its top with the two sodden lumps of cowshit on it framed by
the opening in the branches. Henry hears the door slam but he
can't see the driver. Then he hears the one voice he wishes at
this moment were in Heathen China.

"Come down, boy," Jake Tibbetts says.

It's hard, up here in the tree, to tell just how pissed off he is.
Henry suspects it's a great deal. Jake is not likely to think that
dropping cowshit out of a tree onto passing cars is civilized
behavior, and Jake is big on acting civilized.

They climb slowly down from the tree, he and Bugger, and
Bugger begins to snuffle. Henry's hands feel leaden with the
cowshit caked on them, drying to a crust. He tries to scrape
some of it off on the bark of the tree as he shinnies down, but
there's still a lot, especially on the backs of his hands. Finally,
they stand before Jake. Bugger blubbers a little and Jake stares
at him until he shuts up. Jake isn't much for blubbering, either.

Jake looks them over, takes a long, long time at it, rolls his
cigar from one side of his mouth to the other. Henry dies a good
bit inside, just withers up like a prune.

"What have you got on your hands, boy?"

Henry stares at his hands.

"It smells like cowshit to me," Jake says.

"Yessir."

What happens if you stand around long enough with cowshit on your hands? Does it contain some kind of acid that will eat through your skin? His hands begin to tingle and flush and he feels panic rising in his throat.

It also occurs to him that they've been had. Somebody has come by and gotten bombarded and realized what it was and, knowing it was Bugger Brunson's house, driven down to Biscuit Brunson's cafe and told Biscuit that his kid was up in the big tree in front of the house dropping cowshit on the cars. Jake, sitting in Biscuit's cafe having his afternoon cup of coffee and catching up on the gossip, puts two and two together and comes up with Henry. So he borrows somebody's car (because Jake doesn't own a car) and sets out to spring the trap. Once again he has caught Henry screwing up, and now Jake is going to lay something really miserable on him. Sometimes he wishes Jake would just haul off and slap the pee-turkey out of him, but no, that's not Jake's way. Jake would rather make you miserable, make you want to wither and die inside with shame and guilt. Jake is a master at dispensing guilt.

"Henry," Jake says, taking the cigar out of his mouth, "be a goddamned idiot if you want to. But don't be a goddamned fool." And Jake jams the cigar back in his mouth and gets back in the car and drives off and leaves Henry standing there with cowshit on his hands.

So, there it was, at least what there was time for. There was, of course, a lot more, but it was a representation, anyway. The only loose edges were a few questions, like what's the difference between an idiot and a fool? And another—can moonlight be held legally responsible? And the big magilla—why? But if a life could be capsuled in a few representations and then forgotten, so could questions. And he didn't want a lot of unanswered questions floating around when he was gone. There would be ghosts and lost souls enough here in the snow under the towering firs of the Ardennes without Old Henry's haint. Old Henry, who had so frequently screwed up, owed the world that much. He would leave behind a boy and a woman and a double handful of guilt, but no haints.

So Old Henry forgot it all, representations and questions and the rest, wiped his mind completely clean, as blank as the last white powdering of snow. He forgot his life, and it was all so easy, he wondered at the last if he should feel guilty about that, too.

THREE

JAKE TIBBETTS thought of it as an inherited town, a place where men generally did what their forebears had done, where families carved out a little slice of the town's life and passed it on. It was fitting that the town was built on a square around the courthouse, neat lines and angles crossing back on themselves much the way people did, geometry imitating life.

To carry it a step further, the concentric squares of the town were a sort of local pecking order. If you were a merchant of the first rank, your business was on the main square, with a view of the courthouse out your front window. It meant the business had been there a long time, generally through at least two generations. If, on the other hand, you were located on a side or back street, it marked you as a newcomer or a business that by its nature didn't enjoy courthouse square status, like the mule barn. Just about the only exception Jake could think of was his newspaper, the *Free Press*, which had started, and remained, in its own building a block from the square because of the room it required for the print shop with its big Kluge press and storage for reams of newsprint. Then, too, Jake thought with some satisfaction, the newspaper was a street removed from the "establishment'' in the way a newspaper ought to be in order to view it with some detachment.

Still, it was an inherited business. Jake with his newspaper, detachment or not, shared with the town's leading men the distinction of doing what his father and grandfather had done, however reluctantly he had come to the enterprise.

The courthouse square was not much changed in a couple of generations. Biscuit Brunson was the second in his line to run the cafe. Two doors down, Tunstall Renfroe's grandfather had founded the bank right after the Civil War, just about the time Jake's grandfather had put out the first issue of the *Free Press*. Rosh Benefield's father had been the mayor in his time, and like the old man, Rosh was a lawyer. Rosh's office was next to City Hall and had a somewhat proprietary look about it, as if the two were connected. Everyone assumed that Rosh's boy, Billy, would come home after the war and study law and become mayor.

There were exceptions, of course. Some businesses had changed over the years, like Fog Martin's gas station and garage on the northwest corner of the square, which had been a livery stable for several generations back in Fog's family before Fog recognized the permanency of motorized travel. And people changed too, broke the mold. Take Hilton Redlinger. He hadn't wanted to be an undertaker like his father. He just didn't have the temperament for it. So Hilton's brother, Cosmo, had the funeral home to himself when the old man passed on, and Hilton became the police chief. Each grew to fit his job. Cosmo was like the old man—tall, dark-jowled, with a long bony neck that stuck up out of his collar like an egret's head—gaunt and somber, serious and solicitous. Hilton, on the other hand, had fleshed out. He had a healthy paunch, a solid reassuring face. Cosmo sort of hovered around folks like a dark spirit. Hilton carried himself like a lumberjack—a simple, direct man who knew his responsibility and felt at home with it. Let a man find his natural element, and he would grow to it until it fit him.

Occasionally, you would get somebody new. George Poulos, for instance. He was a Greek fellow, came from immigrants. George had passed through selling ladies' ready-to-wear about thirty years back. He liked the place, so he went back to the city and got his family and moved in. He bought out the Jitney Jungle Super Saver Store (a courthouse square establishment), and as soon as folks saw that George wasn't a fly-by-night sort, they took a shine to him. He had, in fact, been elected to the Town Council the year before.

And there was Ollie Whittle, who had come from the next county to start the radio station just before the war. It was the most progressive thing that ever happened to the town, people said, having their own radio station. Most towns twice their size didn't have a radio station. It was competition for the newspaper, but as Jake told folks, you couldn't remember from one minute to the next what you had heard on the radio, so it didn't make much sense to advertise on it. Still, Ollie had caught on. He had radio shows like the "Swap Shop of the Air" and Ideal Benefield's local news program and the quartet from the Baptist Church. And, Ollie had a gift of gab, a way of saying things that would make you chuckle, like the morning he had said it was so cold it would freeze the balls off a pool table. He was about the closest thing they had to a celebrity in town. Not that he could get elected to the Town Council, though. He hadn't been there long enough for that. And his radio station, though located on the courthouse square, was not on ground level. It was upstairs over the bank, the way the telephone exchange was upstairs over City Hall. A new business, especially a newfangled business, just did not occupy ground level on the courthouse square.

So, it was mostly an inherited town with a little room for a man to maneuver around in if he wanted to. People and things didn't change much. It was a solid town, dependable, predictable. The way people liked it. There was the red brick solidity of the courthouse in the middle of town sort of anchoring things down, with a double door on each of the four sides connected by big wide hallways that crossed in the middle like the spokes of a wheel. The courthouse was eighty-something years old and from its beginning it had acted like a magnet, drawing the town up around it as men left the land and congregated to do business with each other and with those who still tilled the land. It was the place where the county recorded its transactions—births, deaths, marriages, business arrangements, land exchanges, legal disputes. It surged with life—the building and the courthouse square—when court was in session, or on the first Saturday of every month, which was Trade Day.

Court session was good for everybody's business, especially at Biscuit Brunson's cafe. Lawyers came in from all over the county for court, some even from the cities if it was a big enough case. They crossed the courthouse lawn to Biscuit's place for their meals, or for coffee during recess, and sat in genteel conversation in their three-piece suits and starched collars and wingtip shoes. When trials went far into the night, Biscuit always stayed open until the last light in the big upstairs courtroom had winked off. Biscuit had told Jake once that he sometimes wished he had gone ahead, no matter what his wife, Iris, said, and changed the name from Brunson's Cafe to Brunson's Restaurant. It would be more fitting for the courthouse crowd. But as Iris said, you couldn't get too far ahead of folks, and court session came only four times a year.

Trade Day, now, was nothing special for the cafe business. The country people brought their food with them in hampers or paper sacks and ate off the backs of their wagons or trucks and drank tap water out of mason jars. But it was important to the other merchants. The farmers, red-faced and weatherbeaten men in faded overalls, slouched against their tailgates, cheeks bulging with Bull Durham chew, and haggled over the price of hunting dogs, farm implements, knives, guns, an occasional cow or litter of piglets. The women sold quilts, jams and jellies, chickens and eggs, butter, fresh vegetables in season. The men crossed the street to haggle with Tunstall Renfroe at the bank over their loans or to buy a piece of harness or a roll of baling wire at the hardware store. The women filled the dry goods store, picking carefully over the bolts of cloth and staring gape-mouthed at the ready-to-wear dresses on the wire-framed busts in the front window. Packs of their skinny kids roamed the square, tussling on the grass of the courthouse lawn. By sundown they were gone, the whole roiling hard-bitten lot, leaving the square limp with the lingering smell of manure and chicken feathers.

No, as Biscuit often told Jake Tibbetts, you couldn't depend on either court session or Trade Day to make a living at the cafe business. It was the regulars who kept you going—mercantile people who didn't go home to lunch, traveling drummers, a steady group of widows who paid by the week and marked off their meals on the big Crazy Water Crystals calendar on the wall behind the cash register. The widows were so regular that you knew something was wrong if one of them didn't show up. One Wednesday, when Ida Flournoy, who was eighty-two, didn't appear, Biscuit had sent Hilton Redlinger around to see about her. Hilton found Ida at the bottom of the stairs in her back hallway with her neck broken.

Then, to break up the empty hours between meals, there was the midmorning and midafternoon coffee and pie crowd, like Jake and Fog Martin and Rosh Benefield and Hilton Redlinger, drifting in and out for an hour or so, long enough to check up on the pulse of the town and on each other. If there was anyplace that was central to the town, Jake told Biscuit, it was the cafe. It, not Jake's newspaper nor Ollie Whittle's radio station, was the central means of communication.

That's why, Jake told him, you couldn't turn it into a restaurant. In a restaurant, Jake allowed, you had to spend a lot of time and attention on the frills like cloth napkins and thin, fancy plates and cups and saucers that broke if you looked wrong at 'em. In a cafe, you could serve chili to a workman from the Harsole Bingham Bolt Factory and make him feel just as at home as the starch-collar lawyer from the city who sat at a table with a red-checked tablecloth and a napkin dispenser and salt and pepper shakers. No, what this town needed was a cafe, not a restaurant. As Jake told Biscuit, a business, like people, should fit. Jake congratulated himself on possessing, if nothing else, the gift of unassailable logic. It was a boon and comfort to the community.

———————

Right now, at midmorning on Saturday, the day before Christmas, the courthouse square was nearly empty. The day was almost blindingly bright and clear, but there was a sharp, biting wind that pushed people along quickly on the sidewalks. Biscuit Brunson stood behind the counter next to the front window of the cafe, drying thick white coffee mugs with a dish towel and lining them up neatly on the shelf against the back wall, getting ready for the midmorning coffee and pie crowd. There was only Tunstall Renfroe at the counter, down at the last stool, sipping his coffee and being awfully quiet about it. Biscuit had tried to stir up a little conversation, but Tunstall was full of grunts and mumbles this morning, so Biscuit had let him be. Tunstall looked a little weary-eyed, like he had been up all night playing Santa Claus. But that wasn't supposed to be until tonight, and besides, Tunstall's daughter Alsatia was twenty or so and too big for Santa Claus, though Biscuit thought if he were Santa Claus he would sure like to come down the chimney to see Alsatia Renfroe. She did indeed fill up a pair of britches, and there was just a whisper of gossip.

Tunstall Renfroe was in fact thinking of his daughter Alsatia and more particularly about the silk handkerchief he had found plastered on the hood of his Packard when he had walked out of the house this morning to go to the bank.

"Jism," he said to himself after he had peeled off the handkerchief, held it up gingerly by a corner, and studied it. That's what it was, all right—jism. It was slick, slightly off-white. Where had it come from? Some love-struck young pervert, skulking around the place in the early morning, trying to get a peek at Alsatia. But who? Lonnie Tibbetts? He was the closest. Jake's house was maybe a hundred yards away. But Lonnie was only twelve. So. Some over-juiced stripling, morals corrupted by rampant passion, loose on Partridge Road, spilling his jism on silk handkerchiefs and leaving them plastered on the hood of an upright man's automobile. It was the curse of a man with a daughter.

But what to do? You didn't go to Hilton Redlinger and say, "Look, Hilton, I found a silk handkerchief full of jism on my hood this morning and I want you to do something about it." And you didn't march into the house and say, "Alsatia, do you know any young boys who might be masturbating about the yard, dear?" Unthinkable. He shuddered at the thought, deeply offended by the whole business, and then realized he had been standing there holding up the jism-soaked handkerchief for several minutes. He walked quickly to the toolshed, got out a long-handled shovel, and buried the handkerchief behind the shed next to the coal bin. Then he sat down on the back steps and tried to compose himself. He felt sick at his stomach. Not that he blamed Alsatia. A young woman of ripe charms could only do so much to avoid arousing the beast of passion. Alsatia dressed primly, was the soul of decorum behind the teller's cage at the bank, where she had been working since she finished high school. No, it was the fault of morals cut loose by the war, the way people's lives were uprooted and flung to the far corners of the globe. It was as unsettling to the folks back home as it was to the boys at the front. The uncertainty of the thing . . . Tunstall Renfroe, being a banker, abhorred uncertainty. And he recoiled at the thought of impropriety of any sort, not only as a banker, but as one who had helped rescue his own family's bank from the shame of embezzlement. A scandal, any kind of scandal, would kill him.

So now, as he sat in Biscuit Brunson's cafe on the morning before Christmas, with his coffee getting cold in his cup, he was in a fit of gloom, and it showed on his face. The last thing he needed right now was Jake Tibbetts, and here he came.

Jake never walked through a doorway, he blew through it like a little sawed-off tornado, as if he were testing the door to see if it would hold together. The door of Biscuit Brunson's cafe was easy to open, mainly on account of all the widows who came in for dinner every noon, and it was no match at all for Jake Tibbetts. He flung it open and the door banged back against its rubber doorstop. The glass in the upper half rattled. Jake was short and stocky and paunchbellied with big bushy gray eyebrows and a squared-off little bulldog face that flushed bright red in the cold midmorning that followed him in. Lonnie was right behind, a little out of breath from the brisk walk down Partridge Road from Jake's house to town.

"Mornin', gents," Jake said, shucking out of his overcoat, hanging it on the rack next to the door, hoisting himself up on a red-leather-covered stool at the front of the counter. Lonnie crawled up on the stool beside him. Tunstall nodded at them from the end of the counter.

"Biscuit, how about two cups of stout coffee for a pair of weary travelers," Jake said.

"Good morning, Jake. It gettin' any warmer out there?"

"Colder, if you ask me," Jake said. "Lord, I do hate cold weather. Pastine starts nagging me about wrapping the pipes again."

Biscuit poured two mugs of coffee from the pot simmering on the hotplate behind the counter, sat one in front of Jake, the other in front of Lonnie.

"Lonnie, how's the world treatin' you this morning? You use sugar and cream?"

"Fine Mr. Brunson. A little sugar, that's all." Lonnie heaped his teaspoon with sugar and dumped it into the coffee.

"What's Santa Claus gonna bring you tonight?" Biscuit asked.

"Surprise, I reckon."

"And you, Jake." Biscuit wiped his hands on his apron. "What's Santa Claus bringing you for Christmas?"

"Switches," Jake said. "And some stuff to wrap Pastine's pipes." Jake leaned past Lonnie and called down to the end of the counter. "Tunstall, you look like you've been up all night with a sick calf."

Tunstall smiled weakly at Jake.

"I know what it is," Jake said, "you've been out on air raid business again." He turned to Biscuit. "You seen Tunstall's air raid get-up?"

"No, Jake."

"Well, now," Jake said, inhaling a chestful of air, "let me tell you about Tunstall Renfroe's air raid get-up. Tunstall has him a little platform on the top of his toolshed out back of the house. And he has him a pair of binoculars. And he has one of these charts the Army Air Corps sends out that has the silhouettes of all the Jap and German planes. And that's not all, Biscuit. Tunstall has him a fine brass whistle on a cord that he hangs around his neck AND"—he slapped his hand on the counter, just missing the mug of coffee Biscuit had set before him—"a PITH HELMET, by God. Looks like one of the King's Hussars, ready to defend the Khyber Pass. Ain't that right, Tunstall?"

"Now Jake . . ." Biscuit started. Tunstall was staring into his coffee mug.

Jake forged on. "Tunstall goes up there on that platform every night, rain or shine, sleet or snow, and keeps his eagle eye peeled for the INVASION, by God." Jake took a sip of the steaming coffee and batted his bushy eyebrows. "Almost had himself some Nips the other night, so I hear, Biscuit. He rang up Central and told Em Nesbitt there was a flight of Zeroes headed straight for the Heartland of America." Jake paused and leaned over the counter, lowering his voice. "Turned out they were geese. I understand you could hear 'em honking two states away when the Army Air Corps shot 'em down. Just wouldn't believe they were geese. When Tunstall Renfroe tells 'em he's got a flight of Nips in sight, you better believe he's got a flight of Nips. Ain't that right, Tunstall?"

Tunstall sat up straight, stared Jake in the eye. "Not a word of it, Jake."

Jake Tibbetts was an affront to his dignity. He could badger a man to distraction. And the older he got, the worse he was—

irascible, argumentative, acid-tongued. The real crime of it was, he owned a newspaper, a mouthpiece for all his blather. The only reason he got away with what he did was that there was the faintest scintilla of truth at the edge of what he said. Yes, Tunstall was the air raid warden, but everybody in town would have forgotten it by now except for Jake. Rosh Benefield had come to him right after Pearl Harbor, back when there was genuine fear of enemy air attack, had explained how the town needed someone of stature to rally public support for an air defense program. And Tunstall had taken on the responsibility with the gravity he gave to all things of moment. Yes, he had in fact acquired a pith helmet with WARDEN stenciled across the front. But Jake had made such a hoot of the thing that it had undermined whatever chance there was for serious effort. People would pass Tunstall on the street and make siren sounds. And when Tunstall slipped and fell off the roof of the toolshed and broke his ankle, Jake had headlined it on the front page of the *Free Press*: "WARDEN CRASHES, TOWN SURVIVES." And then the man just wouldn't let it drop. Only last month, Jake had nominated Tunstall for citizen of the year in his front-page column:

> In four long and difficult years of war, our town has not once been attacked by enemy aircraft, and that is a singular tribute to the diligence of Air Raid Warden Tunstall Renfroe.

Yes, Tunstall thought, Jake Tibbetts was a threat to people's dignity, and when you took away their dignity, you invited sloth and loose living. The old verities, genteelness and civility, broke down. Decorum became the object of ridicule. So Jake Tibbetts was largely to blame for the kind of loose living that left jism-soaked silk handkerchiefs on the hood of an upright man's car. That, and the war, and the fact that people were making astronomical sums of money working at the Harsole Bingham Bolt Factory on war contracts.

Look at what it had done to the bank, at the class of customers it had brought in. You had people who used to have a hard time keeping clothes on their backs, now opening *savings* accounts, for goodness' sake. Making so much money they couldn't drink it up. On Friday afternoons the bank would be packed with them, poker-faced men in khaki and gray work clothes or over-alls, with the grime so deep in the creases of their skin you couldn't cut it out with a knife, clutching yellow paychecks. Some of them even had two paychecks because their women worked over there, too, right alongside the men. The farms were going to weed and seed. Even old men who had never known anything except the rear end of a mule had thrown down their plows and gone to Harsole Bingham. Greed, that's what it was.

". . . can tell you the difference between a Zero and a Stutz Bearcat in a jiffy," Jake was saying. He just rambled on and on like a windmill driven by his own hot air. The old fool.

The door blew open and Fog Martin and Hilton Redlinger bustled in, Fog in his big red flannel overjacket and his hunting cap with the flaps pulled down over his ears, Hilton in an old brown overcoat and wearing his blue police chief's cap.

"Hark, the gendarme," Jake called. "Tunstall here was just telling us he has a German spy living at his house, Hilton. Morning, Fog. Merry Christmas."

Fog and Hilton stamped their feet and hung their coats on the rack by the door, then climbed onto stools at the counter. Hilton hitched up the wide leather belt that strapped his holstered Colt revolver to his hip. Biscuit shoved mugs of steaming coffee in front of them, along with a platter of Victory Donuts. They were Biscuit's special contribution to the war effort. Every nickel he collected from Victory Donuts went for war bonds. He kept the change in a glass jar on the counter by the back wall.

Fog Martin picked up a donut, stared at it, then dunked it into his coffee and bit off a quarter of it. "Every time I see one of these things now," he said, chewing, "I think of a tire."

Hilton Redlinger laughed, spearing a donut of his own. "They ain't *that* bad, are they?"

"Naw, that's not what I mean," Fog said. "They're round, with a hole in the middle, that's the trouble. Just like tires. And I am wore out with tires. Seems like all I do is patch tires and try to keep enough air in 'em to get folks where they're going."

Hilton ate his donut in two bites. "I ain't seen a new tire in this town in three years."

Tunstall Renfroe opened his mouth to speak, but stopped himself. He had four new tires stashed away in his toolhouse. They had been there since the war started, and dry rot had probably gotten them by now. By the time his car had needed new tires, it was too late to put them on. People would have noticed. It would have caused a lot of snotty questions. A banker couldn't afford snotty questions. So, like everybody else, he rode around on bald tires (when he could get gasoline) that Fog Martin kept patching.

"When do you figure we'll see tires, Fog?" Tunstall asked.

"I don't know. The fellow from Esso came through here last month, he said there doesn't seem to be an end to it. Everything's going to the front, and as long as there's any fighting going on, we ain't likely to see tires, or any more gasoline than we're getting now."

"What you fellas need to do is get rid of your cars," Jake said. Jake had never owned a car. He walked where he went, and had his groceries delivered from the Jitney Jungle Super Saver by Fog Martin's brother Herschel on a three-wheeled bicycle.

"Well, I'll tell you for sure, I'm getting too old to be climbing around under folks' wore-out automobiles on a cold morning," Fog said.

"Old!" Biscuit laughed. "You ain't old, Fog. What do you mean, *old?"*

"Of course I am," Fog said. "I'm getting old, you're getting old. Hell, all of us sitting here are getting to be a bunch of old farts. Young Lonnie excepted, of course. I'm sixty-one years old, Biscuit. How old are you?"

"Fifty-seven."

"And you, Hilton?"

Hilton Redlinger passed his hand over his thinning hair. "Sixty-eight," he said.

"See. One of these days the Town Council is gonna come around and say it's time you handed over the badge to a younger man."

"The hell!" Hilton said hotly.

"Tunstall"—Fog turned to the far end of the counter—"how about you?"

"Ahem." Tunstall cleared his throat. "Ah, sixty."

"And you, Jake?"

"I forgot," Jake said.

"Oh, come on, Jake."

"Yes, Jake," Tunstall said from the end of the counter, "you needn't be sensitive about your age."

"All right," Jake said, "I'm ninety-three."

"No, you ain't," Lonnie said, "you're sixty-four. That's what Mama Pastine said."

Jake glared at him, then winked.

"Well, anyway," Fog Martin said, taking another donut from the Victory platter, "you see my point. We're all getting old as hell."

Well, maybe they were, Jake Tibbetts thought, but it was not anything he cared to dwell on. They might be getting a few gray hairs, but his generation was still running the town, the way they had for thirty years or so. They had no choice, really. The young men, the ones in their twenties and thirties, were off at war or building B-29s in Seattle or Liberty Ships in Pascagoula. And as for men in their forties or fifties, there was a whole lost generation in there—the ones who had left during the Depression. There were a few around, like Ollie Whittle, but he had moved in from the next county. The young bucks, the ones who survived the war, now they would be coming home before too long, fresh from having done important things, and they would want their place. Yes, they would shove old men like Hilton Redlinger aside. Hell, the old knocker was beginning to look a little seedy, anyway. He didn't even shave on Saturday morning anymore. Jake studied him, the white stubble grizzling Hilton's fleshy cheeks and chin, the dry skin flaking off his eyebrows, the long black hairs growing out of his ears. Hilton's wife was sickly. She stayed in bed most of the time. And Hilton was going to seed. But the rest of them had a few good years left. They wouldn't give things up without a struggle. Jake Tibbetts might have turned sixty-four the month before, but there was still a lot of piss-and-vinegar in his bloodstream, by God. And anyway, there was nobody to push him out of the paper. There wasn't anybody to hand it over to, even if he wanted to, which he didn't. God knows, Henry would never make a newspaperman.

"Lord, Biscuit," Fog Martin boomed, slapping his belly, "by the time we lick the Japs I'll bust a gut from eating donuts."

"You'll die a patriot," Jake said. "We'll lay you in state over at the courthouse and I'll run an obituary that says, 'He busted a gut, but saved the country.' We'll put up a statue on the courthouse lawn with a hole in its belly."

Biscuit Brunson leaned over and propped his elbows on the worn linoleum top of the counter. "Well," he said, "I guess we'll need *some* kind of statue on the courthouse lawn when this business is over.''

"What do you mean?" Jake asked.

"You know, something to honor the fighting men."

"Why the hell would we want to do that?" Jake snorted. "I'd think everybody would just want to forget the damfool business and get back to being normal. Besides, there's no statue over there for the First War people."

"No, but . . ."

"Your daddy was in the First War, wasn't he, Biscuit?"

"Yeah, but . . ."

"So, the town ought not to play favorites."

"Well," Biscuit insisted, raising up, "maybe we could do a statue for all the fighting men from all wars. Go clear back to the Revolution."

"Hah!" Jake boomed. "What few people there were around here in the Revolution were a bunch of renegades and outlaws. They didn't give a damn who won the war, as long as folks left 'em alone. Hell, this was the frontier during the Revolution."

"Okay, then," Biscuit forged on, "you could go back to the Civil War." He thought a moment. "Your grandaddy was in the Civil War, Jake."

"Damn right, and he wouldn't have stood for any statues on the courthouse lawn, either."

"Well, just the same, I think we ought to have a statue," Biscuit said. "What do you think, Hilton?"

Hilton Redlinger shifted around on the counter stool and reached for another donut. "What kind of statue are you talking about, Biscuit?"

"I don't know, I guess some kind of statue of a soldier," he said, describing it in the air with his hands.

"Hey," Fog Martin broke in. "How about the sailors, Biscuit? Lots of us got relatives in the Navy. Your own boy's a Seabee."

"Yeah, and what about the Army Air Corps and the Marines and the merchant seamen?" Hilton said.

Biscuit wiped his hands briskly with his dish towel. "Okay, then, how about a cannon."

There was a moment of silence and then Jake guffawed. "A *cannon*! God knows, that's what we need on the courthouse lawn, boys. A *cannon*! We could put the air raid warden in charge of it, and then the next time a flock of Zeroes comes over, Tunstall could blow 'em out of the air! How about it, Tunstall?''

Tunstall Renfroe gave them a sour look. "I think General MacArthur can take care of the Japanese, Jake.''

"Speaking of Japs, you-all heard about the Germans?'' Hilton Redlinger asked.

"We've been hearing too much of 'em the last few days,'' Biscuit said, wiping the counter where Hilton had slopped his coffee dunking a donut.

"Some of 'em are gonna be right here in town tonight,'' Hilton said.

"My God,'' Jake exclaimed. "Tunstall's been right all along. It's the *invasion*, by God. Tunstall, you better get home and grab your pith helmet and organize the militia.''

"Naw,'' Hilton said. "They're coming for the Christmas program. A bunch of 'em from the POW camp over at Taylorsville. Rosh Benefield invited 'em.''

"I'm not so sure that's a good idea,'' Tunstall said. "Folks might be a litle sensitive about Germans, what with this breakthrough in Belgium. Are you going to deputize any extra men tonight, Hilton?''

"No need to do that,'' Hilton said. "There's only going to be a handful of 'em, and they'll have a bunch of MPs from the prison camp guarding 'em. There won't be any trouble.''

"When did you find out about it, Hilton?'' Jake Tibbetts asked.

"Last week,'' Hilton said.

"Well, why the hell didn't you tell me about it so I could get it in the paper?''

Hilton shrugged. "Rosh didn't think we ought to get folks stirred up.''

Jake snorted. "Stirred up? I'll tell you when they're gonna be stirred up. That's when they get to the auditorium tonight and see a bunch of Heinies sitting there enjoying themselves.''

"I'll tell you what,'' Fog Martin broke in, "I think they ought to stay out of the refreshments.''

Jake slapped his hand on the counter. "You well-meaning public servants are gonna be the death of us, trying to protect us from ourselves.'' He jabbed a stubby finger in Hilton's direction.

"Now, Jake," Hilton said, his voice rising, "you wouldn't want to get over to the school tonight and have some trouble over these Germans, would you?"

"I'd rather not back into anything," Jake said. "And if a fellow doesn't know something, he's backing up. There's only two things standing between man and perfection, gents, and that's meanness and ignorance. You can't do anything about meanness because man got that in the Garden when woman sneaked the apple in on him. But you *can* do something about ignorance. Mankind would be half-perfect if he wasn't so god-damned dumb."

They all laughed at that, and Biscuit filled up their coffee cups again and Fog Martin had another Victory Donut and they watched Ideal Benefield pass by on the sidewalk headed for the radio station two doors away to do her Saturday morning "Club News and Community Views" program.

After a few minutes, Ollie Whittle came in, coatless, shivering from the short dash from the radio station. Ollie took a stool between Fog Martin and Tunstall Renfroe. "Top of the morning to you, gents," he boomed. Ollie had a strong, resonant, glad-to-meet-you voice. He was tall and wavy-haired with a big hawkbill of a nose that he pulled on all the time. Biscuit shoved a mug of coffee in front of him and slid the donut platter down the counter. Ollie would have a half hour to drink coffee and visit while Ideal Benefield did her program on the radio.

"What's the latest on the Belgium situation?" Tunstall asked him.

"From what little they're saying, it looks pretty grim," Ollie said, taking a slurp of coffee. "The Germans have driven almost to the Meuse and they've still got Bastogne surrounded. I get the impression our boys have gotten cut up pretty bad. I think they caught Bradley with his pants down."

Ollie Whittle was sort of a local authority on war developments because he had a news ticker up in the radio station and some big Rand McNally maps of Europe and the Pacific tacked on the wall where he plotted the course of the latest action.

"Well, what are Montgomery and Patton doing about it?" Fog Martin asked.

Ollie pulled at his nose. "Montgomery sent reinforcements right off. In fact, it was some of his folks that got cut off at Bastogne. But nobody's heard a peep out of Patton."

"You can bet he's itching to get in the middle of it," Fog said. "I wonder why Ike don't cut him loose?"

"He may be waiting for the weather to clear," Ollie said. "It's been miserable all week. The Air Corps is grounded. They can't get a thing in the air."

"Well, the whole damn thing is Montgomery's fault," Jake said.

They all turned to stare at him. "What do you mean, Jake?" Ollie Whittle asked.

"Montgomery's a ninny. He won't budge an inch unless he's got all the odds in his favor. He wants all the troops, all the supplies, perfect weather, and a band of bloody bagpipers to skirl when he steps off to the march. It has to be done in grand style and on a grand scale, or Montgomery's not your boy." Jake tapped his spoon on the counter for emphasis. "And Ike, the idiot, just keeps mollifying old Monty. Lets him sit up there in Belgium fat and warm through the winter with his tootsies roasting and his pudding baking."

"Now wait a minute, Jake," Tunstall Renfroe protested, "Montgomery's a brilliant general."

"Brilliant my ass," Jake said. "We've been bailing the English out from the beginning. They got themselves in a pickle because they wouldn't call Hitler's hand early on, so they came squawking to good old Uncle Sam, and now the whole damn Limey island is afloat with U.S. greenbacks. And Montgomery struts around like the Duke of Dundee when he and his boys would be bare-assed without a pot to pee in if it hadn't been for us. The tea-drinking sonofabitch."

"That's ridiculous," Tunstall said.

But Jake blasted right on. "The trouble with us Americans is, we never got over being hillbillies. We can fight like hell and hold our liquor with the best of 'em, but we still haven't learned which fork to use. So you put us in with a bunch of folks who've got more manners than sense, and we just turn to jelly with embarrassment. I'll bet old Ike's got to the point that when he's around Montgomery, he feels like he forgot to wash his hands the last time he took a pee."

Ollie Whittle laughed, a deep chuckle that rumbled up out of his stomach. "Jake, that's the damndest discourse I ever heard. I can't decide if it's brilliant or just pure horse manure."

"Horse manure," Tunstall Renfroe said.

Hilton Redlinger scratched at the white stubble on his chin. "What gets me is the way you carry on about the war, Jake. It's the first time I've ever heard you speak much about it. I didn't know you took much interest."

Conversation froze. It hung in the air of the cafe like a pall. Biscuit cleared his throat and began wiping the counter with his towel. The rest of them stared self-consciously at their coffee cups, all except Hilton Redlinger. Hilton hitched himself around on his stool and looked directly at Jake, and Jake thought to himself, The sonofabitch did it on purpose. Every man there knew that Jake Tibbetts had a profligate son off at war somewhere and that Jake thought Henry a goddamned fool and the war a damfool business. But it was Jake Tibbetts's private agony and they had left it alone. Why now? Why Hilton?

"I'm interested in any case where mankind is making an ass of himself," Jake said evenly, returning Hilton's gaze. "Wars are made by men who are too old or fat to fight. The trouble with this one is, we let their fat old men tell our fat old men how to fight it. And when we're supplying all the troops and the ammunition, that's making an ass of yourself."

Jake and Hilton looked at each other for a long moment and finally Hilton said, "Well, it's for sure *we're* too old and fat to fight."

That broke the tension and there was a little smattering of nervous laughter. Biscuit refilled their coffee cups and everybody had another Victory Donut while they waited for the awkward moment among good, old friends to pass.

———————

Lonnie Tibbetts heard and saw it all from his stool next to the door, understood that something uncomfortable had passed between his grandfather and Police Chief Hilton Redlinger. But he catalogued it as another half-fathomed transaction in the mysterious secret code of grown-up men, to which he was again silent and uninitiated witness.

What interested him more than this secret code just now, though, was the thought of the Christmas program tonight. Everybody would be there at the high school auditorium. Em Nesbitt, the telephone operator at Central, would sing "O Holy Night" and Mayor Rosh Benefield, Lonnie's other grandfather, would read the Christmas story from the Bible. Then one of the ministers would deliver a Christmas message. The Methodists and Baptists took turns at that. Finally, Mrs. Eubanks's Rhythm Band from the elementary school would play "Jingle Bells" and "Up on the Housetop." Lonnie would play the wood block and his best friend, Bugger Brunson (Biscuit's grandson, properly known as Lee Mason), would play the flutofone. It wasn't a long program, just enough to get folks in the right mood. There would be punch and cookies in the school cafeteria after the program, and then everybody would go home and get ready for Santa Claus.

And now, Germans. He could picture them in his mind—tall, stern-faced men in gray uniforms, goose-stepping down the aisle of the auditorium, the Army MPs guarding them with tommy-guns. Lonnie agreed with Fog Martin. The Germans ought to stay out of the refreshments.

He thought about all of this as he sat staring out the big plate-glass window of Biscuit Brunson's cafe at the bright, bitter day, seeing the red brick courthouse and the empty street as a picture framed by the window, every line etched in thin, precise pen strokes—the naked branches of the pecan tree, where the old men played pinochle in warm weather, the brown stub of the banana tree that Fog Martin's brother Herschel had planted next to the courthouse years ago. In summer, it shot out thick green stalks and broad leaves and even, one year, a bunch of tiny bananas no bigger than your thumb. You could, if you wanted your imagination to do so, turn the picture into summer and imagine the banana tree green and taller than your head, imagine the sidewalk scorching the bottoms of your bare feet and the heat phantoms shimmering off the slate roof of the courthouse. The pecan tree would make a big puddle of shade on the green lawn where four old men argued over their pinochle cards at a rickety table. Herschel Martin would putter around the banana tree, talking to it as if he were the father of those tiny green bananas. And people would move slowly, gliding like vapors in and out of the cool dark hallways of the courthouse.

But that was summer, good for its own savoring. Now, the picture in the window was bright and sharp and bare, tinged with the delicious anticipation of the day before Christmas.

Just now, in this morning's picture, a man in overalls, flannel jacket, and battered felt hat started down the steps of the court-house, then stopped abruptly, threw up his arms, and dashed back toward the door. An automobile, a Chevy coupe, the only car Lonnie had seen that morning, slewed sideways in the street directly in front of the cafe, jumped the curb, and careened up on the brown grass of the courthouse lawn, throwing lumps of sod from beneath its spinning rear wheels. Lonnie stared, spellbound, wondering if what he was seeing was a picture embellished by his imagination.

And then the airplane roared by, its wheels barely above the pavement, swooping through the space between the cafe and the courthouse.

"What we ought to do is buy out the goddamn Limeys and finish off the job . . ." Daddy Jake was saying as the roaring explosion of the airplane drowned him out.

"What the hell!" Hilton Redlinger bellowed.

And then there was the crash of falling glass as the big plate-glass window at the front of the cafe caved in, followed by a blast of frigid air. Everything shook and rattled like Judgment Day and the noise was enormous. Lonnie Tibbetts fell off his stool.

"My God, it's an air raid!" Tunstall Renfroe yelled.

They all dived for the floor, shouting. Jake grabbed Lonnie around the waist and pressed him down on the cold linoleum.

"They've shot out the window!" Biscuit screamed. "My plate glass! Lordy, they've shot it out!"

Hilton Redlinger had his pistol out now, the big Colt revolver that no one had ever seen him fire. "Christ, they've shot Fog," he said. Fog Martin sat on the floor, staring at them dumbly, blood trickling down his face from a cut on his forehead. He wiped his face with his hand and gaped at the blood. Hilton took aim, bracing his gun hand with the other, and fired two shots through the gaping hole where the plate-glass window had been. The roar filled the room. Lonnie jerked his head up and he could see people running from the courthouse across the street.

"They're gonna bomb the radio station," Ollie Whittle cried. "They always go for the radio station! My God, Ideal Benefield is up there!"

Lonnie thought fleetingly of plump, powdered Ideal, interrupting her club and society news to describe an air raid attack. Lonnie could feel the panic in the room, could see the men's eyes wide with fright, even Daddy Jake's. His breath was coming in short gasps next to Lonnie's ear. Hilton Redlinger let fly with two more shots and one of them struck the window frame and ricocheted off with a whang and buried itself THUNK in the top of the counter.

"God, stop it, Hilton," Tunstall Renfroe said. "You're going to kill us all."

Lonnie bolted up out of Jake's grasp and ran for the door.

"Lonnie!" Jake yelled after him, but Lonnie was through the door and out on the sidewalk, looking down the street and watching the plane becoming a speck just above the horizon east of town. Ollie Whittle charged past him on the sidewalk, sprinting for the radio station upstairs over the bank, where Ideal Benefield already had the window open and was shouting down, "You men there, what's going on? You there. What was that noise?"

———

He had just gotten too low, that was all. He hadn't meant to get that low. He just wanted to see if he could catch a glimpse of Tunstall Renfroe through the front window of the Farmers Mercantile Bank, because he would prefer not to land his plane in front of Tunstall Renfroe's house and spirit Tunstall's daughter away if Tunstall was home. Marvel, he thought he could handle. She giggled a lot and might think it was enchanting, a young man coming in a plane for her daughter. But not Tunstall.

But Billy Benefield had just gotten too low and before he knew it, there was nothing to do but go under the electric power lines instead of over them, and so he had swooped down between the courthouse and the row of stores on the north side of the square and luckily the poor fool in the Chevrolet coupe had gotten out of the way in time. A Curtiss Stearman was a maneuverable plane, but you didn't just stand it on its tail, or you'd stall out and then it would be goodnight, nurse. So he had dipsy-doodled under the power lines and for the split second when he was down between the buildings, he could hear the throaty roar of the Pratt and Whitney engine bouncing back at him off the brick storefronts to his left and he could see the red blur of the courthouse to his right and the flash of the stark-limbed pecan tree just out of reach of his wingtip. He had known exactly where he was, that there was another brace of power lines down at the end of the street and that he had to get the nose up quickly and put some distance under the wheels of the Stearman before he reached the next intersection. And he did. The Stearman responded powerfully, the great blades of the propeller swallowing chunks of air as he felt the thrill of danger race through his own body—his heart in his throat, his fanny puckered up like a prune. He held his breath for a long moment and then he pulled back smartly on the stick and cleared the power lines and gained altitude as he passed over the Jitney Jungle Super Saver and the hardware store, and then he let his breath out with a whoosh. He looked back over his shoulder as he climbed away from the downtown, and he could see people running out of the courthouse and the stores, ants swarming from a stepped-on hill.

Billy hadn't meant to cause all this commotion. He really should have left well enough alone, he told himself. Things had gone quite perfectly until now. He had filed the flight plan for his training flight so that it would take him directly over his hometown on the outbound leg, and that was opportunity enough to drop a little remembrance over Alsatia Renfroe's house. But the idea had come to him as he flew. Inbound, he would be fifty miles or so to the west of the town, headed back toward base. He quickly calculated his fuel and figured that, yes, he would have enough to change course, buzz the courthouse square to make sure Tunstall was in the bank, frocked and proper, waiting for his Saturday morning customers, then land out on Partridge Road, spirit Alsatia away, and drop her off at the airport in the city. He would make it back to his air base on nothing but fumes, and they would bitch about him being overdue. But he could tell them he got a little off course and doubled back once when he shouldn't. Let 'em bitch. It was worth it. It was worthy of a woman like Alsatia Renfroe, who loved a little spice in her life.

Oh, did she ever—as Billy had learned almost six months before when he had asked her out on impulse. She was three years older, and there was, in the way she carried her trim body, a wordly-wise self-assurance that would have given pause to a young man who was less forthcoming. But Billy Benefield was nothing if not forthcoming. He might lack judgment, as his father often told him, but it never deterred him from doing whatever he wanted to do.

Billy had spied her through the window of the bank as he passed by on the sidewalk, just her head and torso visible behind the teller's cage, hands quick and sure as she counted out money for a customer, brow knitted in concentration. Billy stopped in his tracks and stared as she finished the transaction and shoved the money under the bars of the cage, then reached up with the same quick motion and brushed a wayward strand of her short brown hair away from her forehead. Billy stood transfixed for a moment, feeling the heat of the July sun on his neck spreading warmth into the pit of his stomach. Then she disappeared, back into the bowels of the bank, and he went home and called her on the telephone.

"This is Billy Benefield," he said forthcomingly.

"I saw you staring at me through the window," she said, knocking his composure into a cocked hat.

He stammered for a moment (he could never remember stammering before) and then said, "Will you go out with me tonight?"

There was a dead silence on the other end of the line and Billy began to feel miserably stupid. Then she said, "All right." Just like that. And she laughed the little tinkling laugh that gave him a rush of pleasure mixed with a delicious trace of apprehension.

Billy got his father's car with a full tank of gas (unheard of unless you happened to be the mayor's son because the mayor always had his means, though he cautioned you not to flaunt your good fortune) and he picked up Alsatia and they drove around for a while, making small talk, sparring. Billy decided she was a bit flip and cocksure in a somewhat unfeminine but very enticing way. She looked straight at you and spoke her mind about any damn thing she pleased.

"I'm thirsty," she said after a while, and when he asked if she wanted a Coke, she laughed and said, "Not by itself." Her voice had a bit of a taunt in it, as if she had asked him if he still wore knee pants. So he drove by Lightnin' Jim Haskell's house and bought a pint and they parked on the courthouse square, sipping whiskey and Coke from paper cups, listening to Ted Weems and His Orchestra on KMOX in St. Louis. The whiskey left him breathless. It was pure and raw and it seemed to suck all the oxygen out of his lungs. It was late by now and there was nobody there but them. It was still hot, the day's warmth radiating from the asphalt and concrete as it can only at midsummer, giving way to the dark grudgingly. Billy propped the bottle on the dash and they leaned against the opposite doors of the front seat, facing each other, nipping at the strong amber whiskey, their talk limp and vague like the night air.

Billy raised his cup. "Is it okay?"

"Fine," she said. "Just the usual."

"Oh, yeah," Billy said. "I know. I buy it all the time."

"A real regular customer," she said, smiling.

Billy nodded, knowing she was mocking him, not really minding it for some reason, sensing there was in her an unspoken and exotic wellspring of experience. Alsatia Renfroe *knew* things, by God, but she did not tell. It made Billy Benefield a little giddy.

"Do you fly-boys have a few belts before you go up?" Alsatia asked, laughing her little bell-laugh.

"God, no. I wouldn't touch the stuff before a mission. You've got to have all your reflexes intact. The least little mistake and WHAM! you can plow it in."

"Plow it in?"

"You know, crash. Or get caught with a Jap on your tail."

"Right," she said.

"I mean, you know, I've read about it," Billy said. "I've never been there." He stopped, fumbling with his words, the whiskey playing with his tongue. Then he laughed. "Hell, I've never even been up in a goddamned airplane."

She laughed with him, reaching for the bottle of whiskey on the dash, pouring it neat into the cup, no Coke.

"But," Billy said, "I'm going to be the best goddamned pilot in the whole Army Air Corps."

"I'll bet you will," she said, and something in her voice changed. There was no mocking now. "I bet you'll be one helluva pilot."

Billy could feel himself getting drunk, mind and body separating, his thoughts floating in and out of the open window of the car like dust motes. His lips moved, he could hear sounds bubbling out of his throat, but he lost track of what he was saying, what she said. Then they were quiet for a long time and Billy drifted deep down inside himself. Ted Weems and His Orchestra were playing "Cherokee" and some uninhibited sucker with a big ballsy golden cornet was ripping into a shimmering solo, high and a bit sad like a fast plane all alone in the thin upper reaches of air, making its own currents and leaving a precise white trail of condensed sound in its wake where the air parted and then billowed back in on itself.

He realized that her hand was on his arm and he stared, seeing her for the first time really, the finely chiseled bones of her face softened in the glow of the light from the dashboard radio. Then he smelled her perfume, a mere breath of something like mint. He could feel her warmth, a different quality than the close air, radiating from the soft flesh of her face and neck. She reached over and turned off the radio with a click, leaving the cornet solo shimmering in the lost upper reaches of air. Then she moved to him, unbuttoned the top two buttons of his shirt, reached inside and ran her slim hand over the sweat-slickness of his bare chest. ''Oh,'' he said softly. She slid away from him suddenly and he reached for her, but she was out of the car, crossing in front around to the driver's side. She leaned in the window and kissed him deeply, one hand behind his neck pulling him into her mouth, her tongue darting, forcing his teeth apart, mingling with his tongue, teaching him.

And then, by God, she had pulled him out of the car and led him across the narrow strip of courthouse lawn and pulled him down with her under the spreading green canopy of Herschel Martin's banana tree, and she had given him everything she had right then and there with the warm soft midnight breathing on his bare bottom and the wind rushing in his ears even though there was no breeze stirring, and the echoes of the cornet solo burning everything out his mind. She was wild. She threw her strong sturdy legs around his back and squeezed him into her and she went WHAM-WHAM with a little cry. He was numbed by the raw liquor and the shock of it. She went WHAM-WHAM again, then a third time, and then she started to whimper. She reached up suddenly and grabbed him by his left nipple and twisted sharply and hissed into his ear, ''Come!'' And the thrilling pain of it raced down into his groin and he went WHAM-WHAM and collapsed on her, near fainting.

It took a moment for him to come to himself and realize what he had done. Jesus Christ, he thought, I have screwed my first woman under Herschel Martin's banana tree on the courthouse lawn at midnight.

''I love you,'' he croaked.

''Don't get carried away, Billy,'' she said.

He pulled back, started pulling his pants up, feeling panic

rising in his throat. Any moment, somebody could come along and see them here, the mayor's son and the banker's daughter with their whoozies hanging out. Alsatia sat up and began composing herself.

"Come on," he said, pulling at her, "we've got to get out of here."

"Oh, don't get in a twit, Billy," she said, laughing her tinkly laugh.

God, he thought, the woman is mad. Then he thought of something else. "My gosh, you'll get pregnant."

"I doubt it," she said, brushing her hair back from where it had tumbled about her face.

"Oh? You know so much?"

"More than you do."

So, he thought, it wasn't just idle talk. He was not the first boy she had diddled, maybe not even the first under Herschel Martin's banana tree. Who were the others?

He helped her up and they lurched back to the car, both drunk, and they sat apart on the front seat for a long time, not saying anything. Then Alsatia said, "You think I do that with all the boys?"

"I don't know," he mumbled.

"Well, I don't," she said, tossing her head.

"Hey"—he reached for her, but she pulled away. He could see that she was hurt, that she had taken his long silence for scorn. She began to sniffle now and Billy stared at her, dumbfounded, then pulled his handkerchief from his back pocket and offered it to her. She took it, dabbed at her eyes, then looked at him defiantly. "I just wanted to do it with *you*!" she said.

And so she had. He honestly believed that whomever she had done it with before, she now just wanted to do it with him. And she had done it again and again before he staggered off to Basic Flight Training a week later with the scent of Alsatia seared on his brain and the delicious terrifying memory of lovemaking in forbidden, often public places—the stage of the high school auditorium, the narthex of the Methodist Church, his parents' bed, her parents' bed, even standing up beside his father's car parked in the middle of the Whitewater Creek Bridge at three o'clock in the morning.

Alsatia Renfroe had risked everything. And that was why

Billy Benefield was here in his Curtiss Stearman on Christmas Eve morning.

He made one low pass over the downtown, but the way the sun hit the big plate-glass window of the Farmers Mercantile Bank made it difficult to see inside. So he swooped down again and all of a sudden he was in trouble, down where only fools flew. So the only thing to do was dip down under the wires and skim the street and pray while his fanny puckered up like a prune.

When he was up, out of danger, he realized he hadn't even looked in the front window of the bank to see if Tunstall was there. He smacked the flat of his hand against the cockpit wall angrily, then jerked the stick around to the left and headed out toward Alsatia's house. To hell with it. Tunstall or no Tunstall, he was landing.

It occurred to Billy that this was no way to become mayor, as his father, Rosh, deeply desired and as family tradition dictated. This, in fact, could put your ass in a permanent sling. But he had been in scrapes before, and so far there hadn't been anything Rosh Benefield couldn't get him out of. If Rosh really wanted him to be mayor, then Rosh would find a way to help him out of this one.

Besides, he might never have another chance like this with Alsatia. The war was almost over. He would never see combat, never cover himself with glory in battle in a way that would make Alsatia's creamy thighs tingle. No, all of the guys who had made it to the front already would come rushing home in a few months, dazzling folks with their ribbons and their war tales, grabbing up the Alsatias and the political offices. Campaign ads would be full of photos of rock-jawed young men in daring poses on the turrets of their tanks and the wings of their planes and the bows of their PT boats. There was only the Pacific left (no matter this temporary business at Bastogne), and not much there. The Navy would simply surround the Nip islands and let the yellow devils starve themselves into surrender. And Billy Benefield would be the kid who got there too late. So it was here and now as far as Alsatia Renfroe was concerned. One thing the war taught you, whether you made it to combat or not, was that you had to rip off a hunk of life while you could, because there was no such thing as destiny, only odds. And the odds told him to land in front of Alsatia's house and spirit her away and let the devil take the hindmost.

There was a clear, straight stretch of road alongside the pasture just before you got to Jake Tibbetts's house, with no trees on either side or power lines to worry about. A good two hundred yards of nothing but open, straight, hard-packed red clay roadway with at least twenty yards of brown winter-deadened grass between the road and the fences on either side. Plenty of room for a landing, plenty for a takeoff once he had Alsatia in the rear seat.

Billy throttled back as he came in low over the trees that bordered the road just before the big open spot. He cut the engine back all the way as the wheels cleared the trees, and dropped it down onto the roadway with a gentle thump.

One thing Billy Benefield could do, he thought, was fly an airplane. It was a natural act. He would have been hell in combat, with the damp warm rot of jungle and the smell of bougainvillea under his wings and quick death spewing from the barrels of his Avenger. He could shut out the roar of the engine from his mind, feel the essence of the plane's power and grace. He had heard pilots talk about the plane becoming an extension of yourself, but this was more than that. In the purest experience of flight, man became machine. It was not the engine that throbbed, but the core of your manhood. It was Billy Benefield himself who thumped down softly on the hard-packed red clay road next to the pasture. The plane, all that metal and wiring and fabric and fluids, was simply along for the ride.

He coasted, tapping lightly on the brake until the plane slowed, then eased the throttle forward a bit and taxied down the road under the stark leafless limbs of the trees on either side of the roadway, past the Tibbettses' house with Pastine standing open-mouthed on the front porch, wiping her hands on her apron. Billy gave her a big friendly wave as he lumbered past, but she just stared at him and Billy knew she didn't recognize him under the leather helmet and goggles. He was creating a small tornado here under the trees, the propeller kicking up a cloud of dust and leaves. He could see Pastine Tibbetts shiver in the prop wash, then disappear into the house.

In town, there was pandemonium.

The courthouse and every store on the square had emptied and there was a good-sized crowd milling about in the space between the front of Biscuit Brunson's cafe and the spot on the courthouse lawn where the Chevrolet coupe had slewed to a stop. The driver, a woman in a brown coat, was sitting on the ground next to the open door of the car, fumbling with the clasp on her purse and jabbering, "My God, it was an airplane. He almost killed me. An airplane, can you believe it?" Nobody seemed to be paying her much attention except for Jake Tibbetts, who had his reporter's pad in hand and was taking notes.

"What happened?" he asked the woman.

"What happened? Well, I was going to get my mama a Christmas present and an airplane ran over me, that's what happened."

"Did you get a good look at it?"

"I could tell it was an airplane, if that's what you mean. Wings, propeller on the front. An airplane. I could see that much." She had a small cut on her cheek, but it wasn't bleeding much. She finally got the clasp on her pocketbook undone, pulled out a tissue, and dabbed at the cut. She looked up at Jake. "All I wanted to do was get Mama something for Christmas, and Ernest told me not to take the car because it's close to the end of the month and we've almost used up the gas ration and Ernest has to have the car to go to Taylorsville next week, but I said, 'Ernest, I ain't going to walk downtown in this cold wind to get Mama a Christmas present, I'm taking the car, it ain't worth catching pneumonia over it, I got enough to do without getting sick.' But who would have believed I'd get run over by an airplane?"

A small knot of people hovered around the car, but most of the crowd was over in front of the cafe, crunching around in the glass that littered the sidewalk and peering inside through the gaping hole where the window had been.

"Look here, a bullet hole!" one man yelled, pointing to a hole in the wood on the inside of the window frame. "Hey," the man called up to Ollie Whittle, who was leaning out the upstairs window of the radio station, microphone in hand. "A bullet hole, Ollie. They were shooting at the cafe."

"A new development here, folks," Ollie said into the microphone. "We've just learned that the attacker fired shots at Brunson's Cafe. This reporter was inside the cafe when the attack occurred, and I can tell you for sure, folks, an enemy air raid is nothing to be scoffed at. We sure can appreciate what the men at the front go through. The attack, as we said, came just a few minutes ago, totally unexpected. At least one aircraft dived on the courthouse square. An automobile wrecked on the courthouse lawn and Brunson's Cafe had its front window shot out, but that appears to be the extent of the damage. This news bulletin, by the way, is brought to you by Redlinger's White Angel Funeral Home. . . ."

Across the square, Em Nesbitt had the window open in the telephone exchange upstairs over City Hall. "What's going on out there?" she called. "What was that noise?" Em had a clear, strong voice, a good singing voice, and it carried like an aria on the cold air of the morning.

"We've had an air attack, Em. Sound the fire siren," Tunstall Renfroe called back.

"A what?"

"An air attack. Turn on the siren."

Em disappeared from the window, and in a moment the siren on the roof of the fire station on the opposite side of the square moaned to life. The siren was new—an electric device that could be triggered by switch from the telephone exchange. Rosh Benefield had gotten it through some connections at the air base north of Taylorsville a few months before. It replaced the old handcranked siren, and it cut a good ten or fifteen minutes off the response time for the volunteers. Already it had saved the Methodist parsonage. Now it wailed like a banshee across the town.

Tunstall Renfroe and Fog Martin headed for the fire station, and in a moment, the big front door of the station rolled up with a clatter and the fire truck rumbled out of the gaping maw of the bay, Fog at the wheel and Tunstall beside him on the front seat. Tunstall was wearing the extra pith helmet he kept at the firehouse and Fog had a strip of white cloth wrapped around his head to stop the bleeding from the cut on his forehead. Fog turned on the truck's own siren, a low, throaty growl.

Hilton Redlinger appeared in the open front door of Brunson's Cafe, the big Colt revolver in his hand, just as the truck, gears clashing, pulled up in front. "What the hell's going on?" he said, gawking at the truck and the growing crowd spilling out across the sidewalk and the street, perhaps fifty or so now. People were arriving in cars and on foot, most of them men, several armed with rifles and shotguns. One man carried a huge double-bitted axe.

Tunstall stood up in the front seat of the fire truck, yelling over the wail of the fire siren, "Now everybody go home! This is folly, standing around here in a crowd. We're sitting ducks! Everybody, go home and fill your bathtubs with water. Ollie," he called up to the radio station, "you get that on the radio, you hear? Tell folks to stay home and fill up their bathtubs."

"Right, Tunstall," Ollie yelled down. "Folks . . ."

"Now wait just a damn minute!" Hilton Redlinger bellowed. "Ollie, you just hold your horses." Ollie stopped in midsentence. "You trying to start a panic here, you and Tunstall? Stop broadcasting about that airplane right this minute. Put some music on or something. Put Ideal Benefield back on. No, don't do that. Put some music on."

"But Hilton," Ollie protested, "we've got to let folks know what's going on."

"Hell, we don't *know* what's going on. Now you put some music on that radio station or I'm coming up there and shut it down and arrest you for creating a public disturbance."

Ollie disappeared inside the radio station.

"Hilton, you're making a serious mistake," Tunstall protested from the fire truck. "You're taking a chance with people's lives here. We've got to alert the town."

"To what?" Hilton moved through the crowd to the fire truck, waving his pistol and clearing a path.

"The air raid," Tunstall said. "My God, man, are you blind?"

"One airplane, Tunstall. One goddamned airplane," Hilton glared up at him.

"But what about the damage?"

"What damage, Tunstall? We've got a car run up on the courthouse lawn and a window busted out." Hilton grabbed a man next to him. "Run over to the telephone exchange and tell Em Nesbitt to cut off the fire siren." He gave the man a shove in that direction and turned again to Tunstall. "Now you fellows take the fire truck back to the station. Fog, get that thing out of here."

"Right, Hilton. How about I take a turn around town on the way to see if there's any more damage?"

"Fine, but keep the siren off," Hilton said. "Tunstall, you

go with him. Survey the damage and give me a report.'' He grabbed another man standing in the crowd. ''And you go get Doc Ainsworth. We can't reach him on the phone. His line's busy. Tell him Biscuit's had a little spell here. I think the excitement just got to him.''

The phone was ringing inside the cafe and Hilton went back inside to answer it.

Across the street on the courthouse lawn, Lonnie Tibbetts was tugging at Jake's sleeve.

''It was one of ours,'' Lonnie said.

''What?'' Jake stared at him.

''It wasn't no Jap or German. It was a Curtiss Stearman.''

''What the hell is a Curtiss Stearman?''

''It's a training plane. It ain't even got any guns on it.''

''How do you know?'' Jake asked.

''I know a Curtiss Stearman when I see one. I was looking straight at it when it flew by. I got a good look. Besides, I know all the silhouettes of the Jap and German planes. Mr. Renfroe let me look at them when I was helping him on lookout. It's a Curtiss Stearman. Honest.''

''You sure?'' Jake asked.

''I'm sure.''

''Hey, Hilton,'' Jake yelled across the street, just as the wail of the fire siren died, leaving the square strangely hushed. Hilton stuck his head out of the gaping hole of Biscuit's window. ''Lonnie here says it's a Curtiss Stearman,'' Jake said.

''A what?''

''It's one of ours. A training plane. It's unarmed, that's what he says.''

''Well, who shot out the window?'' Tunstall Renfroe shouted, still standing on the seat of the fire truck. ''Just tell me that. If it was an unarmed airplane, who shot out the window?''

''Chief Redlinger must have done it,'' Lonnie said.

''Lonnie says Hilton shot out the window,'' Jake called across the street.

Hilton stared at the Colt revolver in his hand and shoved it into his holster. ''I didn't shoot out the goddamn window,'' he said hotly. ''I didn't fire a shot until the window was already gone.''

Fog Martin started backing the fire truck out of the crowd.

"Hold up, Fog," Hilton said. "Let's try to figure out what the hell's going on here."

A man next to Hilton stuck his head out of the window of the cafe. "Hey, Jake Tibbetts," he called, "you got a telephone call in here. It's your wife."

"Lonnie," Jake said, "go see what Pastine wants."

Lonnie trotted across the street to the cafe. "It was a Curtiss Stearman," he said as he passed Hilton Redlinger.

Ideal Benefield called down from the radio station, "The mayor will be right here, Hilton. I just talked to him on the telephone. He says to keep everybody calm."

"Is Ollie playing music up there, Ideal?" Hilton asked.

"The Radio Luxembourg Orchestra," Ideal answered. "It sounds like funeral music."

"Tell him to put on something cheerful. And see that he doesn't say anything else about an air attack."

Lonnie dashed out of the front door of the cafe and pushed his way through the crowd across the street to where Jake was finishing his interview with the woman in the Chevrolet.

"Mama Pastine says a plane just landed on the road in front of our house," he said breathlessly.

"Christ Almighty," Jake said.

A moment later there was a whole fire-truck-load of them— Hilton, Tunstall, Biscuit (pale but recovering), Fog, Jake, and Lonnie—headed out Partridge Road at full speed with the siren whining WOOOAHHH, WOOOOAHH. They stopped briefly at City Hall while Hilton ran in and got the Thompson submachine gun he had kept locked away since the city bought it back in the early thirties, when desperate men were knocking over banks like bowling pins. Hilton sat up high on the long folds of hose on the back of the truck with the tommygun nestled in his lap, wiping off the Cosmoline with a rag. Lonnie huddled beside him, teeth chattering from the excitement and the biting wind. They almost ran over Mayor Rosh Benefield as they turned the corner from the courthouse square onto Partridge Road, Rosh massive and lumbering with steam rising off his overcoated body from the Saturday morning bath that Ideal's frantic call had summoned him from. His eyes bugged in terror as the truck, wailing like Judgment Day, rounded the corner and bore down on him. He lurched to the side and the truck swerved away and then squealed to a halt. They pulled Rosh aboard and now he sat up front on the wide red leather seat with Tunstall and Fog, thin strands of black hair plastered wetly against his skull. They all felt better with Rosh there because he was a solid man, unflappable, quick-witted—a wiry, sharp-minded man tucked away inside the body of a hippopotamus. Rosh was the only man in town that Jake Tibbetts did not consider to have a touch of the fool in him, and that said a lot.

The truck slowed as they approached the Tibbetts house and Jake, standing on the rear platform, leaned around the side to see what was ahead. But there was no airplane there, no sign of Pastine, either, and he wondered for a moment if she had been snatched up and taken away. Then he thought how foolish that was, how foolish and absurd the whole business was, the thought that they were under enemy attack, here at the end of the war, with the Japanese and the Germans all but defeated and the continental United States unscathed through the entire affair. But then he thought how the war had changed everything, had in fact made almost anything possible if you turned the world upside down and shook it enough. There was of course no enemy aircraft on Partridge Road this cold Saturday morning, the day before Christmas. But there *could* be. And the possibility of it made them dash about like characters in a Buster Keaton movie, dead serious, grim with the fear that turned slapstick into drama into slapstick. There was a fine line there. And he, Jake Tibbetts, who of all men loathed feeling foolish, whose job it was to examine the foolishness in men and events, was smackdab in the middle of it. He could at least appreciate the irony.

They heard it before they saw it, the angry whine like a sawmill gone berserk. They passed Jake's house and rounded the big curve in the road and there it was, sitting sideways in the road, nose pointed toward Tunstall Renfroe's house, engine roaring, propeller kicking up a hurricane of dust and leaves. The pilot was standing up in the cockpit, yelling something at the house. Marvel Renfroe and Alsatia were on the wide banistered front porch and Alsatia was yelling back. Then the pilot turned and saw the fire truck bearing down on him and he sat down in the cockpit and revved up the engine and spun the plane around so that the whirring blade of the propeller was pointed toward the approaching truck.

"Stop!" Hilton yelled, and Fog mashed down on the brakes

and they all pitched forward, holding on desperately as the truck squealed to a halt about thirty yards from the airplane.

"See, I told ya it was one of ours," Lonnie Tibbetts cried. "It's a Curtiss Stearman." It was, indeed, clearly marked with stars and bars on the wings and fuselage.

"A spy!" Tunstall yelped. "Shoot out his tires, Hilton, so he can't get away."

"Nobody's shooting anybody," Rosh Benefield ordered, heaving himself upright in the cab of the fire truck. "That's my boy there."

They all stared at the plane, past the silver blur of the propeller blade, and yes, they could see that the young man behind the leather helmet and goggles was indeed Billy Benefield. He cut the engine back to a throaty idle, but when they all clambered down from the fire truck and started toward the plane, he gunned it and then let out on the brake just a touch and eased the plane toward the advancing crowd to let them know he was holding them at bay and would not be trifled with. They stopped in their tracks with Rosh Benefield's massive bulk in front and Hilton Redlinger at his side with the tommygun in his arms and Jake Tibbetts right behind, wishing to hell he had had time to grab the Speed Graphic from the *Free Press* office because this was a picture story if he ever saw one, a story that cried out for evidence against disbelief.

Then all of a sudden Tunstall Renfroe broke from the pack and sprinted toward the house, skirting wide around the plane—yes, actually sprinting, a figure of lithe grace where they would have expected to see a bouncing scarecrow, arms akimbo, legs lurching. But Tunstall's wing-tipped feet seemed to barely touch the ground and his elbows were tucked in close to his sides like a fleet young foot racer's. It was marvelous, and Jake thought instantly about how he would write a sidebar to this story, a little piece about the elegant poetry of Tunstall Renfroe's bold dash to protect his home and his women, about how he defied age and gravity and was, at least this once in his life, unselfish and courageous—and about how there was that capacity in every man to take up his life in his own hands and shake it for all it was worth.

Billy Benefield stood up in the cockpit and screamed at Tunstall, but Tunstall didn't falter. He reached the broad front steps of the house and stopped and turned and faced the airplane, feet planted wide, face defiant, with his women behind him up on the porch. "Beautiful," Jake muttered to himself. "Beautiful."

"Billy, what the hell is going on here?" Rosh Benefield thundered over the roar of the Pratt and Whitney.

Billy yelled back, "I've come for Alsatia."

He turned to look at her and she cupped her hands around her mouth and called down to him, "Fool!" and Billy flinched as if he had been shot. "Fool!" she called again, "go away."

Alsatia was a straight-shouldered, sturdy-legged young woman with clear skin that gave off a glow of fresh-scrubbed ruddiness and a strong voice that pealed across the yard like the bell of the First Baptist Church. "You're crazy, Billy Benefield."

"I did it for you!" he yelled, waving his arms.

Alsatia threw back her head and laughed lustily. "I know. It's wonderful!" She clapped her hands in delight.

Billy bowed from the waist. "Come on, then."

"I don't go flying with fools," she called back. "Go away. Come back when the war is over."

Billy's face fell. "You won't go?"

"No. But you're marvelous." She blew him a kiss.

Jake Tibbetts looked back and saw that a big crowd had gathered behind the fire truck. People had come by cars in twos and threes, so excited they had left their cars in the road with the doors open and engines running, rationing be damned. Guns bristled in the crowd, muzzles skyward like stubble in a cornfield.

"Billy," Rosh Benefield called. Billy jerked his head around and stared at his father. "Billy, I'm coming around to talk with you." He turned to the rest of the crowd. "Stay here. Let me take care of this."

Jake bristled. "The hell with that. I'm coming, too."

"All right. But the rest of you stay put."

Rosh and Jake walked around the plane's wing and stood on the ground just under the cockpit, looking up at Billy with the dust of the road swirling up around them. The thin strands of Rosh's hair had dried and were billowing in wisps around his head.

After a long moment, Billy said, "I guess I screwed up."

Rosh said nothing. Billy looked around at the crowd in the road, at Marvel and Alsatia standing on the porch, at Tunstall planted at the bottom of the steps with his arms folded across his chest.

"I guess the shit's gonna hit the fan," Billy said. Billy raised the goggles off his face and shoved them up on his leather helmet, leaving big white circles around his eyes.

Still, Rosh was silent for a long time while Billy looked at him, waiting. Finally Rosh sighed—a great, body-shaking sigh—and said, "I'll see if I can fix it. Jake, let me talk to you." He turned on his heel and the two of them walked twenty yards or so off to the side of the road and stood in the grass.

"Don't print it," Rosh said to Jake.

Jake's mouth fell open.

"I'm asking you," Rosh said. "Don't print it." Rosh blinked his small bright eyes, small eyes in a large face in a huge body, a big, proud, solid body. Rosh was a tough man. Jake had seen him in a courtroom literally strip a witness of his composure and confidence with his stare and his quiet, unrelenting voice. But there was no malice in him. He was also proud in the way a man ought to be proud. He knew himself and gave himself no quarter and measured up to his own stern yardstick. He did not ask easily, and he rarely blinked those small, bright eyes.

Jake looked over at the plane, still kicking up a cloud of dust and leaves, Billy standing in the cockpit, the engine a steady idling roar. He thought how events often dragged men in their wake, making fools of them all.

"They'll find him out," Jake said after a moment.

"Maybe not."

"There's the radio. It's been all over the radio."

"So, who believes the radio? It's here one instant and gone the next."

"Somebody'll tell," Jake said, thrusting out his jaw. The whole business offended him. Especially this.

"Maybe not," Rosh said. And Jake realized, as crazy as it was, he might just be right. That was the thing about this god-damned town, you didn't mess with it if you were an outsider. And you didn't mess with Rosh Benefield, who was liked better than any man in town. And too, the town had raised Billy Benefield, the way a small town raises all its young, watches them, brags on them, kicks their butts when they need it. This town might do this thing for Rosh Benefield. They might help him work it out, even with Ollie Whittle's hysterical broadcast and

Biscuit Brunson's smashed window and all the rest. Unless Jake ran the story in the paper. Then the jig was up. Rosh was right about the radio. But once it was in the newspaper, it was real.

Jake glared at him. "I've been in the newspaper business forty-odd years and I've never pulled a story. Not one goddamn story. I've been offered bribes, I've been threatened with bodily harm and worse. But I've never pulled one goddamn story. Now what the hell makes you think I'm gonna pull this one?"

"It never happened, Jake," Rosh said calmly.

"Horseshit! I'm standing here and I'm seeing a kid in a United States Army Air Corps airplane parked in the middle of Partridge Road with the engine running, trying to get Tunstall Renfroe's hotpants daughter to go for a ride with him, and you say it never happened? Why, Rosh?"

"Because it's my boy."

Jake was struck by the great weight of it, by the notion that a man would risk pride, credibility, respect—a lifetime of them—for his son. Once you had asked for a thing like this, you had no more right to ask for anything. The price was staggering, yet Rosh hadn't flinched. Jake, of all people, knew just how staggering it was, because he knew in his heart he would not do the same thing for his own son. He had not ever bailed Henry out. He never would.

But it was not enough. "Rosh, you make a fool out of yourself if you want to. But I've got a newspaper to put out." Jake turned to go, but Rosh grabbed him by the arm.

"There's one other thing, Jake."

Jake swung back around to him and felt his jaw go rigid and his head tilt back as if a great force were pushing at him. He wanted to throw up his arms and shield himself from what he knew was coming, but he didn't.

"You want me to beat you over the head with it, don't you," Rosh said.

They stood there glowering at each other and finally Rosh let go of Jake's arm and shrugged his massive shoulders.

"You owe me, Jake."

Jake's face went slack and the strength drained out of him and puddled on the red clay of the roadway. Rosh didn't have to spell it out because Jake Tibbetts had been living with it for a long time. Plain and simple, it was the fact that his boy had married Rosh's daughter and it smelled of death and destruction from the beginning and that's the way it ended, with Hazel dead and Henry a drunken shell of a man. Now, after all this time, it was laid open like a festering boil pricked with a needle, pus running out of it smelling like death. It had remained unspoken for a long time because it would be an act of dishonor to speak of it. You went on living in a place and living with people despite indiscretion and disgrace because they were the only place and the only people you had, and you had to put some things away for life to go on. Speaking of it now was another terrible price for Rosh Benefield to pay, because it violated unspoken law. This, too, was an act of courage.

It was no matter of winning or losing here. Rosh had simply called in a debt and in doing so had wiped the slate clean between them. But Jake felt a great sense of loss and violation, because to pay the debt meant conceding his one inviolate possession, the integrity of his newspaper. He felt unclean now, standing on the side of the road as Rosh left him and walked back to the plane. He was a man who was about to pillage the sanctity of his own mind, and nothing would ever undo that.

Jake followed Rosh, who was beside the plane now. Billy leaned over the side to hear him.

"How long are you overdue?" Rosh asked.

"Less than an hour."

"All right. Go back. Tell them you had engine trouble. Tell them you landed here, called me, I got it fixed for you. I'll call your base on the telephone while you're on the way and tell them the same thing."

"What kind of engine trouble?" Billy asked.

"How the hell do I know?" Rosh shook his big head impatiently. "I'm a lawyer, not a mechanic. Think of something. Something that's easy to fix. Something Fog Martin could do. A loose wire—I don't know. Do you have enough gas?"

"It'll be close, but I think I can make it."

"And Billy . . ."

"Yes sir."

"Give it a week or so to settle. Then get out."

Billy looked at him, puzzled. "What do you mean?"

"Get out of this airplane business."

"But why?" Billy protested.

"Because you lack judgment, son."

Billy pulled the goggles down on his face again, covering the white circles around his eyes. "I'm the best pilot in the Army Air Corps," he said flatly.

"I said, get out," Rosh repeated.

Billy peered at him through the goggles. "I'm sorry, you know that."

"I know. Now get out of here."

"Yes sir." Billy turned around and looked again at the porch of the Renfroes' house where Marvel and Alsatia stood. Alsatia shook her head, smiled, blew him another kiss.

They got the road cleared and the people and cars out of the way with a great deal of shouting and running about, and Hilton Redlinger sent Fog with the fire engine down to the other end of Partridge Road to block it off so no more traffic would get through. Then Billy settled back in the cockpit and strapped on his parachute harness and gave everybody a wave and eased the throttle forward. The plane lumbered down the road, kicking up a terrible dust storm in the bright cold midday, until it rounded the big curve. Then Billy turned the plane at an angle in the road and locked the brake down and revved the engine to a high whine, checking it, testing the controls until he was satisfied that all was in good order. He pointed the nose at the long straightaway and gave another wave and gunned the Stearman down the road and lifted it majestically into the air, leaving the road swirling with a storm of debris. The plane cleared the trees nicely, gaining altitude, then Billy banked sharply and roared back over the crowd of people standing in the road. It was then that they saw Lonnie Tibbetts, waving gaily from the rear seat of the Stearman, unseen by Billy Benefield, and all their frantic calling could not bring him back to earth.

FOUR

BILLY yelped and jerked his head around and stared at Lonnie with a stricken look when he tapped Billy on the shoulder as they taxied down the ramp at the airfield. "Holy smokes!" he cried. "What are you doing back there?" And Lonnie Tibbetts, who had enjoyed his first airplane ride immensely, just grinned at him.

"It's okay. I buckled myself in," Lonnie said. Indeed, he had figured out the seat strap and shoulder harness and had buckled himself to the plane, loosely so he could raise up in the seat and see over the side. "You could have done acrobats and I wouldn't have fallen out," Lonnie said.

"There's not even a parachute back there," Billy said, shaking his head back and forth, as if he could will Lonnie away.

"So, you weren't gonna crash, were you?"

"Christ!" Billy slumped down in the front seat and stared straight ahead and kept taxiing for a while. Then he turned back to Lonnie and said, "You just keep your trap shut, you hear? You don't say nothing. I mean, nothing."

"Okay," Lonnie said.

They rolled to a stop and several men ran out. Lonnie rose

up in the seat and peered over the side of the cockpit, and they stopped and gawked at him and then started yelling.

The lieutenant who was Billy's flight instructor was madder than hell to begin with. Rosh Benefield had called ahead and told them Lonnie was in the backseat, so that was no surprise, but still the lieutenant was plenty steamed about Billy being overdue on his cross-country flight and not calling in when he had engine trouble. He yelled and screamed and Billy hung his head like he had got caught cutting a fart in church and Lonnie listened and learned a few new words. Eventually they took Lonnie to the flight shack and sat him in a corner and gave him a cup of coffee and a donut while Billy went off with the flight instructor. After a while a major came out of a back room, a tall sandy-haired crinkly-eyed fellow, and said, "You the stow-away?"

"Yep," Lonnie said, before he remembered that Billy had told him to keep his mouth shut.

The major stood tall and straight-shouldered over him, hands on hips. "I oughta court-martial you, buster."

"You cain't," Lonnie said. "I ain't in the Army Air Corps."

"Consider yourself a prisoner of war, then," the major said. "You know what we do with POWs?"

"Some of 'em's coming to the Christmas program tonight," Lonnie said.

The major looked at him quizzically. "What's your name?" he asked after a moment.

"Tibbetts."

"Well, Tibbetts," the major said, "since you're a POW, I'm gonna put you on a work detail."

Lonnie imagined a rock pile and a group of sweating, swarthy Germans. But as it turned out, he rode around with the major in a jeep for an hour or so, holding the man's clipboard while the major checked the flight line. The major bundled him up in a fleece-lined flight jacket that swallowed him and put an olive drab stocking cap on his head, and he was quite warm in the front seat of the open jeep despite the sharp wind that whipped across the open tarmac. The planes were lined up in neat rows on the apron next to the runway, a few old bi-winged Curtiss Stearmans like Billy had been flying, several newer trainers, even a couple of fat-bellied Thunderbolts. They sat waiting, silent, chocks under their wheels, canvas lashed over the open-cockpit Stearmans, plexiglass canopies latched tight on the others. Mechanics worked on one of the Thunderbolts, its cowling stripped off to bare the huge engine, the men on ladders tinkering with its innards, blowing on their bare hands to keep them warm. The major stopped the jeep under the nose of the plane, so close that Lonnie could reach out and touch the gleaming silver blade of the propeller. A young sergeant climbed down from one of the ladders and walked over to the jeep, gave a halfhearted salute. He had a big grease smear across one cheek and his nose was red and raw from the cold. The sergeant stared at Lonnie.

"How's it coming?" the major asked.

"It's a bitch."

"How long?"

"Two hours, maybe three. Fuel line's clogged. We got to take it out, see where the trouble is. Then put it back in."

The major scratched his head. "Colonel wants it ready by morning."

"Yes sir."

"But hell," the major said, looking straight up at the sky, "I'll betcha there's a part you need to fix that airplane that we just haven't got. And there's no sense keeping the men out here on Christmas Eve when they can't get the job finished." He looked back at the sergeant. "I suppose the colonel will just have to fly something else."

There was a trace of a smile at the edge of the sergeant's mouth.

"Knock off, sergeant. You just make sure you've got that bird ready to fly by twelve hundred hours Monday. I'll see you get that part in time."

"Yes sir!" The sergeant stepped back, snapped off a smart salute, and the major threw the jeep into gear and roared off.

"You believe in Santa Claus, Tibbetts?" the major asked as they drove back to the operations shack.

"No, sir. He's a phony."

The major shook his head. "That's where you're wrong, buster. Just like a POW to say something like that. Guys like you, you been fooled by the propaganda. You think Santa Claus is some old fart with a white beard and a red suit who comes down the chimney. Then you get about your age, you start thinking how dumb the whole thing is, and bingo, you got no more Santa Claus. Right?''

Lonnie looked over at him, saw how crinkly his eyes were around the edges under the stubby bill of the shapeless cap he was wearing. ''Yes sir. That's right.''

''Well, let me tell you something, Tibbetts. When I get through putting this godforsaken place to bed in a couple of hours, I'm gonna hitch up my britches and get my ass to town, and I'm gonna see Santa Claus. The real magilla. On the way, I'm gonna stop and buy a bottle of the best hooch I can find, and Santa Claus and I are gonna pass it back and forth awhile until things get good and mellow, and then Santa Claus is gonna haul my ashes. You ever had your ashes hauled, Tibbetts?''

''Mama Pastine makes me clean out the fireplace every morning,'' Lonnie said.

The major threw back his head and roared with laughter. ''That's the ticket, Tibbetts, that's the ticket. Anybody gets his ashes hauled every day has got to believe in Santa Claus.''

His two grandfathers, Daddy Jake and Rosh Benefield, were waiting for them at the operations shack, having driven the hundred miles to the air base on preciously rationed gasoline in Rosh's car. Rosh described again how Billy had had engine trouble and landed his plane and called Rosh, and Rosh had had a local mechanic, a whiz of a fellow with engines, fix whatever it was that was wrong with Billy's plane, and somehow little Lonnie here had crawled up in the back seat while they were working on the plane, nobody noticed him, and well, here he was. Rosh explained it all very matter-of-factly, as he would to a jury, and the major just looked at Rosh with his crinkly eyes. While Rosh was talking, Daddy Jake kept the evil eye on Lonnie, making sure he kept his mouth shut. When Rosh was finished, the major looked over at Lonnie and told him to keep the olive drab stocking cap and to remember about Santa Claus, and then Rosh and Jake and Lonnie piled into Rosh's car and headed home. Jake didn't have much to say. He mostly stared out the window, and Lonnie could see that he was thinking about something real hard the way his brow furrowed and every once in a while his jaw got hard and wiggled as if he were grinding his teeth. He didn't even chew Lonnie out. But when Rosh dropped them off at the house, Mama Pastine took Lonnie straight upstairs and whaled the daylights out of him with one of Daddy Jake's broad leather belts.

As he sat that night on the stage at the high school auditorium, tapping his wood block in the front row of Mrs. Eubanks's Rhythm Band at the Christmas program, his rump and the back side of his legs still stung. But he said to himself that if that was the price you had to pay for a little old airplane ride, so be it.

Lonnie suspected it was all pretty awful. He had heard the Philadelphia Orchestra concerts on the radio, and Mrs. Eubanks's Rhythm Band couldn't even keep time as well as the guys in the Philadelphia Orchestra. But the high school auditorium was packed and there was an air of Christmas excitement mixed with the delicious undercurrent of all that had happened that day. Em Nesbitt sang "O Holy Night" while Mrs. Eubanks accompanied her on the piano. Reverend Ostrow Willis of First Methodist (it would be the Baptists' turn to run the show next year) delivered the Christmas Eve message, all about the hope represented by the Baby Jesus and how Mary and Joseph had wrapped him in squabbling clothes. Rosh Benefield, because he was the mayor and had a good speaking voice, read the Christmas story from the Bible, and you could tell from the buzz and hum in the auditorium when Rosh rose to go to the podium that the whole town *knew*, and more than that, *was in on it*. But Rosh looked them in the eye and read the passage from Luke strong and clear, and when he sat down there was a lot of nodding out in the audience, except from the couple of rows down front where the German POWs were seated. Lonnie was astonished at how ordinary they looked in their plain gray uniforms. A couple of them were very young, no older than Billy Benefield. You couldn't have told they were German POWs except for the military policemen seated behind and to the sides of them. There had been a lot of oohing and whispering and a few baleful stares when they shuffled in just before the program started, but they looked so harmless there was almost an air of disappointment, as if people had been expecting a Panzer Division.

The Rhythm Band played last, and they went boldly through "Good King Wenceslas" and "Jingle Bells" and "Up on the Housetop," with Lonnie keeping up a good strong beat on the wood block and anticipating the hot chocolate and brownies in the cafeteria after the program was over and trying not to squirm in his seat to ease the stinging in his rump.

When they finished, they got a nice solid round of applause, but before Reverend Willis could get to the podium to pronounce the benediction, one of the Germans, an older man with close-cropped hair, stood up right there in the front row and said in a loud voice, "Dat iss the verse shit I haff effer heard."

There was a huge appalled silence and then Daddy Jake leaped out of his seat like a little berserk bulldog, bellowing, "You sonofabitch!" and crawled over people in a frenzy, out in the aisle and down into the middle of the German POWs before anybody could stop him. Jake hit the Kraut three times before the man could get his dukes up. The German crumpled and went down with blood spurting from his nose. Lonnie jumped up in his chair and yelled, "Git 'im, Daddy Jake, whup the bastard!" while the auditorium just went crazy, a wild flailing swarm of bodies down at the front as several other local men leaped into the fray, women screaming, one surging mass of people trying to get down front tangled with another surge toward the rear as others tried to get out of the way, the kids on the stage yelling with delight while Rosh Benefield stood there and watched it in fascination and Reverend Willis wrung his hands and murmured, "Goodness, goodness."

Then Lonnie saw Chief Hilton Redlinger bulling his way through the crowd, pushing people out of the way until he got down to the front of the auditorium, where the mass of heaving men had sort of collapsed on itself in a grunting, cursing pile while the MPs danced around the edge pulling at bodies, trying to get them separated. Chief Redlinger had his huge Colt pistol in his right hand, and Lonnie thought, My God, he's going to start shooting again like he did this morning at Biscuit's. But Hilton had his whole meaty hand wrapped around the pistol, shielding the trigger guard, ready to use the Colt to whack heads if he had to. He reached into the pile and grabbed Jake Tibbetts by the rear of the britches and yanked hard, and Jake came loose like he had been pulled from a mud hole. Jake spun around suddenly and somehow—unintentionally, Lonnie thought—Hilton's revolver caught him just above the right eye and blood spurted bright red from the gash and streamed down his face. Jake stopped short, stared at Hilton for a moment, then reached up and felt the cut and brought his hand away and looked at the smear of blood on it. He was almost serene. Lonnie, standing at the edge of the stage, heard it quite plainly when Jake said, "Hilton, I'll get you for that."

"Jake, get the hell out of here!" Hilton said. "Get out before I throw you in jail for starting a riot."

Jake pulled a handkerchief from his back pocket and folded it carefully and pressed it over the cut, gave Chief Redlinger a withering look, and stalked off. By this time, the MPs had things calmed down a bit. There wasn't much damage, really. The German with the loud mouth had a busted nose and a few of the others had scrapes and bruises. The MPs hustled the Germans out the back door of the auditorium and the Christmas Eve program broke up quickly. There wasn't much stomach for hot chocolate and brownies.

They walked home, Lonnie and Daddy Jake and Mama Pastine, in a dreadful silence. Mama Pastine didn't say a word, but she was puffed up like a bullfrog and Lonnie could almost smell the bile rising up in her. Lonnie was so excited he could hardly keep his feet on the ground and his mouth shut, so finally he got tired of trying to hold it in and raced off down Partridge Road ahead of them and ran around the house several times and whooped and hollered and then sat down on the front steps to wait for them. They hove into view presently, Daddy Jake strutting like a bantam rooster, holding the handkerchief over his eye, Mama Pastine marching in terrible high dudgeon beside him.

They had sent him straight to his room and for a long time he could hear Mama Pastine's voice rising and falling like a bullwhip in their room across the hall. Finally she wore herself out and the house got quiet enough so that he could think back over all that had happened and sort it out in his mind.

It was then that he began to worry about Santa Claus. Recounting his deeds this day, it came to him that he had been at the center of enormous folly and that perhaps a mere blistering of his rear with Daddy Jake's belt would not atone for it. Perhaps Mama Pastine had decided to take his punishment an unspeakable step further—to just leave the Daisy Red Ryder BB gun and the other gifts in the back of her closet. Maybe he would be that one solitary boy in all of recorded history who got *nothing*.

Mama Pastine had lectured him often on pleasure and pain, good and evil, the agonies of Hell and the glories of Heaven. He believed her, believed fervently that God and the devil made war over his mortal soul, that somewhere in the neighborhood of the Heavenly Throne sat an archangel presiding over a huge ledger on which he totted up every good and evil thought and deed. You could always ask for forgiveness, as Lonnie did enthusiastically every night, at least concerning those things about which he was truly sorry. Still, he figured, everything remained in the ledger just the same—the archangel simply made a check mark beside every black deed for which forgiveness had been sought—and someday there would be a great accounting. It just didn't make sense that you could wipe the slate completely clean. Why, that way an old reprobate could sin like sixty all his life, then wiggle out of it with his dying breath and waltz through the Pearly Gates alongside the Baptists and Methodists. Surely God wasn't that dumb. Surely he spotted the old reprobates trying to mingle in with the crowd and thundered, ''Whoa there, Buster! Not so fast!''

But Lonnie thought how horribly unfair it would be if he were lumped in with the old reprobates, and wished passionately this night for the accounting to be postponed. He began to pray and he prayed so hard that his head began to hurt. He went at it for a long time, and finally he heard a stirring in his grandparents' room, Mama Pastine poking around in the closet. Then the door opened and he heard her measured *clomp-clomp* down the stairs. She stayed for a few minutes and came back and when the house was still again, Lonnie let out his breath with a great whoosh and said quietly, ''Thanks, Lord.''

He lay there, listening to the house noises for a while, and then the thought of his father bubbled up, unbidden, from the secret places of his mind. Henry Tibbetts might be taboo here, thinking of him might be a very great sin in this house, but he clung stubbornly to the place, a great unspoken mystery. Lonnie wondered where his father was this winter night. Was he warm? Did he have enough to eat? Did he have friends? And did he ever suffer secret agonies deep in his soul, the way his son so often did?

Lonnie puzzled over his father for a long time in the dark empty midnight. And when he finally drifted into sleep, Henry remained—a sad shadow at the edge of his fitful dreams.

There was only a hint of light in the room from the last pink and orange embers of the coal fire, and Captain Finley, like the light, seemed more a feeling than a presence. He sat deep in the wing-back chair near the hearth, one gray-trousered, leather-booted leg swung over the other. Young Scout noticed first the movement of his hands as he wiped the blade of the glistening saber with a cloth, stroking it with long sweeping motions. Even in the faintest of light, the blade gleamed softly. Captain Finley's broad-brimmed cavalryman's hat and leather gloves lay on the floor next to the chair.

Young Scout stopped in the doorway of the parlor, confused for a moment over why he had come. He stood for a long time, watching Captain Finley, waiting, listening to the wind outside. It was from the north and it moaned at the windows. Then there was another sound, muffled by the wind, the restless snuffling of horses and the stamping of feet—the Lighthorse Cavaliers at muster in the dark, waiting for their captain.

Finally he spoke, and the rich weariness of his voice seemed to rise like coalsmoke from under the curve of his moustache.

"They tried to make me a major today. Can you imagine that, Young Scout? A major! Why, a major is a goddamned fart blown by the wind. Useless, like tits on a boar hog. The next thing, they'd want me performing menial duties on some goddamned general's staff, the sort of trifling things majors do. By God, I'd rather be a private than a major. A private has more honor to him."

"You said no?" Young Scout asked.

"Damned right I said no. They'd have taken my Lighthorse Cavaliers and given them to some dunderhead barely out of his diapers. Some young fool who'd get them slaughtered trying to glorify himself. Let me tell you, Young Scout, the Army of Northern Virginia is the finest collection of fighting men in the history of combat, but it is a human enterprise and thus has its share of idiots and pettifoggers. Many of them are majors."

"But you wouldn't have to be a major forever," Young Scout protested. "You could get to be a colonel and even a general. And then you could command a whole slew of cavalry. Like Jeb Stuart."

"Hah!" the Captain spat. "Stuart. A dilettante. An egomaniac. The greatest glory-seeker of them all. Brilliant, granted. But he spends as much time plucking plumes for his campaign hat and dancing with the ladies in Richmond as he does fighting the Federals. Besides, he was a major once, wasn't he?''

"I guess so," Young Scout conceded.

"Well, there you have it. A man can't be a major and escape unscathed.'' Captain Finley finished wiping the saber, tucked the cloth inside his tunic, slipped the gleaming blade back into its scabbard, and laid the scabbard on the floor next to the chair with his gloves and hat.

"Anyway," he went on, "a hundred men is the most effective cavalry force. Any more than that and you lose speed and flexibility, and thus forgo the elements of shock and surprise, which are the essence of horse tactics. Tonight, for instance. We ride on Hanover Courthouse, where two companies of Federals are asleep like innocents in their bedrolls, dreaming of sugarplums. We will be upon them before they have time to say 'Scat.' And we will carve them up for Christmas dinner.'' His eyes glowed, fevered, in the dying firelight. "They will bleed this night, Young Scout, at Hanover Courthouse. And McClellan will wake in the morning to the awful truth that nowhere in his lines is safe from the Lighthorse Cavaliers! A hundred men, Young Scout. A hundred good and lusty men will loosen McClellan's bowels like a dose of salts.''

"May I come?" Young Scout asked.

"No. I have more important things for you. Wait and listen. Orders will come.'' He stopped, sat deep and silent in the chair for a long time while the wind cried at the eaves of the house and the room grew chill. Then he stood stiffly, reached and picked up the sword, buckled it onto his wide belt, slipped the thick leather gloves onto his hands. "While you wait,'' he said, his voice heavy, "pray for the poor souls asleep in their bedrolls at Hanover Courthouse. Pray for them, Young Scout. They are damned this night.''

Then he was gone, and Young Scout could hear the sharp voice outside in the yard, the barking of commands, the stamping of horses and creaking of leather as the Lighthorse Cavaliers mounted. Young Scout watched at the window as they rode away, Captain Finley on the black horse at the fore, leaning into the night and the wind. There was a full moon, a hunting moon. He stood for a long time, long after the horsemen had melted into the dancing shadows of the wind-whipped trees, until he heard the knocking at the front door.

When he opened it, he saw the woman standing there on the front porch. She had a thin, pinched face, the flesh drawn tightly over the fine bones, an enormous belly covered partly by a threadbare gray coat. She had a piece of paper in her hand. She was shivering. It was miserably cold and the wind whipped nastily around the edge of the house and plucked at the strands of her hair.

"Jake Tibbetts," she said.

"No'm . . ." Lonnie started to say, then his grandfather's voice was suddenly at his back.

"I'm Jake Tibbetts."

The woman thrust forward the piece of paper she was holding. "I'm Henry Tibbetts's wife. Here's the marriage license. And I'm about to have this baby on your porch."

Lonnie stared at her, then turned to look at Daddy Jake, whose face was hidden in shadow in the doorway behind him.

"Jesus H. Christ," Jake Tibbetts said softly.

BOOK
TWO

O N E

JAKE TIBBETTS was proud of the fact that he had written only one editorial in his life.

It had been just after the death of his father, when Jake had taken over the paper.

He had written that he came to the business reluctantly but with a sense of the role the newspaper had played in the life of the town since Jake's grandfather had founded it—that it was as indispensable as the undertaker and the mercantile store to the functioning of a civilized community. He would, he said, attempt to keep the paper honorable and curious. The editorial ran only a few lines and it had caused no particular comment, but the longer he edited the newspaper, the more he prized it. He had no greater ambition for the paper in his sixty-fourth year than he had had in his nineteenth, and he could think of no better way than that editorial to say it.

The week after that first editorial, when he had written all the news he could think of, he sat down to write another one and found he had nothing to say. Nothing, at least, that should carry the weight of the entire paper behind it. Later, Jake began a weekly column that ran without fail on the left side of the front page. But that was Jake himself speaking. He put his own name to it. An editorial, now—that was the voice of the *paper*. And that meant all the honor and curiosity and credibility it had earned since its very first issue. Jake Tibbetts might speak of many things, and he might be taken seriously or lightly. But the paper was no trifling thing. When it spoke, it must be a thing of moment.

Over the years, Jake's column had brought him a measure of notoriety. He was nothing like William Allen White of Emporia, Kansas—who hobnobbed with presidents and princes and wrote of the great tides that sweep man's destiny before them—but his columns appeared in several of the state's newspapers, including the big daily in the state capital. He called the column "Folly" because that was what he wrote about. It was wry, skeptical, caustic. It caught the mood of people sobered by Depression and war. He wrote about the things around him—the minutiae of a small town, the foibles of common folk. Jake Tibbetts was quoted. And when he made one of his rare appearances at the state Newspaper Association convention, he was treated with a bit of awe and deference, accorded the role of seer.

But that was all long after he had come to grips with the paper, after he had learned that he was meant to be a newspaperman, not an engineer as he had originally intended. It was after he discovered, by doing it, that he had the natural curiosity and passion and gift of expression that made a good newspaperman. It was there in his genes, waiting to be tapped.

At first, he knew only that he had no choice but to give up his engineering, come home from college and run the newspaper. It was a family obligation. His mother could not handle it alone, and it would be some years before he could turn it over to Isaac, his younger brother. His mother had put it to him quite plainly as they sat in the parlor after they had buried Jake's father, Albertis: Come home and take over the paper, or she would put it up for sale. And much as Jake loathed the place, that would not do.

He set out at first, not knowing he had any gifts for the newspaper business, trying to understand it as an engineer would methodically research a problem of angles and stresses. He was not looking so much for insight into the mechanics of the trade—he picked that up naturally enough from the old printer who ran the shop. Rather, he wanted to know the process of how events became news, what was worth telling and what wasn't, how event became copy, what strange chemistry it was that linked the paper to the town.

During the first months he struggled during the day just to get the paper out once a week, learning the ancient craft of printing—the strange smooth feel of type, the odd way the type cases were laid out, the noisy maddening intricacies of the Linotype, the quirks of the massive Kluge press and the folding machine. Then at night he spent hours in the yellowing back files of the *Free Press*, reading the words of two generations of Tibbetts newspapermen, waking often at dawn with the sun slashing through the window of the newspaper office, body cramped and aching, head resting on the pages of the large bound volumes he had been reading when sleep took him.

He found that it had been, in its best of times, a fierce newspaper—uncompromising, blunt, often judgmental. It printed warts and all and made no apologies for it.

Take the bank, for instance. Jake learned that it was actually Tunstall Renfroe's great-uncle who had founded it just after the Civil War. He had managed it with apparent good sense for ten years and then had suddenly absconded with most of the assets, accompanied by a young male teller, never to be heard from again. It was all there in the paper, unvarnished. Tunstall's father had taken over the ruined bank and over a period of some thirty years he had slowly, painfully, repaid the town's losses and rescued the Renfroe family name. There were small evidences of the bank's return to respectability: News that assets had grown, announcements of new services, and finally coverage of the grand opening of the bank's new offices on the courthouse square, an event of such moment that it included a parade, fireworks, and speeches. There was, as the *Free Press* reported, "a huge throng, virtually the entire populace of the incorporated community and many from the surrounding countryside, overflowing the sidewalk and street in front of the grand new bank building and covering the courthouse lawn like locusts." It had been one of Jake's father's rare flights of fanciful prose. The article also noted that "the crowd braved a sweltering sun and the speech by Mayor Arthur Benefield, which ran upwards of two hours."

It was from the paper and from his mother that he learned about his grandfather, Captain Finley, who had died when Jake was small and who existed in his memory as a short, stocky man with big graying eyebrows and leather suspenders and a powerful, gamy smell about him that Jake first associated with his growling monologues at the dinner table and that he later came to know as the odor of whiskey and cigars. Jake, barely able to see over the edge of the table, his plate of food at eye level, sat at Captain Finley's left. He rarely understood the conversation, but the memory of the old man's smell, the confident, rumbling rise and fall of his voice, was powerful. In later years, strong good talk, spirited argumentation, always evoked the bittersweet aroma of his grandfather. Captain Finley was a man who knew his own mind.

Jake's mother's memory was more detailed, but similar: "Captain Finley. He always wanted to be called Captain. He loved Tuesdays, because that's when he set type. It was all done by hand back then, before your father put in the Linotype machine. Captain Finley would go to the paper very early in the morning, and he would stop off on the way at Lightnin' Jim Haskell's house and pick up a quart jar of whiskey. He'd lock the door to the paper and work all day, drinking whiskey and setting type and singing bawdy songs. You could hear him out in the street when you passed by. Then sometime in the late afternoon he would get through setting type and finish off the jar of whiskey and lay down on the floor and go to sleep. He was something of a town scandal.''

That had been when Jake's mother was a girl, in the years after the Civil War, in which Finley Tibbetts had fought as a captain in Pickett's cavalry. Captain Finley had come home from war with nothing but his saber and his horse and the clothes he wore, a man approaching middle age with a wife and a half-grown boy and not much prospect for employment. He had been a railroad man before the war, but the railroads were mostly gone, ripped up by Union raiders, their rolling stock either demolished or stolen and taken up North. Finley had sold the horse, borrowed a little money, and started the newspaper. Years later, when Jake took over, no one could tell him why Finley Tibbetts had gone into the newspaper business. He was a literate man, though he had never been to college, but there was no history of newspapering in his family. He seemed simply to have filled a need. The community had no newspaper, so Finley Tibbetts started one. He hung his warrior's saber over the fireplace of the small house he built on the outskirts of the crossroads farming community, the house that had sprouted wings and a second story over the years until it was the rambling, disjointed white frame hulk of Jake's youth. In the beginning, it had been three rough-hewn rooms. That was even before the courthouse had been built.

Jake deduced, from reading the early issues of the *Free Press*, that the town had stolen the courthouse. Or, more precisely, had stolen the county seat. The courthouse followed.

Another community, thirty miles away, had been the seat of government before the war, but it was located on the railroad line and had been pretty well ravaged by the Union raiders who came to tear up the tracks. So as soon as the Reconstruction legislature was formed, peopled with newly freed Negroes and Northern carpetbaggers, Captain Finley and other locals mounted a campaign to have the county seat moved. They argued that their town was more centrally located in the county, and thus more accessible to a farming population whose labors left precious little time for conducting legal and commercial affairs. The *Free Press* was filled with exhortatory editorials trumpeting the superior qualities of the town and citizenry, the unassailable logic—real and imagined—of making it the seat of county government. But when the deed was done, Captain Finley Tibbetts's account left no doubt that logic had little to do with the business:

This newspaper is reliably informed that the decision to relocate the seat of government to this community was aided and abetted by liberal amounts of cash, crops, and other inducements, to which our Legislature is uncommonly susceptible these days.

Let it never be said that our citizenry (both here and in the Capital) do not know how to strike a bargain.

Debate on the measure in the General Assembly was virtually non-existent, a fact that may be due in part to the absence from the proceedings of the representative of our rival community. It is reported that he was at the moment in the clutches of a band of ruffians who accosted him on the outskirts of the Capital City and incarcerated him incommunicado, bound and gagged at the bottom of a well, during the period of the Assembly's discourse.

We trust that such carryings-on will result in better protection for members of the Legistlature in the future, and that those responsible will be brought to Justice. If God wills it.

The former county seat, of course, screamed foul. The federal governor-general investigated. But the decision stood, and Finley speculated in print that the governor-general had been persuaded by the same "overpow'ring logic" as had the General Assembly. The future of the town was assured. A new courthouse was built and the railroad, when it was reconstructed, followed the new county seat, which became a bustling mercantile center serving the surrounding farmland. The town grew up around the courthouse, and as it prospered, the *Free Press* thrived.

Captain Finley Tibbetts had not been content to observe and comment. He served on the Board of Education, held posts in the powerful Masonic Lodge. In the pages of the paper, he spoke of himself in the third person:

Reports having reached the community that a gang of thieves and rogues had seized control of the Whitewater Creek Bridge and were accosting the good citizens of the area and were relieving them of their worldly goods and affronting their Personages, an armed force led by Captain Finley Tibbetts, formerly of General Pickett's horse troop, moved against the marauders.

Following a brisk engagement in which two of the ruffians were dispatched on the spot, the remaining three were hung from the bridge railing until dead.

Captain Tibbetts's force suffered the loss of one horse.

As Jake pored through the back issues of the *Free Press* in search of its soul, he came to identify the newspaper largely in terms of Finley Tibbetts, because Jake's father, Albertis, had left little of his mark on it. And when he pictured Finley Tibbetts in his own mind, it was the picture of a warrior. The only photograph of him in existence was a daguerreotype showing Finley in his cavalryman's uniform—close-set, intense eyes like live coals under the bushy eyebrows, staring out from under the perky bill of a campaign cap, nose slightly large for the square face, bold curving moustache that made the thin mouth seem to turn down at the edges as if Finley were about to spit.

The photograph had been taken in Richmond near the beginning of the war, when the Confederacy was in full blush, the Army of Northern Virginia recognized as the finest assemblage of fighting men in history, before Finley had witnessed the insane hope of the Confederacy go glimmering on the blood-soaked slopes of Cemetery Ridge as his horse company attacked through a nightmare of gore on Pickett's left flank. Jake had been only six years old when Finley died in 1886 at the age of fifty-seven, so all that lingered were the photograph (which he kept now on his desk at the paper) and the vague but insistent memory of the bushy eyebrows and leather suspenders, the rumble of the strong confident voice like a cannonade rolling across the dinner table, the smell of cigars and whiskey. That memory, and the Finley he discovered in the pages of the *Free Press*, convinced Jake that his grandfather had brought home a cast of personal devils from the slopes of Cemetery Ridge, and that he had spent the rest of his life spitting in their eyes.

His editorials were proof enough that the warrior remained. Of the Town Council he had written:

> The most unnecessary rank in the Military Forces is that of Major. It is the Captains and Lieutenants and those in the enlisted ranks who do all the work, whilst Colonels and Generals get all the glory. Between the two classes is the rank known as Major, holders of which have no other responsibility than to jump through their skins upon the command of the Colonels and Generals and on the whole make life discommodious for the Captains, Lieutenants, and enlisted men.
>
> Pity, then, the community whose entire Town Council is composed of Majors. They are at the beck and call of that odious minority known as the Landed Gentility and manage to needlessly complicate the lives of the General Populace.

There was the occasion in 1883, three years before Captain Finley's death, when—as Jake learned from his mother—the captain had gone on an especially lengthy and devastating drinking binge, had barricaded himself inside the *Free Press* office in

defiance of family and constabulary, and had come to his senses
on Thursday morning to find he had not gotten out an issue of
the paper for the week. To avoid loss of his postal permit, he
had met the weekly mailing requirement by simply reprinting
the previous week's issue with a new dateline and a bold headline above the masthead: "REPEATED BY POPULAR REQUEST."
It was a story still told with knee-slapping relish in the state's
newspaper circles.

Toward the end, when the years of heavy drinking and bat-
tling with his private devils had begun to eat at his mind, Finley
had become savage. He wrote:

> Congressman Llewellyn visited this community on Fri-
> day last to participate in the Independence Day celebra-
> tion. Despite that, the festivities went on apace.
> Congressman Llewellyn came disguised as a hot-air bal-
> loon and floated throughout the day above the assembled
> celebrants, tethered only by the weight of his overwhelm-
> ing pomposity.

And:

> This journal hereby notes the passing of a local citizen of
> some notoriety, one Emmanuel Haislip, who, being
> stupefied by spirits, fell from the porch of the Majestic
> Hotel, and, striking his head against a hitching post, was
> killed instantly.
>
> Said Haislip is survived by his wife and seven young
> innocents, who exist in utter destitution.
>
> The ladies of the Methodist Missionary Society, noting
> the sorry state in which the late Haislip was wont to keep
> himself, have refused to render aid to the family of the
> departed.
>
> Mr. Haislip was a servant under arms of the late la-
> mented Confederacy, which he served with distinction
> and courage. The ladies of the Methodist Missionary So-
> ciety are not worthy to lick his boots.
>
> We know whereof the Bible speaks when it invokes
> blessings upon the POOR IN SPIRIT. It does not mean
> Mr. Haislip.

Jake could see that the paper had been a sharp-witted conscience for the young town in its early years, but that as Captain Finley aged, it had become simply the old man's vituperative mouthpiece, full of his own dark hauntings. Jake resolved not to let it happen again. A man might have his own prejudices and the paper might have its own voice, but the twain must not be confused.

There was little evidence of Albertis Tibbetts, Jake's father, in the pages of the *Free Press* in the years before Albertis had succeeded to the editorship. Captain Finley had dominated the paper totally. The only mention of Albertis was a brief announcement in 1873 when Albertis, at age eighteen, had entered the paper's full-time employ. "The editor," Captain Finley had written, "notes the addition to the staff of this journal of Albertis Tibbetts." That was all. No title, no mention of Albertis's duties, no comment on the editor's expectations.

Albertis had, in truth, been consigned to the back shop, to the ink pots and type cases, and there he stayed until the day they found Captain Finley bug-eyed and stiffening in the parlor of the house with a whiskey jar in one hand and his Confederate saber in the other. There was a deep slash across the flowered brocade of the parlor sofa, cut through to the springs, a final bluecoat Captain Finley had faced and slain. Jake's mother told him how Finley's face, in its death pose, had been twisted into a grotesque, vicious snarl that Cosmo Redlinger, Senior, the undertaker, could not expunge. Jake had been a small boy at the time, but he had a vague, troubled recollection. Henrietta Tibbetts, his long-suffering wife, looked at him one last time before they bolted the casket lid and shuddered. In his last years, Captain Finley had been a hard, hard man.

Albertis was not. There was a deep tinge of melancholia in the Tibbettses' family history—a tendency toward fits of depression, dark imaginings, night sweats, purple fevers, overactive dreams. This sullen strain in the family psyche would vanish for generations, then suddenly fester and erupt as it had in Albertis.

He was a doe-eyed, gentle, forebodingly quiet man, given to great silences when time seemed to hang suspended about his thin, bent shoulders. He had seen his father bedeviled by liquor, so he had never taken a strong drink. But there were times when his melancholia was stronger than whiskey. For days, he would be incapacitated by whatever dark and secret fears he harbored, when he would sit immobile in the deep-tufted wing-back chair in the parlor, facing the open window, staring into the day or night as if waiting for the visit of an archangel. He had always been a moody boy, but the fits of depression began to surface regularly after Captain Finley died and Albertis, at the age of thirty-one, took over the paper.

No one had to tell Jake Tibbetts about Albertis. He knew firsthand, because he watched his father slowly wither and rot from whatever it was that sucked away his vitality.

Albertis was a sensitive craftsman in the print shop. He set type flawlessly. His layout of the paper was pin-neat, a beauty of composition. But the soul of the paper, what was *written* in it, utterly confounded him. He had none of Captain Finley's natural affinity for words or his keen sense of man's fickleness and folly that made the pages of the *Free Press* fairly dance with excitement. The paper under Albertis was a pleasure to look at, but it was as dull as dishwater.

What Albertis did do was modernize the paper's physical plant. He went to St. Louis and bought a typesetting machine, the first to be installed in a newspaper in the entire region. The Linotype clattered and rumbled as Albertis sat hunched over its keyboard, making it sing with the columns of copy that passed through his fingers into its keyboard and were transformed into slugs of type ready for layout. Albertis rarely made an error. His concentration was total. He and the machine seemed to become as one, as if the hot metal coursed for a time through his own veins. The machine was an early model, and temperamental. Periodically it would belch in protest and suddenly spit a stream of molten metal toward the ceiling, sending everyone within range scurrying for safety. Albertis would patiently clean it up, make minor adjustments, sit down at the keyboard, mutter to the machine, and resume typing. Jake's earliest and most basic consciousness was embedded with the tart smell of the Linotype metal cooking in the machine's bowels, the rich shop smells of ink and glycerin and paper, the clink of metal against metal, the vision of sweat pouring down Albertis's face as he stroked the machine, his countenance serene, the only time he ever seemed at peace with himself.

The paper prospered, even more than it had under Captain Finley. It was not burdened with the old man's raging passions, the feuds with advertisers and subscribers that kept somebody mad with the paper almost constantly. Under Albertis, it was bland, predictable, safe, and utterly lacking in personality. But then there was little of his father anywhere. Albertis Tibbetts did lonely battle in the agonized arena of his own soul.

Albertis had always been quiet and withdrawn, so in the years of Jake's childhood it had not seemed particularly odd that he became more so. But about the time Jake was entering adolescence, Albertis's periods of gloom and silence and immobility began to stretch into days, and the running of the paper became something of a crisis. Jake's mother, Emma, began to take on more and more of the duties. Out of desperation, with Albertis incapacitated for longer periods of time, she hired a printer, a grizzled ink-stained gnome named Turbyfill, who, when provoked by the ornery Linotype machine, could spew forth streams of profanity that were works of beauty in their inventiveness.

Emma put the boys to work in the shop, Jake proofing galleys and setting headlines and advertising copy in movable type, Isaac stacking paper and running errands. And Jake began to resent the paper. He saw nothing but tedium and confinement in it. He began to hate the sight of his father hunched over the Linotype keyboard, on the days when he was well enough to work, turning babble into metal. He had no understanding and even less patience with the notion that a man's private devils could eat at his innards. He assumed that it was the paper that did it, and he resolved to never, never let that happen to him. The paper could go to hell. He thought of it as a gaping black hole, stinking of sweat and ink, that could swallow a full-grown man.

Emma, because she couldn't depend on her husband, became the paper's de facto editor. Albertis's name never left the masthead, but she was in fact running the place without pretense of being a newspaperwoman. Jake and Isaac helped, but it was not much. As months passed, Jake could see the newspaper sapping her strength, and that made him hate it even more. Emma kept the paper together, protected its name and reputation because she had two sons who would inherit it. But the paper was slowly defeating her. Seeing it, Jake would stand in the back shop shaking with a rage that left him weakened and faint of vision. He wanted to throw his work violently to the floor and run screaming out the front door. But to do that he would have to pass his mother, who would peer up from her work with strained, faded eyes. And he couldn't face that. Years later, he would see in the back issues of the paper what a haunted shell of itself it had become under Albertis Tibbetts, how much the paper had become like the man. But at the time it was happening, when he was there watching it, he felt only rage. He vowed to have done with it as quickly as he could, even if it meant running away.

As Albertis's melancholia deepened, his isolation from the family became almost total. Days stretched into weeks when Jake's only notion of his father was a presence behind a locked door, the measured tread of footsteps pacing the floor of the upstairs bedroom, the pall of a deeply troubled spirit in the house. A doctor came and went periodically, but there would be no change in Albertis's condition for a week, two weeks at a time. Then, unannounced, he would emerge from whatever black chamber he had been inhabiting, mumble a few words to wife and sons, and steal quietly back to the newspaper office, where he would hunch over the keyboard of the Linotype, sweating the rancid sweat of a man whose vital juices were poisoned and curdling.

When Jake was seventeen and on the eve of graduation from high school, Albertis called him into the parlor during one of his rare moments of lucidity to talk about Jake's prospects. The sight of his father caused Jake's breath to catch in his throat. He had seen little of Albertis for weeks. The man was a ghost in his own home. His flesh was pale, parchment-thin, drawn tightly around the deep-set eyes and sharp cheekbones. There was a kind of fever about him, the smell of wasting flesh and spirit. His hands trembled in his lap, alive with their own uncontrolled electricity.

"Jacob," he said, and it was the voice of a stranger, a wayfarer lost in the desert of his own soul, a voice so dry and barren and robbed of life that it was more silence than sound. Albertis was sitting deep in the wing-back chair and the chair was turned so that it faced the window, away from the rest of the room. His eyes never left the window, never stopped staring out at the yard, where spring was beginning to wither under the hot breath of June. "Jacob," he said again, "will you take over?"

Jake's mind tumbled in confusion for a moment. What in hell was the man talking about? And then he realized Albertis meant the paper, and his stomach took a sickening lurch. "No," Jake said.

There was a long silence and Jake searched Albertis's face for some flicker of emotion, even anger, but there was nothing.

"I plan to be an engineer," Jake said. "I'm going to college. Mother says there's enough money to get me started, and I'll figure out the rest."

"What about the paper?" Albertis asked, still staring out the window.

"Let Isaac have it."

The thin hands trembled, the pale eyes blinked. "Does he want it?"

"I don't know. He's only eight years old. How the hell would he know?" Albertis's gaunt head jerked slightly.

"Did you know that?" Jake went on, hearing his voice rise, feeling the rage beginning to thrash about in his gut. "Did you know that Isaac is eight years old? Or that I'm seventeen? Or that Mother is getting old? Huh? Did you know that?"

He wanted to lash out with his hands, grab the bony shoulders, cuff Albertis about the head, shake the dry brittle body until pieces came loose and fell on the carpet. But he held himself ramrod straight beside the fireplace next to the chair, arms rigid at his side.

Then for the first time Albertis turned to look at Jake. If he had spoken sharply, Jake would have struck him. But Albertis's voice was calm and steady. He lifted a quavering hand and stroked his chin. "Young man, you speak like a fool. You have been in league with phrenologists and soothsayers and exorcists and that idiot doctor who comes here poking and farting and mumbling. What, by God, do you know of succubi?" He gave a hollow laugh, then went on, his voice fevered. "Would an infant cling to its mother if her fangs were dripping with poison? Hah! Field mice know their own hiding places." He looked out the window again, nodding to himself, his eyes dancing about in their sockets like dervishes. Then suddenly he seemed to collapse upon himself. His shoulders sagged, his face went slack, he sunk back into the deep reaches of the chair. Again, his voice was ancient, barely a whisper. "An engineer. Ah, yes. Your mother's doing. Well, be done with your engineering."

Jake started to protest that it was his own idea, that his mother wanted him to stay and take over the paper, that she literally begged him with her weary eyes. But he hung fire, seeing for the first time how truly mad Albertis was, and how near death.

So Jake ran, lurching with the burden of a deep, pained, irretrievable sense of loss and betrayal. A man owed more to his family than to just give up and take refuge in bedlam. A boy was owed a father. That was the least he could expect.

Jake spent two years at the university in a state of constant dread, waiting for the inevitable. He learned the art and craft of the engineer, took small refuge in the neat confinement of lines and angles, logic and natural law. But he was certain he would have to give it up. And he did.

When Albertis died, they discovered that he had been living with a steadily growing brain tumor that had, during the last miserable year of his life, turned him into a violent madman. At the funeral there was a livid bruise on Emma Tibbetts's forehead, the result of Albertis's final slobbering paroxysm. Like his father before him, Albertis had become a hard, hard man.

Jake came home from college and buried his father and took over the paper and wrote his first editorial, then began to discover the soul of the newspaper that Albertis had never known. In the still, quiet hours of the early mornings he leafed through the back pages of the *Free Press* and found his grandfather, the warrior-editor. By God, the man breathed fire in print. He wrote at full gallop, the flashing silver saber of his wit slicing air and flesh. Finley had left powerful reminders of himself: his words; the daguerreotype; and the saber, which still hung in its silver sheath above the parlor fireplace in the white frame house out Partridge Road that now served as home for its third generation of Tibbettses. Jake lifted the sword from its hanging place, restored its luster with neat's-foot oil and silver polish, made a weekly ritual of cleaning it. The touch of the cool smooth metal was a physical link with the man who had wielded it in hot battle, as he had later wielded a slashing pen. Jake came to worship him. Captain Finley was the father he would have chosen for himself. Albertis had simply gotten in the way.

As Jake began to mold himself to the paper, as he remolded the *Free Press* in Captain Finley's original image, he discovered painfully how difficult it was to write simply and well, how impossible it was to describe anything exactly or to recount any event with perfect faith. At first, words dumbfounded him. He was a bumbling, inarticulate lout with deadlines nipping at his heels. He cried in frustration, hurled pencils, wadded paper.

But eventually, it came to him like some long-neglected animal instinct, the essential secret of all writers: Most of the business involved having something worth saying, and the rest depended on saying it simply. He discovered that his engineer's love of logic wasn't entirely wasted on the process, that good writing was the natural expression of an organized mind. A man had to organize his thoughts, get to the heart of things, and not clutter up the place with excess verbiage. After one particularly frustrating bout with the language, the floor about his desk littered with scraps of paper, he composed a line that he typed on a fresh sheet of paper and thumbtacked to the wall above his desk:

CHEW ADJECTIVES THOROUGHLY AND ESCHEW ADVERBS ALTOGETHER

and then went on to write a straightforward, unadorned account of the event he had been trying to describe. It made him grunt with satisfaction.

The paper became a sort of cocoon in which he underwent a metamorphosis from engineer to newspaperman, a tight circumscribed world of metal and ink and words, a world in which a cauldron of heat and light and sound and smell bubbled and stewed and finally gave forth that most marvelous of creations, a newspaper, in which the editor was seer and alchemist.

Jake came to realize that his genes, however muddled, had done him a favor, that he had that rare combination of skills and instincts it took to edit a weekly newspaper. From Captain Finley (though it took him a while to realize it) he had inherited some talent with words, natural curiosity, innate skepticism, the touch of arrogance that told him he had a right to observe and comment on mankind's affairs. From Albertis (loath as he was to admit it) he had gotten a mechanical sense, a feeling for the print shop that was the other half of the paper's personality. A newspaper needed both talents. It had its voice, and then it had its means of mechanical expression. Both masters had to be served.

In a small town, hundreds of miles from a mechanic who could service a Linotype machine or a Kluge press, you had to be able to fix things yourself, often with makeshift parts and ingenuity. And that was where Jake's engineering instincts served him well. He had an ear and a feel for the machinery. He could sense the certain, almost imperceptible shudder in the innards of the Linotype just before it belched forth a spurt of hot metal. He could hear the slightly off-key rumble of the big press that let him know when a bearing needed grease. He had an inborn curiosity about how things worked that served him well as both printer and editor. The human machine was messier and less reliable than the Linotype or the Kluge, but it too operated within certain natural bounds, within the laws of push and pull. And a newspaper was one of those pushers and pullers that kept the human machine on track.

At the turn of the century, Jake had been editor of the paper for a year and he was beginning to admit he liked it. The day came when he was able to dismiss the ill-tempered old printer, Turbyfill. Late in the afternoon, after the man had gathered up his coat and stomped out the door, Jake stood in the middle of the ordered chaos that was the print shop and breathed deeply of the intoxicating richness of smells and said to himself that if he was nothing else, he was, by God, a printer. And he admitted that he might someday be a newspaperman, even a good one.

The next afternoon, as he was beginning his weekly press run, the first pages of newsprint starting to feed through the monstrous Kluge and stack neatly at the far end ready for folding, the press broke its main crankshaft. The Kluge screamed with a horrific shriek of metal and shuddered to a halt, scaring the hell out of Jake. He looked around wildly for Turbyfill and then realized he was all alone in the grip of more trouble than he had ever known.

"You sonofabitch!" he bellowed at the press, bringing his mother running from the front office.

"Jacob, for God's sake!"

"It broke!" he cried. He climbed down from his perch atop the press, the small bucket seat where he sat to feed the big sheets of newsprint into the Kluge's maw. He stalked around the press, trembling with anger and fear, glaring at it, stunned by the way it had turned on him.

"What the hell am I gonna do now?" he yelled.

"Fix it, I suppose," Emma Tibbetts said, and turned on her heel. He could hear her humming at the desk up in the front office while he stomped around, fuming, kicking at the unyielding metal.

His first impulse was to run for help, and he ran first to the boardinghouse where Turbyfill had lived. The old man was gone, and nobody knew where. Then he stood in the street outside the boardinghouse for a moment, thinking where he might turn next. Another editor? They had their own papers to put out. It would be the end of the week before anyone from another paper could come to help. One thing for sure, there was nobody else in *this* town who knew the first thing about fixing a printing press. Neither did Jake Tibbetts, but it appeared he would have to learn.

He went back to the newspaper office and rummaged around until he found the diagrams for the press tucked away in the bottom of a drawer, studied them, and tackled the press with wrenches and hammers, still in a hot rage over the machine's stupidity and stubbornness and his own incredible bad luck. He did everything wrong at first and then had to undo his errors and start again. Eventually, curiosity began to wear at his anger and he became absorbed in the work, the engineer taking over. It was late afternoon before he finally got the crankshaft out. It was deep in the innards of the press and he had to practically dismantle the machine to get at it. He took the broken pieces to the blacksmith shop down the street and paid the man to work into the night forging a shaft that would hold until he could get a new one shipped in by train. It was midnight when the smith finished, and then Jake hauled the shaft back to the newspaper office and went at the press again. He put the Kluge back together piece by piece, getting it all wrong again and taking it apart and doing it over until he got it right, learning more about the machine than he could have gleaned from years of studying the diagrams. Jake scarcely noticed as night turned into day and the day wore on to afternoon and evening. At the end, faint with fatigue and lack of sleep, he climbed back up on the bucket seat on top of the press and gave the huge flywheel a vicious turn. The Kluge groaned and shrieked in protest and then, like a dinosaur emerging from centuries of sleep, it began to rumble with life, growling over the way its bowels had been meddled with. Jake started feeding in sheets of newsprint, yelling at the top of his voice, ''Go! Go! Eat that newsprint, you sonofabitch! Go!''

When he finished the press run it was two o'clock in the morning and as he shut down the press he heard the front door slam. His mother leaving. She had come and gone during the two days of his agony, he could hear her humming in the front office, a soft undertone at the edge of his absorption in the job, but she had not spoken to him once.

He got the papers folded and stuck on the mailing labels, moving like a ghost in a fog of utter exhaustion, then wheeled the bundles of papers in a cart to the post office and left them on the doorstep, where the postmaster would find them when he opened up. Friday was dawning. It had been early afternoon Wednesday when the crankshaft snapped. The *Free Press* was a day late this week, but it had published.

Suddenly, he felt a surge of new life, a rush of pride, an impulse to run up and down the street yelling, "I did it! I whipped the sonofabitch!" But then he stopped and reflected soberly on the issue of who had whipped whom, and walked instead to Lightnin' Jim Haskell's house and bought a fruit jar of whiskey and took it back to the newspaper office. He sat on the floor with his back to the cold metal of the Kluge and toasted the old monster that had owned his body and soul for the past two days. He held the jar of whiskey up to the light pouring in the windows of the front office and watched the way the light made small rainbows through the prism of the strong clear liquid. He thought of his grandfather, Captain Finley, sitting on this same floor years before, after a day of typesetting, drinking this same whiskey. And he thought of his father, gaunt shoulders hunched over the keyboard of the Linotype, bony fingers racing over the keys, oblivious to the rivers of sweat streaming down his neck and making a broad, dark band down the back of his shirt, at peace with his tortured soul for a few moments. For the first time, he linked the two men—his forebears—men so violently different as to defy kinship, but each bedeviled in his own way by the strange alchemy of turning metal into words. He was too tired to hate anymore. He slugged on the whiskey for a while, feeling no effect from it until he passed out. The last thing he remembered was a sense of loneliness, of regretting that he had no one with whom to share his small triumph and his tiny nugget of wisdom.

Now here he was trying to write his second editorial, at six-thirty in the morning of Christmas Day, 1944, with the light coming strong and gray through the windows of the newspaper office, drained of color, washing out the yellow glow of the single bulb that hung above his typewriter. He thought back to the morning forty-four years before when he had sat on the floor of the print shop, drunk with a mixture of pride and sadness. He thought of another morning, two years after, when he had come here to the newspaper after they had buried Isaac, dead of typhoid. He had sat at his desk with another bottle of Lightnin' Jim's Best, thinking that now there truly was no one else to run the paper but himself. He had grieved for Isaac, but it came to him in his grief that he and the paper had already formed an unbreakable bond. It was his life's work. He had grown to fit it.

But this Christmas morning, he was just a tired old man. His fingers were stiff with cold and he realized that he was still wearing his overcoat, that he had not lit the oil heater when he had reeled in the door five hours before, numbed and driven by his own craziness after the woman—Henry's woman—had appeared on his front porch.

Somewhere, a block or so away, he could hear the erratic fevered popping of firecrackers. They must be from some youngster's secret prewar hoard, because there hadn't been any firecrackers for a long time. Powder was used these days for bullets and bombs and artillery shells, not firecrackers. They seemed to set off small explosions in his brain and he sat back a moment from the old Underwood, feeling a bit faint and disoriented. He breathed deeply several times.

Jake felt very much older than his sixty-four years, very much used and abused. And it was a new feeling. He had always *appeared* older, had cultivated a look of rumpled frumpiness. He wore celluloid collars and garters on his sleeves long after they went out of style. And he kept a cigar jammed in the corner of his mouth like a period at the end of a declamation. Nature had given him bushy eyebrows and prematurely graying hair and a short, stocky build. At thirty, he had looked forty-five, and that was fine with him. It gave him the patina of age a man needed if he was to be a wry, detached observer of mankind's folly. Despite all that, he was vigorous in mind and body. Since he refused to own an automobile, he walked—a mile to the paper in the morning, back home at lunch, back to the paper for the afternoon, and finally home again in the evening. It was an article of faith, weather be damned, done at half-canter, arms swinging, calves pumping, shoulders thrown back to allow his lungs their full extension. Physically, he was sound.

But this morning, he was whipped. He was driven by things he couldn't control, and that violated his most basic premise about life. He believed that the one thing a man must do was to *TAKE HIS LIFE IN HIS OWN HANDS AND SHAKE IT FOR ALL IT WAS WORTH.* A man had to take responsibility for himself and his destiny. Up to now, he had. But sixty-four years of believing that had been shaken in one mad day.

He meant to write an editorial apologizing to his readers. He meant to tell them that he was deliberately keeping something out of the paper for the first time in its history, violating his own most precious possession because another man had called in a terrible debt that he had no choice but to pay. It was the kind of thing that had to be said in an editorial, not in Jake Tibbetts's own front-page column. It was the voice of the *paper* that he had sullied, and the readers deserved to know it. After all these years, it was time for another editorial. But after five hours, he was no closer to writing it than when he began.

He heard again the sporadic popping of the firecrackers outside, and it brought him back to the notion that had been tilting about in his head since he sat down at the typewriter hours ago: It was the war that had him spooked. He had thought about it long and deeply through the night. He realized, as Captain Finley Tibbetts must have realized in the gore of Cemetery Ridge, that there were times and circumstances when a man might be denied the right to take his life into his own hands, when a man himself might be taken up and shaken like a rag doll and tossed away. A war might, as he had told Hilton Redlinger the day before, be made by men too old or fat to fight. But once made, it assumed a life of its own and it swept young and old along with it. It left nothing unsullied.

He, Jake Tibbetts, had held this particular war at arm's length for a long time. He refused to acknowledge it in the left-hand front-page column of the paper, his private domain.

Still, the rest of the paper was full of it because the paper belonged to the town, and they could wallow in the war if they wanted to. . . . *Technical Sergeant Mason R. Daniel has completed the Advanced Bombsight Calibrator's Course at Nellis Army Airfield. . . . Mrs. Zouella Beacham has returned from a visit with her daughter, Mrs. Ella Fay Carmack, in California.*

Mrs. Carmack's husband, First Lieutenant Horace D. Carmack, is stationed with the Army artillery at Fort Ord. . . . War Bonds Chairwoman Mrs. Marvel Renfroe announces that Brunson's Cafe has led all local business establishments. . . . and on and on, filling the precious columns of the *Free Press* week after week, the trivial backwash from powerful currents that were changing the country. Young men gone to places like Port Moresby and Salerno and Fort Ord were indelibly marked and altered by it. Young women tagged along after them as far as they could go, snatching moments in tiny rented rooms—women who in past wars would have been scorned by polite society as camp followers, but who were now polite society's daughters and sisters.

The goddamned war reached into every crevice. A man could not buy a decent cigar anymore, because the best of the tobacco went overseas, and what was left smelled like it had been pissed upon when you set match to it. Every window had a gold star, every home a scrap-metal collection box, every face a pinched look because they knew someone for whom death meant a delivery boy with a telegram or a fuzzy-cheeked young officer scuffling his feet at the front door.

The God-damned war. Surely God must be as sick of it as he was. Surely it must prove that God was a mysterious and ironic God, not the meddler the church crowd made him out to be. If He were a meddler, He would have meddled by now, when ultimate depravity had taken the world by the short hairs.

Just as it had Jake Tibbetts by the short hairs. Try as he might, he could not stop it from intruding on him. Every so often, some ass—through ignorance or perversity—would ask him, "How's Henry these days?"

And Jake would reply, "He's in the Army," and do it in such a way as to wither the inquiry. It did not keep asses from asking, but it usually kept the same ass from asking twice.

Now the war had intruded on him again, a beast that leaped from behind, a thief that violated his inner sanctum. It sent Billy Benefield in his Curtiss Stearman, and that had led to the compromising of his newspaper. And now, out of the night, it sent a pregnant woman, a refugee, who was just now giving birth in an upstairs bedroom of his home to his grandchild, a war baby.

Henry had played another dirty trick on him, and it was the war that enabled him to do it. Jake had long ago dealt with

Henry, or thought he had. But now he was back like some wandering ghost, smelling of decay and the stench of war. Ghost-Henry and his Texas bride and the God-damned war had taken over Jake Tibbetts's house and blown away his sense of self-destiny like a fart in the wind. It had driven him out of the house in the dead of night after Henry's wife had been put to bed upstairs and the doctor had clumped in from the cold, sleep-bleared and sardonic, a man who had run out of surprises. It had driven Jake down the wind-whipped road with the cold slicing at the edge of his mind, peeling away layer after layer until it got to the raw, bleeding core of things. It had driven him, crazed from the shock and cold, to the old Underwood typewriter in his newspaper office because he told himself it was time for another editorial, after all these years. But in that, too, he failed.

As morning broke, Jake admitted his failure and muttered, ''To hell with it.'' Why try to tell people something about the war they already knew? Why try to deal with the ghost of Henry Tibbetts, who—exempt from service at thirty-one years of age and with a child at home—had gotten drunk and joined the National Guard a heartbeat before Pearl Harbor? And what good to publicly anguish over the sullying of the paper's name? It was a private grief. At the bottom of it, he was what he was—a man who pissed into the wind, who still believed that a man had to take his life into his own hands, insofar as he was able. Once he began to make excuses, his nuts were in somebody else's pocket.

That decided, Jake replaced the tattered cover of the Underwood, apologizing to an old friend for having kept him up all night listening to the babbling doubts of an old man.

TWO

*T*HEY had ridden all night and they were flushed with victory, a bit maddened by the blood-spilling. Captain Finley was at the point with a small group of riders. They came hard into the walnut grove beside the creek bank, pistols drawn, bodies low-slung in the saddle, guided by the black smoke from the pine knots Young Scout had heaped on the fire. They were followed closely by the adjutant, Muldoon, and the main body of the Lighthorse Cavaliers. The ground trembled with their coming, a phantom troop in the gray half-light of daybreak. Young Scout rose from the fireside to greet them, his joints stiff from cold and waiting.

The troop boiled in around him, the horses splashing out into the stream, roiling the water, bending to drink with a great gasping noise. The creek was no more than waist-deep here where it widened at a bend. There was a narrow sloping sandbar on the near side and thick brush on the other down to the stream's edge. Several horsemen galloped into the thicket on the other side, thrashing around in the brush to satisfy themselves it was clear. Breath came in sharp white puffs from the horses' nostrils and steam rose from their heaving flanks.

They were lean, somber men—born to saddle, honed like saber blades, able to fight at full gallop, teeth bared to the wind. They wasted no motion. As their horses finished drinking, the riders urged them back up the bank of the stream into the walnut grove, dismounted, began uncinching saddles, tethered the horses in a picket line. Young Scout stood, barely breathing himself, watching them, watching their fevered eyes shot through with bottomless fatigue and the imprint of what they had seen and done at Hanover Courthouse. They made camp quickly. It was the mark of a good cavalryman that he could be off his horse and into his bedroll within minutes, dropping instantly into a death-sleep that knew no nightmares. Oh, to be like them, Young Scout thought. To ride and do battle and then sleep a just sleep.

Captain Finley moved among them, his black horse stepping gingerly as he made a full circle of the camp, speaking quietly to the troopers. When he had finished and satisfied himself about them, he allowed his own horse to drink at the stream's edge. Young Scout followed him on foot to the sandbar and stood there watching him. Captain Finley sat slump-shouldered in the saddle, head bowed, unseeing, deep inside himself. Then he raised up, turned abruptly to Young Scout. "It was an abattoir," he said. "No place for a boy. No place for a gentleman." Then he dug his heels into the black horse and urged him back up into the woods, where he dismounted and handed the reins to a trooper. He knelt beside Young Scout's fire, extending his hands to its meager warmth.

Young Scout followed, hunkered next to the fire across from Captain Finley, watching, seeing the great weariness in his face, the rust-colored stains splattering the front of his tunic. There would be stains, too, on the great curving blade of the saber that hung from Captain Finley's belt. An abattoir, he had said.

Young Scout had waited through the dead of night, as Captain Finley had told him to, and the message had come, as he had known it would. The Lighthorse Cavaliers had indeed caught the Federals in their bedrolls at Hanover Courthouse and had made bloody work of the garrison. But when they turned to withdraw, they found that a force of bluecoat infantry had moved with uncharacteristic swiftness to block their escape. There was a brief chaotic firefight in the darkness and then Captain Finley wheeled and headed to the east, deeper into enemy territory. By the minute, the situation grew more grave. It was a matter of time until the Union cavalry would be barking at their heels. So Captain Finley had summoned him from his bed to find them a temporary hiding place. Young Scout had gone eagerly into the cold dark because his captain had called.

"You've done well by us, boy," Captain Finley said.

Young Scout flushed with pleasure. Maybe now . . . now that he had proven himself . . . they would let him fight . . .

"But we have got ourselves into a fine stew," Captain Finley went on. He drew a map from inside his tunic and motioned Young Scout to come around to him. He spread the map on the ground with a rock on each corner to keep the wind from plucking at it. Then he reached into the breast pocket of the tunic, pulled out a stump of a cigar, jammed it into the corner of his mouth.

"See here," he said, his stubby finger poking at the map. "We have managed to get the main body of McClellan's army between us and our own lines. And General Lee needs us. He's hatching a mighty attack. Within hours he will send Jackson's corps against McClellan's right flank and attempt to drive him south and east away from Richmond. Longstreet, who is on Jackson's right, is to hold fast and allow Jackson to pivot the enemy around Longstreet's front. But if Jackson is successful, that will keep the Federals between him and us."

Young Scout could see the brilliance of it. A bold attack by Jackson, the stumpy-legged bulldog of a general who moved entire regiments as if they were platoons, a master of feint and jab. Jackson might turn McClellan's entire army to the east toward the sea, rescue Richmond from imminent danger, possibly even entrap McClellan against the James River and chew him to pieces.

Young Scout nodded. "Then we're out of it."

"The hell," Captain Finley said. "The hell we are."

"But . . ."

"What would you have me do, boy? Hunker here while the war goes on without me? Waste these hundred good men?"

Young Scout flushed. "No, but . . ."

"A man proves what he's worth when the cards are stacked against him." He fixed Young Scout with his red, weary eyes. "He doesn't cut and run like a faint-hearted ninny, he hitches up his britches and gets on with the business. You understand that?"

"Yes sir," Young Scout said, chastened.

Captain Finley studied the map for a long time, chewing on his cigar, rolling it from one side of his mouth to the other.

Finally, he said, "We'll go east."

Young Scout stared at the map. "But that's away from our lines."

"Exactly. The Federals will think they have us at bay. They'll occupy themselves with trying to capture the fox at the back door while the bull smashes through the front. If we keep them busy awhile, Jackson will have a fine day of it." He punched the map, showing how he would do it. "We'll ride clean around McClellan's rear, nipping at his haunches as we go. We'll drive him to distraction. He'll think he has at least a division on the loose at his backside."

"What about Jackson?" Young Scout asked. "How will he know what we're up to?"

"You'll tell him," Captain Finley said, and Young Scout's entire body tingled.

"Me?" Young Scout whispered.

"If I sent a grown man and the Federals caught him, they'd have him dancing at the end of a rope. But they won't suspect a poor farm boy, and even if they did, they probably won't hang him for it." Captain Finley winked. Young Scout felt his stomach lurch.

"You risk everything," Young Scout said.

"No," Captain Finley said. "These hundred good and lusty men"—he jerked his head, indicating the Cavaliers huddled in exhaustion in their bedrolls in the walnut grove—"risk everything when they rise from their blankets and put on their boots and ride off with me to do battle." His voice was a deep rumble, like slow rolling thunder. "They risk life, and more than that, honor. I can't guarantee their lives, Young Scout, and I can't be the keeper of their mortal souls. All I can do is protect their honor. And I do that by being bold." He paused for a moment, studying Young Scout. "Remember this, boy, if ever the Lord gives you the terrible burden of leading good men: Take matters in your own hands and shake them for all they're worth." He leaned close and Young Scout could smell his powerful gamy man-odor. "Be careful, but don't be timid. Consider McClellan, who creeps and parries like an aging lover, and whose losses are appalling. Don't stand about smelling your own farts. Be bold! And whatever the consequence, take complete responsibility for it. Making war is the devil's own business. You'll not save your own soul by shrinking from it.''

Captain Finley sat back and sighed deeply. He took the cigar from his mouth and tossed it into the dying fire, then rose abruptly and walked to the sandbar at the edge of the stream. Young Scout sat gape-mouthed. "Come here,'' the captain said after a moment, his back still to the boy. "Let's talk about your mission.''

They walked out on the narrow sandbar at the edge of the stream.

"You'll have to keep your wits about you,'' Captain Finley said. He fished another cigar stub from the pocket of his tunic and stuck it between his teeth. "If the Federals stop you, tell them your mother has sent you to cut firewood for your aunt in Mechanicsville. Can you remember that?''

"Yes sir,'' Young Scout said.

"Ride directly through the Union lines as if you know exactly what your business is,'' Captain Finley went on. "Go straight to General Jackson at Savage Station and tell him what we're up to.''

Young Scout nodded.

"Now. You need a sign.'' He slipped the plain gold wedding band from his finger and pressed it into Young Scout's palm. "Jackson knows it. Guard it well, and I'll retrieve it from you in Richmond on the weekend.''

Young Scout felt the thrill of fear race through his chest. It was a dangerous business, almost foolhardy. No matter what Captain Finley said, the Federals could hang him as a spy because he was on a military mission dressed in civilian clothes. But Jackson's success might well hinge on it. If he knew the Lighthorse Cavaliers were raising Cain at McClellan's rear, he would strike even more boldly, throwing his reserves into the attack. And if Jackson succeeded this day, it could save Richmond from grave peril. The Confederacy could fight on.

"I'll get through,'' Young Scout said, looking up into the weary face.

But then he felt a rush of despair, struck suddenly by the realization that Captain Finley and his hundred good and lusty men would ride out to do battle while he again became a message boy. It was unfair! Captain Finley was sending him back there, back where there was nothing but confusion . . .

"You damned well better get through," Captain Finley said, "or I'll be ridiculed as a fool or worse for having tried it. Better to be thought a fool than a pissant, though." He threw back his head and laughed, his fine teeth bared to the wind, framed by the bold black slash of his moustache.

Young Scout felt the first bullet cut the air between their faces even before he heard the report of the rifle from across the stream—a nasty click of a noise like the jaws of a small vicious beast snapping shut. Then there was another shot that tore a piece from the brim of Captain Finley's campaign hat, and suddenly Captain Finley was grabbing him by the waist, scrambling madly back up the sandbar to the thin cover of the walnut trees, where all hell was breaking loose, men coming out of their bedrolls, eyes wild with sleep blasted by sudden shock and fear, grabbing rifles, firing toward the creek. Across the way, the bushes down close to the water's edge erupted with rapid fire, and Young Scout knew instantly what was there—Federal cavalry armed with the new Sharps repeating rifles, a handful of men creating the chaos of a hundred. A small patrol that had stumbled onto Captain Finley's sleeping troop.

The captain jammed Young Scout down into the ground behind a thick walnut tree and knelt, whipping out his pistol from the holster at his belt. He fired, taking careful aim at the brush line across the creek. A bluecoat tumbled from the bushes and splashed into the stream, sprawled half-in and half-out of the water, his boots still in the brush. The pistol bucked and roared again like a cannon erupting just over Young Scout's head. He heard screams behind him in the walnut grove as men took bullets and fell, the frightened bellowing of horses, a wall of exploding rifle and pistol fire, lead smacking into tree trunks and cutting through the bare limbs of the trees, sending a shower of branches and bits of bark tumbling down through the storm of fire.

Young Scout flipped over on his back and looked up into the crazed face of his captain, contorted with rage at the craven stealth of the ambush, at his own slackness in having let them creep so close. Captain Finley detested ambush as a cowardly form of warfare. He showed no mercy in battle, but he was no bushwhacker.

Suddenly he leaped to his feet and unsheathed the gleaming silver sword with a long, flowing motion of his arm. "Charge the skulking bastards!" he bellowed. "Charge! Take no prisoners!" He was down the narrow sandbar and into the water in the flick of an eyelash, wading furiously into the stream with great raging steps, booming away with the pistol in one hand and waving the sword with the other, screaming his fury as a hail of bullets churned the water and sand. The Lighthorse Cavaliers erupted from the walnut grove with a roar, following him. Then Captain Finley went down and Young Scout's heart lurched and he, too, was on his feet, yelling, storming down the sandbar. "Sonofabitch! Sonofabitch!" he screamed, not knowing whether he meant the blue-coated sons of bitches across the creek or the maddened bantam-legged sonofabitch who was rising again now in the water in front of him, waving the sword and blasting away with the pistol.

Young Scout splashed into the water and felt his feet go out from under him as he stepped into a hole. He went under, flailing with his arms, and the shock of the icy water took his breath. Through the rush of water in his ears and the wild pounding of his heart, he could hear the roar of the firefight going on overhead—the splat of bullets hitting water, screams of agony and anger, the steady rattle of guns. The water was numbingly cold. Cleansing. He could feel it sucking the life from him and he felt a sudden great joy. Oh, to die nobly for God and the Lighthorse Cavaliers!

Then he felt strong arms around his waist, pulling him to the surface.

Shit, he thought. Saved again.

THREE

J_{AKE} had not intended to go home, not just yet. In fact, he had intended to prop up his feet on his rolltop desk, rear back in the swivel chair, put his chin on his chest, and take a nap.

But as soon as he got his feet propped and the chair reared back, the telephone rang.

He despised the instrument. He preferred to look a man in the eye when he dealt with him. He detested people who hid behind the telephone's anonymity. People who called to complain without identifying themselves were cowards. ''Meet me in the street!'' Jake would roar at the caller—man or woman— as he slammed down the receiver.

He had once written a column about the telephone:

The main folly of the instrument is that it foreshortens time in a way the Creator never intended. It gives a man no time to think.

Consider the poor man who receives a telephone call informing him that his mother-in-law has died suddenly and tragically, and rushes to the rooftop of his house and flings himself off in a fit of grief. Had he more time to consider the matter, he might decide he was better off without her, or might—Happy Day!—learn that the dear woman had left him a sizeable share of her estate.

But the telephone was a necessary business evil. This morning, it had destroyed his plans for a nap. He picked up the receiver.

"Jake, come home," Pastine said on the other end.

"Presently," Jake answered.

"Now," she said. "Lonnie's fallen in the creek."

"What!"

"Biscuit Brunson just brought him home, sopping wet. He won't tell me anything. You'll have to come home and deal with him. I've got my hands full."

There was a long pause. "With what?" Jake asked.

"The baby."

"Oh."

Another long pause. "It's a girl. You can tell it's a Tibbetts. She's got a big mouth."

Pastine hung up and Jake put the earpiece on the hook and sat there staring at the telephone for a while, thinking about the man who threw himself off the roof of his house in agony over his mother-in-law. Then he got up and put on his coat and headed for home.

He was halfway down Partridge Road, arms swinging briskly, when Herschel Martin, Fog's younger brother who tended the banana tree on the courthouse lawn, came by on the Jitney Jungle Super Saver Store delivery cycle. It was a three-wheeled pedal contraption with a big wooden bin behind the seat where Herschel carried sacks and boxes of groceries. Herschel had found his place in life. He knew where every soul in town lived and he was single-mindedly faithful about delivering groceries from George Poulos's store. Winter and summer, he wore a red baseball cap with the white letters USN on the front that another brother, Carlton, had sent from the carrier *Midway* in the Pacific. This morning, he was well bundled against the cold in a flannel jacket, earmuffs, and a pair of rubber fishing boots that came midway up his thighs.

"Hey, Jake," he called as he pulled alongside, pumping hard on the pedals, the rubber boots squeaking in rhythm as he pedaled, "that Hitler, he's a dumb sonofabitch."

"Where'd you learn a word like that, Herschel?" Jake asked without breaking stride.

Herschel slowed to match Jake's speed and rolled alongside him. "Heard it from Fog," he said. "Fog's allatime saying stuff like that. Hell, he thinks I'm crazy and don't pay no attention. Him and his buddies, y'know. Hell, I ain't crazy, I'm just a little slow, y'know, Jake."

"Maybe not even that," Jake said.

"Biscuit Brunson, he helped me work it all out. He's been a big help to me, y'know. Biscuit Brunson, he says I got plenty of sense, lest I wouldn't be able to find everybody's house, y'know. Biscuit Brunson, he says I'm making a worthwhile contribution to the war effort. And he says if a fellow's making a worthwhile contribution, he can't be crazy, y'know."

"Well, who told you you were a little slow?"

"Biscuit," Herschel nodded vigorously. "He says if I wasn't a little slow, I'd be off fighting. Anyway, that Hitler, he's a dumb sonofabitch."

"Yeah, I guess you're right, Herschel," Jake said. "Where are you going with the groceries?"

Herschel stopped pedaling and pulled over to the side of the road. "Ain't going no place now. I'm outa gas." It was a favorite of his, running out of gas. Jake stopped, walked over to the delivery cycle, pretended to pour gasoline from an imaginary can into Herschel's imaginary tank.

"Why is it," Jake asked, "that you're always running out of gas when your big brother runs a service station? Tell me that, Herschel."

"Hell," Herschel laughed, "it's the war, Jake. Don't you know there's gas rationing?"

"I don't have a car," Jake said.

"Well, there's a war on," Herschel said. "They're sending most of the gasoline overseas, y'know. Everybody gets a little, but not enough to get 'em where they're going. And Fog, he don't play no favorites, y'know." He laughed again. "Funny thing about it, though. Can't nobody find enough gas to get where they're going, but they always got a little extra for old Herschel. Figure that." And he pedaled off, pumping madly.

"Where you going with the groceries?" Jake called after him.

"Your place. Got lots of stuff for the new baby. Hey, you know that Hitler, he's a dumb sonofabitch," Herschel yelled back, and then he was gone around the big curve, out of sight. So, the story was out. If Herschel Martin knew, then George Poulos knew. Pastine had obviously rousted him out of bed on Christmas morning to fill an emergency order. And if George Poulos and Herschel Martin knew, the whole town would soon know because news like a new baby at Jake Tibbetts's house would travel like a locust storm. Damn the telephone.

By the time Jake reached the house, Herschel had the groceries stacked neatly on the sideboard next to the sink and was sitting at the kitchen table nursing a steaming mug of coffee. Biscuit Brunson was sitting across from him, looking rumpled and frazzled, a cup of coffee untouched on the table in front of him. And Lonnie was in a chair next to the stove, swaddled in blankets, feet stuck in a tub of hot water, hair tousled and damp. The smell of Vicks Vapo-Rub was strong in the room. Ollie Whittle was muttering on the Atwater-Kent, ". . . at this season of unbounded joy and universal hope, the management of Redlinger's White Angel Funeral Home want to thank you for your patronage . . ." Upstairs, Jake could hear the baby squalling her head off and the *clump-clump* of Pastine's feet as she moved around.

Jake stood in the doorway looking at them for a moment. Lonnie ducked his head and stared at his feet.

"You look like you been out all night, Jake," Biscuit said.

Jake grunted, and then he heard Pastine clomping down the stairs behind him. She had a big armload of bloodstained towels and sheets. Pastine looked frayed about the edges. Wisps of graying brown hair escaped from her tight bun and floated about her head and face. She shot Jake a murderous look. "Fix some more coffee," she said, brushing by him. She crossed the kitchen and opened the back door, letting in a blast of cold air, and dumped the linens on the back porch. Lonnie stared.

"Well, don't just stand there," she said, turning back to Jake with hands on hips. "We need a fresh pot of coffee. And when you get through with that, see if you can figure out what Mister Crazy Horse here is up to." She pointed to Lonnie, who grimaced. "Tell him what happened, Biscuit." And she stomped out, leaving the kitchen chilled in her wake. Upstairs, the baby was making the air dance with her bawling.

"Well . . ." Biscuit started to say.

"What's all the blood for?" Lonnie interrupted.

"That's from the baby," Herschel Martin said. "Babies come

with lots of extra blood, y'know. That's what Doc Ainsworth told me when George Poulos's wife had her last one. Babies . . .''

"Shut up, Herschel," Jake said.

"Awright, awright," Herschel said, "but that Hitler is one dumb sonofabitch if you ast me."

"Don't you have some more deliveries to make, Herschel?" Biscuit asked.

"Nope. This is the only one. George Poulos, he says we don't go out on Christmas morning for nobody but babies."

Biscuit rolled his eyes toward the ceiling. "All right. Well, anyhow," he said to Jake, "I was up early, about six-thirty like I always am, and I went out to the henhouse to get some eggs. You know, my henhouse is down in the back, not far from the creek, and well, all of a sudden I heard this yelling and thrashing around back by the creek and I ran down there to see what was the matter. Then I saw Lonnie here just run pell-mell into the water, cursing—I mean CURSING—at the top of his voice, like he had somebody chasing him. Only I didn't see anybody else there. I mean, he just ran pell-mell into the creek with all his clothes on, and it not much over freezing this morning." Biscuit waved his arms to show them how incredible it was. "Beat anything I ever saw, Jake. Then he stepped off into a deep place and went under, and I waded in and pulled him out. I asked him what in the dickens he was up to, but he wouldn't say a word. So I took him up to the house and dried him off and put some of Lee Mason's clothes on him, and he still wouldn't say a thing. He just stared at me. I went back down to the creek after a while to see if I could find anything, and I did find a place where somebody had built a fire. The ashes were still warm. I wondered if Lonnie here had happened up on a tramp or something. Whatever it was, it must have scared him pretty bad. He hasn't said a word since I got him home 'til just now."

The silence hung heavy over the room for a long time, then Lonnie raised his head and looked at Herschel Martin. "Herschel, was you out here yesterday when Billy Benefield's plane landed?"

"Nope," said Herschel, "I run out of gas downtown, y'know. Couldn't get NOBODY to help me. Everybody was just so busy runnin' out here to see the airplane, they couldn't stop to help old Herschel. And you can't tell me there wadn't gas to be had, neither. Rationing and all, folks still got a little gas for old

Herschel, except when they're in such a fool hurry they ain't got TIME to help a fellow," he huffed. "I seen you jaspers come by on the fire truck, and I waved and tried to get you to stop and give old Herschel some gas, but you made like you didn't even see me. You just kept agettin' it."

"If I'd seen you, I'd have stopped, Herschel," Lonnie said earnestly.

"Dammit, shut up!" Jake bellowed. "I'm trying to figure out why a twelve-year-old boy with supposedly good sense is wallering around in Whitewater Creek at six-thirty on Christmas morning, and all I get is goddamn gasoline!"

Herschel drew himself up out of the chair with great dignity. "I can tell," he said sonorously, "when I ain't wanted. It don't take no dummy to know that."

"Aw, sit down and drink your coffee," Jake waved him back to the chair.

"Okay," Herschel said, and sat down, his rubber fishing boots making tiny squeaks.

"Now," Jake turned back to Lonnie. "Let's have it. What's going on here?"

Lonnie shrugged.

"Was somebody chasing you?"

"I don't know." He squirmed in his chair, his eyes darting from Biscuit to Jake to Herschel. Everything was quiet in the kitchen except for the Atwater-Kent, which was playing "It's Beginning to Look a Lot Like Christmas."

"That won't do," Jake said.

"What if I told you I saw some gold on the bottom of the creek," Lonnie said hopefully.

"Uh-uh."

Lonnie thought a minute. "Went to rescue a fair damsel?"

"You see any fair damsels in the water, Biscuit?" Jake asked.

"Any *what*?"

"Pretty women."

"Lord, no. There wasn't anybody else around, like I said. Lonnie just ran down off the bank pell-mell into the water like he had fire in his britches. And I never heard the like of cussing from a young'un."

"What kind of cussing?" Jake asked.

Biscuit looked around, then lowered his voice. "He said 'son-ofabitch.' Several times."

"Who were you 'sonofabitching,' Lonnie?"

Lonnie looked up into Jake's face, his eyes pained.

"Was anybody chasing you, Lonnie? Did anybody try to mess with you?"

"No, sir."

Jake paused for a moment and then he said gently, "Was there anybody else there?"

"Yes . . ." Lonnie started to say, and then he hung fire. "I mean . . ." and his face scrunched up and Jake could see that he was about to cry.

"Biscuit," Jake said, "could I talk to you outside for just a minute?"

Biscuit got up from the table and put on his coat and they walked outside on the front porch, where the morning was gray and cold, the kind of morning you ought to have on Christmas when it looked like it might even snow if you were lucky, but probably wouldn't. It hardly ever snowed until late February or March, sometimes not even then. Jake remembered that there had been only one white Christmas on record: 1865. The year the men came back from war. Captain Finley Tibbetts had written about it in one of the very first issues of the *Free Press*.

"Biscuit," Jake said, "I think what we got here is just a case of overactive imagination."

"You mean," Biscuit said, "he ran in the creek on a freezing morning and there WASN'T ANYBODY THERE?"

Jake nodded. "I think that's the case, yes."

"Good Lord."

Jake put his hand on Biscuit's shoulder. "Biscuit, I really appreciate your taking care of Lonnie. I think he'll be okay now. We'll get him warmed up and send him up to bed." He gave Biscuit's shoulder a squeeze.

"Jake," Biscuit said earnestly. "I hope you'll take this thing seriously. It's not like it's an isolated case, either. I mean, this is two days in a *row* he's pulled a caper like this. Yesterday, he went flying off in Billy Benefield's airplane. Today, he's thrashing around in an ice-cold creek and cussing at the crack of dawn. Things is, it seems to me, a little out of control."

"Out of control." Jake nodded again.

Biscuit stared at him a moment. "You don't see anything wrong with it, do you."

"Now, I didn't say that, Biscuit. I just think the boy's imagination runs away with him sometimes. You know how kids are. You may not remember it, but you were a kid one time. Hell, I remember me and some of the older boys caught you and another squirt peeing off the Whitewater Creek Bridge onto a man and a woman in a rowboat.''

Biscuit blushed. "Jake, I'm telling you," he went on doggedly, "when a twelve-year-old boy runs pell-mell into the middle of a creek at six-thirty on Christmas morning, cursing like a wild savage, that ain't overactive imagination. That's a SERIOUS PROBLEM. I just don't think you see it. Not a bit.''

But he did see it, Jake thought. You had to live in bedlam to get the point, but he did indeed see it. If you were a sixty-four-year-old man who had sat up all night in a frigid newspaper office trying to write an editorial you never really intended to write in the first place; if you had a pregnant woman on your front porch at midnight and a caterwauling baby in the back upstairs bedroom by daybreak; if you had a profligate, reprobate son who had wiped out one wife and sent another one home heavy with child from some tawdry wartime union—when you had all that going on, then a grandson who stowed away in airplanes and went dashing into Whitewater Creek on Christmas morning was not so grievously insane after all. In fact, those might qualify as the sanest acts he had seen in the past twenty-four hours.

God, he thought, how the Tibbetts clan must confound the rabble. They were all reincarnations of Job, visited with plague and pestilence. But they refused to cover themselves with sackcloth and ashes in penitence for whatever curse it was that invited misery down on their heads. The Tibbettses were like the man who visits the bank to find that he has been wiped out, then walks out the front door and pisses on the sidewalk in defiance. Four generations of them now had been pissing on sidewalks. The drunken, raving Captain Finley and the haunted Albertis had gone right on being their eccentric, bellicose, unreconstituted selves. Henry, for all his craven good-for-nothingness, remained defiant about it. He simply would not do what he was supposed to do, and to hell with the world. And now there was Lonnie, who could dash into a creek at dawn and then sit there and refuse to say why he did it. No, it wasn't insanity, it was sidewalk-pissing raised to a new level of art.

"Well, Jake," Biscuit interrupted his thoughts, and Jake realized he had been standing there for a long time squeezing

Biscuit's shoulder, lost in contemplation. "Well, Jake, it's Christmas morning, after all, I've got a family waiting home. Lee Mason will have his Santa Claus all tore open by the time I get there."

Jake released his grip. "Biscuit," he said lamely, "thanks. I mean . . ."

"Sure." Biscuit looked at him for a moment. "Just . . . just get the boy some help. I mean . . . you know, he and Lee Mason play together . . ."

And Jake realized that Biscuit Brunson was afraid, afraid for his own kin, afraid that whatever curse it was that hung over the Tibbetts bunch would touch somebody else with its godawful bad luck.

"We'll pray over it," Jake said, and wondered why he said it.

Biscuit cocked his head to one side. "Jake, tell me straight. Have you ever prayed over anything in your life?"

"Oh, yes. I remember sending up a little signal when Joe Louis was fighting Max Schmeling. I had a little wager on that one. And there was another time, right after I took over the paper. The press broke down and it took me two days to fix it. When I finished and climbed back up on the sucker and got ready to throw the juice to it, I distinctly remember saying, 'Lord, if you're listening, tell this sonofabitch to behave.' "

"Jake, you blaspheme," Biscuit said.

"That's what Pastine tells me."

"How long has it been since you've been to church?"

"Not since the press broke down," Jake said. "When the damn thing ran, I figured I had called in all my cards."

Biscuit looked him square in the eye for a long time.

"Jake," he said, "you may need it one of these days."

"What, church?"

"God."

"It's the same thing, ain't it?"

"No," Biscuit said, "it's not." And that surprised Jake, because he had always thought of Biscuit Brunson as the staunchest of churchmen, a deacon at First Baptist. "You may," Biscuit went on, "have to go to the pit someday. And you can't take a church with you."

"I've been there," Jake said quietly.

"Maybe so."

Maybe not? Jake stood there on the porch and watched as Biscuit walked down the steps and got into the old Ford coupe parked between the house and the big bare-branched oak tree. Biscuit rolled down the window. "Merry Christmas to you, Jake."

"And to you, Biscuit."

Biscuit started the car and pulled out of the yard, made a big circle in the road and headed down Partridge Road toward town. Jake stayed there on the porch after the car had disappeared, hearing the sound of the motor fade, listening to the faint *poppety-pop* of firecrackers from over in town. He stayed there and thought about their two sons, his and Biscuit's, remembered the two frightened faces peering down at him from the branches of the tree in front of Biscuit's house when he had caught them dropping cow turds on passing cars. His Henry and Biscuit's Lee Mason, whom everybody called Bugger. Bugger's face round and fat with the big moon eyes beginning to well up with tears. Henry's thin little face starting already to glaze over with that look of utter impassivity it got when a confrontation was at hand. And Jake wanting to take him by the shoulders and shake him and say, "For God's sake, if you're going to piss on the sidewalk, ENJOY IT." Wanting to, but not doing it.

Bugger had grown up fat, eager to please. He had passed up the cafe business and learned to operate heavy machinery at Harsole Bingham Bolt Company, married, fathered a boy who was inevitably called Little Bugger. Same age as Lonnie. When the war had come, neither Bugger nor Henry had had to serve. But Lee Mason Brunson the First had lost forty pounds, joined the Navy, become a chief petty officer in the Seabees, grinding up Pacific islands to make landing strips from which Curtis LeMay's B-29s could rain hell on the cities of imperial Japan.

And Henry? Well, it had been a relief to them all when the Guard had been activated. Henry disappeared, as far as Jake was concerned, until the Army Hometown News Release arrived at the *Free Press* two years later, saying that Lieutenant Henry F. Tibbetts had been assigned as a platoon leader with the 25th Infantry Division. Jake had thrown it into the wastebasket, but not before wondering how Henry had managed to avoid being cashiered or jailed, and even more, how he had managed to become an *officer*, for God's sake. He wondered if perhaps Henry had come to grips with himself, if somehow in the maelstrom of war he had taken his life in his own hands.

It would have been the most remarkable of miracles for Henry

Tibbetts to have come to grips with himself. This, after all, was the Henry Tibbetts who had run his car off Taylorsville Road in a drunken stupor and killed his wife, and then crawled away and hidden like a craven coward. Ah, yes, Jake thought, I've been to the pit, Biscuit.

Still, the thought of Henry making something of himself had gnawed at him for a long time. Until last midnight, when the woman had shown up ready to have her baby, Henry's baby, on Jake Tibbetts's doorstep. No, Henry hadn't learned a goddamned thing. As Jake stood on the porch, shivering in the gray cold of Christmas morning, he thought, The sonofabitch. He's done it again. Another dirty trick.

———————

Herschel Martin clomped out the back door, his rubber boots squeaking down the steps, and Lonnie was left alone with his dilemma.

What to do? he agonized as he sat there in the warm kitchen wrapped like a seasoning fruitcake in a swath of blankets, his feet in a tub of water turning tepid, carols and Christmas greetings on the radio making antiharmony with the squalling of the baby upstairs, the aroma of bubbling coffee filling the room. What to do about Captain Finley?

He could always tell Daddy Jake a flat-out, bald-faced lie, but that was really no option at all. Telling a bald-faced lie to a person you loved was surely one of those monstrous black sins that stayed in the archangel's book in huge bold letters, no matter how hard you tried to pray it away.

When Daddy Jake had asked him a few minutes before if somebody had been chasing him, with Biscuit Brunson and Herschel Martin sitting there staring at him, he had said, "I don't know." But that wasn't a lie, it was just stalling for time. Now, though, Biscuit and Herschel were gone and Daddy Jake would march back in here in a minute and want some answers. It would be just the two of them. And there would be no more "I don't know's."

So, what to do? Tell him? But how? How to explain Captain Finley, whom Daddy Jake knew only as a face in a picture frame on his desk at the newspaper, a sword hanging over the fireplace, the vague memories he had passed along to Lonnie of an old man who smelled of cigars and bay rum oil? As much as Lonnie might love him, Daddy Jake was part of the chaotic, feverish here and now where airplanes landed in your front yard and people had fistfights at the Christmas program and big-bellied women showed up on your front porch at midnight.

But Captain Finley—he traveled light, rode like the wind, kept his eye on his duty. Out there, out where Captain Finley and his hundred good and lusty men thundered through the fields and woods and creek banks, was a clean and simple place. Be bold! Take matters in your own hands! And be honorable. In such a place, it was not madness at all to be thrashing about in an icy creek on Christmas morning. It was duty. So how to tell Daddy Jake that no matter how much Lonnie Tibbetts loved him, he must go when Captain Finley called, to the secret places where only warriors could go? If he *told* Daddy Jake, it wouldn't be real anymore. And there would be no place to go when the here and now turned upside down and left him reeling.

Lonnie heard the front door open and close and then he looked up and saw Daddy Jake standing in the doorway of the kitchen.

What to do? What would Captain Finley do? A diversion. He looked Daddy Jake square in the eye and asked, "Did Santa Claus come and take all my stuff back?"

His grandfather looked at him for a long moment, then pulled a cigar out of his pocket, rolled it around in his mouth to moisten it, bit off the end, spat the nub in the garbage pail under the sink, and lit the cigar, jamming it in the corner of his mouth. Billows of smoke issued from it, as if it were an old clunker of a car starting up. Daddy Jake hardly ever lit up a cigar at home. Never in the kitchen.

Finally he said, "That was a damfool thing you did this morning, boy."

"Yessir," Lonnie said, looking straight at him.

Daddy Jake pulled out a chair with a clatter and sat down at the table. "In fact, you're building up quite a little list of damfoolishness these past couple of days."

"Yessir."

"Any particular reason?"

Lonnie shrugged.

Jake stared at him a moment, then placed his cigar carefully on the edge of the table, got up and poured himself a cup of coffee from the fresh bubbling pot on the stove, sat back down at the table, dumped in two spoons of sugar, stirred, and took a quick sip, cradling the cup in both hands. On the radio, Ollie

Whittle was delivering Christmas greetings from George Poulos and the Jitney Jungle and sending special holiday wishes to all the fighting men far away from home on behalf of George, whose son was a trooper with the 82nd Airborne somewhere in France.

Daddy Jake set his cup down on the table and stuck the cigar back in his mouth. He sat there for a while, looking down into the blackness of his coffee cup, before he spoke. "Imagination's a wonderful thing, Lonnie," he said. "A fellow can't buy imagination, can't manufacture it. He's either got it or he hasn't." He spoke slowly, choosing his words. "Most of the failures in this world are failures of imagination, Lonnie. Most men who fail are failures because they lack imagination. The first thing a fellow has to do is to decide that something needs to be done. There's plenty that needs to be done in this world, but lots of folks just sit there like a bump on a log"—Jake made a bump on a log out of his fist—"and think everything is just hunky-dory. But even deciding that something needs to be done isn't enough. You've got to imagine *how* it can be done. A fellow who sees a need but has no imagination is just a complainer, and he'll just sit there on his butt. But you take a fellow who sees a need *and* has an imagination, and he won't let a damn thing stand in his way."

Jake took the cigar out of his mouth, had another sip of coffee, put the cigar back, leaned back in his chair and hooked his thumbs in his belt. Lonnie could feel his rump going numb on the hard stool, but he sat very quietly, listening.

"The thing you have to watch for," Jake went on, "is folks who don't have any imagination. Every time a fellow with imagination does something, it makes the other bunch madder'n hell because it shows 'em up. Right off, they'll tell you ninety-eight ways why it can't be done, and if that doesn't work, they'll tell you ninety-nine more ways why it *shouldn't* be done." He took a puff of the cigar, held it for a moment, studying it, then went on. "Take that fellow Seward, when he said the country ought to buy Alaska. Well, they hooted—all those who said he couldn't and the rest who said he shouldn't. They said, 'If it's so bad the Russians don't want it, it must be worse than worthless, because the Russians will take anything.' But Seward just kept to his business and went right on and bought Alaska. Then a few folks with imagination went up there and discovered gold and lived on the edge of peril and proved that a fellow can lick the meanest, coldest, wildest wilderness on earth if he just *imagines* he can. And someday, mind you, they'll find a way to warm the place up, and folks'll be swimming in fancy outdoor pools in the middle of January in Juneau and growing sweet corn and pole beans in Nome. You understand what I'm saying?''

''Yessir, I think so.''

''Now a man with imagination,'' Jake went on, ''he'll make a damfool of himself sometimes. But when he makes a mistake, he's just got to hitch up his britches and go on, don't you see. He's just got to push on through, because at the end of all his damfoolishness he'll find what he's been after. He may not know what shape it is or how it feels or smells. But he knows it's there. And after he's blundered around a bit being a damfool, he may land smack-dab on top of it. And if he doesn't worry too much about being a damfool, he'll have a good time in the process.''

''But what if he just keeps blundering around and never does find it?'' Lonnie asked.

''Some never do. But you just keep trying. If you give up, all you have left is a trail of damfoolishness to show for your time and effort, and that makes you an Absolute Damfool. There is nothing to be more pitied.''

Lonnie wondered then about his father. Nobody had ever come right out and told him much about Henry Tibbetts's damfoolishness, but he had picked up enough to know that Henry had probably broken every tenet of Mama Pastine's notion of Doing Right. He knew that Henry rode dead drunk on the back of the fire truck whooping and hollering when the volunteers went to a fire; that he had been drunk the night Lonnie's mother, Hazel Tibbetts, had been killed in the car wreck, and drunk the night he joined the National Guard. Daddy Jake made no secret of his conviction that Henry was a reprobate and a disgrace. But what Daddy Jake was saying here seemed to put a different light on things. Was Henry Tibbetts just blundering about being a damfool because he was looking for something? If so, there was nothing especially wrong with his damfoolishness. Unless, as Daddy Jake said, he was an Absolute Damfool. The more Lonnie thought about it, the more he wanted badly to ask Daddy Jake about it. But he didn't.

''Is imagination the same thing as pretending?'' Lonnie asked instead.

''Sometimes that's the way it starts, Lonnie. And sometimes

that's all it ever amounts to.'' Then he looked away out the window and stared for a moment through the frost-glazed panes at the bare branches of the trees, and Lonnie knew for dead certain that his grandfather was thinking of Henry Tibbetts, too. He sensed with unerring instinct that a great truth was waiting to be spoken, a mystery revealed, that this was the one moment perhaps never to be seized again when he might learn who he was and where he had come from. He waited, holding his breath until his chest ached and his eyes burned, waited for Daddy Jake to say it. But he didn't.

''But a man with true imagination . . .'' Jake started to say, and then his voice trailed off and Lonnie could see how tired Jake was, how the lines around his eyes and the furrows on his brow had deepened.

It was then that it dawned on Lonnie that Daddy Jake *wasn't going to ask him about Captain Finley.* It had been sitting there between them, just waiting to be asked. But Daddy Jake, God bless his soul, had let it be. Lonnie felt the sting of grateful tears in his eyes and he wanted to leap up and throw his arms around Daddy Jake and tell him how much he loved him—loved him for somehow understanding. But he didn't, because he was afraid that if he did, he might blurt out a question about his father. And that was something Daddy Jake didn't want to talk about, the way Lonnie didn't want to talk about Captain Finley.

So they were even, he thought. Things remained unspoken. Secret places remained secret. At least for now.

Lonnie felt a great weariness creep over him. He wanted to shuck off the blankets and go upstairs and burrow down in the warm cave of his bed and drift off to sleep thinking about damfools and Absolute Damfools, tunneling like a mole through the rich dark underground of his imagination.

Then he noticed the silence. The radio was quiet. Bing Crosby broke off right in the middle of ''Silver Bells'' and there was no sound in the kitchen except for the faint bubbling of the coffee-pot. Upstairs, the baby had apparently cried herself to sleep. The silence lasted perhaps fifteen or twenty seconds, and then Ollie Whittle came on, his voice crackling with urgency. ''Ladies and gentlemen, I have an extremely important news bulletin in my hand from the wires of the United Press. American troops have reached the beleaguered garrison at Bastogne, breaking the thrust of the massive German advance in Belgium. Elements of

General George Patton's Third Army, aided by unexpected clearing weather that allowed heavy aerial bombardment and resupply missions, broke through stiff enemy resistance to relieve the Bastogne garrison, which had been surrounded by German units for five days. Repeating this news bulletin . . .''

And then Ollie was interrupted by Mama Pastine's stifled cry and Lonnie jerked around to see her standing in the doorway of the kitchen, hand over mouth, hair askew, wild-eyed.

"Pastine . . ." Jake rose from his chair.

She pointed at the Atwater-Kent. "Bastogne," she said, her voice an anguished croak. "That's where he is."

"Who?" Jake asked, his mouth already beginning to frame the word . . .

"Henry," she said. "He's near Bastogne. He's all right!" she cried.

"What do you mean?" Jake asked, staring at her.

"His last letter," she said, still looking at the radio, which was now thundering majestically with "Adeste Fidelis." "He mentioned a town named Bastogne. The censors left it in."

"What letters?" Jake asked. "There haven't been any letters."

"Oh, yes." She turned on him, her voice brittle. "There most certainly have been letters. Henry writes me letters."

"But where?" All their mail, business and personal, came to a post office box. Jake picked it up on his way home to lunch. It was part of his regimen. He sorted through it as he ate, opening the personal items, laying aside the business mail to take back to the newspaper with him in the afternoon. If they got mail, he saw it.

"Rosh Benefield," she said after a moment. Lonnie could see the color drain from Jake's face as if she had struck him in the belly. Pastine sat down in a chair at the table and folded her hands in her lap. Jake stood there, immobile.

"They started coming about a year ago," Pastine said, calm now. "Rosh called one morning and said I had a letter addressed in his care and I should come get it. So I went, and it was from Henry. It wasn't much. He just said he was in Texas and he was a lieutenant in a new division. After a month or so there was another one and then they came more often until there was one every week or so. Then they shipped out in August, straight to France, and there was a long time that I didn't hear anything.

Finally there was a letter saying Henry was near the front lines. That's when he mentioned Bastogne. I looked it up on the map.''

"Where are the letters?" Jake asked.

"Locked away in Rosh Benefield's safe," she said. "They belong to me. And someday to Lonnie."

"You wrote him back?"

"Of course."

"And did he tell you he was married?"

"No."

"Maybe he's not."

"Yes," she said flatly, "he's married. I looked at that marriage certificate real carefully last night. And this morning I rousted the probate judge in Loconas County, Texas, out of bed and told him I was calling from the Pentagon and I had to know if Lieutenant Henry Tibbetts was married because he was on a dangerous secret mission. So the good judge got himself down to the courthouse and confirmed it. Henry's wife used to be Francine Wolzinski. She is twenty-two years old and she was born in Cleveland. It's all according to law. They are man and wife."

Lonnie was thunderstruck, listening to it. Not that his father was remarried, but that Mama Pastine had called on the telephone all the way to Loconas County, Texas, and convinced some old judge that she was from the Pentagon.

"When did this all happen?" Jake asked.

"July eleventh," Pastine answered.

"That makes," Jake counted on his stubby fingers, "five and a half months. And that means. . ."

"That means," she cut him off sharply, "that Henry's wife and daughter are here in this house. Your daughter-in-law and granddaughter. Your son is in mortal peril in Belgium. God willing, he has been delivered from danger."

Jake started to speak again, but she went barreling right on by him. Lonnie had never seen her so wrought up. "Now the next thing that is going to happen, Jake Tibbetts, is that you are going to get yourself up the stairs and welcome your daughter-in-law and your new granddaughter into this house." She stood abruptly and pointed at Daddy Jake. "You have been at this business long enough!"

She towered above the table, a fury in a rumpled cotton print dress, hair flying, eyes flashing. For the first time Lonnie could remember in his entire life, she seemed bigger than Daddy Jake—bigger than Lonnie ever imagined she could be.

"Up!" she cried, jerking her arm as if she could levitate Daddy Jake up the stairs.

Lonnie thought suddenly of the Great Waldini, the black-caped hero of the serial now in mid-run at the motion picture show, a man of deep piercing eyes and enormous mystic powers who moved inanimate objects with the sheer force of his will as sparks flashed from his fingertips. As of last Saturday afternoon, the Great Waldini was hanging from the tattered shred of a venetian blind out the window of a New York City skyscraper with Madison Avenue fifty floors of heart-stopping emptiness below him, waiting for Episode Seven. Lonnie could not picture Mama Pastine hanging from a venetian blind, but there was the same powerful electric force about her that filled the room and made the hair on the back of Lonnie's neck tingle.

"Up!" she roared again.

But Daddy Jake, to Lonnie's amazement, not only didn't go, he sat down. It was as if he moved out of the line of sight of Mama Pastine's flashing finger, out of the aura of her powers. But it had taken a lot out of him. He slumped, shoulders sagging. There was a long silence, and then he said weakly, "I'll be damned."

Mama Pastine lowered her arm. "Yes, you will," she said quietly. "If you're not already, you certainly will be. You are a hard and stubborn man, Jake Tibbetts. You are your grandfather's grandson and your father's son."

"I am no drunk or lunatic," Jake muttered.

"Better you were. We could write off your mule-headedness to it and put you away until you came to your senses. But no, you are running loose in the world. Now, you have gone far enough. You may disown Henry, but not his wife and daughter." She paused a moment, brushed back the strands of hair from her forehead. "Go upstairs to them."

Jake stared at the floor, considering it a moment, and then said, "No, I will not."

"You will not?"

Jake didn't raise his head, but Lonnie could see that defiance was stuck in his gut like concrete. His jawline was rigid and the veins on his neck stood out like cords. "I will not," he said again.

Mama Pastine stood over him a moment longer, glaring at the top of his bowed head. "All right, then," she said finally.

And she walked out of the kitchen, leaving them sitting there, Jake staring at the spot on the floor where her feet had been planted, Lonnie staring at Jake, awed by the test of wills he had seen. Mama Pastine, in a fury of which he had never known her capable, had been unable to move him. The mystic power of the Great Waldini had failed.

Then they heard her banging around in the parlor, heard a loud clatter of metal, heard her heading back toward the kitchen, realized at the same instant what she had done, rose up out of their chairs in unison as she filled the doorway, both hands gripping the hilt of Captain Finley Tibbetts's cavalry sword. She raised the long curving silver blade, gleaming from the polish of Jake's chamois cloth, until it was aimed directly at Jake's chest, the wicked tip barely trembling.

"Out!" she bellowed. "Out of the house!"

Jake opened his mouth and the cigar fell out and plopped on the floor. A large-sized rat could have run down his throat.

"You have thirty seconds to be clear of the premises!"

Jake's mouth closed, then opened again. "Put that thing down before you cut yourself, Pastine."

"I will run you clean through with it!" she cried. "I swear I will." She made a quick menacing move toward his chest. Jake flinched.

"Don't stick him there, Mama Pastine," Lonnie yelped. "It'll bounce off his breastbone."

"You keep your mouth shut, buster," she roared at Lonnie, "or I'll run you out of here with this old fool! You have concocted enough devilment of your own to put the Jehovah's Witnesses to rout. And you"—she jabbed again at Jake with the sword. "Move!"

Lonnie knew then that Jake would make a sudden lunge toward her, grab the sword away, and put an end to all this, but to his amazement, Jake began to edge backward. His chair tumbled over with a racket and he lurched, grabbing the edge of the table with one hand to steady himself. Mama Pastine pivoted to give him the open doorway and he edged sideways along the table until he reached the opening and backed through it. "Pastine, you were a lot more fun before you got religion," he said hoarsely.

"Oh no you don't, you old fool. Don't you start in with your words, Jake. You've bamboozled me and the rest of the world long enough with your wit and wisdom. Now you just keep your mouth shut and your feet moving.'' She feinted again with the sword and Jake winced as if he had been cut. ''Move! Save your blather for the rest of the fools who can't tell the difference between good sense and hogwash.''

Jake backed through the kitchen doorway into the hall. He reached behind him to open the front door, still keeping an eye on her. Lonnie watched it all in open-mouthed amazement, then got up out of his chair and followed them, dropping the blankets on the floor and making small puddles with his dripping feet as he walked. Daddy Jake backed on through the front doorway, pushing the screen door open with his hand. Mama Pastine was close behind him, the sword held straight and unswerving in front of her, arms locked with some powerful force. Jake kept moving, easing sideways down the front steps. Lonnie stood just inside, behind the screen door, seeing how quietly furious they both were—Jake all red-faced at the bottom of the steps, eyebrows bobbing violently, Pastine glaring down at him from the top.

That was just how they were when Rosh Benefield pulled up in the front yard in his Packard, switched off the engine, sat staring at them for a moment, then opened the door and eased his great bulk out of the car. He closed the door behind him softly and stood there, taking it all in. ''Merry Christmas,'' he called finally. He waited a moment for an answer, and when none came, he shrugged his massive shoulders, walked around to the back of the car, opened the trunk, reached in and lifted out a shiny red bicycle. He sat it on the ground by the car and kicked down the kickstand so that it stood by itself.

''Billy's,'' he said, looking up at them. ''You can't buy a new bicycle for love nor money these days. They just aren't making any new bicycles, I guess. But I found this one of Billy's in the back of the garage and I got Fog Martin to fix it up. He did a real nice job on it, don't you think?'' He patted the seat and looked at them again, again got no comment. Jake and Pastine just stood rooted in place, staring holes in each other, ignoring Rosh. ''A young fellow like Lonnie ought to have a bicycle, don't you think?'' Still no answer. Rosh looked up at Lonnie standing behind the screen door. He cleared his throat. ''Lonnie, don't you think you ought to get some clothes on there?''

Lonnie looked down at himself, remembered for the first time that he had been naked beneath all that swaddling of blankets. Now he shivered in the cold and bent forward a little bit and covered his dingle with his hands. Naked or not, freezing or not, this was too good to miss. Out on the porch, Mama Pastine gave him a withering look, then turned back to Jake.

There was another very long silence, and then Rosh Benefield said, "Well, are you folks having a good Christmas?"

"Shut up, Rosh," Mama Pastine said. "Can't you see I've got two fool idiots on my hands?"

"Well," said Rosh affably, "what seems to be the matter, Pastine?"

"Jake won't go upstairs and welcome Henry's wife and the new baby."

"Ah," Rosh said, "I see."

"You've heard all about it by now, I suppose?" she asked.

"Ahem. Well, Herschel Martin's pretty well spread the news, I guess."

"Yes, I suppose he has," Mama Pastine said. She sighed an enormous sigh and then lowered the sword slowly until the tip touched the wood at the edge of the porch, leaned on it for support. Lonnie couldn't see her face from where he stood inside the house, but he could see how her jaw sagged with fatigue.

Then suddenly Jake lunged back toward the steps and in a single beautiful rippling motion worthy of Captain Finley himself, Mama Pastine brought the sword up and hauled back like a baseball batter and swung, carving a great curving slice of Christmas morning out of the air, the tip of the blade passing just inches short of where Jake seemed to hang in midair on the third step, the force of the swing taking her clean around until the rushing blade—CHHHUUUNNNGG—hit the post next to the steps and bit a good inch and a half into it, rattling the galvanized tin of the porch roof like musket fire. She jerked on the hilt mightily with both hands and pulled it free as Jake bellowed in fright and leaped back to the ground at the bottom of the steps, ashen-faced. Pastine pointed the blade again at Jake and screamed, "OUT! I said OUT!"

"My God, you could have cut my head off!" Jake hollered. He turned to Rosh Benefield, who was frozen in place next to the Packard, hand resting on the seat of the red bicycle. "Did you see that? Did you see what she nearly did to me?"

Lonnie's heart leaped into his throat. He could see, even though Mama Pastine had her back to him. He could see the terror in Daddy Jake's eyes that told him *she would have done it*. It would have been a monstrous thing, but she would have done it. Lonnie felt his knees go weak and he wanted to cry out in horror but his throat was locked by the big lump of his heart.

Grandaddy Rosh blinked his small bright eyes and stood there looking first at Pastine, then at Jake. "I think," he said finally, "that you might ought not to try getting back in the house again, Jake." His voice was slow and measured, as if he were carefully explaining a point to a jury. "And Pastine, don't you think it would be best if you went back inside and put the sword up? And got some clothes on young Lonnie there? Let's just try and get ourselves organized here and work this thing out like sensible folks."

"You call that sensible?" Jake yelled.

"I'd call it pretty persuasive, Jake," Rosh said.

"Well, what the hell am I gonna do if I can't live in my own house?"

"Stay at the newspaper," Pastine spat. "Stay down there with your printing press and your cranky Linotype machine and your ink and all your precious words. Talk to your typewriter. Just sit there and laugh all you want at everybody who's not as wise and witty as you are. Call us all fools the way you love to do. Then every once in a while, get up and go back to the washroom and look in the mirror and say, 'Fool, fool, fool.' Because that's what *you* are, Jake. Fool, fool, fool."

"Is that what you think?"

"You're an arbitrary old man," she said. "You have no milk of human kindness in you."

"That's not true."

"Well, mostly."

Jake's shoulders slumped. "All right, Pastine. If that's what you want."

"That's just the way it is," she said. "If you change your mind about Henry's wife and baby, let us know. Until then, just live at the newspaper."

Jake turned to Rosh Benefield. "She's throwing me out, Rosh," he said.

"Well, there does seem to be some ground for compromise there, Jake."

Jake thought for a moment, and then his jaw hardened. "No. Hell, no. Nobody's gonna tell me how to think."

Rosh nodded slowly, his great head bobbing up and down. "Then I guess you're right. She's throwing you out."

"Do you think I'm an arbitrary old fool, Rosh?"

"About some things, yes."

"About Henry."

"That, mainly."

"What did I do that was so wrong, Rosh?"

Rosh shrugged. "Maybe you didn't forgive him enough."

"I forgave him a helluva lot," Jake said stubbornly.

"But maybe not enough."

"The way you forgive Billy?"

"It's what a man does, Jake."

Jake turned back to Pastine. "Is that what you think, too?"

She stood there for a moment, leaning on the sword, looking down at him, then said, "Yes."

Jake squared his shoulders. "Well, you can all go straight to hell. If raising a damfool makes me a damfool, then so be it. I'm going to town." He turned and started off across the yard, then stopped and yelled back to Pastine, "I'm gonna freeze in this weather. Can I have my coat?"

Pastine walked back in the house, brushing by Lonnie, got Jake's old brown overcoat off the rack in the hall, went back to the edge of the porch, and tossed the coat down to the bottom of the steps. Jake walked over and picked it up, brushed it off, and made a great show of putting it on, pulling the collar up tight around his throat, buttoning all the buttons one by one while they watched him. Then, without looking at them again, he stalked off toward town, arms swinging briskly, shoulders thrown back, legs pumping. Acting like it didn't matter. Knowing better.

Lonnie sagged to his knees in the doorway and watched him go, feeling very small and alone, wondering in despair if somehow he had brought it all down on their heads with all his damfoolishness, wondering most of all if it would ever be right again.

BOOK
THREE

ONE

*H*_{*E*} was twenty-six, unmarried, when he looked up from the Linotype one summer Tuesday afternoon, sweat pouring down his face and back, the Linotype grumbling with the indigestion of a week's worth of copy it was turning into metal, to see her standing over him, fresh-scrubbed and peach-complexioned in a middy blouse and white organdy skirt and pert sailor hat. He felt suddenly grotesque and rancid, like a ruined ancient prisoner kept overlong in a dungeon and visited at long last by a lady.

"My God," he said aloud, "the Royal Navy." He had a way, he was aware, of confounding people with his directness. But not this one. He studied her as she studied him, all coolness in the fetid heat of the print shop.

"Dante in his inferno," she said. He had never seen her before, not that he had paid more than passing attention to the young women hereabouts. He was married, by God, to the newspaper. But he had never laid eyes on this one, and in fact she didn't have the look of the local girls. There was a certain air of . . . what? Refinement? That, yes. But more—a sense of being quite sure of herself, quite capable. She was a sturdy girl with fine high cheekbones and strong blue eyes, a bit too tall perhaps. Not the Royal Navy, the Norwegian Navy.

"What is this thing?" She indicated the machine with a flip of her hand.

"It's called a Linotype."

"Tell me how it works."

"It casts fools' words into metal," Jake said.

She tossed her head and the twin ribbons on the back of the sailor hat danced in the close air of the shop. Jake felt something catch inside him, deep in a place he had almost forgotten. "Then better you should shut it down," she said with a trace of a smile.

"Even fools love to see themselves in print," Jake said.

She looked around at the dimly lit print shop, every machine and workbench and wall coated with four decades of grime and grease and ink, absorbing light, rich and fevered in the August heat. Jake expected her to raise her eyebrows or give a little twitch of her nose to show him how dingy she found it. But she didn't.

"Out of the darkness . . ." Jake started to say, and then the Linotype, envious perhaps because of his inattention, suddenly groaned and hissed and exploded with a spurt of molten metal that shot toward the scarred ceiling. Jake leaped up with a cry, his chair clattering backward, and shoved her away as a shower of metal droplets rained down on the floor. She gave a small quick cry of fright and indignation. "Jesus . . ." he yelled, and then he looked and saw the dirty gray handprint across the front of her blue middy blouse, just over her breast.

Jake felt a bit faint. He knew he was blushing and he shoved his hand in his pocket. She drew herself up and gave him a withering stare.

"I'm sorry," he muttered, shuffling his feet like an idiot. "The damned thing is cantankerous. It doesn't know when to keep its mouth shut."

"Its owner doesn't know where not to put his hands," she said icily, reaching into her small blue purse (the same fabric as her navy blouse) to withdraw a white handkerchief, which she used to dab at the ink stain on her front.

"I didn't want you to get burned," Jake said, recovering a bit, staring at her firm full bosom as she worked at the smudge. "I'll get it cleaned for you."

She looked up, saw him gaping open-mouthed. He blushed

again, feeling the hot rush of blood engorging his ears and cheeks. She stopped, lowered her hands, opened the purse, shoved in the handkerchief, and took out a five-dollar bill. She thrust it out to him. "Renew our subscription, Mr. Tibbetts," she said, and then turned and walked out the door, the ribbons of her hat flouncing behind her.

Jake caught up with her two blocks away, breathless from the run. He didn't know how to stop her, didn't want to touch her arm and run the risk of having her strike him down in the street, so he just leaped ahead of her and planted himself in the middle of the sidewalk, right in front of the Farmers Mercantile Bank.

"Good Lord," she said, and stopped.

"Who are you?" Jake blurted. He held out the five-dollar bill. "I can't renew the subscription unless I know who you are."

She studied him for a long moment and he stood there frozen to the sidewalk, knowing what a ridiculous, godawful sight he must be with his hair matted with sweat, every inch of exposed flesh covered with the grime of his labors, wearing a filthy shop apron over his undershirt. He blinked in the afternoon sunlight, chest heaving from his dash. He wanted to melt into the sidewalk, leaving only a black puddle of ink and sweat. But he stood his ground. By God, he would be a fool if he had to.

"Pastine Cahoon," she said finally. "I think you will find the subscription in my father's name."

"Your father."

"Henry Cahoon."

Then she swept past him, left him standing there like an egg frying on the sidewalk. He stood for a moment, rooted to the spot, and turned just in time to see her round the corner at the end of the block and throw a quick glance back at him, a mere flick of her eyes. "Well, I'll be goddamned," Jake muttered.

Henry Cahoon's daughter. Henry Cahoon was something of an eccentric—a farmer of sorts with a good bit of rich bottom-land bordering Whitewater Creek several miles north of town, but more than that a tinkerer and inventor. Several years past he had created and patented a mechanical stump puller, which he manufactured now in a converted barn on his property. He employed perhaps thirty or forty men and the stump pullers were sold all over the South and Midwest, wherever men were still tearing down forests to make cropland. Henry Cahoon had been one of the first men in the county to own an automobile, not because he was one of the wealthiest (which he might well be by now) but because it gave him something else to tinker with. He was a quiet, tall man who kept to himself. Jake Tibbetts had never known him to have a wife, much less a daughter.

Jake marched into the Farmers Mercantile Bank, ignoring the staring eyes of the customers, into the glass-walled back office where Tunstall Renfroe sat hunched over a ledger book.

"Good Lord," Tunstall said, peering up at Jake through his wire-rimmed glasses.

"What's the matter?" Jake demanded. "Everybody keeps looking at me and saying 'Good Lord.' "

"You look like you just walked straight out of the print shop," Tunstall said. He looked at Jake's grime-smeared arms and hands. "Without washing up."

"Well, I did. Tell me about Henry Cahoon's daughter."

Tunstall leaned back in his chair and gave Jake a thin smile. "Henry Cahoon's daughter. Weeelllll. What brings on all the interest in Henry Cahoon's daughter?"

"None of your business." Jake folded his arms across his chest.

"All I know is," Tunstall scratched his chin, "her momma died about eight years ago and Henry Cahoon sent her some-place to school. To get 'finished,' you know."

"Well, she's back," Jake said.

"Seems like I heard that, yes. Got her degree and came back home. I think I heard somebody say she was helping Henry with his business. He's got quite a little operation going out there." Tunstall smiled again, clasped his hands behind his head. "You interested in the stump puller business, Jake?"

"Hell, no."

Tunstall's grin widened. "You interested in a wife, Jake?"

"*Hell*, no."

Tunstall fairly beamed. "Well, what's got you running all over town in your dirty apron asking about Pastine Cahoon then?"

"It's a perverse fascination with the Norwegian Navy," Jake retorted, and left Tunstall Renfroe hiked back in his swivel chair, grinning like an idiot.

Jake went back to the newspaper and thought about it. He went through the mechanical motions of setting type, proofing the galleys, making corrections, laying out the front page for the next day's press run, all the time thinking about Pastine Cahoon in her middy blouse with the smudge on the front right over her breast.

And he thought about himself. He had arrived at a watershed of sorts in his life. Now was the time to decide what he intended to do with the rest of it.

He would be a newspaperman, that much was set in stone. He had, at twenty-six, surrendered himself to the paper, and having done that, had mastered it. Isaac had died of typhoid, and Jake's mother did little more than keep the books and take in a few subscription renewals during the few hours she spent at the paper each afternoon. She made it plain that he was the editor, that whatever the *Free Press* became, it was Jake Tibbetts's responsibility.

It was just the two of them at home, in the house at the end of Partridge Road that by now was a two-story frame with a wide front porch and a big oak tree in the front yard. Albertis, before the melancholia had disabled him, had had the second story added and had rearranged the downstairs so that it had a parlor and a dining room where the bedrooms had been. Now, the house yawned with a great emptiness. They took their meals at the small table in the kitchen, and in the warm months they sat after supper on the front porch, wrapping their desultory conversation in cocoons of long silence while the evening gave itself over to the music of crickets and night birds. Emma Tibbetts was a tired woman. She had lost a husband and a son and she wanted no more of whatever foolishness the world was ready to dish out. She seemed to hunker down in the front porch rocker, giving fate a low profile.

So Jake began to consider Pastine Cahoon; or, more generally, to consider the notion of a wife. It hadn't occurred to him much before. Not that he was uninterested in women as a species—he just hadn't given much thought to living with one. He had taken sexual solace a few times from a middle-aged widow in Taylorsville, but now it came to him that it might be a regular thing, part of that enormous regularity that came with looking across the breakfast table at the same woman every morning for the rest of his life.

What kept him from pursuing Pastine Cahoon at first was just this, the thought that pursuing any young woman might lead to the finality of marriage. But after a few weeks of mulling that over, he became accustomed to that possibility and then even fascinated by it. It was perhaps time, he decided, to consider a wife, if that's what the natural progression of things brought on. What happened next was that he began to lust in his mind after Pastine Cahoon, and that stopped him dead in his tracks. He began to think thoughts that no young man ought to think about a proper young woman—and be sure, any daughter of a man like Henry Cahoon had by definition to be proper. This proper young woman became, as he told himself, a pain in the balls, the focus of great spasms of passion, a savage outpouring of juices and emotions of which he had not guessed himself capable. Midnights, in his room, he raged in sweaty combat with the laughing satyr in his own mind that kept trying to undress her, to reveal under clutching fingers the sleek belly, full breasts, soft white thighs. When he thought he had the beast under control for a moment, she would spring full-blown and naked before him, full of innocent secrets, undefiled but beckoning, until he flailed at himself, cursing afterward in the hot sweet darkness.

Jake was wretched. All this agony was after one brief encounter with Pastine Cahoon, and more weeks passed while he strove in vain to conquer the devil in his groin.

Suddenly, it was October and he came face to face with her in the Farmers Mercantile Bank one morning. He almost collided with her as he bustled through the door, and she dropped the bank bag she was carrying. Jake stammered an apology and stooped to pick it up, bumping heads with her on the way down. They both backed away, leaving the bag lying there on the marble floor of the bank foyer like the contested prize of two warring armies.

"My goodness," said Pastine Cahoon, rubbing her forehead. "Is this a holdup, Mr. Tibbetts?"

Jake laughed, suddenly at ease, suddenly relieved to realize that Pastine Cahoon, out there on her farm on the banks of Whitewater Creek, had not for some reason guessed at how she had been violated in thought by the wicked beast in Jake Tibbetts's mind. He knelt to pick up the bank bag, and as he stood again he felt wonderfully buoyant, almost giddy, perfectly relaxed, as sure of himself as he had ever been in his life.

"Shall I give this to you now, or bring it out on Sunday afternoon?"

Pastine Cahoon cocked her head to one side, gave him a long and searching look, and said, "You may give me the bag now, and I will expect you on Sunday afternoon at three."

So it began, and it went on for a year. Jake was in no hurry. He reveled in the courtship and in Pastine Cahoon, wanted to savor it at length. She was a fascinating surprise to him. She had opinions, honed by her schooling, and a lively curiosity inherited from her father the tinkerer. Jake had imagined the courtship of a young woman to be all billing and cooing, but this young woman could *talk*, for God's sake, and she challenged him. She knew all about the gold standard, Philippine independence, Kaiser Bill's expansionism. She considered Teddy Roosevelt an adventurist tool of capitalist empire builders, and said so. Jake Tibbetts hadn't thought about Teddy Roosevelt at all.

"If Teddy Roosevelt were to offer himself for local office, I might get worried," he said to Pastine one Sunday afternoon as they sat on her front porch. "If he's the kind of adventurist you say he is, he might want to open hostilities against the next county."

"But that's exactly what he's done in Panama," she said.

"So?"

"Don't you care about Panama?"

"I haven't really thought about Panama."

"Maybe you should."

"Well, every time I get around to thinking about Panama, some dear lady from the Methodist Missionary Society calls up and wants something in the paper about their study of Pago Pago. So I'm pretty wrapped up with Pago Pago right now. Maybe you could convince the Methodist Missionary Society to take a look into this Panama business."

"Jake Tibbetts," she said coldly, "you are mocking me."

"No," he said, smiling, "I may be mocking the Methodist women, but I am not mocking you, Miss Cahoon."

They courted fitfully through the winter months, Jake renting a buggy from Martin's Livery Stable on Sunday afternoons to make the drive out to Henry Cahoon's factory-farm. He met Henry Cahoon only once—a tall reed of a man who stooped as he went through doorways. He came from a back room as Jake arrived for his third visit, weak eyes blinking behind thick glasses, thinning white hair askew as if he had been standing in a gale. He grabbed Jake's hand with a powerful callused grip, muttered a few unintelligible words, and disappeared as quickly as he came. Pastine didn't seem to think there was anything out of the ordinary about him.

"Daddy's perfecting his stump puller," she said when they had sat a respectable distance apart on the living room sofa.

"Is there such a thing as a perfect stump puller?" Jake asked.

"Not yet," she said. "But there will be."

When the weather turned warm in the spring, it became a ritual for Jake to pick her up in the buggy and drive back to town, where they would walk in the small park on the riverbank and then sit on the steps of its white band shell. Their conversation became something of a comfortable ritual.

"The railroads," she said to him one spectacular Sunday afternoon, the air freighted with the aroma of budding, leafing things, "are the tool of the robber barons."

"So?"

She gave him a disgusted look.

"Railroads are neither good nor bad," Jake went on. "They're simply functional. They move things. Chickens. Lumber. Corsets."

"But they're controlled by a few greedy men who use them to amass unconscionable wealth."

"What kind of wealth is unconscionable?" Jake asked. "And what does a robber baron look like, anyway? I've never seen one get off the train. I've seen lots of chickens, lumber, corsets, the like. I've seen preachers, lyceum speakers, ladies' ready-to-wear drummers, even a United States congressman one time. But not a single robber baron. Do they have fangs? Do they carry vials of plague in their money belts? Now if I was expecting a load of corsets and got a load of robber barons instead, I'd be upset. But as long as the corsets arrive, I'm pretty near satisfied."

She brushed impatiently at a strand of hair, a small delicate gesture that made Jake's heart lurch. He was still having night sweats, worse than ever. The banter helped keep his mind off this lust he harbored for Pastine Cahoon.

"Have you no conscience, Jake?" she said, shaking her head. "The greed of these people has made virtual slaves of an entire class of citizens."

"Greed makes the world go round. Self-interest is the root

of human nature. Ask any woman who's standing at the train station waiting for a shipment of corsets.''

She rose from where they sat on the band shell steps, exasperated, walked a few paces away on the grass, turned and stamped her small foot. "You are the most hopelessly provincial person I have ever met," she said. "Why an obviously intelligent man such as yourself refuses to take an interest in the affairs of the world is quite beyond me.''

Jake grinned at her. "I jes tries to git from sunup to sundown, Miz Pastine. Jes hoes de cotton and plows de mule and tries to fine a little fat to go along wit de lean. De big massah, he make enuf fool of hisself wifout old Jake stirrin' de pot.''

"I say again," she said, her voice rising, "you are a provincial man.''

"I run the *Free Press*, not the *Harper's Bazaar.*''

"I would think any editor would have a responsibility . . .''

"To show fools the foolishness of their ways," he interrupted. "And there are quite enough local fools to go around.''

She stood there for a moment glaring at him, eyes dancing, and Jake thought to himself how foolish he was, sitting here and challenging this marvelous young woman whose very presence made his heart pound. His mouth would get him in trouble yet.

"Your trouble, Mr. Tibbetts," she said after a moment, "is that you talk too much. You have a rejoinder for everything.''

He looked away from her, stared for a time at another couple in a rowboat in the river next to the park. The young woman had a bright green ribbon in her hair that flashed in the sunlight as she tossed her head back and laughed at something the young man had said.

"Why did you come back here?" he asked finally.

"Why, indeed, not? This is my home.''

"But doesn't it bore you?''

She cocked her head to one side and laughed, a bright sharp bell note. "Gracious, no.''

"But the people you were around at school, they must have been infinitely more interesting than we local bumpkins.''

She laughed again. "Ha! *Now* you're talking about bores. They're so *smug*. And they all think alike. Everyone there thinks Teddy Roosevelt is an adventurist. All they do is sit around and nod at each other. There's no one to argue with because there's nothing to argue *about.*''

"Surely, though, after such a rich intellectual and cultural atmosphere you must find this humble community a trifle backward."

"Oh," she said, tossing her head again in the way that made Jake want to lunge for her, "it has possibilities."

And so it went, on through the spring and summer. Jake Tibbetts paid regular suit, but only up to a point. Physically, he was the most timid of men, afraid to trust himself beyond brief moments of hand-holding. But they talked and talked, and on that level came to a certain intimacy. Jake began to give up bits and pieces of himself to her—the things he had learned about the newspaper, about his Confederate ancestor Captain Finley Tibbetts, about writing and publishing in a small town where you had to face on Thursday the people you wrote about on Wednesday. He told her of his contempt for pompous fools, especially those who wrote in national magazines, of his relish for grappling with local affairs in good wholesome argument, of his profound belief that a man must take his life in his own hands and shake it for all it's worth and take final and ultimate responsibility for it. He even told her about the dark strain of madness that ran through his ancestry—Captain Finley, dead with a ghastly grimace on his face and a slash across the brocade of the parlor settee, where he had dispatched one last bluecoat devil; Albertis, haunting the upstairs, mired in melancholia. He told her all these things, unburdened himself to her as he had never done with another person. But he was afraid to touch Pastine Cahoon. And so, he almost lost her.

The first inkling of trouble was on a Sunday afternoon in early September, still hot with the afterbreath of summer, dust-choked from a dry spell the crop-gathering farmers had welcomed. Jake was sweaty and gritty by the time he drove up in the yard of Henry Cahoon's home in his rented buggy to see another rig parked by the front door. He climbed down, hitched the horse's reins around a sycamore tree, and knocked. Henry Cahoon came to the door and Jake stood there for a moment looking up at him.

"Ahem. Is Miss Pastine home?"

"She has company," Henry Cahoon said, blinking behind his thick glasses.

Jake opened his mouth to speak, couldn't think of anything

to say, and closed it again. "Well," he got out after a moment, "could I speak to her?"

Henry Cahoon closed the door without a word, leaving Jake sweating like an idiot on the front porch. He stood there, feeling more and more like a fool, angry and embarrassed, and finally turned to go. Just then, Pastine opened the door a crack and peered out.

"Oh, hello," she said, her voice musical. She looked perfectly cool and dry and that made him feel even grubbier, the way he had felt that hot afternoon more than a year ago when he had dashed down the street in his ink-stained apron to find out her name.

"You have company?" he asked.

"Yes." She looked just the slightest bit smug, he thought. Trying not to be, but not quite bringing it off.

"Who, might I ask?" The Baptist preacher, perhaps? An old friend from school?

"Rosh Benefield, if it's any of your business."

My God, he thought. Rosh Benefield. His best friend. The sonofabitch.

"But didn't you know I was coming out?" he protested, feeling the heat rising in his face, making him sweat even more.

"No," she said.

"But I come every Sunday . . ."

"Perhaps," she said airily, "you take me for granted. Perhaps you presume too much."

"Yes. Yes, I guess I do." Jake started backing away from the door, staring at her in confusion, feeling horribly stupid.

Pastine just stood there. "Are you all right?" she asked after a moment.

"Hell, yes, I'm all right," Jake bellowed, humiliation washing over him in hot waves. "I'm just by-God fine!" He bolted for the buggy, and he didn't even look back as he whipped the horse out of Pastine Cahoon's yard in total rout.

Jake drove like a madman back to town, went straight to Lightnin' Jim Haskell's, and got a pint jar of Jim's Best. He took it to the newspaper office, pulled the blinds, sat there in the darkness of the front office with his feet propped up on his cluttered desk, and drank fiercely. Halfway through the jar, he got hold of himself enough to think coherent thoughts. He railed for a while in his mind at the inconstancy of women, banging his fist on the desk for emphasis. Then he vented his anger on the fickleness of friends. Damn them both—Pastine Cahoon and Rosh Benefield—for sneaking around behind his back. Especially Rosh Benefield, the closest friend he had ever had. They had grown up together, gone off to college together—the only two young men from their graduating class to do so. When Jake had had to quit and come home to run the paper, Rosh had stayed, gone on to law school. But when he came back and set up practice with his father, the mayor, he was the same old Rosh: quick-witted but deliberate, slow to anger, easygoing. They had drifted into the comfortable habit of good conversation, Rosh dropping by once or twice a week in the late afternoon after his day at the law office, settling his already portly frame into the chair beside Jake's desk for a drink and some spirited talk. Jake would pull a jar of Lightnin' Jim's Best and two tumblers out of the bottom drawer, pour two fingers apiece, and they would sip and banter until it was gone, and when Rosh had left he would wash the tumblers at the sink in the back and put them away. By unspoken agreement, they took turns buying the whiskey. It was never at the law office that they met, always at the newspaper, because Rosh shared his own office with his father and Jake's domain was entirely his.

They talked about the town, about people, about matters of public portent, sensing their place as young men whose opinions would increasingly matter as time went on. They talked about their lives, their aspirations, their philosophies. But they had not talked much about Pastine Cahoon. Jake Tibbetts was reticent when it came to Pastine Cahoon. Obviously, he thought now, too reticent. He should have warned Rosh Benefield, the skulking sonofabitch, that Pastine Cahoon was his girl. *His* girl. He thought about it for a long time, sitting there in the gloom while Sunday afternoon faded outside. No, she wasn't his girl at all. He had been too goddamned timid. He had sat around sweating with indecision until she had given up on him. That was the plain and simple truth of it. He, Jake Tibbetts, the most decisive of men, who had chased Pastine Cahoon down the street, had not pressed his case because he was timid and because he thought he had all the time in the world. Jake thought for a moment about going back out there, banging on the door and declaring himself. But he was pretty drunk now, and he didn't want anybody else—especially Pastine Cahoon—to see him as more of a fool than he really was. So before he began to wallow in self-pity, he screwed the top on the jar of Lightnin' Jim's Best, stuck it in the bottom drawer of his desk, and lurched home and straight to bed for a fitful, tortured sleep.

He was a bit surprised when Rosh Benefield turned up on Wednesday evening just after Jake had finished his weekly press run and had carried the neatly folded stacks of papers to the long worktable that filled the middle of the print shop, ready for labeling. The front door was locked, as it always was on Wednesday evenings when Jake was busy up on the big Kluge press. But Rosh knocked loudly and Jake saw him through the glass upper half of the door, standing there on the sidewalk with a brown paper sack tucked under his arm.

Jake went to the door, unlocked it, and opened it a crack. "I'm not finished," he said. "I don't have the labels on yet, and I've got to get 'em down to the post office."

Rosh blinked. It was the only movement in his face. If you were going to whip Rosh Benefield in a courtroom, Jake thought, you would have to figure out what his blinks meant. If he didn't want you to know what he was thinking, it was his only expression.

"I'm not in any hurry," Rosh said. "I'll just wait while you finish up."

Jake didn't want to drink whiskey with Rosh Benefield this Wednesday evening, not when he was still seething over the man's duplicity. But for God's sake. Here he stood like a walrus on the sidewalk with a paper sack under his arm, as patient as sunrise.

"All right, come in." Jake closed and locked the door behind him and Rosh eased into the chair beside Jake's desk like a berthing ship, placed the paper sack on the desk, and folded his arms across his spreading middle. Jake looked at him, grunted, and went to the back shop. He took his sweet time putting the labels on the papers, all 585 of them, stopping to bundle them with twine by rural route numbers the way the government required. When he was finished with that, he hauled them to the back door and stacked them in his dray cart. Then without a word to Rosh Benefield, he closed the door with a bang and pushed the cart the three blocks to the post office, opened the door with the key the postmaster had given him, and deposited the bundles on the sorting table in the mail room, where the postmaster could get at them early the next morning. Jake locked up, then stopped for a moment outside and took out his pocket watch. Almost seven. It had been an hour and a half since Rosh Benefield had arrived. Well, he thought, let the sonofabitch marinate.

Rosh was still sitting there, hands folded, when Jake got back. Jake took off his apron and spent several minutes at the sink in the back, scrubbing at the grime that blackened his hands and arms, then dried himself and went to the front office. He sat down in the swivel chair at his desk, feeling the sudden rush of satisfied fatigue that always came with putting the paper to bed for the week. It was something he liked to enjoy by himself. Rosh Benefield never came this early on Wednesdays.

But here he was. Jake opened the bottom drawer of his desk, took out the two tumblers and left the half-empty jar of Lightnin' Jim's Best he had been working on Sunday. He placed the tumblers with a thump on the desk, took Rosh's jar of whiskey out of the paper sack, unscrewed the lid, poured two fingers apiece, and recapped the jar. He shoved one of the tumblers over toward Rosh, who had been watching him with those small slow-blinking eyes. They raised their glasses to drink, and just when Jake was about to take a good mouthful of the strong, raw whiskey, Rosh said, "Let's drink to Miss Pastine Cahoon."

"Goddamn!" Jake bellowed, red-faced. He slammed his own tumbler down, splashing whiskey across the desktop, spattering the front of Rosh's vest. Rosh calmly finished taking his drink, then set his glass down, reached for the handkerchief in the inside breast pocket of his coat, and blotted the droplets of whiskey. Jake glowered at him in a high rage.

When Rosh was finished, he put the handkerchief back in his pocket, smiled at Jake, and said, "I'm in love with Miss Pastine Cahoon." Jake wanted to kill him, but he gripped the arms of the swivel chair and kept his butt jammed into it. "I have asked her to marry me," Rosh went on.

"How . . ." Jake croaked, the words barely coming out, ". . . how long have you been seeing her?"

"Oh, about six months," he said. "On Thursday evenings. We go to prayer meeting."

Jake almost lost control then, imagining them sitting there on their pious rumps listening to the Baptist preacher mouth religious hokum, and then riding side by side to the Cahoon farm on the narrow seat of Rosh's buggy while he . . . oh, God. And this had been going on for *six months*. While he dawdled, unsuspecting.

Rosh took another sip of his whiskey. "I think we are what you refer to as rivals, you and me."

"Did you know. . ."

"Yes."

"And still, you . . ."

"Yes. Miss Cahoon is a singular young woman. Quite capable, I think, of making up her own mind. Which she has done."

Jake slumped in the chair. So, that was it. He felt a great ache welling up in him, a sense of something indescribably precious, irretrievably lost. He wanted Rosh Benefield to get the hell out of here so he could die quietly.

"She turned me down," Rosh said.

It took Jake a moment.

"I said, she turned me down."

"What?"

"I asked Pastine to marry me and she said no. Nicely, but quite flatly." Rosh's poker face broke just a little then, just a flicker. He started to say something else, but the sound died in his throat and he picked up the tumbler and tossed off the rest of the whiskey with a gulp, then sat it down again on the desk with a long, deliberate motion. "Wheee," he said. "I think Lightnin' Jim must be straining that stuff through an old horse blanket." He wiped his lips with the back of his hand.

"Rosh, I . . ."

Rosh waved him to silence, then reached and got the whiskey jar in his meaty hand, unscrewed the cap, and poured three fingers in his glass. He took another big sip and coughed, his eyes watering. "I think she's got her mind set, Jake."

"Huh?"

Rosh leaned forward, heaving his bulk toward Jake, got up close to his face and breathed a great cloud of whiskey fumes on him. "I think," he said, "if you would get off your goddamn butt and ask her, she'd have you."

Jake stood up, bent over, and kissed Rosh Benefield on the cheek. Then he went straightaway and did what Rosh told him. And she married him.

They had been married for five delicious months when Pastine decided to build the library—not for their home (though she had filled the place with books and magazines) but for the town.

Jake Tibbetts was still congratulating himself on his incredible good luck. Pastine had said to him straight off, on their honeymoon in Memphis, "Jake, I want you to know that I will show no modesty in making love to you." And she didn't. There was no question that she hadn't had the slightest experience with it. But she came to the marriage bed delightfully curious, explorative, uninhibited. Jake Tibbetts floated down Partridge Road each morning to the newspaper office, *knowing* there must be a joyously wicked aura about him that people could see. Surely, he was the only man alive—well, certainly the only man in this straightlaced town—who had a shamelessly lusty wife at home.

She was a straightforward young woman, to be sure. She had a strong, clear voice that hailed people from across the street, a way of fixing people with her eyes when she spoke that was mildly disconcerting. People were hard-pressed to speak of any Eastern airs cultivated by her schooling; rather, she was if anything too thoroughly democratic in the way she insisted on approaching everyone—man or woman, adult or child, prominent or obscure—with the same unsettling directness. The best they could summon was the notion, discreetly shared, that Pastine Tibbetts was a trifle *forward* for a young matron. The stuffiest of folk objected most to her opinions, which she hadn't the good grace to keep to herself.

There had been no clash at all at the white frame two-story house at the end of Partridge Road where Jake took Pastine to live. Quite the contrary. Emma Tibbetts summarily turned over the management of the house to Pastine and retired permanently to her front porch rocker, glad to be rid of the responsibility of the house and Jake. She also announced that she was giving up the bookkeeping duties at the *Free Press* and that if Jake wanted to know whether he was going broke or making a living, he would have to do his own figuring. "My Lord," Jake protested, "I'm a newspaperman, not a business tycoon!" He had no patience for it. So Pastine took over the books, too. She was quick with figures, and one afternoon a week was enough for her to balance the ledger sheets, get the bills out, and do the banking. Jake went right on letting his correspondence stack up on the corner of his desk until Pastine could dispose of it. Pastine kept him organized in his work and happy in his home. She brightened up the house with the intimate touches it had never known—new curtains in their bedroom, a fresh-cut rosebud in a small pewter bud vase on the table just inside the front door. Yes, she had changed his life in every way, quite remarkably. Jake Tibbetts was a satisfied man.

Then, there was the library. There was none, save for a few shelves of books at the high school. Pastine decided that it was an abominable situation. A town without books courted dimwittedness and quackery, and she told the Town Council so in person. She had thrown their meeting into an uproar when she rose to ask for the floor. It was the first time in the community's history that a woman had addressed the council. In fact, it was the first time the members could remember a woman even attending. But Pastine Tibbetts was there, and she was politely determined to be heard; not knowing what else to do, they heard her. She let the Town Council know precisely what she thought about the lack of a town library while the honorables sat slack-jawed and fidgeting in their seats and Jake hunched in a chair in the corner chewing on his cigar, jotting down notes on the folded sheets of newsprint that served for his reporter's pad, wearing a bemused expression. He recounted the meeting in full, writing that it "was hastily adjourned in some disarray following Mrs. Tibbetts's presentation."

At the end of the week, after the *Free Press* had hit the street and the town had had time to absorb the novelty of the situation, the council sent Cosmo Redlinger to see him. Cosmo was the council member closest to Jake's age, a promising young man already established in his father's funeral home business and now occupying the council seat his father had recently given up. Jake laughed in his face. "You pompous farts looked like a bunch of penguins with your feathers plucked," Jake said. "That's Pastine's business, Cosmo. I don't tell her how to save the world from sin and ignorance, and she don't tell me how to run the goddamn newspaper."

That was what he told Cosmo Redlinger, but Jake believed otherwise, and he broached the subject with Pastine that night after dinner as they sat in the parlor, Jake polishing Captain Finley Tibbetts's sword, Pastine reading *Harper's Bazaar.*

"Ahem." Jake cleared his throat, and she looked at him over the top of the magazine.

"This, ah, library business," he said, rubbing the sword briskly, its blade gleaming in the lamplight.

"Yes?"

"You, ah," he laughed, "sure have thrown the Town Council into a tizzy."

"Probably." She went back to her magazine.

"You, ah, feel pretty strongly about it."

Pastine put the magazine down in her lap. "A community without a library is like a church without a hymnbook. The Town Council has a duty to tend to the cultural and intellectual life of the community."

"They don't see it that way," Jake said. He put the sword down, picked up the scabbard and began polishing it. "They figure their business is to keep the town safe from ruffians and keep horse droppings off the streets."

"A library is no less a matter of the public's welfare than lawfulness and cleanliness."

Jake nodded. "Maybe."

"But?"

"Well . . ." he hung fire.

"What's bothering you, Jake?"

"It's, ah . . . well, the wife of the newspaper editor . . ."

"What about it?"

Jake put the scabbard down on the floor and stood up, facing her. "I try to keep a neutral stance in the community."

"For goodness' sake, why?" she asked, raising her eyebrows.

"So people can depend on the paper. So they can make up their own minds."

"Well," she said, picking up her magazine again, "you and the newspaper can do what you like. But I intend to see that the issue of the library remains stuck in the craw of the Town Council."

Jake could feel the heat rising in his face. "You make my job difficult," he said. She didn't answer, and after a while he sat down and finished his work, put the sword back on its hooks above the mantel, and went to bed, miffed and a bit hurt that she had dismissed him so abruptly. But when Pastine came up later, she snuggled in next to him as if nothing had happened, and they made love and he forgot everything.

Pastine did not. The next Monday afternoon as Jake was slaving over the Linotype, sweat streaming down his face and back and stinging his eyes, the machine in one of its especially temperamental moods, Pastine walked into the back shop and handed him a sheaf of papers.

"What's this?" he asked, edging his swivel chair back from the keyboard of the typesetter and glancing over the four pages covered with her neat, economical handwriting.

"An editorial."

Jake handed the papers back to her. "We don't print editorials."

Pastine jutted out her chin. "This is important, Jake. It's about the library."

"We don't print editorials," Jake said again, keeping his voice even. "And if we did, that would be *my* job."

Pastine's eyes flashed. "Don't you think this town needs a library?"

"I haven't thought much about it," Jake said. He pulled a fresh cigar out of his shirt pocket, bit off the end, took a kitchen match out of his pocket, struck it on the side of the Linotype machine, and lit the cigar. He took his time, concentrating on the work, took several deep puffs to get the cigar going. Then he looked up again at Pastine.

"Does this newspaper have a social conscience?" she asked.

"Well," he drawled around the cigar, "we have a society page, if that's what you mean."

Pastine stamped her foot. "Don't mock me!" She waved the sheaf of papers in his face. "This town needs a library. Any community that wants to call itself a place of reasonable thought needs a library. And the Town Council just sits there and blinks. Jake, you're the only means of public expression. You have a duty to speak out."

"Oh, no!" he roared, leaping to his feet. "That's where you're wrong. The duty of this newspaper is whatever the hell I *say* it is. And I say its duty is to print *facts*. That's all. *Facts*. The way things are, not the way some do-gooder supposes they ought to be. People will act like idiots and fools, but it is not the job of this newspaper to correct their behavior by foisting its opinions upon them. Now if you want to speak out about the library or the presidential election or the heathen Filipinos or any other cockeyed thing you've got on your mind, then stand out there in the street and rave 'til the sun goes down. Assassinate the Town

Council if you wish. This newspaper will print a full account of the deed. But we will not editorialize upon it. Or the library. Or anything else. Goddammit!'' He ended at the top of his voice and the young printer's devil he had hired to replace Isaac, working at the back of the shop, dropped a full galley of Linotype slugs onto the floor with a clatter.

"Don't you curse and bellow at me, Jake Tibbetts," Pastine yelled.

"Don't make a fool of yourself in my newspaper office," Jake shot back.

They stood there for a long moment glaring at each other. "Then you will not run the editorial?"

"No," he said, "I will not run the editorial."

"Fine," she said. "I will buy an advertisement to state my position."

"The hell you will. Advertisements are for the purpose of selling goods and services, not pandering propaganda."

"You are a stubborn ass, Jake," she said softly.

"Guilty on both counts."

"You are a provincial, unprogressive, close-minded mule."

"Correct again. And I'm one other thing."

"What's that?"

"I am the editor of this goddamn newspaper. Now get the hell out and let me edit. OUT!" He flung his arm in the direction of the front door. She gave him an absolutely murderous look, shook her fist under his nose, and flounced out.

"Holy cow," the printer's devil said from the back of the shop, where he had stood thunderstruck watching them.

Jake spun on him. "Be celibate," he roared. "It's simpler."

Their house was an icy, silent battleground for more than a week. Jake went home from the newspaper that Monday night prepared to apologize for his outburst and patch up the quarrel, but when he tried to broach the subject lightly at the dinner table, Pastine calmly picked up her glass of iced tea and poured it over Jake's head while Emma Tibbetts sat there in stunned amazement. Jake leaped from his chair and flung out of the house and didn't come home until well after midnight, lurching up the stairs under the influence of Lightnin' Jim Haskell's Best to find the door to their bedroom locked.

He slept on the parlor sofa and dreamed fitfully of Captain Finley Tibbetts dispatching blue-coated demons with his sword.

For several days, they didn't speak. They sat down together at meals, but the kitchen table was a gulf of enmity between them. They stared at their plates, avoiding each other's glances, eating with quick, angry bites. Jake left the house without a word immediately after dinner each night, went back to the newspaper office, where he puttered and drank and cursed to himself, then came home when the house was quiet and dark and slept in the back bedroom that had been Isaac's. Several times, he was struck with remorse and started to blurt out something that would break the awful hostile silence, but then he would glance at her tight-lipped, iron-jawed, unforgiving face and the thought of what she had done would well up like a raging beast and devour him with rancor that left a bitter taste of bile in his throat. She had . . . She had . . . He was hard-pressed to put a name to it. Well, what the hell. She had *crossed* him. She had invaded his private domain, which she might have done innocently enough, but once there, she had challenged his right to it. She had tried to tinker with the one thing in Jake Tibbetts's life you just damn well did not tinker with—his newspaper—and then had called him a mule when he bowed up his back. And then she had poured iced tea on his head. Humiliated him in front of his mother. Made him a skulking stranger in his own house. He seethed at the thought of it, and as the week went on, the anger and sense of betrayal festered and grew until they threatened to consume him.

Emma Tibbetts ignored them both for several days, hoping they would work it out. But when the end of the week approached and the air in the house seemed electric with their hostility, she took matters into her own hands. She talked to Pastine and then she left.

When Jake came home late Saturday afternoon, he saw that Emma Tibbetts's rocking chair on the front porch was empty. He stood for a moment in the yard, regretting there was no excuse to delay the dread of going into the house. He let himself quietly in the front screen door and stopped in the hallway, thinking how in the space of a few days it had become a house where you did not speak. Then something, a tiny movement, caught his eye and he turned and saw Pastine sitting naked there on the floor of the parlor. He stopped, dumbstruck, in the doorway. He just stared at her for a long time, a curving statue of flesh and shadow in the fading light. Then he thought suddenly of his mother and looked wildly about, up the stairs and in the kitchen.

"Jake," she said softly, the first word she had spoken to him in five days.

He jerked his head back to her.

"Take your clothes off. We're alone."

He hesitated for a moment, confused, and then she reached out her arms to him and he moved toward her in a trance. She stopped him. "Take them off," she said again, and he did, leaving his clothes in a pile on the floor, shivering in his nakedness in the openness of the parlor where people just did not go naked. He was numb.

Pastine patted the floor in front of her. "Sit down," she said.

He sat, feeling incredibly awkward, but when he reached to touch her she stopped him again.

"Now let's talk," she said. "With nothing between us." And they did, haltingly at first and then in torrents, each pouring out hurt and anger, ticking off grievances, opening wounds. They lost track of time. It turned dark outside and Pastine got up and turned on a single lamp in the corner so they could see each other, then sat down again cross-legged on the floor in front of him and they went on and on. And finally, when they were utterly exhausted with lashing at each other, they came to an accommodation.

They agreed that Jake would run the newspaper. It was his business, but more than that, his fiefdom, to do with as he saw fit. He had made the newspaper his own, and that's what it would remain. Pastine, for her part, would champion whatever cause she wished. A woman of her sense and sensibilities could not be expected to stay meekly at home and simply be the newspaper editor's wife, without opinion or prejudice. She would be mistress of her own realm. Neither would interfere with the other. And to hell with what the town thought on either score.

They each gave out of their stubbornness, and then they collapsed sobbing into each other's arms and coupled hungrily, violently, ignoring the lumpy braided carpet beneath them. Then totally spent, they slept where they lay.

They woke on Sunday morning with the sun streaming in the windows, stiff and aching from the hard floor.

"My God," Jake said, suddenly remembering. "Mama."

Pastine laughed. "She spent the night out."

"What?"

"She said she had a sick friend who needed some company, so she spent the night out."

"You . . . she . . ."

"We had a long talk."

"And she . . ."

"Then she left me to my own devices."

"Good Lord, she never spent the night out in her life."

"Maybe," said Pastine, "she never had a good reason."

Emma Tibbetts came home just after noon, spoke to them pleasantly, and went to the front porch, where she spent the afternoon humming and rocking. She died quietly in her sleep a month later. Jake regretted that he never said something, just a little something, to let her know how grateful he was. But he, the master of language, never could find the right words.

Pastine eventually got her library. She assaulted the citadel of the Town Council for a while longer, and the council heard her politely and unbendingly. Then she came to understand she would win no battles with them in their own arena. She would have to construct one of her own.

It took three years. Pastine stopped going to council meetings, stopped making public pronouncements about a library. The council sighed with relief and forgot her. But while they did, she was organizing—a lyceum series, a study club, concerts in the band shell beside Whitewater Creek on Sunday afternoons. She became a bundle of vigor in the Methodist Church (the doors of which the Tibbetts family had barely darkened since the death of Captain Finley's widow, Henrietta, one of the church's staunchest members). She took on the hundreds of small tasks and responsibilities that let the older Methodist ladies know she was properly aware of her role. She began to learn patience, to fit herself into the community. It began to be said of her that while she still left you a little breathless with her energy and enthusiasms, she was not quite so, well, *forward* as she had once been.

But if Pastine mellowed, she had her own agenda. Slowly, with a thousand subtle hints and pressures, she brought a sizeable number of the town's influential women to the notion that their community could be just as refined, cultured, and intelligent as any other, and that a library was just the thing they needed. And before they knew it, the members of the Town Council had been sandbagged. They were in deep trouble with the town's guardian females. It was about the time the woman's suffrage movement was beginning to get a good deal of attention in the Eastern cities, and while the local women were certainly not in sympathy with *that* sort of unladylike business, there was a faint stirring of female militancy in their campaign for the library. Such a matter could not be entrusted to *men*, the kind of recalcitrant dolts on the Town Council who stood in the way of Truth and Enlightenment.

They did it without speeches or demonstrations at council meetings. Instead, they applied pressure in dozens of parlors and bedrooms. The council finally capitulated in a rout, announcing without fanfare that a small room of the City Hall previously housing the records of the Water and Sewer Department would be cleared and shelves installed for the purpose of accommodating a modest lending library. A small sum would be appropriated from the town treasury for the purchase of books, and contributions would also be welcomed. A delegation of ladies made the rounds of the town's business establishment, collecting enough to buy a set of *Encyclopaedia Britannica* and hire a young woman to keep the library open three afternoons a week. One mysterious donor gave the staggering sum of three thousand dollars, which was put in trust to provide continuing funds for books and upkeep.

Pastine stayed entirely in the background, and Jake reported the business without comment. They stood together on the afternoon when the library was dedicated, listening to Mayor Arthur Benefield, Rosh's father, extol the virtues of learning and proclaim the library a repository of the world's wisdom. Jake leaned close to Pastine's ear and said, "There's more than one way to skin a cat."

She tossed her head playfully, just the way he had seen her do that afternoon when she presented herself in middy blouse and sailor hat in his steamy print shop more than four years before. "All you have to do is decide the cat needs skinning, and if you've got any gumption, you'll find a way."

"I'd say this cat was skinned from the inside out," he said. She smiled. "I'd think you would want at least a little of the credit, though."

"Oh," she said, "I'd much rather have the satisfaction."

He was quite proud of her. And very much in love.

━━━━━━━

A library was easier to get than a baby. Calculating patience might defeat the Town Council, but nature was quite another thing.

In those three years while the library project went on quietly, Pastine had two miscarriages and the second almost killed her. Jake found her unconscious in a pool of blood on the kitchen floor when he came home for lunch. He carried her upstairs to their bed, crying with fright, and dashed madly down Partridge Road to Doc Ainsworth's office. They sped back in Ainsworth's buggy to find her pale and lifeless, the red stain spreading around her on the bed sheets. Jake huddled sobbing in the hall for an hour until Ainsworth emerged, shaken, to say he had stopped the bleeding and she might live. She was terribly weak, but Jake hovered over her for days, feeding her broth and warm milk, massaging her listless arms and legs, until she finally began to stir. It was two months before she got out of bed. And Charlie Ainsworth said, "No more of this baby business."

So in 1910, Jake Tibbetts resigned himself to the notion that there would be no offspring, no heir to pass along the newspaper to, now that he had it so embedded in his gut that it was the most essential thing about him. He thought to himself, I'll just have to run the sonofabitch until I croak.

He tried hard not to fix blame. He told himself that Pastine had been more than willing, that she had risked her very life to bring them a child. But as time went on, the thought began to eat at him that he had done his part. His seed was fertile. It was the soil that would not support life. Was she too damned brainy to be a proper mother? After all, she had been away, had been exposed to exotic ideas and philosophies, had an obstinate mind of her own. Perhaps it went deeper than that. Her father was a tinkerer, an inventor, a cerebral man. Had the accumulated genes of the Cahoons conspired to short-circuit those of the Tibbettses?

Jake didn't expect a big family. The Tibbetts women had never been great child-bearers. Captain Finley had fathered only a girl besides Albertis, and she had become a sour old maid. Albertis, in turn, had begat only Jake and Isaac. So now there was only Jake, of the entire line, and if he did not particularly wish to father a nation, he at least had the right to expect a single heir. But Pastine seemed incapable, and the thought of it rankled and in turn made him feel guilty for thinking it.

However, Jake's mental agonies came to an abrupt halt when Pastine became pregnant again. Now Jake was terrified. She was fearfully, wretchedly nauseated, and Jake himself was sick with worry, having blamed her in his own heart for her failure to bear a child, now having impregnated her in a fit of sweating passion against all advice of Charlie Ainsworth. If she died, it would be his fault. *All his fault.* Ainsworth glowered at Jake accusingly and ordered Pastine to bed. And they waited.

Then one day in Pastine's third month, Jake arrived home in the late afternoon to find her sweeping the front porch, a gingham apron tied across the slight swell of her belly, strands of hair loose around her head as she wielded the broom vigorously.

"Good God, woman, back to bed!" he yelled, dashing up the steps and wresting the broom from her.

Pastine tossed her head. "Go to bed yourself, Jake. You've been looking a little peaked lately."

"What the hell are you trying to do . . . ." His voice trailed off before he could say *mess it up again*? and he felt the cold grip of panic in his gut.

"This one's going to be all right, Jake," Pastine said, smiling. "Don't ask me how. A woman just knows these things. I woke up this morning and I said to myself, 'This one's going to work out. It's my time.' "

"But Charlie said . . ."

"Charlie Ainsworth is just a doctor." She patted her stomach. "I'm in charge here."

She was indeed. She began to blossom with a beautiful fullness, to hum with some secret reservoir of confident energy. Dust flew. The house fairly squeaked with cleanliness, was aromatic with the rich smells of nesting. Pastine became especially playful in bed, as if her body sought affirmation of her condition. Jake was both delighted and frightened, fearing their frenzied thrustings and thrashings would disrupt the awakening life in her womb. But she took control of him as she had taken control of herself. Jake sensed an awesome strength in her. She would deliver a baby, by God, and once she had decided that and captured her own body in the fierce grip of her mind, nothing could sway her. She swept everything, Jake included, before her. So he finally gave up protesting and worrying and gave in to the overwhelming delight of it.

It was a cesarean. The baby had gotten himself twisted around ass backward and tangled in his own umbilical cord, and there was nothing for Charlie Ainsworth to do but go fetch him. Henry came ill-tempered and bellowing into the world, flailing his arms in protest. Ainsworth's nurse, who helped with the delivery, washed him up, wrapped him in a blanket, and stood in the doorway of the room so that Jake, who had been pacing like a madman in the hall, could get a look at him. The nurse said, shaking her head, "That boy's got a spark in his eye, Mr. Tibbetts. Just you watch out for that young'un."

"Yeah," Jake said, grinning. "Ink in your blood will do it every time."

Pastine lay ghostlike in the sheets when they finally let him in a couple of hours later. As he bent to kiss her, she whispered, "There's more than one way to skin a cat, Jake." Jake felt a great rush of joy and pride and love. And yes, awe. Some sort of vehement grit had brought her through it. She would do, he thought happily. She would do.

Charlie Ainsworth told them that this was the end of it. No more babies. This one had been sheer luck, a miracle, against all odds, and it had left her with a lot of damage that couldn't be fixed. So he had tied things off so there would be no more risk of pregnancy.

Jake wouldn't let the finality of it take anything away from his immense pleasure. They named the boy for Pastine's father and for Jake's grandfather: Henry Finley Tibbetts. For weeks after Henry was born, Jake would slip into their room after supper each night, carrying Captain Finley's Confederate saber, and sit for a long time in the darkness while Henry slept and muttered in his crib, wiping the blade of the sword with a soft smooth cloth, thinking of the Tibbetts men—the fire, the madness, the pride, the courage and shame —and how it had all come finally to this. There was, for this small sleeping baby, both a kinship and a magnificent aloneness. All things old and new. Alpha and omega. Amen. Pastine would often find him there, asleep in the chair with the sword on his lap and a smile on his face, and take him to bed.

———

But Henry was a disaster from the first. He developed a terrible case of colic at one end and diaper rash at the other, and together they kept him squalling and red-faced. He slept at most for an hour or two at a time and then awoke screaming and rattled the windows with his fierce cries. Nothing they tried helped his angry stomach—not Pastine's own milk, not store-bought formulas, not even the goat's milk Jake got from a local farmer. His raw, red bottom broke out in ugly blisters and defied every medication. Charlie Ainsworth said he had never seen another case like it. There was nothing to do but keep Henry's rump greased and force food into him so he wouldn't starve to death, then walk the floor with him bawling and shaking with rage until he finally exhausted himself and fell asleep. He was eighteen months old before he slept through the night, and by then Jake and Pastine were gaunt and battle-weary.

At two, Henry was a terror. He threw, spilled, screamed, kicked, bit, upset, and rejected. Jake he especially rejected. If Jake tried to pick him up, Henry would bellow at the top of his lungs and lunge for Pastine. And Jake recoiled in astonished hurt. The worst of it came one night after supper when Jake picked him up to take him upstairs to bed. Henry was heading across the parlor for an empty whatnot stand that had once held an assortment of figurines and doodads until Henry had broken some and the rest had been put away.

Jake scooped him up and lifted him high in the air, and Henry flailed out with a small hard fist and smashed Jake in the eye. Jake roared with pain and staggered to the parlor sofa, where he sat with a thump, turned Henry over his knee, and gave him two resounding whacks on his diaper-padded rear. Pastine, sitting dumbfounded in the wing-back chair next to the fireplace, leaped up, screamed with fright, and snatched Henry away from him.

"Don't you *ever*!" she cried, clutching the astonished Henry to her breast.

"Goddamn!" Jake roared. "The little sonofabitch put my eye out!"

"Don't you curse! Don't you dare curse! Don't you call this baby a sonofabitch!" Pastine was near hysterics now.

The pain was excruciating. Jake slumped on the sofa, holding his hand over his eye while Pastine stormed from the room and pounded up the stairs. He sat for a long time, hoping it would stop hurting, but when it didn't, he finally left the house and walked the mile and a half to Charlie Ainsworth's, tears streaming from the injured eye.

"Nothing serious, but my God, what in the hell did you tangle with?" Charlie said when he looked at it.

"Henry," Jake muttered.

"Henry?"

"Yeah. I picked him up and the little bugger bashed me in the eye." Jake looked at him plaintively. "Charlie, he's the meanest kid I've ever seen."

"Hell, Jake, it's just a stage," Charlie said.

And it was, but it was just the beginning of many stages. As a child of five and six, Henry was sullen and uncooperative. For days, he refused to eat. He would get frighteningly pale and weak, and just when they were ready to take him to Taylorsville to the hospital, he would suddenly break his fast as if nothing had happened. They would go for weeks with no problem and then Henry would sit down at the kitchen table for a meal and look across at them over his full plate and his eyes would glaze over and he would go on strike again. Jake would yell and threaten, Pastine would wheedle and cajole, and Henry would go right on doing what he damn well pleased until he was damn well ready to eat again.

In his elementary school years, he was bright enough, but

he disrupted his classes with the same obstinate behavior and was constantly in dutch with his teachers. He was whipped, lectured, and occasionally sent home. But he simply stared at them with a stubborn set to his little jaw and went on about his business. He wasn't mean, he didn't fight, he had friends. He didn't seem especially angry at anyone, not even at Jake, who tried mightily to make him toe the line. But he played his own tune and to hell with the rest of the world. When Jake fussed, Henry simply clammed up and hunkered down inside himself. He never cried.

In adolescence, he stopped giving anybody a hard time. He simply stopped giving a damn. Jake tried to interest him in the newspaper, but it was a disaster. Henry was all thumbs in the print shop. He dropped things, broke things, messed up printing jobs and machinery. He stood for hours in front of a box of hand-set type, looking at a diagram of the box Jake had made and slowly, piece by agonizing piece, setting a headline with half the letters upside down, never learning the layout of the box so that he could do it quickly and deftly. Jake had hated the paper in his own adolescence, but nevertheless he had learned the layout of a type box in a single afternoon.

Finally, one day as he watched Henry going through the agonizingly slow motions of setting type for an advertisement, Jake walked over and took the stick of type out of his hand and said, "Henry, why don't you go home." Henry turned and looked at him, gave him a tight little smile, took off his shop apron, and walked out.

"I can't talk to him," Jake complained to Pastine. "He never says anything back. He just stands there and looks at me as if I've got antlers growing out of my head."

"You preach, Jake," she answered. "Just talk to him. Don't preach. Do you ever ask him a question?"

"Hell, yes. I ask him questions all the time. I try to find out what's inside that head and he just mumbles. Yes or no, that's about all I get."

"But you preach a lot, too," she said.

"How the hell will he ever learn any of the things a father is supposed to teach his son if I don't tell him?"

"Just let him watch," she said. "He'll pick it up."

"Hah!" Jake exploded. "Like I did."

Jake was confounded. What had he done to make this son of his a rebellious idiot? What had he ever done except try to make Henry, at every difficult step of the way, learn to take responsibility for himself? That wasn't too much to ask, was it? He was haunted by the specter of his own father, Albertis, pacing the floor of his upstairs room in the grip of melancholia while Jake stumbled through his boyhood trying to find his own way. Henry would not be like that, by God. Henry would have some idea of what a man did to fend for himself and take his life in his own hands. But nothing seemed to sink in. Henry was just one big aching disappointment in the pit of Jake Tibbetts's soul.

As for Pastine, she simply stayed with it.

"My God," Jake told her, "you hover over him like he's going to fly away. Give him some room. Don't spoil the boy."

"I'm not spoiling him," she answered quietly. "He just takes more work than most. We've just got to have patience, Jake."

And she was patient. She focused the same relentless energy on raising Henry that she had brought to having him in the first place. He tried her to the point of absolute exasperation, but she plodded on, coaxing, bullying, cajoling. Sometimes it worked. Often it didn't. But she didn't give up. She became incredibly weary with it. She gave up many of her community activities and gave herself over to ornery, difficult Henry.

Between the two of them, Pastine and Jake, Henry became a hard sore spot, a canker that would not heal. They argued frequently and acidly, and Jake could feel something essential going out of his marriage. There was a distance between them now, a gulf across which they could not touch—for Jake, a source of deep, bitter resentment.

When Henry finally found something he was truly interested in, it was Hazel Benefield.

She was eighteen, a senior, when sixteen-year-old Henry discovered her. He followed her about the halls of the high school like a small dog and she ignored him at first while her girlfriends giggled and the senior boys mocked him, barking as he passed, oblivious. And then to everyone's astonishment, Hazel Benefield—the sauciest and most popular girl in the senior class—decided she *liked* Henry Tibbetts, for gosh sakes. And she began to devour him.

Henry became meekly obedient around the house, took to keeping himself and his room neat, silently did what he was told, kept his grades up. But he had a glazed, slack-jawed look about him. He slept fitfully. They could hear him moving about in his room in the middle of the night like a haunted spirit. He left the house early every morning to walk Hazel to school and returned late every afternoon glassy-eyed and exhausted. And he absolutely refused to talk about Hazel Benefield with either of them.

"He's sick," Pastine said, genuinely alarmed. "Don't you think he's sick?"

"I'd call it an advanced catatonic state," Jake answered, relieved that something had finally jolted Henry.

"No. Don't pass it off like that, Jake. It's not healthy. It's not just that Hazel Benefield is two years older than he is. She's . . . she's . . . well, she just *knows* too much."

In Jake and Pastine's presence, Hazel Benefield was a model of demure girlhood. But she had a way of taking Henry's arm possessively, her eyes dancing with a secret mischief, while Henry turned pale. Pastine was right, Jake thought to himself. This girl knew too much. Certainly, too much for Henry Tibbetts.

They thought it would end when Hazel went off to college the next fall, but it didn't. The letters passed in the mail every day—one arriving, one leaving. And Henry was in agony. Whatever Hazel was doing at school, they suspected she was teasing Henry by long distance. He burned the letters as soon as he read them. He lost weight, became gaunt and holloweyed.

"You're right," Jake said. "He's sick. This is serious."

"It's like a disease," Pastine said, her hands clenched tightly in her lap, her brow creased with worry.

"We can intercept the mail," he said. "Both ways."

"No," she said, shaking her head. "He'll find another way."

"I can have a talk with Rosh."

"And tell him what? That his daughter is making a zombie out of our son?"

Jake sat there for a long time next to her on the parlor sofa, staring at the floor. Then finally he raised his head and said, "Pastine, Henry has been making a goddamn fool of himself in one way or another since he was old enough to hold his head up. The one thing about it is, he always graduates from being one kind of fool to being another."

"Jake," she said, clutching his hands in her own, "don't give up on him."

Jake couldn't answer her, because in a way, he already had.

But then it changed. Hazel went to visit a cousin in Minnesota during the summer after her freshman year, the letters stopped, and Henry came out of it. He seemed older, stronger, as if whatever Hazel Benefield had done with him had left a tough callus. Jake saw it, but he left Henry alone, having decided by now that the boy would have to come to grips with himself.

In the spring of his senior year, Henry announced at the dinner table one night that he wanted to go to the state university in the fall.

Jake stopped in midbite, his fork poised above his plate. "And study what?"

"Psychology."

Jake put his fork down. "Horse manure."

"Jake . . ." Pastine started, but Jake waved her to silence. "Why?" he asked.

"Because I'm interested in it," Henry said, meeting his eyes.

Jake picked up his napkin out of his lap, wiped his mouth, and laid it beside his plate. "Psychology is the study of why people make fools of themselves."

Henry nodded, a touch of a sardonic smile around his mouth. "Yes. That's part of it."

"What's the rest?"

"I don't know," Henry said. "That's what I want to find out."

"Well, I will send you to that great citadel of higher learning if that's where you want to go," Jake said. "But I will not send you there to study psychology."

It was the first argument Jake and Pastine ever had about money. Pastine's money. She had enough to send Henry to college, she let him know straight off when they were alone in the parlor later. Henry Cahoon had bestowed a dowry of ten thousand dollars on Pastine when she married Jake, but Jake refused to have anything to do with it. "If a man can't support his wife," he said, "he's got no damn business getting married." So they had agreed that what Pastine did with her money was her business and Jake was never to hear of it. He suspected that the three-thousand-dollar founding contribution to the library had come from her private funds, but they never spoke of it.

Henry Cahoon had died when Jake and Pastine had been married for ten years, and by then he had built his stump puller business into a modest enterprise. Pastine was the only heir. She tried to talk to Jake about her inheritance, but he refused. "I'm no business tycoon," he said. "Go see Rosh Benefield." She did, and Henry Cahoon's business was sold to two young locals, Oscar Harsole and Rupert Bingham, who transformed it over the years into the Harsole Bingham Bolt Company. It was the town's largest employer. The only remote benefit Jake Tibbetts had ever seen from it was the yearly two-column-by-three-inch advertisement Harsole Bingham took in the *Free Press* to wish its employees a Merry Christmas and Happy New Year. How much money Pastine got from the sale or what she did with it Jake never knew—didn't want to know. But now, she was telling him she was going to use part of it to send Henry to college.

"No you won't," Jake said, tight-lipped. "*I'll* send Henry to college."

"No, you won't," she said. "You just said you wouldn't."

"I said I wouldn't send him up there to study why people make fools of themselves."

"Well, that's what he wants to study."

"No."

"You don't even know anything about it."

"I know . . ."

"Nothing," she interrupted, wagging a finger at him. "You are a fine, perceptive newspaper editor, Jake, but about many things you are plainly ignorant. And concerning those things about which you are ignorant, you are mule-headed."

"It seems we've had this conversation before," Jake said, grinning. "Want to take your clothes off?"

"Don't mock me!" she snapped. "And don't try to out-talk me, either. You're bad about that, Jake. Sometimes you talk and talk and talk until you just wear me down and I wonder afterward what it was you said that was so persuasive. And then I realize there wasn't anything persuasive, it was just the weight of all those words that finally did me in. Well, this time I won't be talked out of it."

There was a long, long silence as they stared at each other across the parlor—he on the sofa his grandfather had slashed with the Confederate sword, she in the wing-backed chair where Albertis had once sat, mocking Jake's own plans for college. Engineering it had been. Something useful.

"Psychology," he said. And then he got up and went to bed.

So Henry went off to college to study psychology. When he had been there for six months, he married Hazel Benefield.

The telephone. Calling him like a thief from sleep in the dead of night. He stumbled downstairs, cursing Pastine for having insisted on a telephone in the house, where it could violate a man's privacy at a forsaken hour.

"Yeah," he said into the receiver.

"Jake?"

"Who the hell else?"

"Rosh here. Are the kids with you?"

His mind worked sluggishly, like a swimmer fighting through murk.

"Henry and Hazel," Rosh said. "Are they there?"

"No. I don't think so." Jake laid the receiver down, walked to the front door, peered out. The yard was empty and still in the moonlight.

"No. They're not here."

He could hear Rosh's heavy breathing on the other end, the deep noisy breath of a fat man. "They went to a dance in Taylorsville. They should have been back by now."

"What time is it?" Jake had left his pocket watch on the bedside table upstairs.

"Three o'clock. Ideal just woke me up. We thought they might have gone to your house."

"Did you try to call their place?"

"No answer over there," Rosh said. "They've been gone almost eight hours, Jake."

"Where's Lonnie?" Jake was awake now, awake enough to feel the dread beginning to build in his gut.

"He's here. They left him with us about seven."

"Where was the dance?"

"Taylorsville."

"I know. But where?"

"The National Guard Armory, I think. That's where they have all the dances in Taylorsville."

"Have you tried calling over there?"

"No," Rosh said. "I thought I'd call you first, just to see, you know."

"Yeah. Well, do you want me to call Taylorsville?"

"No," Rosh said, "I'll do it. I'll call the police station over there, see if they've had any word."

"Okay. Call me back." Jake hung up and sat down on the stairway to wait. Henry and Hazel. The thought of them made him bone-weary. Hazel was crazy—probably certifiably so—and Henry was a bigger goddamn fool now than he had ever been. Together they were the most chaotic mess he had ever seen. They had come home from college in Henry's junior year with Hazel pregnant and Henry in an absolute fog, like a man shipwrecked. Ideal insisted they move in with the Benefields, but that lasted until Lonnie was born and Hazel's constant whining and bitching drove Ideal to distraction. So Rosh and Jake had found them a small three-room house and made the down payment and moved them in. They had been there for four years now and their screaming fights had become a town scandal. Lonnie spent a lot of time with his grandparents. Henry had been through two jobs—as a shipping clerk at Harsole Bingham and as a burial insurance salesman—and had failed miserably at both. At the moment he was looking, and in 1936, looking for a job was no piece of cake. Henry and Hazel could barely buy groceries, and here they were going to a dance in Taylorsville. They were wretched. Hopeless.

The phone rang again and Jake snatched the receiver from its cradle.

"Nothing," Rosh said.

"Okay. Rosh, come get me and we'll try to find 'em."

"But they've got my car," Rosh said.

Jake thought a moment. "Call Hilton Redlinger, then. You're the mayor. Get him up and get him rolling. The two of you come get me."

It was still very dark when they picked him up in front of the house. He had left Pastine sleeping. She had never awakened, even when the telephone jangled downstairs. It was cool with the first hint of autumn, the sound of Hilton's police car and their voices swallowed by the last remnants of night. They drove first past Henry and Hazel's small house. It was dark and there was no car at the curb in front. Henry owned a ruin of a Model A Ford, but it was parked behind Fog Martin's service station these days, waiting for Henry to scrape together enough money to get the block re-bored. When Henry and Hazel needed transportation, they borrowed Rosh's Packard, as they had done this night.

They cruised the town for a while, searching the square and the side streets, then lurching through the potholed streets of Haskell's Quarter, where Lightnin' Jim and the other Negroes lived. Nothing.

"Maybe they had car trouble on the way home," Hilton said.

"Yes," Rosh said. "The car's in good shape, but anything can happen."

"You want to drive a ways out Taylorsville Road and see if we can find 'em?" Hilton asked.

"Before we do that," Jake said, "swing back by their house. Just in case they've come in."

There was no sign of them, but Jake had Hilton stop the car and he got out and walked up the buckled sidewalk to the front door, feeling a rush of anger at the unkempt grass and Lonnie's scooter, one wheel gone, lying against the front steps. He tried the door. It was unlocked and he pushed it open, stepped into the house, fumbled along the wall next to the door for the light switch, found it with his hand, flipped it on, and saw Henry sprawled in a chair in the darkness, head slumped to one side, covered with more blood than Jake had ever seen. It scared the hell out of him. He thought at first that Henry was dead, thought crazily of his own safety, half expected Hazel to rush in from another room and slash him with whatever instrument had opened the terrible gash across Henry's forehead.

"Rosh! Hilton!" he bellowed out the open door, and they scrambled out of the car, Rosh lumbering behind Hilton up the sidewalk and into the house.

"Good Christ!" Hilton said softly, pushing by Jake, crossing the room. He knelt by the chair, examining Henry's gaping wound. There was a powerful odor of whiskey in the room. The floor beside the chair was slick with vomit.

"Is he . . ." Rosh started to say.

"No," Hilton said, and then Henry moved a bit in the chair and moaned, opening his mouth just enough to expose a bloody pulp of broken teeth.

Jake shook himself from his paralysis long enough to peer into the other two rooms of the small house, turning on lights. There was no one there.

"Henry," Rosh said tentatively, "Henry, where is Hazel?"

Henry moaned again and turned his head away from them, cradling it in his arms and drawing his legs up, shivering like a wet dog.

Jake was on him in two strides, grabbing him by the arm. "Where is she?" he shouted. Henry cried out in pain and jerked his arm back, holding it against his side.

"Where is Hazel? What have you done with her?"

"Jake. Hold on there," Rosh said, but Jake waved him off. He reached down and grabbed Henry by the chin and pulled his face around to the light.

"Ahhhhhh . . ." Henry groaned in agony. Jake gave his chin another twist, and finally he said, "Caaaa . . . caaa . . . ," the sound bubbling out through the bloody mush of his mouth.

"The car?" Jake demanded. Henry nodded, his face contorted with pain. "Where?"

But then Henry's eyes rolled back in his head and he went limp.

"He's passed out," Hilton said, rising.

"Let's go," Jake said.

"What about Henry?"

"Leave the sonofabitch where he lies," Jake said.

"Jake, for Christ's sake. He's hurt pretty bad. Look, we

don't know what's happened here. Let's just take one thing at a time.''

Jake stood rooted to the floor, staring at Henry, loathing him, while Hilton found the telephone and rousted Charlie Ainsworth out of bed.

"You think we ought to call Ideal and Pastine?" Hilton asked then.

"No," Rosh said. "No sense worrying anyone until we know what's going on."

They drove in silence across the Whitewater Creek Bridge and out the state highway toward Taylorsville, and it was Rosh, peering into the hole the headlights carved into the darkness, who saw it first—the strip of plowed-up grass and dirt on the shoulder of the road at the near end of the big looping curve.

"There," Rosh cried, and Jake and Hilton saw it at once and knew what it was. Hilton jerked the steering wheel around and stopped the car sideways in the road, headlights pointing toward the furrowed gash and the blackness beyond where the shoulder dropped off abruptly.

They piled out of the car, Hilton carrying a huge silver flashlight. When he cut on the beam, it took a huge slice out of the blackness below the shoulder of the road and showed them in terrible detail the crumpled, still-steaming hunk of metal that had been Rosh Benefield's Packard. It was clear what had happened. The car had missed the curve, its wheels biting hungrily into the grassy shoulder, slewing it sideways until the wheels clawed nothing but air. Then it somersaulted fifty feet down the embankment toward the red clay of the gully below and smashed with such awful force that it snapped a foot-thick pine tree like a matchstick and rammed the car's engine completely back into the passenger compartment.

"Hazel!" Rosh screamed. "Hazel!" But there was no sound in the cool night air except the methodical hiss of liquid dropping onto the hot engine block.

"I can't go down there," Rosh cried in anguish, and it took Jake a moment to realize he meant that he was physically unable, with his huge bulk, to make it down the bank. So Jake and Hilton left him there on the shoulder of the road, moaning and hugging himself, while they scrambled down, grabbing at clumps of grass to steady themselves. The tortured smell of battered metal and burned rubber and death rose up to choke them.

At the bottom, where it leveled off, Hilton grabbed Jake by the arm and jerked him up short; then Jake could smell the gasoline. A lot of it. They could hear it dripping steadily from the ruptured tank. "It could go up any minute," Hilton said softly. Hilton swept the car from rear to front with the white-hot beam of the flashlight, resting finally on what had once been Hazel Benefield, a shredded pulp in green taffeta. She had gone through the windshield and had smacked head-first into the pine tree, and then the car had caved in on top of her.

Jake stared, paralyzed. Then he heard Hilton retching beside him, and above them, Rosh's high wailing sob, keening like a woman. Hilton threw up for a long time and then he looked up at Jake, tears streaming down his anguished face. "God, Jake," he sobbed. "God. Oh, God. Rosh. It'll kill him."

Jake nodded dumbly. "Henry did this," he said, and it seemed the words came from somewhere far off.

Hilton shook his head. "Nobody knows."

"Henry does," Jake said.

Jake never told anyone what Hilton did to spare Rosh Benefield the agony of what oozed from the green taffeta dress on the blasted hood of the Packard. After he and Jake had climbed back up the bank and helped huge, broken Rosh into the police car, Hilton disappeared for a moment into the thicket on the high side of the road and came back with a pine knot, then took out his cigarette lighter and held the flame under the pine for a long moment until it caught, and hurled the flaming piece of wood into the gully. There was a tremendous roar as the gasoline caught and the fading night erupted like midday and Rosh, who was crumpled in the front seat, raised his head and said, "What was that?"

Jake cradled him in his arms like a baby. "It blew up, Rosh. There was a lot of gasoline around. It just blew up."

Henry never told them what happened. He said he couldn't remember. Not the wreck, not what had gone on in the car before. They could only guess. For Jake Tibbetts, the details didn't matter. What mattered was that Henry had killed his wife through his drunken blind stupidity, and what's more, had run away from it. Jake disowned him.

Rosh and Ideal Benefield were devastated. When they came out of seclusion a month after the funeral, Ideal was in a furious frenzy and she turned it on Pastine Tibbetts. Ideal was by now, as the mayor's wife and through the force of her own dominating personality, an arbiter of the town's social code. Ideal and Jake had locked horns before, but now she went after Pastine. And Pastine quietly capitulated. She resigned her memberships in the Study Club and the Methodist Missionary Society, her place on the Library Board. Jake was enraged, but she wouldn't talk about it.

"I'm not getting any younger. It's time somebody else did it," was all she would say.

It was as if the fight had gone out of her, after all the years of struggling and agonizing. She was tired. She wrapped a cocoon of quiet about her in the house on Partridge Road, closing off the world as if she had closed the shutters. They seldom spoke of Henry. It was simply something they had ceased to share as a part of their lives together, and that—the fact that there was something, no matter how painful, they could no longer share—was tragedy enough.

Henry became a sodden wreck. He was dead drunk when he joined the National Guard unit, and the government did them all a favor by mobilizing Henry's unit on the eve of Pearl Harbor. When he shipped out, leaving Lonnie with Jake and Pastine, Jake hadn't seen him for almost two years.

It was a year after the accident before Rosh Benefield and Jake exchanged more than a cursory word in passing. Then Rosh showed up late one Wednesday afternoon at the newspaper office just as Jake returned from delivering the weekly edition to the post office, brown paper sack under his arm, looking older and fatter and frayed. They resumed their weekly ritual and they never spoke of Henry and Hazel, or of their wives. It was enough to know that each had suffered in his own unspeakable way, and that none of them would ever be the same again.

TWO

JAKE TIBBETTS was still trembling with fright and humiliation when he arrived at the courthouse square on Christmas morning, 1944. He had decided, as he hightailed it down Partridge Road, that no woman who chased him out of his own home and tried to cut off his head with his own grandfather's sword would tell him where to live. He goddamn well would not go to live at the newspaper, at least not straightaway.

How the hell was a man supposed to live at a newspaper office, anyway? There was no place to eat, sleep, or bathe in a newspaper office. It was a business establishment, not a habitation. Living at the newspaper would be as ridiculous as living at the Jitney Jungle Super Saver Store or the dry cleaner's. Better he should set up housekeeping at Redlinger's mortuary than at the *Free Press*.

But the only alternative he could think of on the spur of the moment was the Regal Hotel, which was mostly a boarding-house, filled with itinerant preachers and traveling drummers and 4-f farmhands who had come to town for the scandalous wages at the Harsole Bingham Bolt Company. Jake wanted nothing to do with a fleabag.

So Jake Tibbetts came to the courthouse square on Christmas morning with no place to reside except in his overcoat. The square was deserted, the courthouse a raw, red, wind-chapped sentinel guarding the boarded-up front of Brunson's Cafe and the dignified darkness of the Farmers Mercantile Bank and the lighted window upstairs over the bank, where Ollie Whittle's radio station was playing Christmas music. He felt himself watched by the awning-lidded eyes of the drugstore and the barbershop, whose candy-striped pole was the only splash of Christmas color downtown this year.

In the years before the war, multicolored lights were strung between the electric power poles on the square—a marvelous twinkling of reds and greens and yellows and blues, a sight to make your spirit tingle. But in the panicky days of December 1941—after the Japs had blasted Pearl Harbor—Tunstall Renfroe, newly appointed air raid warden, had ordered them all taken down.

"Can you imagine," Tunstall said, "the target we'd make with the square all lit up like the World's Fair? We're sitting ducks! Just asking for it!"

"Besides," Biscuit Brunson added, "the spirit of Christmas is in here," he thumped his chest, "not strung up on poles."

So they had taken down the lights, but not before Jake had had his way with them in his front-page column:

This newspaper is reliably informed that Santa Claus is considering a cancellation of his appointed rounds this year because the enterprise is so fraught with danger.

The Old Elf is quoted as saying he does not mind vying for airspace with German Junkers and Japanese Bettys, but the alarmed citizenry hereabouts has compounded his usual navigational problems by removing the colored lights around the County Courthouse that serve as his favorite landmark.

Santa is an elderly gentleman and his mission is difficult at best. He has, we are informed, no relish for making it more so by having to bump about in the dark, risking life and limb and precious cargo.

He was heard to exclaim, the last time he drove out of sight, "God save us from air raid wardens!"

The column caused a commotion, and copies of the paper were hidden from the town's young. It provoked heated debate over coffee at Brunson's Cafe and caused a meeting of the Town Council to dissolve in uproar. But soon the issue was moot. Christmas had come and gone and the next year nobody bothered because by then the war was full-blown and grim and no one seemed to fancy colored lights on the courthouse square.

It broke Herschel Martin's heart, because the Christmas lights, along with the banana tree that was now just a winter-browned stub against the red wall of the courthouse, had been Herschel's pride. He spent most of the year fussing over the lights, checking the bulbs and connections. Then the day after Thanksgiving he would supervise the stringing of the wires, dashing back and forth from one side of the square to the other on his Jitney Jungle delivery cycle.

Now, on this Christmas morning, there was only a small committee of grackles huddled on the electric wires at the edge of the courthouse lawn, not a single car in the parking spaces that paralleled the curbs on either side of the street.

Jake stood on the corner by the barbershop for a moment, wondering where the hell he would stay the night. He decided that the matter needed some careful consideration. So he headed for Lightnin' Jim Haskell's house.

Lightnin' Jim's was a small white frame house that presided over the part of town they called Haskell's Quarter. White folks mostly called it "the Quarter," but they recognized it as Lightnin' Jim's domain, where he ruled as arbiter, rector, and patriarch. White folks went to the Quarter to pick up their maids or buy Jim's whiskey, but they didn't meddle in his business. Most of the houses in the Quarter were unpainted, their boards warped and weathered gray, the roofs tarpapered, the yards hard-packed clay that would turn to goo when it rained. Jim's place had a fresh coat of white and a neatly trimmed little patch of grass in front, brown now with winter, rimmed by carefully spaced whitewashed rocks. There were thick nandina bushes, heavy with red berries, on either side of the front steps. There was a screen porch across the entire front of the house.

Jake knocked at the screen door. Rule Number One. You did not go onto Lightnin' Jim's screen porch unless you were invited. If you stepped onto the porch without invitation, Lightnin' Jim figured you were up to no good and he would shoot you dead. He had dispatched one of the Quarter's ruffians that way, and that's all it had taken to establish the rule. There was no sign on the porch, but everyone—black and white—knocked first.

After a moment the door to the house itself opened and Jake peered through the screen. "Yas?" A woman's voice. Young and throaty.

"Is Jim here?" Rule Number Two. You did business with no one but Jim. Try to transact with someone else on the premises and Jim would cut you off, which was as bad as shooting you dead.

"You mean Mr. Haskell." A soft laugh, teasing.

"I mean that decrepit bag of bones Lightnin' Jim Haskell who sells rotgut whiskey," Jake said, raising his voice.

Then he could hear another voice, deep and rumbling, inside the house. "Shut the door, bitch woman."

The door closed abruptly and in a moment the curtain on one of the front windows was pulled back an inch or so. There was a long pause and the door opened again.

"Come in the house, Jake." Rule Number Three. If Lightnin' Jim invited you *into* his house, you were among the elite. Most customers he served on the front porch. Some—black and white—he made come to the back of the house. Jim had established a hierarchy, based entirely on whether he liked you or not.

It was a small neat room, neat despite the piles of magazines everywhere—on the floor, on the mantel above the fireplace with its coal fire flickering in the grate, on the lamp tables, filling two-thirds of the space on the brown sofa—splashes of color in the warm brownness of the room. Thick stacks of *Life* and *Look* with their black-and-white war photo covers, *Saturday Evening Post* with its puckish Norman Rockwell characters, *Collier's*, and yellow-spined *National Geographic.* There was just the sofa and a butt-sprung brown easy chair and Jake took the empty space on the sofa, resting one elbow on a stack of *Scribner's*, noticing a 1938 date on the top issue. It was a tight little house. The room was warm. An ancient clock, nestled among the magazines on the mantel, passed time methodically.

"Not a newspaper in the place," Jake said. "The goddamn floor sags from the weight of all these magazines, but not a single newspaper. Don't you care about what's going on in the world?''

Lightnin' Jim was ancient. He shuffled in slopped-over bedroom slippers, flannel shirt and thin gray trousers hanging from his bony shoulders and hips, ruined face a mass of creases beneath a magnificent explosion of wiry white hair. He picked up an open magazine from the seat of the easy chair, turned down a page to mark his place, then dropped it softly onto the threadbare rug beside the chair and sat down. He waved a hand weakly.

"Newspapers are triflin' things," he said. "Newspapers are full of gossip and slander. There's nothing uplifting about a newspaper. My woman back there reads the newspaper.''

Jake could hear, behind the closed door of the next room, the throaty young voice of the woman and the soft babble of a child and a radio playing Christmas music. And there was the exotic smell of collards cooking in pork fat, mixed with the rich dusky aroma of Negroness.

"Don't you care what's going on out there in the world? Don't you know there's a war going on? Tunstall Renfroe says we could be bombed tomorrow.''

"And what can a pore nigger bootlegger do about the war?'' Lightnin' Jim laughed a short, dry laugh. "Let 'em bomb. I'll be here. They hit this place, they'll just ruin a lot of good whiskey and tear up a lot of magazines. But I'll be here, just the same. Newspaper won't do me no good. By the time the war gets to the magazines, it's done passed by enough so you can get a good look at it. Newspapers just deals with trifles. They's nothing uplifting in a newspaper. Just triflin' stuff. Magazines, now, they take time to uplift a man.''

Jake picked up a copy of *Look* from a stack at the end of the sofa and read, " 'New York's Daring New Fashion Look.' Now that's real uplifting.''

Lightnin' Jim shrugged. "All those magazines is printed by white folks,'' he dismissed it. "You can't keep white folks from triflin' altogether.'' Then he turned and called, "Hey, woman,'' and in a moment the door to the adjacent room opened and the woman was there, and a small boy at her knees, staring at Jake.

"Bring us a cordial,'' Lightnin' Jim said. She turned away, leaving the door ajar, and the boy stood there. "Come,'' Jim said, patting his knee, and the boy scrambled into Jim's lap, nestling up against him, still looking at Jake, eyes bright and bold, very curious. Jake could see the resemblance, the faint residue of the ruined old face in the very young one.

"What's your name?" Jake asked.

"Jim Haskell," the boy said.

Another Lightnin' Jim, Jake thought, to carry on the business the way generations of Jim's family had done. There had been a Lightnin' Jim in his grandfather's day, serving that generation out of the predecessor to this neat white frame house, passing along the secrets to the next and the next. Mostly, the secret of where they got the whiskey. It was not raw moonshine and it was not rotgut bootleg, either. It had some age on it, a bouquet and a patina that suggested a reverence for the passage of time. There was always the whiskey and there was always a Lightnin' Jim.

"You teaching him the business yet?" Jake asked.

"No," Lightnin' Jim shook his head. "Not this one."

"You got other boys?"

"He's the only one. Only one left. There was another one some time ago, but he wasn't a whiskey man. He drank too much of it. This one, he's going into real estate." The boy burrowed deeper into the crook of Jim's arm.

"Here?"

"No. Buffalo, New York."

"What kind of real estate?"

"Mine. And his."

"Good Lord," Jake said softly. He could see it all of a sudden, how Lightnin' Jim had taken the money they had paid him for his good whiskey and sent it north, and he could imagine what it had bought—store buildings, two-story tenements, vacant lots. Good, solid real estate that a black man could quietly own and that would blossom in value in a place like Buffalo, New York, under the hand of a bright-eyed young Jim Haskell with a degree from someplace like Cornell or Columbia where Negroes were being accepted now.

"How'd you do it?" Jake asked.

"I got good advice," Jim said.

Jake laughed, thinking of his grandfather wading with his slashing saber through the gore of Cemetery Ridge while the first Lightnin' Jim Haskell learned to make whiskey on some white man's doomed plantation. Then he remembered very vividly his grandfather at the dining table, thundering, "The Confederacy didn't fight over slaves. Not a tenth of the men who rode at my side ever owned a Nigra. We fought because we were trifled with. We fought for the honor of it!'' He could almost feel his grandfather in the room with them—the powerful rumble of his voice, the gamy smell of his cigars and whiskey, the angry batting of his bushy eyebrows. It was a memory like a body long buried and suddenly unearthed, and it took Jake's breath for a second.

"Well, I'll be damned," Jake said. "Why Buffalo, New York?"

"I like the sound of the place," Jim said simply.

"What about your business?"

Jim laughed his little short, dry laugh again. It bubbled up like water out of dry, cracked ground. "Don't worry yourself, Jake. I'll be around awhile yet. Even if I wasn't, folks find a way to get what they want."

The woman came back then with a crystal decanter and two tumblers on a green metal tray, the decanter half-filled with golden whiskey, crystal facets reflecting flickers of the coal fire in the grate. The very look of it made Jake warm and for the first time that morning he could feel the knot of anger and hurt in his gut beginning to loosen.

Lightnin' Jim poured elegantly from the decanter while his wife held the tray, filling the tumblers a third of the way and handing one to Jake. Then he settled back, the boy still on his lap, and raised his glass. "Merry Christmas to you, Jake Tibbetts."

"And to you, Jim Haskell. To your health and good sense."

They sipped at the smooth, strong whiskey and talked, and Jake could feel the room closing in around him like a warm blanket, keeping time with the ticking of the mantel clock, the smell of the whiskey keeping the vivid image of his grandfather strong in his mind, holding him halfway between distant past and contemplated future where a young black man named Jim Haskell traded in real estate in Buffalo, New York.

He dozed, and when he woke, his mind was heavy with sleep and accumulated fatigue and the poison of anger and the narcotic of the whiskey. His eyes snapped open and he looked around in confusion for a moment. Jim was still sitting in the battered easy chair across from him, slowly turning the pages of a magazine, whiskey tumbler empty on the table at his elbow. The boy was gone.

Seeing him awake, Jim closed the magazine and placed it on the table.

Jake felt a flush of embarrassment. He blurted out, "Pastine tried to kill me this morning!" Jim just stared at him. "She tried to cut my head off with my grandfather's sword," he went on. "She stood at the top of the steps and swung that sword around so hard she took an inch-deep hunk out of the porch column. Another six inches and she would have killed me." He stopped, stared into the tumbler still clutched in his hands. There was a quarter-inch of amber liquid still in the bottom. He drank it quickly and the gulp of whiskey burned his throat as it went down. Lightnin' Jim was still watching him, inscrutable as a prune-faced Buddha. "Henry sent a new wife home. She showed up at midnight on the front porch, ripe as a melon, and went upstairs and had a baby girl. The sonofabitch killed one wife and now he sends another one home ten months pregnant and us not even sure the baby's his. Now Pastine wants me to go upstairs and say how-d'ye-do and welcome and everything's all right." The words tumbled out and Jake could feel the heat rising in his cheeks, the anger welling up in him again. "Well, I'll be goddamned if I'll do it. I'll just be goddamned . . ." He broke off, embarrassed again, and sat for a moment huddled down deep inside the overcoat he had never taken off.

"White folks," Jim said, as if he were spitting on the floor. "White folks tell me all their business. I coulda been a rich man offa gossip alone. I s'pose you figure a bootleg nigger ain't gonna tell on you. Well, you're right. But this bootleg nigger knows what kind of fools they is walking around wearing white faces. Jake Tibbetts and all the rest." He sneered. "White folks too goddamn smart to be careful. White folks is *triflin'*. Like newspapers."

Jake got up and placed his tumbler on the table next to Jim Haskell's own and gathered his overcoat about him.

Jim sat there and looked up at him for a moment and then asked, "You want whiskey?"

Jake nodded, and Jim called to his woman, who came with a pint jar of Lightnin' Jim's Best from the dark secret recesses of the house. Jake pulled two rumpled dollar bills from his pants pocket and handed them to Jim, then bade them good day and went back to his newspaper, where he spent the night curled up on a stack of newsprint, well insulated from the cold.

———————

The banging on the back door waked him and he sat upright with a groan, stiff and aching, his head throbbing from the first hangover he could remember in years. My God, he thought, I've drunk enough of Lightnin' Jim's Best to fill Whitewater Creek, and I've never had it do me like this. Either that whiskey nigger was putting out some bad stuff, or else Jake Tibbetts was getting old. He was cold down to his bones and he could feel a raw tickle at the back of his throat that he knew would have him wheezing and coughing and dripping within twenty-four hours.

The banging was louder now. "Awright, goddammit!" he bellowed as he swung his feet down off the stack of newsprint and wrapped his overcoat tight around his body, shivering and miserable. He stood, but the room swam around him and his stomach lurched sickeningly. Jake leaned back against the stack, gripping the edges of it with his hands until things began to settle down. He breathed deeply and stood upright again, then shuffled through the press room to the back door, unbolted it, swung it open.

It was Lonnie, bundled against the cold in his flannel jacket, nose and ears red, holding a paper sack. The back alley was empty and quiet. Jake remembered. It was the morning after Christmas. Lonnie thrust the sack toward him. "I brought you some stuff," he said.

"Your Mama Pastine know you're here?"

"Nosir."

Jake reached in his pants pocket and pulled out his watch and squinted at it. Eight-thirty. He stared at Lonnie for a moment, blinking painfully in the morning sunlight, then shoved the door wide open. "Well, come on in out of the cold."

Lonnie followed him through the press room and the back shop, their footsteps echoing in the emptiness, into the front office, where Jake opened the blinds on the front windows and then sat heavily in the chair at his desk.

"It's cold in here," Lonnie said, setting the paper sack on the edge of the desk.

"Yeah," Jake said, then got up and lit the kerosene stove in the corner of the office, fumbling with the matches and muttering at the tart smell of the kerosene that made the bile rise in his throat. He could feel Lonnie's eyes on his back. The burner on the stove finally caught and Jake turned back to Lonnie. "What you got there?" he pointed to the sack.

"Underwear, mostly."

"Underwear."

Lonnie shrugged. "I figured you'd get persnickety about your underwear. Besides, Mama Pastine says if you don't change your underwear, your bottom will rot off."

Jake reached over and opened the sack and pulled out the items: five pairs of boxer shorts; five undershirts; a pair of suspenders; Jake's shaving mug, brush, straight razor, and strop; a pair of summer-weight gray pants; a porcelain-handled hairbrush; two cigars. He placed it all in a neat pile on his desk, then sat back in the chair and folded his hands in his lap and looked at it for a moment. Lonnie stood there, silent, expectant.

"What happened yesterday, I don't want you to worry about that," Jake said after a moment.

Lonnie didn't say anything.

"I love your Mama Pastine, you know that?"

"Yessir."

"Even after yesterday, you understand?"

"Yessir."

"She just got overwrought. She's been putting up with me for a long time, and I guess she just got overwrought."

He looked at the boy and thought, Ah, Lonnie. How you do haunt me with your father's enormous brown eyes and that way of looking at me as if you are waiting for me to tell you something. God knows what. I have no answers. Had none for Henry, have none for you.

"Are you sick, Daddy Jake?" Lonnie broke through the hard shell of his thoughts.

Jake sniffled. "I'm just coming down with a cold, that's all."

"You been drinking that old corn whiskey, too. I can smell it." He wrinkled up his nose.

"Yeah, I been drinking that old corn whiskey. So what?"

Lonnie's eyes flashed. "You ought not to. If I'd done it, you'd have whipped my butt."

And that was the difference, Jake thought, between father and son. Henry would give you some lip, but if you barked at him he'd get that whipped-dog look and clam up. But this one. This one just rocked back on his heels and came right back at you. He had too goddamn much of his grandmother in him, that was what.

"You got a big mouth, boy," Jake said.

"Yessir." Lonnie looked around the newspaper office. "You gonna live here?"

"Hell, no, I'm not gonna live here. This is a newspaper office, not a boardinghouse. For God's sakes."

"You could go to the Regal, I reckon."

Jake snorted. "I've got no truck with itinerant riffraff."

"Well, you gotta live someplace. You got no place to sleep or take a bath."

Jake thought for a moment. "I'll think of something." He would, by God, think of something. He would *not*, by God, live at the newspaper office. Pastine was out of her mind.

Lonnie stood there, arms folded across his chest, head cocked to one side the way Pastine did when she was giving him that don't-give-me-any-foolishness look.

Jake wiped his face with his hand. "Don't you worry about me, boy," his voice rose. "I'll do just fine. By God, I'll make out." His head hurt like the dickens. Little flickers of light danced before his eyes.

There was a long silence, and then Lonnie said, "You could come home, I reckon."

"No," Jake said quietly. "I can't come home."

"Well," Lonnie said, "I can't say as I blame you. That baby squalls all the time and when she messes up her diaper, you can smell it all over the house."

Jake studied him for a moment. "They give it a name yet?"

"Nosir. I heard 'em talking. They're gonna wait until Henry comes home to give it a name." Not *Daddy*, but *Henry*. It had been a long time, Jake thought.

"Ah."

Lonnie waited, then said, "They talk all the time. They're thick as thieves already."

"Thick as thieves."

"Yessir."

Jake understood then how bewildered Lonnie must be by the whole business. It came to Jake, sitting there cold and stiff and hung over, how upside down Lonnie's small world had always been. And how unfair it was. A boy ought not to be torn. He ought to have a place that was safe and warm and somebody around who had some answers, or at least thought he did. And Jake Tibbetts felt small and lost himself because he didn't know what the hell to do about it. It was just such a godawful mess they had all made of things.

Jake wanted to cry. But he didn't. Instead, he said, "Lonnie, I love you."

Lonnie looked at him in surprise.

"Your Mama Pastine loves you, too. We're gonna get this thing straightened out. We've just got to give it some time, you hear?" Lonnie nodded.

Jake turned away from him, stared out the window at the morning after Christmas, bright with expectation, and he thought about giving things some time. How much time did they have?

"You ever tried pissing into the wind, Lonnie?" he asked.

"Nosir."

"You'll get it all over you."

"I reckon."

He turned back, put his hand on the stack of things Lonnie had brought in the paper sack. "Thanks for the supplies, boy. I'll be okay, don't you worry. You just help your Mama Pastine. She's got her hands full right now."

Lonnie walked over to the front door and stood there for a moment, then asked, "Can I come help you down here?"

Jake held his breath, then let it out slowly. "Doing what?"

Lonnie swept his arm around, indicating the back shop. "All that stuff you do back there."

"You want to be a newspaperman, boy?"

Lonnie shrugged. "I don't know."

"You'll get your hands dirty."

Lonnie nodded.

"And sometimes folks'll raise hell with you."

He nodded again.

"Well," Jake said, "it's all right with me if it's all right with your Mama Pastine. I don't want you getting caught in the middle of this little row we're having. I don't want this newspaper business to have anything to do with that. You understand?"

"Yessir. It don't."

"Doesn't."

"Yessir."

"But if you want to come down here and hitch up your britches and pay attention and work hard, okay. I'll pay you ten cents an hour.''

Lonnie's eyes widened.

"But you'll have to work it out with Pastine. Whatever she says goes. If she'll let you come an hour after school every day, fine. Saturdays, that's fine, too. But she's the boss on this. You go home and talk with her and let me know."

Lonnie opened the front door, still keeping his eyes on Jake. "Thanks for the BB gun," he said.

Jake waved him off. "Don't thank me, thank Santa Claus. He flew through shot and shell . . ."

"Oh, bull," Lonnie said, smiling. "I ain't a kid no more, Daddy Jake."

"Well . . ."

And then he was gone and Jake sat there for a long time and stared out the window at the morning, feeling some warmth creeping back into his body, listening to the small sounds in the back shop, the rustling of the mouse that lived under the shelves on the back wall and ate small holes in the stacks of paper he kept for job printing, the tiny metallic clink of the Linotype machine that had never been allowed to cool down completely since Albertis Tibbetts had installed it years before. Jake thought about his father, imagined him hunched there over the Linotype keyboard, fingers dancing flawlessly over the keys, brow creased in concentration. Albertis could set galley after galley of type and never make a mistake. He was a printer, but he was not a newspaperman. Old Captain Finley, from what they said, had been both. Jake was both. Henry had been neither. And now there was Lonnie, who might be both or neither or somewhere in between. He might even be the best of the lot. God bless him if he wanted to become a newspaperman. And God save him, too. Thinking about it, Jake decided suddenly that he was hungry, and he remembered that he hadn't had a bite to eat since dinner on Christmas Eve, right before Henry's wife had appeared. By God, he could eat a horse. He could almost smell the rich aroma of eggs and bacon and coffee at Biscuit Brunson's cafe, where by this time they would have heard about how Jake Tibbetts had been routed from his own home at the point of a sword on Christmas Day, would be smacking their lips over the juiciness of it. What the hell, he thought, and went to face the music.

He was right. He could tell it the minute he opened the door, the way they all stopped talking and turned and stared at him as if he had leper's spots all over his face instead of just a two-day stubble of beard. Tunstall Renfroe put his coffee cup down in its saucer with a soft clink. Fog Martin stared, then reached for a Victory Donut and bit off half of it. Hilton Redlinger hitched his big butt around on the counter stool and hauled up on his sagging pistol belt. Biscuit wiped the counter furiously and said, "Howdy, Jake!" a bit too loudly.

Jake bowed. "Gents," he said, and made an elaborate show of taking off his overcoat and hanging it on the coatrack next to the door while they sat there and watched him. Then he turned back to them. "Well" he said grinning and slapping his hands together, "let me tell you what happened to me yesterday."

"Come on, Jake," Tunstall said, "don't take the fun out of it for us."

They all laughed then, taking the edge of embarrassment off of it, and Jake sat down on the stool next to the front window.

"Well, you've all heard the story by now, I'm sure. Complete with embellishments. My version would be dull by comparison. Suffice it to say I've still got all my limbs if not my wits. Pastine, good woman that she is, dispatched me from the house at sword point, and that's the whole of it." He grinned at them. "My God," he slapped the counter, "I could eat a horse."

"I'm fresh out of those," Biscuit said.

"Then gimme two eggs over light, sausage, grits, toast, and coffee. And hold the marmalade."

"How 'bout a donut?" Fog said, raising the glass lid from the platter of donuts and taking another one for himself.

"Naw, I'm afraid I'll ruin my appetite. I just want to sit here and savor the smell of Biscuit fryin' up my breakfast and suffer in anticipation."

"Coming up," Biscuit said, turning to the griddle behind the counter, where he cracked two eggs and plopped them sizzling on the hot surface, then placed two thick circles of sausage beside them and, over to one side, two pieces of white bread to brown into toast. Biscuit cooked all his short orders on the same big griddle here in the front of the cafe, the juices of eggs and bacon, sausage and pancakes, mingling richly. If you came in later in the day and ordered a grilled cheese sandwich, it would taste faintly of the breakfast you had had several hours before.

Jake looked over at the boards Biscuit had nailed over the bombed-out window and thought about Billy Benefield and the airplane. It seemed like eons ago. So much had happened. There was a strange quality to their even being here this morning, like men who had wandered through a time warp and staggered exhausted up on the far shore, weighted with the baggage of their journey. Jake felt for a moment as if they were all sitting here holding their breaths, waiting to see what calamity would strike next. Or was it just he who felt that way?

Hilton Redlinger finished his plate of blueberry pancakes with a great sigh of satisfaction, placed his knife, fork, and spoon neatly in the middle of the plate, and wiped his mouth with a paper napkin. He looked over at Fog, who was making quick work of another donut. "Fog, you must have paid for enough bonds eatin' those donuts to arm a division."

Fog nodded. "Patriotic duty," he said thickly.

"Biscuit, how many war bonds you reckon those donuts have bought?" Hilton asked.

"Four hundred and twenty-five dollars' worth," Biscuit said over his shoulder. "That's bought and paid for. And I got some change in the drawer back in the kitchen. Maybe another ten bucks' worth."

"Lord, can you imagine that. Four hundred and thirty-five dollars' worth of donuts at a nickel apiece. That's . . ."

"Eight thousand, seven hundred donuts," Tunstall said, doing a quick calculation in his banker's head.

"And you been selling 'em how long?"

Biscuit thought back for a moment. "Almost three years exactly. I started just after Pearl Harbor. December of forty-one."

Hilton turned to Tunstall. "Figure that, Tunstall. Eight thousand, seven hundred donuts in three years. How many is that a day?"

"Wait a minute, boys," Jake said from his end of the counter. "Let me run back to the paper and get my Speed Graphic so I can get a picture of the Human Adding Machine in action."

Tunstall reached for a paper napkin and took his fountain pen out of an inside coat pocket.

"Oh, no," Jake said. "Do it in your head."

Tunstall put the pen away, smiled at them, leaned back in his chair, closed his eyes for a few moments while his lips moved almost imperceptibly. Then he opened his eyes and said, "Figuring that Biscuit is open six days a week, that's three hundred and twelve days a year, and he has sold eight thousand, seven hundred donuts in three years, that comes to just over nine donuts a day. To be precise about it, nine-point-three donuts a day, slightly rounded off."

"Is that *right*?" Hilton asked the rest of them.

"How the dickens would I know?" Fog said. "There ain't another man in this room can find the square root of fifty, even using paper."

"Seven-point-oh-seven," Tunstall said, "slightly rounded off."

"You're pretty good at figuring, ain't you, Jake?" Hilton said. "You had some college."

"Lord, no. I'm a newspaperman, not a financial tycoon. We of the press deal in approximations."

"Well, I guess we'll have to take your word for it, Tunstall," Hilton said.

"Hell, he figures loan interest that way," Jake said. "No telling how much folks in this town overpay the Farmers Mercantile because Tunstall sits there and smiles and does tricks in his head."

"I'll be glad for you to check me any time, Jake," Tunstall spoke up. "Anyway, it'll be time to retire those Victory Donuts before long. From the news on the radio this morning, I'd say the war's just about over."

"Yeah," Hilton said, "I heard Kaltenborn last night. He said the big fight in Belgium was the Germans' last gasp. The only thing to decide now is who gets to Berlin first—us or the Russians."

Tunstall got up from his table, walked behind the counter and poured himself another cup of coffee from the steaming pot. "I hope it's our boys. The Russians are a barbaric lot."

Hilton hitched himself around on the stool again. "Yeah, but they fight like hell. I'd hate to think we had to whip the Germans all by ourselves."

Biscuit poured Jake a cup of coffee and Jake spooned in sugar and cream, stirred, and took a noisy slurp. "Personally, I think we should have sat back and let the Germans and the Russians kick the doodoo out of each other and then walk in and pick up the pieces.''

''That wouldn't be fair,'' Tunstall said. ''The Russians have lost *millions*.''

''Good riddance,'' Jake snorted.

''Well, anyway, it looks like the Germans are pretty much whipped,'' Tunstall said. Tunstall fancied himself something of a war strategist. He spent considerable spare time at the radio station, poring over the big war maps that Ollie Whittle had mounted on the wall.

''You ain't forgetting the Japs, are you?'' Fog Martin asked. His brother Carlton was on the carrier *Midway* in the Pacific.

''Heck, we'll whip the Japs in thirty days,'' Hilton said, nodding for emphasis. ''We'll just turn Georgie Patton loose on 'em.''

''I wouldn't count on it,'' Fog said. ''Carlton says the Japs are fanatics. He says they tie themselves to trees so they can't run away and they'll have to die fighting. And he says they strap hand grenades to themselves and run right into the middle of a group of our boys and set the grenades off. They just don't give up. I hate to think what'll happen when we invade Japan.''

There was a long moment of silence while everybody thought about that, and then Tunstall said, ''Well, maybe we won't. Maybe we'll just surround Japan and starve 'em out.''

''That could take years,'' Hilton said gloomily. ''The little buggers don't eat much, anyway. They can grow enough rice to keep going, I imagine. And they eat bamboo, don't they?''

Biscuit gave Jake's eggs and sausage and toast a flip, let everything sizzle for another half-minute, and then scooped it all up with his spatula and deposited it on a plate, which he placed in front of Jake along with a steaming bowl of grits with a puddling pat of butter in the middle. The aroma hit Jake full force and he fell on the breakfast, eating ravenously while the talk went on, a quiet babble at the edge of his slowly satiated hunger.

''Everything okay, Jake?'' Biscuit asked.

''Mmmmmm,'' Jake answered, feeling the pit of his stomach beginning to warm and fill. He was oblivious to the rest of them and their talk of starving the Japanese. ''More grits,'' he said after a while, and Biscuit refilled the grits bowl and plopped another pat of butter on top. Jake ate with relish and then he slowed down and began to savor every mouthful, feeling the last vestiges of his hangover swept away by his gorged belly. He finished finally and wiped his mouth on a paper napkin. Biscuit refilled his coffee cup and he sat there on the stool, reveling in an overwhelming sense of well-being and taking note of the novelty of it—eating breakfast at Brunson's Cafe instead of his own table, a man on his own, footloose and fancy-free for the first time in . . . Lord, how many years? In a few minutes, he would get up and pay his bill and get a toothpick from the small glass container on the counter and amble leisurely back to the paper, picking his teeth and contemplating the business of getting the paper out for another week, the honest labor of an honest man. Not the kind of man who would live in a damned newspaper office, by God.

". . . be coming home all of a sudden," Fog Martin was saying. "They'll be busting a gut to get out of uniform and settle down."

"What I wonder is, is it safe?" Tunstall asked.

"What do you mean?"

"Well, all these boys running around loose. Trained killers, so to speak. I mean, we don't know what combat has done to them. You could have a young fellow standing on a street corner and a car backfires and he grabs the nearest gun and starts shooting at everything in sight. What do you think, Hilton?"

Hilton pondered that for a moment, slack-jawed. "Well, I reckon it's something we ought to consider. I guess maybe the sheriff should be careful who he issues pistol permits to, but you can't deny a man the right to have a gun. It ain't constitutional."

Biscuit leaned over the counter toward them. "I 'spect the last thing any of those boys wants is a gun, after what they've been through." There were nods all around. "In fact, I think instead of worrying about them shooting up the place, we ought to be thinking about a proper memorial."

Jake sat up on his stool. "What do you mean, memorial?"

"I mean something to honor all the boys who fought. Especially the ones who won't be coming back." There was a glint of moisture in Biscuit's eyes.

"You're still hung up on a *war memorial*." Jake strung out the words. They had been debating it just two days before, on Christmas Eve morning, when Billy Benefield had come swooping down on them and turned the courthouse square into a war zone. You would think after that foolishness, folks would be content to let the war well enough alone.

"I'm not hung up on anything, Jake." Biscuit picked up his cloth and started wiping the counter. The dishcloth was Biscuit's security blanket. Any time you got him the least bit agitated, he'd pick up that damned dishcloth and start trying to rub the top off the counter. "I just think we ought to do something to let the boys know we appreciate what they've done."

"Best thing we can do for the boys," Jake said, slapping the counter with a bang, "is to let 'em alone. Let 'em forget the goddamned war and get back to living normal lives."

They all stared at him, a little taken aback at his vehemence.

Tunstall cleared his throat. "Ahem. Well, I think Biscuit's got a point." He looked at Fog and Hilton expectantly.

Fog nodded. "I reckon. Yeah, I reckon Biscuit's got a point, all right."

"Well, you both got a point," Hilton said, noncommittal. "It's something we ought to think about." Hilton, always the public servant. Teetering between the whims of the dolts on the Town Council and every jackleg common citizen who thought he knew how to enforce the law, serving at the caprice of both, and getting no younger. Hilton's once-hard jaw sagged now and his hair was all white and thinning badly so that the mottled pink of his scalp showed through. He was spreading on the bottom and thinning on the top and if his wild shoot-em-up response to Billy Benefield's air attack was any indication, he was losing his grip.

"Aw, what the hell, Hilton," Jake said. "Take a stand for once in your life. Do you or do you not think we ought to have a war memorial?"

Hilton turned on him, startled. "Well . . ."

"Yeah?" he demanded.

The color rose in Hilton's neck then, and for a second he looked like the Hilton Redlinger of old who could lay a grown man out on the sidewalk with one roundhouse swing. "I think," Hilton said, "we ought to have a war memorial."

Jake looked at them a moment, his eyes moving from Biscuit behind the counter to Fog and Hilton on the stools next to him to Tunstall sitting at the table. "Well, you're all full of horseshit."

"Jake . . ." Biscuit started. This just was not the way you

ran a friendly argument in Biscuit Brunson's cafe. They had been sitting here, the five of them, jawing over one thing and another for forty years or so, digging at each other in more or less good humor, with rarely a truly heated word, taking even Jake Tibbetts's barbed wit in stride. Nobody had ever told them they were full of horseshit.

"Horseshit," Jake said again. "Hell, we're just a bunch of goddamned old men sitting here on our fat butts. We didn't fight the goddamned war. We don't know a fool thing about war—with the possible exception of Tunstall, who thinks he knows more about strategy than Dwight D. Eisenhower. Not a damned one of us ever killed a man, including our esteemed police chief, whose only victim is a plate-glass window." He could see the surprise, the hurt in their faces, but he barged on, lashing out at them. "So what the hell do we think we're doing, sitting here debating a war memorial? We got no damn business putting up a war memorial. If the boys come back and want a war memorial, let them do it. It's their war."

"It's everybody's war," Tunstall said, the heat rising in him. "Everybody in this town took part in the war in one way or another."

"Yeah," Jake shot back, "we went around wearing our air raid helmets and taking down the Christmas lights and eating donuts, all right. But none of us *fought*. Them that *fights* gets to *memorialize*."

"Jake," Biscuit said, "I think you're dead wrong on this."

"You may damned well be right. But I know what I think. And me and my newspaper are dead set against a war memorial."

There was a moment of stony silence, and then Fog Martin, gentle Fog, said, "Jake, don't make a horse's ass out of yourself over this just because of your boy."

Jake stared at him for a moment, unblinking. Then he pulled his dirty handkerchief out of his back pocket and blew his nose noisily, then put the handkerchief back, still looking at Fog, and fished a dollar bill out of his front pocket. He laid the bill on the counter, got off the stool, put on his coat, and walked out the door without another word being said.

By early afternoon, the word was out—at least around the court-house square, where Jake was making his usual rounds of the merchants, gathering advertising copy for the week's edition of the *Free Press*. Nobody came right out and said anything to Jake about it. But the looks they gave him let Jake know the breakfast set-to in Biscuit Brunson's cafe was common talk among the rab-ble. Jake Tibbetts was against a war memorial and he had cussed out four of his best friends over it. Used the word "horseshit." Conversation stopped in midsentence when he walked in the front door of the Jitney Jungle Super Saver or Alvah Foley's barbershop or Hamblin's Mercantile, and they went scurrying about finding something terribly interesting in a cantaloupe or bolt of cloth, cutting funny looks at him out of the corners of their eyes.

At the Jitney Jungle, George Poulos was a little distant, but then George had a boy in the paratroopers somewhere in Europe and he might be a little touchy about a war memorial. Then, too, he was on the Town Council, and that was where any flap over a war memorial would end up eventually. George took his usual quarter-page ad and jotted down a list of his specials on the back of a brown paper sack while Jake waited, but he didn't have much small talk today.

"I'll get your proof over to you tomorrow morning, soon's I set the type," Jake said, folding the paper sack and tucking it into an overcoat pocket.

"No need," George said, then hung fire for a moment. "But you got the chickens wrong last week."

"Huh?"

"The chickens. I had the chickens down for nineteen cents a pound. Whole fryers. You ran it eighteen cents a pound." George sounded a little testy. "I had to sell 'em for eighteen cents. Seems like every woman in town was in here wanting whole fryers for eighteen cents a pound."

"I'm sorry, George," Jake said. "Figure up how much it cost you and I'll take it off your bill."

"No," George shook his head. "No need."

"I insist," Jake insisted.

"Folks see something in the paper, they figure it's right," George said.

"Sure. How much did you lose?"

"Coupla dollars, I reckon."

"It's done. And I'll bring you this week's proof tomorrow."

"Well, maybe you better."

Jake stood on the sidewalk outside the Jitney Jungle for a few minutes, thinking to himself that yes, George Poulos was upset over the war memorial. George had never asked for a proof of his ad before. It was a little ritual with them. Jake would say he was bringing over the proof and George would say no bother. It was one of those million small gestures in a day's transactions with your fellow supplicants that could go either way: I trust you or I don't. Jake had no doubt made mistakes on George Poulos's ads before—all those items, all those numbers. But over the years, it probably all evened out. This was the first time George had ever mentioned it. He had even asked for a proof, for God's sake.

Whit Hennessey at the post office likewise had a bit of a burr under his saddle. Whit was sitting in the little back room of the post office, but when he saw Jake's box open and the hand slide in to get the stack of envelopes, he came to the window and peered out.

"Jake."

" 'Lo, Whit. How are you?"

Whit blinked behind his thick glasses. "Pretty busy. Still got a lot of Christmas cards. Some folks always wait too late to mail their Christmas cards and here I am the day after, with more mail than I oughta have."

"Mail's mail, I guess," Jake said, shuffling absently through his own stack.

"No, not at all," Whit said. "A Christmas card is first class. I got to give priority to first class."

Jake looked up at him.

"Take for instance some business sends a bulk mail flyer and it arrives the day after Christmas," Whit went on. "Regulations say I got to get the first class taken care of first. That's why they call it first class. So some businessman's trying to make a living and his bulk mail flyer has got to sit there while I take care of folks who didn't mail their Christmas cards on time." Whit seemed affronted by the untidiness of it.

"I see what you mean. Yeah."

"Regulations are regulations. I got a letter from Arthur this morning."

"Oh?"

"He's in France now. Just made staff sergeant not long ago,

and now they're sending him to Officer Candidate School. He says there's a big shortage of lieutenants.''

Jake tried to conjure up an image of Whit's boy Arthur, but all he could remember was a kid of ten or so in overalls, no shirt, bare feet, hanging around the back door of the post office because Whit wouldn't let him inside. Regulations.

"He'll make a good officer," Jake said. "He's a good boy."

"Yeah," Whit said, nodding. "I just want to get him home. You know what I mean?" He looked at Jake closely, waiting for something.

"I'll be glad to see all the boys home myself," Jake said evenly. "I'll be glad to see things get back to normal."

"Normal. That's right. I just want everything to get settled down again." He said it fervently, so much so that it took Jake aback.

Jake thought about it as he walked the block to the newspaper, unlocked the door, turned the sign in the window from the side that said GONE to the side that said BACK, hung his overcoat on the rack by the door, and sat down at his desk to sort through the stack of notes and papers he had brought back from his rounds.

He thought about "normal," and he thought that there was no such thing anymore and probably never would be again. The war had changed all that. The war had taken what people had been used to and turned it upside down. People had lived in this town and a thousand others like it in pretty much the same way for years and years. And then suddenly the war had changed it all completely and irreversibly in the space of a few months. Jake suspected that the changes themselves were only the half of what bothered folks. It was the suddenness of it, the enormity of it, and the suspicion that once things could change this drastically, they could change again, that lives would never again operate on an even keel. "Normal" went right out the window.

Now, if H. V. Kaltenborn was right, they were about to get an inkling of just how right their suspicions were, because the war would soon be over and the boys would be coming home, bringing with them all their baggage: the wounds, the fears, the wonders, the places they had been, and the things they had seen. They would be forever and profoundly altered by it, and they would bring all that baggage back and set it down in this town and then the town would undergo another upheaval. Some of the boys would stay around awhile and then they would get antsy about things, having seen something of the world, and they would leave—taking some of their baggage with them, but leaving some behind—and there would be still more upheaval. And then those who stayed would have their own ideas about things, some of them strange and troubling perhaps, and they would be making a place for themselves and their ideas. That meant that folks like Whit Hennessey and George Poulos and the coffee crowd at Biscuit Brunson's cafe would have to make room or be shouldered aside. These men who had *been* the town would become boring old farts who sat around and scratched at their dandruff and talked about the past, but whose experiences paled in comparison with all the young men had seen and felt. They would be surplus goods, like old tanks and airplanes rusting in the weeds, another kind of leftover from the war. And that hurt. It was hard enough growing old, and hard enough going through the upheaval of war and the end of war, but to have them happen together . . . well, little wonder that folks might get riled up at the thought of a flap over a war memorial. It wasn't so much the memorial itself, he suspected, as it was all the other.

But should that make a damn to Jake Tibbetts and his newspaper? Should he pull in his horns on this thing he felt strongly about, just because it got folks upset? No, he had had the town's bowels in an uproar over one thing or another for as long as he had been running the *Free Press*. He had always spoken his mind, even when it hurt, even when he had been dead wrong. That was what a newspaper was supposed to do.

Ah, but there was this other thing, and gentle Fog Martin, who would never hurt a fly, had gone right to the heart of it. Just why was Jake Tibbetts opposed to a war memorial? Was it on sacred principle or was it because of Henry, that wretched ghost who had suddenly come to life so that he could confound Jake with his mess and confusion all over again? Come now, Jake, be honest with yourself.

He sat there a long time, trying to be honest with himself, then realized suddenly that it had gotten dark outside. He was hungry and grubby. He hadn't had a bath in more than two days and the stubble of beard on his face felt like a wire-bristle brush. The tickle at the back of his throat had gotten steadily worse during the day. And he still had made no provisions for lodging himself for the night. He thought of the stack of newsprint in the back shop and shuddered. And then his anger came flooding back, the humiliation of being routed from his own home by a bull-headed woman. No, by God, he would not spend another night on top of a stack of newsprint. He would not, by God, live at the newspaper.

———————

Jake pushed open the heavy oak and leaded-glass front door of the Regal Hotel and stood for a moment in the empty entrance hall, thinking that he had not been in the place since he was a boy.

It had been known then as the Widow Whichard's Boarding-house and Jake remembered it as a warm, casual, cluttered place with rich smells wafting from the kitchen just back of the big dining room, mingling with the aroma of the boarders' cigars. It had a wide front porch where, in the warm months, the guests could take the air after supper in green wicker rocking chairs, protected from the setting sun by dark green lattice blinds that rolled up and down and gave the house, when they were extended, the look of an aging gentleman with droopy eyelids.

Now, in winter, the rockers and blinds had been stored away and the porch was bare, the windows shuttered against the cold. The place had changed hands several times over the years, and the present owner was a widower named Grayson who had re-named it the Regal Hotel and hung a neatly lettered wooden sign from a metal post out front to prove it. Inside, it was cold, austere, proper. Grayson had regalized it. There was a coatrack, coatless, just to the right of the front door; an umbrella stand, umbrella-less, next to the coatrack; a plain armchair upholstered in a shiny bottle-green material next to the umbrella stand. To his right, an archway opened into the dining area—the table as empty as his stomach—and to his left was the hotel desk, apparently another Grayson touch. It had a broad wooden counter with a bell and a guest book, and behind it on the wall was a shelf divided into numbered pigeonholes. There was a key in one pigeonhole, a small stack of mail in another.

Jake walked over to the desk, turned the guest book around, examined the entries. The last had been four days ago, an E. Thurmond Broadus of St. Louis, representing the Foot-Pleasure Company. Shoe salesman. Jake had met him before in Hamblin's Mercantile, a red-faced beefy man with a big nose and the faint smell of leather about him.

Jake turned the book back around and tapped on the bell. Its echo dingled tinnily off the polished wooden floor and the plastered walls. He waited perhaps a minute and then tapped again, harder this time, and after a moment the door behind the desk opened a crack and a woman peered out—plump-faced, hair in curlers, face shiny with cold cream.

Jake said, "I need a room."

"How long?"

"The night. For starters."

The woman eyed him suspiciously. "You aren't local, are you?"

"Why?"

"We don't let overnight to locals," she said.

"Why not?"

She sniffed. "We got our reputation to think of. You start letting overnight rooms to locals, first thing you know they'll be using 'em for things besides sleeping, if you know what I mean."

Jake nodded. "Brings out the beast in a man, don't it."

"What?" she asked.

"Lust," Jake said. "And who might you be, madam?"

"Mrs. Grayson," she said, with a lift of her chin. "The new Mrs. Grayson. We was married Christmas Eve."

"You're not from these parts?" Jake asked.

"Taylorsville," she said. "And who are you?"

Jake drew himself up. "I am the Reverend Sylvester Pomfret of St. Louis. Your hostelry," he indicated the premises with a wave of his hand, "has been recommended to me by a member of my congregation, E. Thurmond Broadus, who I believe lay under this very roof not four nights ago. Represents the Foot-Pleasure Company. Admirable fellow, though I've never seen a bigger nose on a man. Anyhow, Brother Thurmond speaks highly of your accommodations and your table. Have I got the wrong Regal?"

Mrs. Grayson didn't say anything for a moment. She just stood there and looked at Jake, and then she leaned over the counter and looked down at his feet. "Where's your satchel?"

"Ahem. My valise was . . . ah . . . stolen. Yes, stolen. On the train. I am as you see me. I require only a bed for the night and then I shall quit this miserable place."

Mrs. Grayson gave him a good once-over. "You don't look like a minister," she said finally.

"Oh," Jake said, rolling his eyes toward the ceiling, "if you only knew what I have been through these last few days."

"And what's that?"

Jake leaned over the counter toward her. "My good woman, I will tell you the whole sad story if you could find it in your Christian heart to give me a bit of bread and a glass of cold milk. I am faint with hunger."

"Well," she looked him over again, "you can't be too careful these days, you know, what with the war going on. Especially with these young fellows. But an older gentleman like yourself . . ." she trailed off. "Well, I had to ask. Mr. Grayson is laid up with a cold, and he told me not to let overnight to no locals."

"How right you are," Jake nodded. She took his two dollars and had him sign the guest book, which he did with a flourish, affixing the initials D.D.M. after his name for a bit of academic flair, and then she took him to the kitchen and warmed a plate of turkey and dressing, cranberry sauce, and carrot cake. Jake tried not to wolf it, but he bore down on the plate hungrily, half-listening to the drone of Mrs. Grayson's voice as she launched into a monologue about her sister Erma, who had been afflicted with especially painful female cramps until a young revivalist laid hands on her in a tent meeting and expunged whatever succubus had hold of her plumbing. Erma, it seemed, had gone off with him to continue the benefit of his ministries, but somewhere along the way she had strayed again and had ended it all by jumping from the eleventh floor of a Chicago hotel in 1939.

Jake nodded occasionally and let her drone, and as he finished off the plateful of food, it occurred to him that the Regal Hotel was the most temporary of lodgings. He wouldn't be here at all, with a full belly and a place to sleep, had Grayson himself appeared at the counter. How the hell could he know the Regal didn't let overnight to locals? He never set foot in the place. And if he tried to stay on, Grayson would find out who he was and kick him out on his ass and the whole town would get a good laugh over it. Reverend Sylvester Pomfret. Gad! So he would stay the night, leave quietly in the morning, and let tomorrow night take care of itself. Right now, he was too bone-tired to care much.

"God help us," he muttered.

"That's what I said," Mrs. Grayson sighed. "They said Erma hit feet first and it scrunched her up so bad her ankles was up around her collarbones. They brought her home in a little bitty coffin like they bury babies in." She paused, pondering it for a moment, then gave Jake a long look. "What are you here for, anyhow?"

"I had a vision," Jake said, before he caught himself.

"A *what*?"

Ah, shit, Jake thought, forging on. "I was laying there in my bed in St. Louis two nights ago, and I awoke from a sound sleep to find an angel of the Lord sitting on my portmanteau."

"What?"

"My suitcase. The good fellow had apparently dragged it out of the closet and was sitting there on it with his arms folded across his chest. Like this," Jake showed her. "And he said to me, as clear as you please, 'Sylvester Pomfret, go witness.' And then he vanished. Well, what was I to do? I leaped from my bed that instant, packed my valise, and made my way to the train station."

"But what happened to you?"

"What do you mean?"

"You said something about a sad story."

"Ah, yes." Jake rose from his chair, picked up his coat, and began edging toward the doorway. "Already, the hand of fate was upon the venture. I had barely seated myself on the train when a voice in my ear said, 'Go to the last car.' I did, and there I found a young man, in the depths of despair from riotous living, about to fling himself from the rear platform to a certain death. So I fetched him a blow upside the head"—Jake smacked the air with his fist—"and when he came to his senses I preached the grace of God to him. I am sorry to say that when he left the train in Cairo, Illinois, he took with him my portmanteau and I was left with the clothes on my back and a small sum of cash in my pocket."

"Good Lord," Mrs. Grayson said.

"It has left me feeble from fatigue," Jake said, letting his shoulders slump wearily. "I must get my rest."

"Shall I see you up?" she asked, handing Jake his key as he backed out of the kitchen into the hallway.

"Oh, no. I can quite manage."

"Second room on the right," she called after him as he

climbed the stairs. "You want me to bang on your door in the morning?"

"God bless you, no," Jake called back.

The second-floor hallway was dark, but he found the room with the aid of the dim light filtering up the stairs from the first floor, let himself in, closed the door, felt along the wall just inside for a light switch, found none, then opened the door again and stood there and let his eyes get accustomed to the semidark-ness until he could just barely make out the naked bulb hanging by a cord from the ceiling. He pulled the string, glanced around at the stark furnishings of the room—flaking iron bedstead, mar-ble-topped washstand, battered chifforobe. Regal, my ass, he thought. The ministry is hell. He shuddered in the chill, then switched the light off again, put on his overcoat, pulled back the covers, climbed into bed, and slept.

He could tell the instant he awoke that it was late. The light around the edges of the yellowed window shade was strong, the flat iron-gray light of an overcast morning well along. He groaned, and then winced with pain from the raw open wound his throat had become. While he had slept like death itself, the cold had seized him full force. Now he was bathed in sweat, flushed with fever. His eyes burned and his head felt as if it had been stuffed full of lard. Aw my gawd, he tried to say, but nothing came out. He sat up in bed, shuddering with a sudden chill. He drew the overcoat around him and tried again to speak. Aaaarrrgh. Nothing. His voice was gone. He sat there in agony for a moment, staring at the window shade, then extricated him-self from the tangled bedclothes and set his feet gingerly on the floor. Every joint ached. He slumped, face in hands and thought of what a pitiful sack of manure he had become in two short days. Vanquished from his own home, gossiped about in every kitchen and business establishment, forced to take refuge in a flophouse posing as a preacher, filthy, smelly, stubblefaced, and now feeling his vital juices ebbing from every agonized pore of his body. He thought fleetingly of death, surcease from sorrow. He could just lie back in the bed, pull the covers up to his chin, and let death steal quietly over him like a gray shadow.

And then suddenly, for some reason, he thought about the war memorial. He remembered that he had dreamed of it, some-time during a night purpled by feverish dreams—a hideous giant obelisk on the courthouse lawn, casting an enormous shadow across the sidewalk in front of Biscuit Brunson's cafe. People stood all around gazing up at its marble face, etched with the names of millions of dead, growing up, up out of the ground like a haunted beanstalk until it was taller than the courthouse itself. Jake was somewhere in the crowd and Hilton Redlinger drove by in the fire truck, scattering the throng, stopping next to Jake, pointing up at the memorial. "Where's Henry?" he cried. "Where's Henry?" Jake tried to speak, but nothing came out.

Goddamn 'em all. They wanted a war memorial, did they? A monument to the waste and misery of war? A tribute to upheaval and anarchy? Well, they wouldn't get it without a fight!

Jake jerked upright, head pounding, heart racing. He gasped for breath and felt a wave of dizziness sweep over him and fell back on the bed while the room whirled around him, tilting crazily like a carnival ride gone haywire. He lay there for a long time with his eyes clinched tight until it slowed and then stopped. Then he calmed himself, thinking as he did that he was a sick old man approaching sixty-five and that there might not be too many fights left in this pitiful sack of manure, so he better get his ass up and out of the Regal Hotel and gird himself for battle.

Easier said than done. It was not quite as late as he at first thought—his pocket watch said seven-thirty—but it was the worst possible time for him to be stirring about in the Regal. The hallway was empty when he opened the door to his room, but he could hear a droning chorus of voices from the dining room down below. It sounded like half the town down there, talking with their mouths full. He looked down at the other end of the hall. There was no back stairway, only a window. He considered it fleetingly, then imagined himself crashing through the roof of the back stoop while one of the hired cooks screamed in terror, or impaling himself on a nandina bush. No, there was no way out but the front stairs, and they emptied into the entrance hall just at the opening to the big dining room. It would have to be quick.

But she caught him. He was halfway across the lobby, hat in left hand shielding his face from the tableful of babbling gluttons, when Mrs. Grayson's voice rang out. "Reverend Pomfret!"

He took another long stride toward the door, but she grabbed him by the arm and spun him toward the dining room. He had a glimpse of her plump face as she called out, "Gentlemen, I want y'all to meet Reverend Sylvester Pomfret from St. Louis!" Conversation stopped in midmouthful and the entire table turned and stared at Jake. There were at least twenty and Jake knew most of them, including Whit Hennessey, the postmaster, and the red-faced man with the enormous nose sitting down at the end of the table: E. Thurmond Broadus of the Foot-Pleasure Company of St. Louis.

"Reverend Pomfret had a vision," Mrs. Grayson announced. And then, spying Broadus, she said, "Of course, here's somebody you know already. Mr. Broadus come in on the early train."

Broadus stared at Jake, then guffawed. "Hell, that ain't no reverend, that sonofabitch is Jake Tibbetts."

The rest of them began to snicker, and then Whit Hennessey said, "Jake, you takin' up a new line of work?"

"What?" Mrs. Grayson jerked her head back and forth, confused, and her ears began to turn red.

"He runs the newspaper," Whit added.

"But he said he had a vision," Mrs. Grayson insisted.

"Hallucination is more like it," E. Thurmond Broadus said helpfully.

"Local!" said Mrs. Grayson, indignant, as if he had peed on the floor. "You get the hell out of here! And don't come back!" She gave him a shove.

Jake glared at them, clamped his hat on his head, and said, "Horseshit." Only it came out as a tiny croak from the depths of his stricken throat. Then he turned on his heel and stalked out, leaving the breakfast table at the Regal Hotel awash with gales of laughter. His ears burned. I have made of myself, he thought, an Absolute Ass. If I keep this up, I will become an Absolute Damfool, and there is nothing to be more pitied. What the hell. I will go live at the newspaper.

━━━━━━━━

Lonnie was waiting for him at the front door of the newspaper office, bundled in flannel jacket, knit cap and mittens, holding a small paper sack in his hand.

"Where you been?" Lonnie demanded.

"Doing the Lord's work," Jake croaked. He was beginning

to get a little of his voice back, but his throat burned like fire and his overstuffed head throbbed.

"What?"

"Never mind."

"What's wrong with your voice? You sound like a frog."

"I've got a cold," Jake rasped irritably.

"Did you sleep outside last night?"

Jake ignored it, fished the key out of his pocket, and unlocked the door. "Come on in."

'I'd love to," Lonnie said. "I'm freezing. I been standing out here waiting on you about five hours."

Inside, Jake pulled up the shade on the front window, letting the strong gray light into the front office, then lit the kerosene stove in the corner. Lonnie watched him silently, still bundled, sack in hand.

Jake turned to him and pointed at the sack. "You bring me something?" he growled.

"Naw. That's my lunch. I come to work. Mama Pastine says it's okay. She says if I'll stick to newspapering and not pay any attention to your foolishness, she don't mind."

Jake nodded. "Well, take your coat off."

They both took their coats off and hung them on the rack next to the door and Lonnie put his lunch bag down on Jake's desk, and then they stood there and looked at each other for a moment.

"Well?" Lonnie said finally.

"Well, what?"

"You gonna teach me to be a newspaperman or what?"

Sweet Jesus! Why the hell would anybody want to be a newspaperman? It was proof positive of the strain of madness that curdled the blood of the Tibbettses.

"You can start," Jake said, "by sweeping up."

"What?" Lonnie looked incredulous.

"Now listen," Jake said evenly. "I can hardly talk and I ain't going to waste any words on you. If you want to be a newspaperman, start at the floor and work your way up. Start at the front door and sweep to the back."

Lonnie put his hands on his hips and glared at Jake for a moment, then shrugged. "Awright. Where's the broom?" Jake glared back, and finally Lonnie waved his arms and said, "Awright. Awright. I'll find it myself."

Lonnie banged around in the back shop and after a moment

he came back with the broom and started sweeping, making a great show of getting into every nook and cranny. When he had finished with the front office and moved into the back shop, Jake slumped in his swivel chair, opened the bottom drawer of the desk, and got out the jar of Lightnin' Jim's Best and took a small swig. He winced as it burned his raw throat and settled like molten lava in his empty stomach. After a moment, his throat felt a little better and he took a couple of more swallows and put the jar away.

He surveyed the wreckage of his desk, piled high with mail unopened, stacks of correspondence unanswered, bills unpaid, things undone. It was the backwash of his business, the place where he put things that had little to do with actually getting out a newspaper. It was, in fact, more Pastine's domain than his own. She came at least once a week, spent an afternoon rustling busily through the stacks, extricating the bills and writing out checks from the thick checkbook she kept in the lower right-hand drawer, mailing out subscription renewal notices, collecting the checks and cash that people sent him, and making a weekly bank deposit. She tended to the most immediate and critical paperwork, stacking the rest for Jake to peruse when and if he took a notion. But just look at it now. She had been here only last Thursday. Or was it Tuesday? Already it was a mess. And God only knew when Pastine Tibbetts would be here again. Maybe never. The paper would pile up until it covered the top of the desk entirely, then spill over onto the floor and grow and grow until it blocked the front door and he had to conduct business entirely from the rear entrance. But it was not anything he, Jake Tibbetts, could handle. He was a newspaperman, by God, not a business tycoon. He must get help.

Then he thought again of the war memorial, or more particularly, what he ought to do about it. That he *would* do something about it there was no question. He would not back down on this the way he had already backed down once this week, when Rosh Benefield had called in an ancient debt. There were no old debts associated with this business of the war memorial. He had it stuck in his craw, and now he had to make a public issue of it, and that meant speaking through the voice of the newspaper. But how to say it? It nagged at him like a toothache, but words wouldn't come. It would just have to fester awhile longer.

"Awright. What next?" Lonnie stood in the passageway between the low partitions that divided the front office from the back shop, leaning against the broom.

"You finished?"

"Yessir."

"Front to back?"

"Top to bottom. Your voice sounds better." Lonnie sniffed, turned up his nose. "You been drinking that old whiskey."

Jake leaned forward in the chair. "Yes, by God, I've been drinking that old whiskey. And if you want to become a newspaperman, you keep your nose out of the personal habits of the editor."

Lonnie cocked his head to one side and gave him a quizzical look. "Well, if you're finished drinking whiskey, what's next?"

Jake stood up and scratched at his crotch, where he was beginning to itch badly from lack of a bath. "Next is, you gotta learn how to set type." Lonnie's face lit up. "Come on." Jake led him to the back shop, where the type cases were stacked in their cabinets against the wall next to a layout table. He slid one of the wooden cases out of its niche and placed it on the table. The pieces of type, black with years of use, lay jumbled in their compartments, separated by thin wooden partitions. Jake picked up a single piece of type. "Type," he said. "What letter?"

"It's a *d*," Lonnie said, looking at the end of it.

"Wrong. It's a *b*. Type is backwards when you look at it. You set it backwards. Right to left."

"Like Chinese," Lonnie said.

"Like what?"

"Chinese. They write backwards."

"Well, sort of. Anyway, it's backwards and you set it backwards, so that when you turn it upside down and print it on a piece of paper, it comes out right. Now." He tossed the piece of type back into its compartment. "Type comes in all sorts of sizes and styles. Big and little, plain and fancy. This here is twenty-four-point Bodoni Bold. Different types for different jobs. Boldface for headlines and ads. Fancy styles with little squiggles on 'em for the society page. But you'll get all that later." Jake stopped, caught his breath, swallowed hard. Speaking was an agony. "First you learn the layout of a type case. Anything strike your eye right off the bat?"

"It's dirty," Lonnie answered promptly.

"It's got ink on it," Jake said. "What else?"

''The compartments ain't all the same size.''

''Bingo. God, my throat is killing me.'' He was seized by a fit of coughing that doubled him over and scalded his throat like a hot poker. ''Be right back,'' he gasped, and stumbled to the front office, where he took another healthy slug of Lightnin' Jim's Best, blew his nose mightily on the dirty handkerchief from his back pocket, and composed himself.

Back at the type case, he said, ''Now where were we?''

''The compartments. They ain't all the same size.''

''Aren't.''

''That's right.''

Jake glared at him a moment. ''Now why do you reckon that is?''

Lonnie studied the type case. ''There's more of some pieces than others.''

''Why?''

''I don't know.''

''Which ones have more pieces?''

Lonnie picked up a piece of type from one of the larger compartments. *''E.''* He examined another. ''And *a.''*

''Right,'' Jake said. ''You use more *e*'s and *a*'s making words. And lots of *s*'s and *o*'s and *t*'s. But not many *z*'s and *q*'s.''

Lonnie picked over the type, then looked up at Jake. ''Why don't they have the letters in order? Here's the *a*'s up here and the *b*'s way over here.''

''There's no rhyme or reason to a type case except what I just said. A type case was designed by a drunk German who was blind in one eye.''

''Then how do you know what's where?'' Lonnie demanded.

''You just learn it,'' Jake said. ''You learn it so well you can set type drunk and blind, which is the way many a printer has done it through the ages. Now I want you to go back yonder and get a piece of poster board off that stack''—Jake pointed to the back wall, where the paper was stacked—''and I want you to draw a layout of this type case. Then I want you to put in all the letters and numbers and punctuation marks and such. And then I want you to set the Gettysburg Address in twenty-four-point Bodoni Bold.''

''Holy cow,'' Lonnie exploded. ''How'm I gonna do that? I don't even know the Gettysburg Address.''

''Find it.''

"Where?"

"That's your business."

Lonnie thought. "The library?"

Jake shrugged. "Sounds good enough." He showed Lonnie how to hold a type stick in his left hand and drop the individual pieces of type into it one by one, *click-click*, right to left, until they became words, separating each word with a blank piece, filling an entire line with words and spaces and then lifting the line out between two long metal slugs and placing it in a form that Jake set up for him next to the case.

"Now," Jake said. "Got it?"

"I reckon." Lonnie looked a little glum.

"What's the matter?"

"Aw, nothing."

"Huh?"

"Well, this ain't what I thought it would be like."

Jake scratched his crotch again. God, he needed a bath. That was the next order of business. A bath. And a shave. And another little nip of Lightnin' Jim's Best, which was already working wonders on his cold.

"Look," he rasped. "What a newspaperman does is turn words into print. You can have all the great words in the world, and if you can't turn 'em into print, nobody's gonna see 'em. And if nobody sees 'em, you got no newspaper. Abe Lincoln's Gettysburg Address would have been forgotten in an hour if some newspaperman hadn't written it down and turned it into print. Just pretend you're that newspaperman, listening to old Abe there on the battlefield with the guidons whipping in the breeze and the soldiers gathered around close with their hats over their hearts. And you there, preserving his words for posterity."

He could see the idea take hold in Lonnie's head. "I reckon I better go to the library first." He headed for the front door.

"Hey, whoa, wait a minute." Jake caught him. "Put on your jacket and your cap and mittens."

"Aw . . ."

"Aw, nothing. You want to go home with pneumonia and have your Mama Pastine put you to bed?"

"Nosir."

"And here," Jake fumbled in the middle drawer of his desk, found what he wanted in the back, under a pile of pens, pencils, paper clips, junk. "Here's a key." He handed it to Lonnie. "I'm gonna go get myself cleaned up, and I may not be here when you get back. Just let yourself in and get to work. And put on one of those aprons back there so you don't get ink on your clothes."

Lonnie held the key in his mittened hand for a moment, staring at it as if it were gold instead of tarnished brass.

"You keep it," Jake said. "You can't be a newspaperman if you don't have a key to the newspaper office."

Lonnie grinned and bolted out the door, and Jake stood in the open doorway and watched him, sneakers flying, until he turned the corner at the end of the block and headed for the library.

He went back inside and got the jar of Lightnin' Jim's Best out of the drawer of his desk and drained what was left, a half-inch or so, letting it trickle down his throat so that it both burned and soothed the raw membranes. His head still felt like an over-stuffed parlor cushion, but the whiskey had considerably eased his misery. In fact, he was beginning to feel positively fine. Maybe even better than fine. Maybe a little foolhardy, like he might be ready to piss into the wind.

He put the empty fruit jar back into the desk next to two other empties and reminded himself that he needed to take them to Lightnin' Jim's the next time he went. It would make the crotchety old sonofabitch easier to deal with if he got some empty jars back. He was always complaining about not having enough jars, about how the war had caught him short. He was always glowering at you and saying, "Don't you white folks know there's a war on?"

Jake slammed the drawer shut, then locked up and walked the two blocks to Rosh Benefield's office, carrying the sack of supplies Lonnie had brought him the day before. The sign on Rosh's front door said he was at the courthouse, so Jake opened the unlocked door and took Rosh's key to the fire station from its hook inside.

He crossed the square at a brisk pace, holding his paper sack as if it contained the heads of vanquished foes, and fired off a jaunty greeting to everybody in sight. They gaped at him, amazed that he had the gall to show his face in public after having made an Absolute Ass of himself. He could see people peering out of the front windows of the stores at him as he cut

across the courthouse lawn, legs pumping. *There goes the lunatic. And what in blazes do you reckon he's got in that paper
sack? You heard the latest, of course. Yes, a preacher, for God's
sake.* He waved and smiled, wondering if he should slobber a
bit for effect.

He went around back in the alleyway behind the fire station,
let himself in the rear door, lit the heater in the small locker
room behind the bay where the pumper sat, took off his clothes,
and turned on the shower. He stepped under the stinging spray
and let it blast his body for a while, washing away the grime
and embarrassment of three days of uncleanliness. He soaped
himself twice, cleansing every pore, then turned off the water
and stepped out. He had no towel, so he dried himself on the
shirt he had just taken off, dressed in fresh clothes, and got out
his brush, mug, and straight razor and shaved carefully. He
looked at himself in the mirror for a moment, turned his head
this way and that, and decided that he looked just fine. Damn
fine, in fact.

Thus cleansed and refreshed, he locked up and paraded again
across the square to the Jitney Jungle Super Saver for supplies.
He bought a package of sliced bologna and another of cheese,
a loaf of white bread, two cans of sardines, a box of saltine
crackers, a small jar of mayonnaise, and a bottle of olives. He
knew the olives would give him heartburn, and that's why Pastine never kept them in the house. But he was no longer under
Pastine's roof, and he loved olives, and if he was going to have
to live at the newspaper, he would by God have olives with his
lunch. Anybody who looked and felt this damned fine should
have a jar of olives if he wanted them. Jake stood in front of the
butcher case whistling tunelessly while George Poulos sliced
and wrapped his bologna and cheese in self-conscious silence.
Then he carried the items to the front counter, where George
totted up the bill by hand on the back of a paper sack and put
the groceries inside.

"Did you hear about the sonofabitch that tried to pass himself
off as a preacher from St. Louis over at the Regal?" Jake asked
as he handed over his money. George almost choked.

It was past noon by the time he got back to the newspaper
office, and Lonnie was hunched over his work in the back shop,
face screwed up with concentration as he drew an outline of the
type case on a piece of poster board, a hand-copied Gettysburg

Address beside him on the layout table. Lonnie stopped and they spread out their lunches on a corner of Jake's littered desk and discussed the relative merits of store-bought versus homemade mayonnaise (Pastine made her own) while they ate, washing down their sandwiches, sardines, and olives with tap water from the sink in back, drunk from the tumblers Jake kept in his bottom desk drawer. Jake ate happily, and when he finished he belched with pleasure, tasting the tartness of the olives already doing mischief in his full belly.

"Whatcha gonna do with the rest of that food you bought?" Lonnie asked as he folded the wax paper from his sandwich and stuck it back in the paper sack he had brought from home. "You leave it laying around in here and it'll spoil and you'll get the toe mange."

"The what?"

"You know, the stomach poison."

"Ptomaine poisoning."

"That's what I said. Toe mange."

There were still several slices of bologna left and most of the bread and cheese, more than enough for his supper. "I'll stick it in the window by the back door," Jake said. "It'll stay cold enough."

It brought him crashing back to earth, just that simple little thing about what to do with uneaten food. Gad, the whole business was complicated. Half the day was gone and he still hadn't made any provisions for sleeping tonight. He had spied an old cot and mattress at the fire station, but he would have to go back and get Rosh's key again later in the afternoon and haul the thing over here to the newspaper office. And he didn't have any sheets or blankets, so he would have to bundle up in his overcoat and leave the kerosene heater on all night. Then tomorrow there would be a whole new set of domestic details to worry with. He didn't feel so damned fine anymore.

"Time's wasting," he said, getting to his feet. "I got a newspaper to get out, and you got to tell the nation what Old Abe said at Gettysburg."

They went back to their work, Lonnie laboring over the type case, Jake firing up the Linotype and wading into the stack of copy that had to be set into metal. He was a half-day behind and it would be late into the night before he got it set, proofed, and laid out in the forms he would have to load onto the big Kluge press by noon tomorrow to print the paper.

He stopped at midafternoon and walked over to the layout table where Lonnie was slowly, methodically, fitting pieces of type into the type stick. *Click-click.* Lonnie looked up from his work. There was a smudge of ink on his forehead where he had wiped it with a grimy hand. "How's it going?" Jake asked.

"He sure did talk a lot."

"One of the shortest speeches a politician ever made." Jake pulled his watch out of his pocket and flipped open the cover. "Three o'clock," he said, "time for you to knock off."

"Do I hafta?"

"Yep. You don't want to burn yourself out in one day. Go get washed up."

Jake was back at the Linotype when Lonnie finished scrubbing himself and he stood behind Jake for a moment, watching him punch the keys. Jake finished the line, then took one of the slugs he had set a few minutes before out of the tray on the machine. It was still warm to the touch. He handed it to Lonnie. "See what's on there?"

"Type."

"Just like you set. This machine does exactly the same thing you're doing over there, only it won't set anything any larger than eighteen-point. But it's all the same. Turning words into metal so you can put 'em on paper."

Lonnie looked over the Linotype, top to bottom. "Can you print anything you want to?"

"Within reason. I try to stick approximately with fact. Let me see your hands."

Lonnie showed him. He still had the smudge on his forehead.

"Not bad. A newspaperman is never one hundred percent clean. But you'll do."

"You smell a lot better yourself," Lonnie said.

Jake grunted. "Coming back tomorrow?"

"I reckon. I can't leave Old Abe in the middle of his speech."

"Okay. You know I've got to get out the paper tomorrow. I can't spend a lot of time with you until that's done."

"That's all right."

Jake looked at him for a long moment. "You can quit anytime you want to." Lonnie didn't say anything. "I didn't have any choice when I was your age or a little older. I had to work here, and I didn't like it a bit.''

''You didn't? Then why are you doing it now?''

Jake smiled. ''I tried it again later and decided I liked it. So there's nothing wrong with you deciding now that it's not for you.''

''I reckon I'll try it some more.''

''As long as your Mama Pastine thinks it's okay.''

Lonnie studied him for a moment. ''You want me to tell her anything for you?''

''No.''

''Okay.''

When he had gone, Jake sat there at the Linotype keyboard for a while, remembering how he had, ages ago, stood sullenly at the same layout table where Lonnie had been working all day, hating the meaningless jumble of the type case, hating the smell of the place and the grime under his fingernails, hating Albertis Tibbetts for being a haunted man who hid from his demons in a darkened room, pacing, pacing. Then he remembered another sullen boy, Henry, standing at the type case, eyes glazed in befuddlement, hands clumsily trying to fit pieces of type into a type stick, and then just standing there and staring for a long time until finally Jake went over and took the type stick out of his hand and told him to go home. He remembered his great disappointment, the empty ache the boy had left when the front door had closed.

Jake shook his head forcefully, thrusting the images away. He looked toward the front window and saw that the gray afternoon was waning fast. He still had the society page to do. And something about the war memorial. It would be a long night.

———

He had quite lost track of the time when he heard the rattling at the front door. He peered through the pool of light around the Linotype machine into the darkness of the front office and saw the door open and the great bulk of Rosh Benefield fill the door-way.

''Rosh?'' he called.

''Do you know anybody else this size?''

Jake got up from the Linotype and pulled his watch out of his pocket. It was after eight o'clock. Four hours had passed since

Lonnie had left and he had been totally absorbed in his typesetting, punching page after page of copy through the keyboard, pausing only to remove the finished type and restoke the machine with metal ingots and relight the cigar he finally felt good enough to smoke. Galleys of bright metal slugs sat waiting on a table nearby for proofing.

"Well, don't just stand there with the door open," Jake said.

"I'm waiting for you to come help me." Rosh disappeared into the darkness and Jake followed him outside and felt the sudden bite of cold air. The sky was clearing and there was a half-moon winking behind the scudding wisps of cloud. There would be a hard freeze tonight. He thought suddenly of Pastine, of the unwrapped pipes outside the kitchen window, wondered fleetingly if he should call and remind her to leave the faucets dripping overnight . . .

Rosh was standing by his Packard, which was parked against the curb, the trunk open and some kind of contraption sticking out. Jake stepped closer and recognized it as the camp cot he had seen earlier in the day in the fire station. Gad. He had completely forgotten about sleeping arrangements. And here was Rosh Benefield with the cot in the back of his car.

"Well, are you going to help me, or do I have to tote it in for you, too?"

They wrestled it out of the trunk of the car and carried it inside, then went back and got the thin mattress that was on the floorboard of the back seat and set the whole business up next to the paper stacks in the back room. By the time they finished, Rosh was grunting with the effort and his forehead was speckled with shiny beads of sweat.

"I'm too old and fat for honest work," Rosh said, pulling a handkerchief out of his back pocket and mopping his brow. He fixed Jake with his small bright eyes. "And you have the look of a man who is fresh out of whiskey."

"Right on both counts," Jake said.

"Well, I thought of that, too." Rosh huffed out the door and came back with a paper sack and sat down heavily in the chair next to Jake's desk, his overcoat flapping open to give his great belly room, while Jake turned on the light in the front office and pulled the shades on the windows. Rosh set the sack down with a soft thump on the desk and sighed. "You'll have to do the rest, my good man. I'm tuckered out."

Jake sat in his own swivel chair and got two tumblers out of the bottom drawer, opened the sack and took out the full jar of Lightnin' Jim's Best, its clear beautiful liquid laced through with a rainbow of colors, fracturing the light from the overhead bulb. He opened the jar and poured three fingers in each tumbler and handed Rosh one; then they lifted their glasses in a silent toast and drank.

"You're a day early," Jake said.

"No, I'm a day late." Rosh wiped his mouth with a huge hand.

Jake grunted. "I assume the rabble are having an exquisite time with my . . . er . . . circumstances."

Rosh nodded. "You couldn't get a man, woman, child, nor beast in town to vouch for your sanity." He smiled. "I think Reverend Sylvester Pomfret put the cork stopper in the bottle, so to speak."

"God be praised," Jake said.

They drank in silence for a while, savoring the whiskey slowly, while Jake thought how many times they had sat here in the shank of a midweek day in this musty, cluttered office, how the ritual of it connected all the years they had been friends and broached the times when they might not have been. There were many reasons why they should not have shared so many fruit jars of Lightnin' Jim's Best for such a long time. There was Ideal Benefield, who did not cotton to drinking or to Jake Tibbetts. There was the anguish of Henry and Hazel, deadened by time to a dull ache. And there was most basically the fact of who they were and what they represented—Rosh the mayor, the lawyer, the pillar of the community; and Jake, who threw rocks at everything. But the simple fact of the matter was that they liked each other and they liked good whiskey and they agreed on a few basic things that ought to guide how a man acts—honesty, diligence, grace. So they created inviolable pockets of time in which they shucked off all their trappings and became just Rosh and Jake, whiskey drinkers.

"It must be fairly good whiskey," Rosh said, taking a sip and raising his glass to let the light play on it. "We've drunk enough of it to have long ago discovered any inadequacy."

"It may not be any good at all," Jake countered. "But it is consistent. I've often wondered why everybody calls it Lightnin' Jim's Best. Is there a Lightnin' Jim's Worst?"

"If there is, I hope it never touches my lips." Rosh smacked his lips. "Perhaps this is simply the best whiskey there is around here."

"It's the *only* whiskey there is around here."

"Well," said Rosh, "there you have it. Maybe it's just right. If it were any better, Lightnin' Jim would be selling it to city folks. If it were any worse, it would have killed us."

"Do you know what that sonofabitch told me Sunday?"

"No, what?"

"He said he's getting out of the business. He said he's the last of the line. That little 'un of his. Jim's going to send him to college up north and let him manage real estate."

"Oh?" Rosh didn't seem surprised.

"Jim says he's got holdings in Buffalo, New York, of all places. Now how the hell does a bootlegging nigger buy real estate in Buffalo, New York?"

Rosh took a long sip of the whiskey. "It helps if he's got a good lawyer."

It took a moment for it to sink in. "You?"

Rosh shrugged his massive shoulders. "I can't, of course, divulge any details of a lawyer-client relationship."

"But why you?"

"He pays on time."

"Well, why Buffalo, New York?"

"I don't know. Maybe he read about it in a magazine."

"Well, I'll be damned." Jake reached and got the whiskey jar, splashed another couple of fingers into their glasses. "I'll be damned," he said again. It was a part of Rosh Benefield he knew little about—who his clients were, what he did for them, what secrets he kept locked away in his safe and in his rich, curious mind. People no doubt trusted Rosh with their most private thoughts and deeds. And Rosh, the great Buddha, sat unblinking as they bared their souls, committed to his keeping their foulest sins.

"What a moral hell-pit," Jake said out loud.

"What's that?"

"Being a lawyer. People ridicule lawyers for being greedy connivers. Maybe they ought to pity you for what you know."

Rosh shifted in his chair, a mountain moving. In a lesser man it would have been a squirm. "Quite unlike your own profession."

"Yes."

"You plumb for man's most private indiscretions and then trumpet them from the steeple top."

"I often say," Jake said, "that man's avarice is exceeded only by his curiosity. And man is never more curious than he is about the avarice of others. I'm simply in the curiosity business."

"You must admit," Rosh raised his eyebrows, "that you newspaper people feed off the bottom, so to speak—mayhem, despair, misfortune . . ." he waved his hand, indicating the ills of mankind.

"True. But we can unburden ourselves. You can't." It brought to mind his vague notions of Catholicism, of the dim flicker of candles in great arched rooms, of the tortured utterances of the confession box.

"What do you do when a scoundrel walks in?" Jake demanded.

"Represent him," Rosh said. "The fact that he's a scoundrel doesn't make him any less worthy of representation."

"But. . ."

Rosh cut him short. "Don't think it doesn't cause an occasional upheaval of my bowels. I once said to myself, 'Rosh Benefield, you are either a pedant or a sophist. You either take refuge in rules or you fool yourself with fallacious argument.' And I quit the profession for several hours."

"For several hours!" Jake snorted.

"Yes, and don't snort." He sat there for a while, staring at his glass, then drank off what was left in the bottom. "I'll tell you a story, Jake Tibbetts, and then you can snort if you want to." He paused again. "A woman came to me once and asked me to help her deceive her husband. It was"—he waved his hand again—"nothing of an amorous nature. She, ah, wanted to relieve the husband of a potential distraction, let's say." He looked at his glass again, then thrust it toward Jake. Jake poured and Rosh took a long swig. "To go on. It was a small deception. The woman had the best possible intentions. I had been privy to far greater evil on the part of others. But it came at a peculiar time, when I had started to fear for my own integrity and sanity. I told the woman I'd have to think about it. Then when she left— it was late in the day—I locked the door to my office and got very drunk. And sometime during the early evening I took a pistol out of my desk drawer and pressed it to my temple. And then do you know what I did?''

"You blew your brains out," Jake said.

"I thought about you."

"You blew my brains out."

"No, dammit, you smart-assed sonofabitch!" Rosh exploded. Jake was stunned. Rosh rarely raised his voice and he never cussed. He looked hard at his friend and he could see that Rosh was deeply moved. This was something very important to him, something so private and delicate and yet so momentous that the urge to tell and the urge to keep faith with a secret warred in his great body and soul.

"I'm sorry," Jake said, chastened.

"I thought," Rosh went on after a moment, when he had calmed himself, "about something you had said. You said a man had to take complete responsibility for himself, that he had to take his life in his own hands and shake it for all it's worth. I thought about that, Jake. I thought about it real hard. Then I looked down the barrel of that gun and I said to myself, 'This isn't taking responsibility. This is just taking off.' So I put the gun away and went home."

There was a long, heavy silence, and finally Jake asked, "And what did you do about the woman?''

"I did what she asked me to do. There was nothing illegal about it, nothing any other lawyer wouldn't do as a professional service. There were some personal qualms, but I decided I would let them be her qualms, not mine. And since then, I've refused to assume anybody else's guilt. I decided that if I could take responsibility for myself, I could expect everybody else to do the same."

"But they won't," Jake interjected.

"Some will. Sometimes. And some won't. But that's their problem, not mine. Anyway, since then I have slept like a saint. And you," he smiled, "what you said, Jake, saved my life."

"My God," Jake said softly.

"I only wish," Rosh said, "that you believed it."

"What?"

"Just words, Jake." Rosh waved his glass, sloshing the whiskey. It caught the light of the overhead bulb and gave off a shimmer of tiny amber explosions. "You don't really believe what you say about a man taking responsibility for himself. If you did, you wouldn't try to tote other folks' guilt around like a peddler's sack. You'd let other folks do their own toting.''

After a moment, Jake said, "You mean Henry."

"Mainly."

"Well, to hell with Henry. I haven't thought about Henry in two years. Maybe longer.''

Rosh laughed. "You put on a big show, Jake. You damn him, you disown him, but you carry Henry around on your shoulders, trying not to let the rest of us see how it makes you stoop.''

Jake opened the fruit jar and poured another dollop of whiskey in their glasses. He was a little drunk. His eyebrows were turning numb. He could feel the whiskey like a thin film between himself and the room, wrapping him in a cocoon. He took a small sip. "You're full of shit," he said.

Rosh drank, then set his glass down on the desk. "Am I? Think about it. Think of everything you've done, everything that's happened to you since the day before Christmas. Starting with Billy's plane landing out on Partridge Road. Think about it, Jake, and then tell me you don't have Henry stuck in your gut like a tumor.''

"You think I'm a goddamn fool, don't you," Jake said bitterly from behind the whiskey film. "You think I ought to forgive Henry everything he's done and tuck my tail between my legs and skulk home to Pastine.'' He was slurring his words now and that made him angry. "And you think I ought to stop stirring up trouble about the goddamn war memorial.''

"God forbid," Rosh sighed, "that I should ever tell a man what he *ought* to do. I just wish you'd follow your own advice.''

"Well," Jake said stubbornly, "I'm not going home. She ran me out of the house with my grandfather's sword, for God's sake. She almost cut my head off.''

Rosh nodded. "That she did.''

"And I am going to have to live here at the newspaper office, just like she told me to do, because I can't find anyplace else and have made an ass of myself at the Regal Hotel.''

"Well . . .''

"And the war memorial . . .'' he trailed off. "Well, to hell with all of it anyway.''

Rosh drew his overcoat over his belly as if protecting himself from the fierceness of Jake's scowl, and then he got up from the chair with a great effort. "A fat man is a menace to himself," he said. "A fat drunk man is a menace to the world."

"Why don't you just kiss my ass," Jake said.

"I can't bend over that far anymore," Rosh said pleasantly. "Can you drive?"

"Of course I can drive. Whether I can drive home or not, that's the question. But since you won't drive—God, you're a backward man, Jake—I'll have to make the attempt. Why don't you get a car, for Christ's sake." He lumbered out the door, leaving Jake sitting there at the desk, and after a while Jake heard the engine of the Packard start up, the clashing of gears, a series of sharp squeals as Rosh drove herky-jerky away from the curb and headed down the street. Jake sat listening until the sound of the engine died away. There was so much of Rosh that he left a great yawning emptiness in the room. Then Jake remembered that he had never thanked Rosh for the cot.

He got up presently and went to the back shop, where the Linotype machine waited for him in the pool of light, hissing and creaking. It was a molten maw into which you poured your soul. He sat down in the chair with a groan, thinking of his grandfather, Captain Finley—how he had come here early on Tuesday mornings in the days before the Linotype machine and set all the type by hand with a jar of a long-dead Lightnin' Jim's Best beside him, curling up on the floor in a stupor when he finished. He would like to have known the old bastard, known what private demons inhabited the dark recesses of his mind, and more importantly, how Captain Finley kept them at bay. One thing about it, demons didn't go away just because you were drunk.

Jake fished in the pocket of his shirt for a fresh cigar and a match, lit it, and jammed it into the corner of his mouth. He belched around the cigar, tasting whiskey and olives. Then he started setting type because tomorrow he had to get out a newspaper, drunk or not.

He worked for a long time, forgetting Rosh Benefield, forgetting Henry, forgetting everything but the words on the pages before him and seeing them only as words, not thoughts. He set tray after tray of type, carrying them hot from the machine to the proofing table, pulling proof sheets and marking them, making the corrections. It was the point where the mechanical part of being a newspaperman took over, where Jake the writer gave up his words. As long as the copy was in his Underwood, he worried it like a dog with a bone, agonizing over phrase and syntax, x-ing out, rewording, slashing angrily with his thick black pencil until the paper was virtually unreadable—all a vain, maddening effort to say something just right for a change. But once he committed the copy to the Linotype, that was that. There was something about casting the words in metal that gave them—wise or foolish—a permanence that you didn't tinker with. The words now belonged to the newspaper, to that entity that you both created and were enslaved to. If there were such a thing as heaven, it would be a place where newspaper editors wrote with perfect clarity and wit and grace, and where nobody took issue with what they said.

He set type until his whole body ached and sagged with fatigue, and when the final page was set and proofed and corrected, he stopped and looked at his watch and saw that it was nearly midnight. He would have to be up again in six hours, laying out the final four pages of the paper and locking them into the heavy forms to put on the Kluge.

It was all done, all except the thing he had been putting off for two days now.

He thought about it for a long time and he thought about what Rosh Benefield had said about a man taking responsibility for himself. He made up his mind finally and decided to compose it directly on the Linotype machine so that there would be no rewriting, no editing, no turning back. He typed:

AN EDITORIAL

The *Free Press* is unalterably opposed to the erection of a War Memorial in this community.

Those who favor such a monument do so with only the most honorable intentions. They see it as a testament to the bravery and dedication of those who serve in the present conflict, especially those who have died.

The *Free Press* thinks otherwise. No monument can honor warriors without honoring war itself. And war is dishonorable.

Let the Germans and the Japanese erect War Memorials. They made the war. Let us get on with the Peace.

He set it without error in two-column slugs that would fit in the space in the upper left-hand corner of the second page, where there had not been an editorial in more than forty years.

Then he went to bed.

THREE

*T*HE weather cleared over Belgium and Luxembourg on Christmas Day, 1944, and as the year ended, so did the great German offensive in the Ardennes forest that came to be known as the Battle of the Bulge. With the clearing weather came the American Army Air Corps—first, General Pete Quesada's P-38s and B-25s, tactical support for George Patton's Third Army, which was driving to relieve the embattled garrison at Bastogne; then "Toohey" Spaatz's big bombers that rained tons of high explosives on the German positions.

But by the time the Air Corps came, the battle was decided. The infantry had done it. They were by now gaunt, hollow-eyed men, frozen and exhausted, numbed from fear and noise and physical misery. But all along the great bulge the Germans had made in their lines, they held—at the bloody ridge guarding Elsenborn at the north; at the blasted village of Bastogne in the south; at Foy—Notre Dame, the tip of the advance, a few miles from the Meuse River that was Hitler's initial target. Two things happened to the Germans: They were outfought and they ran out of gasoline. When a German unit abandoned its vehicles on the road leading to Foy—Notre Dame, the Americans found the tanks all but dry. Hitler's last desperate gamble had failed. The carnage was appalling.

By January 4 of the new year, the Americans had begun to take back the ground they had lost.

Thus it was that a small patrol from a unit of the 82nd Airborne Division came to the clearing on a hillside not far from St. Vith, where Lieutenant Henry Tibbetts and thirty of his men had made their pitiful stand against the German attack.

There were seven of them, led by a nineteen-year-old sergeant from Moncks Corner, South Carolina. He was miserably tired and cold and he would carry the chill of the Ardennes snow in his bones for the rest of his life. But he led the patrol, as many nineteen-year-old sergeants did on that day, because the battle had taken a terrible toll of junior officers. So he tried to keep his numbed senses alert because he had the lives of six other men in his keeping.

He saw the tank first, slewed up on its side against a big rock, its paint blistered from the *Panzerfaust* that had ripped a hole in the side of the turret and turned the tank's innards into a blinding hell. Now it was just a frozen piece of junk. And good cover for an ambush. He dropped to the snow, bringing his M-1 to the ready, and heard the rest of them scattering and hitting the deck behind him. He lay there for a while, looking it over—the ruined tank, the dark lumps in the snow of the clearing. It was awesomely quiet, as if the war had gone on ahead and left them and this white-crusted place in an eddy of time. Then a gust of wind moaned through the tops of the huge fir trees and he started as a clump of snow fell from one of the branches and plopped in an explosion of white. He stifled the urge to fire, to empty a clip into the clearing, where the snow had fallen on the dark lumps. He swallowed the hard ball of fear in his throat and rose to a half-crouch and sprinted for the tank, flattening himself low against the side. He looked back and saw the others watching him, waiting. He pointed to one man and then to a fallen log at the edge of the clearing, showing him where to go. When the man hesitated, the sergeant jerked his arm impatiently, and the man got up and ran low to the ground, his boots crunching holes in the hard crust of the snow, and sprawled behind the log. The sergeant moved the rest of them up the same way, one by one, until they were all in position with the clearing in their field of fire. Then he took a deep breath and eased around the edge of the tank, sweeping the clearing with his rifle, seeing nothing but the snow and the dark lumps, seeing that it was a killing ground.

The sergeant stood up and motioned them in and they rose and came slowly, warily, seeing for the first time what he had seen in the clearing.

"Jeez," one of them said, a kid from Idaho. "There must be fifty of 'em."

"They had a helluva fight."

"Check 'em," the sergeant said.

They made a circle of the clearing, turning over the hard-frozen bodies, avoiding their unblinking eyes.

"One-oh-sixth Division," one of them called, examining the patch on a jacket.

"Yeah, those bastards took an ass-kicking," another one said.

"They were green," said a corporal from Toledo. "First time in action and they lost half the fuckin' division."

"Most of these guys been shot in the head," the kid from Idaho murmured. "Bastards."

They gathered by the tank and hunkered in the snow, lit cigarettes, while the sergeant made his own check. He counted twenty-nine bodies, all but two of them Americans. Then he pulled out the map he was carrying inside his shirt and marked the place so he could report it when they got back from the patrol. Graves Registration would be along in a few days.

"How much farther we going?" the corporal asked him when he put the map away.

" 'Til we find something," he said.

"Ain't nothing to find. The Krauts are gone. Hell, they're probably over there"—the corporal indicated the general direction of the German lines—"inside getting warm. We're still out here in the fuckin' snow trying to find 'em." He spat a stream of tobacco juice from the wad he had tucked in his cheek, making a brown stain on the snow at his feet. The sergeant said nothing.

The kid from Idaho raised his head. "They're probably high-tailing it to Berlin."

"They're finished," one of the others said—an older man, twenty-five perhaps. He was tall and thin and wore glasses. He had been to college for a year before he became a paratrooper and he thought a lot about things before he opened his mouth. "They may hold out another month or so, but this was it." He looked around at the rest of them. "What you want to do now is try to keep from getting your ass shot off while we mop up." They nodded. "And hope we don't have to fight the Russians."

"Do what?"

"I heard the captain say the other day that we might as well go ahead and whip the Russians while we're here. He said we'll have to do it sooner or later."

"The Russians are crazy," the corporal said, and spat another thin stream of tobacco juice. "I heard stories. I heard one of their tank commanders has got strings of what look like dried peppers draped around the turret of his tank. They're German peckers."

"Where did you hear that?" the kid from Idaho demanded.

"Hell, I don't know. I heard it."

The sergeant got to his feet and walked a few feet away from them, to the middle of the clearing, and knelt to look where he had seen a glint of metal in the snow. He picked it up. A dogtag. And under it, where the snow fell away, another one. He brushed away the snow and saw the pile of dogtags, their beaded chains stiff and frozen. "Sonofabitch" he said softly. "Look here." They gathered around him and looked at the pile of dogtags.

"Christ," the kid from Idaho said. "Why you figure the Krauts did that?"

"I don't know. It don't matter. They're all dead, anyway." But it did matter. It made him angry, strangely so, in a way that all the killing and maiming of the last few days had not done. Killing was what they all did, both sides, and nobody had taken any prisoners the last few days. But this. It was stupid. It defiled the dead, as if killing weren't enough. The sergeant laid his M-1 down in the snow and scooped up the pile of dogtags, holding them in both hands. He was shaking and the small dull metal rectangles rattled against each other. "Give every body a dogtag," he said, holding out the double handful to the others. "Give every sonofabitch a dogtag."

"But how's anybody gonna know who's who?" the corporal asked.

"It don't matter," the sergeant repeated. "They're all dead anyway."

They stared at him for a minute, saw the red craziness in his eyes, and then they did as he said. When they were finished, there were four dogtags left over. He stood there, holding them dangling by their chains, and looked around the clearing.

"Check under the tank," he said.

The corporal crunched through the snow and knelt at the spot where the tank's right tread had slewed up on the rock and scooped away the snow, making an opening. Then he pulled a match out of the pocket of his jacket, struck it on the rock, and leaned into the opening, pausing there for a long moment. He drew back and turned to the others and they could see that his face was ashen.

"Yeah," he said softly. "Yeah, they're there."

some time, over the Linotype machine, looking at them, and Lonnie knew from his look that his question would be taken seriously, that Daddy Jake would think about it for a moment the way he always did and then give him an answer. He waited, watching the big bushy eyebrows, the red and watery eyes, the hands that still rested on the keyboard, and then after a moment Daddy Jake turned and looked at him and said, quietly, "I don't know, Lonnie. I really don't know."

FOUR

It came to him as he was setting type for the front-page head-lines, laboring over a case of twenty-four-point Bodoni Bold on a Tuesday afternoon after school, *click-click*, the pieces of type standing like soldiers (or sailors) in the type stick—upside-down backward *w*'s and *o*'s and *m*'s and a *p* that reminded him of "periscope." And he wondered. What makes a submarine stay on the bottom?

He thought about it for a moment and then set the type stick down softly on the layout table so as not to jostle the *w*'s and *o*'s and *m*'s and *p*'s, and he went over to where Daddy Jake was hunched over the keyboard of the Linotype, fingers drumming *clackety-clack* while the machine snorted and wheezed and disgorged slugs of type like small shiny farts.

He waited until Daddy Jake reached the end of a paragraph and then he tapped him on the shoulder. When Daddy Jake turned around and peered out from under his big bushy eyebrows, Lonnie asked, "What makes a submarine stay on the bottom?"

Jake just looked at him for a while, his eyes red and watery from concentrating on the copy, and then he leaned back in the chair and ruminated for another while, batting his eyebrows with the ferocity of great wisdom rumbling around inside his head.

"I think," he said when he was finished ruminating, "that they make everybody sit down." He digested that, blinked once or twice, and went on. "When they want to bob around on the surface, they make everybody stand up. And when they want to go down to the bottom, they make everybody sit down. And that keeps the weight on the bottom of the boat. And if the enemy is overhead, they just sit there and stay real quiet so that nobody can hear them."

"But what if somebody has to get up and go to the bathroom?"

Jake rolled his eyes back in his head. "That's the hardest part."

"Yes?"

"Well . . . they can always let half of 'em stand up and the other half sit down, and that means the boat will be halfway to the bottom. And those that are standing up can go to the bathroom."

"It sounds pretty complicated."

"Timing and discipline," Daddy Jake nodded. "Timing and discipline. Study the lives of the great generals and admirals and you'll find they possessed those virtues in abundance. They knew just when to stand and when to sit. When to fight and when to cut and run."

"Did Captain Finley Tibbetts have timing and discipline?"

"The utmost." One of Daddy Jake's ears began to twitch. "How else do you think he got Ulysses S. Grant's ear?"

"He WHAT?"

"I never told you about that?"

"No, you never told me about that."

"Well, it's not much of a story." He swiveled around in his chair to the Linotype keyboard.

"Daddy Jake!"

"Well, all right." He swiveled back. "It was at Gettysburg. Captain Finley had his troop attacking up Cemetery Ridge and the shot and shell were so heavy that the Confederate charge was beginning to wither. And Captain Finley knew he had to do something to buck up the boys. So he gave that fine black charger of his the spur and galloped straight through the Union lines and took out his big sword and whopped off General Grant's ear. Then he rode out again with hellfire and damnation exploding around his head. He not so much as singed an eyebrow."

Lonnie cocked his head to one side and gave Jake the fish eye. "Ain't so."

"Is so. Go to the library and find a picture of Ulysses S. Grant in a history book. See how his hair always covers his ears." And Daddy Jake smiled with great satisfaction while Lonnie stood there and took in the delicious outrageousness of it, the infinite preposterous possibilities of submarines and cavalry riders and Ulysses S. Grant's ear mixing with the rich warm smells and sounds of the print shop. It was all very, very fine.

He existed these days in a twilight world between the improbable and the outrageous. Between Daddy Jake, living here in the newspaper office, sleeping on a cot back by the Kluge, heating coffee on a hotplate, shaving over the wash-up sink, taking an occasional shower at the fire station, smelling like cigars and bay rum oil and Lightnin' Jim's Best and the nose-tickling, slightly rank odor of bachelorhood—and home, where women dogged his every footstep, traipsing up and down the stairs with armloads of diapers, sheets, gowns, frilly-lacy-doily blankets, smelling of talcum powder and lilac water and Carnation Evaporated Milk, except for the little one, who yelled her head off and just smelled, period.

There was not a quiet place anywhere. Not here, where the machinery clanked and rattled and Daddy Jake bellowed and fulminated; not at school, where the drone of decimals-conjugations-elements-continents buzzed through his head; not at home, where even the deepest hours of night were split with the wails of the little bugger in the room next door. Certainly not in the secret compartments of his own mind, where his imagination ran riot and gave him no peace. It all made him a little dizzy.

It had been almost a month now since the great shebang, when Mama Pastine had run Daddy Jake out of the house and he had taken up residence at the *Free Press*. He seemed to be more or less holding his own. He was a little rumpled around the edges and he didn't shave every day and sometimes he forgot to go over to Biscuit Brunson's cafe for a meal. But since he had gotten over his cold he had been in reasonably good health. And he made a great show of showing no interest whatsoever in what was going on out Partridge Road.

He had plenty to keep him occupied in town, because things were still in a general uproar over the war memorial. It had been three weeks since Daddy Jake wrote the editorial, and the whole town was still in an angry twit over it. He was being given pretty much the silent treatment in Biscuit Brunson's cafe, which was where he was taking all his meals since his first purchase of bologna and cheese and bread had gone rancid and given him the stomachache. Several people had canceled their subscriptions to the *Free Press*. George Poulos, who had a boy in the paratroopers, stopped running ads for the Jitney Jungle Super Saver. And others called on the telephone. One in particular. Lonnie was working in the back shop when Daddy Jake picked up the receiver in the front office, listened for a moment, turned red in the face, and snarled, "Meet me in the street, you son-ofabitch!" then slammed the receiver on the hook. He stormed into the back shop and sat down with a great jolt in the chair at the Linotype machine, turned to Lonnie and said, "Don't ever hide behind the anonymity of a cowardly instrument like the telephone!"

The next morning, as Lonnie was on the way to school, he detoured by the newspaper office and saw Daddy Jake standing out on the sidewalk in front, bundled in his overcoat, doing something to the window. As Lonnie walked up behind him, he could see that Daddy Jake was scraping at the glass with a razor blade. And there was enough of it left so that Lonnie could see that it was a swastika, done in bold slashes of black paint. He stood there for a moment by the curb, watching Jake absorbed in the job, and then he said, "Daddy Jake . . ." Jake whirled around and Lonnie saw the cold flat fury in his eyes. He backed up a step, suddenly afraid.

"Go to school!" Jake barked at him, and he took off running.

But at school there was still the war memorial to be dealt with. Purvis Redlinger saw to that. Purvis was a head taller and a good ten pounds heavier and when he bulled into Lonnie from the back in the schoolhouse yard just before opening bell, he sent Lonnie sprawling, books flying. Purvis stood over him for a moment with a nasty grin curling his upper lip and then he said, "Well, look here who I bumped into. Lonnie Tibbetts, the little Nazi. Well, I'm so sorry, Adolph."

A crowd gathered around them quickly, pushing into a tight little circle, and a nervous giggle went through the throng.

It took Lonnie a moment to get his breath back. He looked down and saw that he had scraped the knee completely out of his pants and the flesh was raw and bleeding underneath. The cold knot of fear in his stomach made him want to roll over and cover his head, but he looked up at Purvis Redlinger and swallowed hard and said, "Kiss my ass, Purvis," and came up swinging. Purvis decked him with a roundhouse blow that caught him aside the head and made his ear explode in pain. Lonnie drew back to throw a punch, but Purvis hit him again, this time with a left that whumped into Lonnie's stomach and sent him down hard on his rump on the frozen raw clay. He sat there a minute, staring at his shoelaces and trying to keep from throwing up, while Purvis hovered over him, slapping at the top of his head; then he just sort of crumpled forward and grabbed Purvis around the ankles and yanked hard, pulling Purvis down on top of him. That was where it ended because Professor Kessler, the principal, pushed through the crowd and grabbed each of them by the jacket and yanked them apart. "See here!" he commanded. And Lonnie could see quite well. He had had his butt whipped.

Professor Kessler took them in his office and spread-eagled them across the front of his desk and gave each of them five blistering whacks with his long flat paddle, then sent them limping down the hall to their room.

Purvis muttered threats at him all day, crowding up against him in the lunch line, taunting him on the playground, but avoiding anything so blatant that it would bring the wrath of Professor Kessler down on them again. The rest of the kids gave him wide berth, even Bugger Brunson, who was his best friend but who was terrified of Purvis Redlinger. Purvis liked to punch Bugger in the stomach and call him "blubber gut."

Lonnie kept to himself and kept his mouth shut. As soon as school was out, Lonnie went to the back of the playground behind the big oak tree, where serious disputes were settled, and waited. Purvis swaggered up a few minutes later, trailing a little band of snottynosed hangers-on who, like Bugger, were terrified of Purvis. Lonnie didn't even give Purvis time to open his mouth. He kicked Purvis in the nuts, and when Purvis collapsed in agony, Lonnie glowered at the rest of them who had gathered to watch the massacre and stalked off. Bugger Brunson was standing on the sidewalk at the edge of the school yard, but Lonnie didn't even look at him.

At the newspaper office, where he went every afternoon for an hour after school, Daddy Jake surveyed his red swollen ear and the rip in his pants and said, "You've been fighting."

"I fell down playing kick ball."

"And fell on your ear."

"Right smack on it."

Daddy Jake ran his hand through his thinning hair and Lonnie could see how his knuckles stood out hard and white. Then he stood there with just his jaw moving for a while and looked at Lonnie, and finally he said, "Well, I hope you kicked the shit out of that kickball."

"Yessir," Lonnie said. "I sure did that."

Lonnie was late getting home that evening because he went with Daddy Jake to the every-other-Thursday-afternoon Town Council meeting. And that's where things came to a head.

Grandaddy Rosh Benefield was presiding since he was the mayor, and things were going along fine until the end of the meeting when Cosmo Redlinger, who ran the funeral parlor, said he wanted to make a motion.

Grandaddy Rosh looked down the long council table at Cosmo and folded his hands in front of him and said, "All right, Cosmo."

"I want to move," Cosmo Redlinger said, "that we build a war memorial."

There was a good little crowd in the council room, more than usual, most of the chairs around the wall filled with spectators, and it got so quiet you could have heard a mouse fart when Cosmo Redlinger said that. Everybody seemed to lean forward a bit toward the rectangular table in the middle of the room where Grandaddy Rosh and the other four members of the Town Council sat. Everybody, that is, except Daddy Jake, who paused barely an instant as he scribbled on the sheaf of folded newsprint he was using to take notes. He finished the sentence he was working on and then held his pencil poised above the paper, waiting to record the next salvo. Everybody else seemed to be making a great effort not to look at Daddy Jake. Cosmo Redlinger, in fact, was making a great study of the ceiling above his chair, where paint was flaking off the plaster around a big brown water stain. The commode in the upstairs telephone exchange would be just about there, Lonnie thought, taking a good look at the stain himself. He took a moment to imagine Em Nesbitt, the operator, sitting on the commode while the switchboard buzzed furiously with someone trying to get through to report an air raid, or worse.

Grandaddy Rosh looked all around the table, fixing each of them in turn with his small bright eyes, and Lonnie noticed again how small Grandaddy Rosh's eyes were in his big face and how bright they were, like little diamonds nestled in a pillow. And he noticed how hard it was to tell what Grandaddy Rosh was thinking because his face stayed the same almost all the time. Only his eyes changed, and now they were hard and bright.

"Councilman Redlinger has made a motion," Grandaddy Rosh said, sounding very formal about it. "Do I hear a second?"

George Poulos mumbled something from his place near the middle of the table, but he had his back to Lonnie, and Lonnie couldn't hear what he said.

"What, George?" Grandaddy Rosh asked.

"I said, 'Second,' " George answered.

Grandaddy Rosh unfolded his hands and then folded them again. "We have a motion and a second. Is there any discussion?"

There was a long breath-holding silence, and then Alvah Foley, who owned the barbershop, spoke up from his side of the council table. "What kind of war memorial?"

They all looked at each other, and then Grandaddy Rosh said, "Cosmo, it's your motion. Do you want to elaborate?"

Cosmo pulled at his long nose for a moment. "Well, a . . . uh . . . monument, I suppose." He thought about that for a while, then added, "Granite."

"A granite monument," Grandaddy Rosh repeated. "Do you think it ought to have any embellishments or appurtenances?"

"Spell that," Orval Middleton said. Orval was the fourth member of the Town Council and the secretary. He wrote laboriously on pages of a loose-leaf binder and later transcribed the minutes of the council meetings into a large leather-bound ledger that had been kept since the town was founded after the Civil War.

"Which one?" Rosh asked.

"Appurtenances," Orval said.

"A-p-p-u-r-t-e-n-a-n-c-e-s."

Orval wrote it down.

Cosmo shot them a blank look. "Any what?"

"Decorations," Grandaddy Rosh said. "I'm . . . ah . . . trying to flesh out your motion, Cosmo."

"Decorations," Cosmo nodded. "Like what?"

"Well, statuary. Inscriptions. The like."

"You don't have to use legal terms, Rosh," Cosmo complained. "We're all just ordinary folks here."

"I'm sorry," Rosh said evenly. "What I mean to say is, do you think our"—Lonnie noticed that, how he said *our*—"war memorial ought to have some kind of figure represented on it, perhaps a statue, or any writing on it?"

"I think a statue would be fine," Cosmo said, placated. "A statue of a soldier."

"Well," Alvah Foley threw in, "there are a lot of sailors and airmen from around here."

"I've got a nephew in the Merchant Marine," Orval Middleton said, looking up from his three-ring binder.

"How about people who work in dee-fense plants?" said a man over in the corner of the room, one of the spectators. Grandaddy Rosh turned around and stared at him, because he didn't allow spectators to just speak up like that, unless it was the part of the council meeting called Remarks from Citizens.

"We can't put everybody on it," Cosmo said irritably.

"Then maybe we ought to think about something besides a statue," Rosh said, in control again.

"Maybe," George Poulos said, "we ought to just have a big granite thing with the names of the boys who died in action on it."

"What about the ones who were wounded?" Alvah Foley asked.

"All right," George said. "The dead and wounded."

There was a moment of somber silence in the room while they all thought about the dead and wounded.

Alvah Foley cleared his throat. "How badly wounded?"

"Wounded *and injured*," Orval Middleton put in. "My nephew hurt his back real bad loading cargo on a freighter and I think," Orval raised his eyebrows, "that a man who was injured in the line of duty ought to be recognized because that cargo was going to Russia.''

Lonnie looked over at Daddy Jake's sheaf of newsprint and saw that the last word on there was ''appurtenances,'' and after that his pencil had meandered off into a series of squiggles. But Daddy Jake was taking it all in, his gaze shifting from one to the other. Every so often his ear, the one turned toward Lonnie, gave a slight twitch.

Cosmo Redlinger was getting a little flushed in the face. ''Well, that's ridiculous,'' he said. ''Every boy that's gone in the service has had some kind of injury or another, I imagine. Where do you draw the line between getting shot and dropping your rifle on your foot?''

''I didn't say anything about dropping a rifle on your foot,'' Orval said hotly. ''I just think when a boy gets hurt bad doing something that helps the war effort, like sending vital cargo to Russia, he's made just as much of a contribution as another one that gets shot.''

Grandaddy Rosh nodded agreeably. ''There are,'' he said, ''all kinds of sacrifice.''

The rest of them nodded with him, except for Cosmo, who turned sideways in his chair and hiked one leg over the other knee, giving them his shoulder. ''I think,'' he said after a moment, staring up at the brown stain on the ceiling again, ''that we've gotten off the subject.''

They chewed on that for a moment and shifted their rumps around in their seats and then Alvah Foley said, ''Truth of the matter is, the war ain't over.''

''That's true,'' Grandaddy Rosh said.

Orval Middleton scribbled some more and then stopped, hung fire, and looked up and down the table. ''I suggest,'' he said, weighing his words as if they were pieces of rationed beef, ''a cannon.''

There was a long deep silence and then Cosmo said, ''A what?''

''A cannon. We could just put a cannon on the courthouse lawn and let it do the whole job. Honor the dead, the wounded, the injured, everybody that comes back—from all the services.'' He thought about it, bobbing his head up and down. ''We could even make it a memorial to all the past wars—the War Between the States, the Spanish-American, the First War, all of 'em. And we could,'' he wound up with a flourish, ''even paint it white. For peace.''

It took a while to digest all that, but finally Grandaddy Rosh said, ''I ought to remind you that anything that goes on the courthouse lawn is the purview of the County Commission. They may have some ideas of their own.''

''They'll want the whole county in on it,'' Alvah Foley said.

''And there's the American Legion,'' George Poulos added.

''Well!'' Cosmo Redlinger exploded, surprising them all with his vehemence. ''I *think*''—he slapped his hand on the council table—''that this body should go on record favoring the idea of a war memorial.'' He turned and looked directly at Daddy Jake, the first time anyone in the room had done so all afternoon. ''We ought to let folks know how we stand on *that*.''

''We can work out the details later,'' George Poulos said, nodding.

''All in favor say 'Aye,' '' Grandaddy Rosh said quickly.

They all said, ''Aye.'' All five of them.

''Opposed?''

Silence.

''Motion carries. Further business?''

Silence.

''Move we adjourn,'' Orval Middleton said. He had been on the Town Council longer than anybody else, and he was always the one who said ''Move we adjourn.''

''Second,'' George Poulos said.

''All in favor?''

''Aye.''

The room emptied quickly and after a moment there were only the three of them—Grandaddy Rosh, Daddy Jake, and Lonnie. Daddy Jake sat there and scribbled a few lines on his newsprint while Rosh shuffled through the papers in front of him on the council table, finally standing them on edge and jogging them against the table to make a neat pile. Through the window at the side of the room, Lonnie could see that the light was fading fast. He was late and Mama Pastine would skin him good—for being late and for having the knee ripped out of his pants and a cauliflower ear. Should he tell her? No, she wouldn't understand, any more than she would understand why a submarine stays on the bottom.

Grandaddy Rosh got up from his chair like an elephant rising from a long sleep and put the papers into a manila folder.

"Lonnie, you ought to come to council meetings more often," he said.

"Not if y'all gonna drag on so long," Lonnie said. "Mama Pastine'll skin me alive."

"Tell her you've been observing democracy in action," he winked. He looked over at Daddy Jake. "Tell her it's not a perfect form of government, but it beats lynching."

Daddy Jake just snorted and got up and walked out.

━━━━━━━

What he didn't tell Daddy Jake—what he didn't *dare* tell Daddy Jake—was that he was consumed with the need to know more about his father.

Henry Tibbetts existed for him as a shadow man, a gray and half-remembered figure who appeared infrequently and smelled of what Lonnie later came to know as Lightnin' Jim's Best and scratched Lonnie's face with the stubble on his cheeks. Lonnie had lived with Daddy Jake and Mama Pastine for about as long as he could remember. His mother, Hazel, he could barely recall, and Henry had moved in and out of his life like a soft-spoken ghost. Lonnie hadn't seen him at all since the National Guard had taken him off to war. But Mama Pastine's outburst on Christmas morning, the way she had turned on Daddy Jake with such wrath, had awakened his curiosity. There was something important going on here, something that made Henry Tibbetts, shadow man that he was, seem suddenly compelling.

The next week, when the library reopened from the holiday break, Lonnie looked up Bastogne, Belgium, in the world atlas, placed his finger over the name of the town, and said to himself, "My daddy is there." Having marked Henry Tibbetts's existence on a map, he had to know more about the man who occupied the place. And with Daddy Jake out of the house, maybe he could.

His father had been a taboo subject for a long time, he knew that. But it was Daddy Jake's doing. So he felt no qualms about asking Mama Pastine, as she tucked him into bed one night, "What was my daddy like?"

She stopped, hands still thrust under the mattress where she had been stuffing the edge of the sheet. "What do you mean, 'was'?"

"I mean when he was a boy."

She stood up and folded her arms over her bosom. "Well, he was a lot like you are. He was smart, but sometimes he didn't act like he had much sense."

"Did he get in trouble a lot?"

She closed her eyes and stood there for a moment as if she were looking back inside herself. Then she said, "No more than most, I imagine."

"Do you have a picture of him?"

"Yes."

"Can I see it?"

" 'May.' "

"May I see it?"

She let him get out of bed then and took him to her own room and showed him the photograph, taken when Henry was fourteen. It was in a brown envelope in the bottom drawer of her bureau. She slipped the photograph carefully from the envelope and handed it to him. He looked at it a long time, trying to make a person out of the image in black and white, but nothing came to him. Henry had high cheekbones like Mama Pastine and thick eyebrows like Daddy Jake, and between, his eyes seemed to be lost in his face. Not small, especially, but lost. Lonnie looked up from the photograph into the bureau mirror and searched for some connection, some evidence.

"Who did—does he look like?" Lonnie asked.

Mama Pastine studied the photograph for a moment. "Hmmmm. Probably more like Albertis than anyone. With a little Cahoon thrown in. The intelligent nose. That's Cahoon. But mostly like Albertis."

"Daddy Jake's daddy."

"That's right."

"Did I know him?"

"No, he died before you were born. In fact, he died when your grandfather was a young man."

Lonnie looked at the photograph again. "And who do I look like?" he asked.

"All of us," she said.

That wasn't enough. Lonnie wanted to look like somebody in particular, not everybody in general. He tried to arrange his face in the mirror to resemble the thin-faced boy with the high cheekbones and thick eyebrows in the picture. But the eyes stumped him. Henry wasn't looking at the camera. He eyes were pointed in that direction, but he wasn't *looking* at it.

"You could never tell what he was thinking," Mama Pastine said, as if she could read Lonnie's mind.

"Was he very big?" Lonnie asked.

"No, not really. About average. A little thin."

"Do you have a picture of my mother?"

She sat there very quietly on the edge of the bed for a time and then she said, "No, I don't." But the way she said it made Lonnie dead certain there was a picture of his mother, Hazel Benefield Tibbetts, somewhere in this house, perhaps in a box in the dust-encrusted attic, perhaps a picture of Hazel in her wedding dress with her arm entwined in Henry's. And he was just as dead certain that Mama Pastine, whatever her reason, would not show it to him.

"She was killed in the wreck," he said. He knew that much.

"Yes."

"And what did he do?"

"Well, he was very sad," she said softly and Lonnie could see how sad *she* was, how whatever had happened had left a deep hurt place in Mama Pastine that she had tucked away like the picture in the bottom of the bureau drawer. She stood up and busied herself rearranging things on the top of the bureau so that Lonnie wouldn't see how close she was to crying. But he did. He stared at the picture awhile longer and then handed it back and she put it away.

"Can I look at it again?"

"You *may* look at it anytime you want. Just handle it gently."

"Why is Daddy Jake mad at him?"

"He, uh, hmmmmmm," she started and then trailed off and closed her eyes again, looking inside. "They had a disagreement," she said finally.

"What about?"

"They disagreed about a lot of things, actually."

"Like what?"

"When you're old enough, I'll tell you about it."

So, that was that. Mama Pastine knew *everything*. But some of it she wouldn't tell because it made her sad, and some of it she wouldn't tell because he was too young. Lonnie didn't want to hurt Mama Pastine, and there was no way he could make himself any older than he was, so that was that. He might glean bits and pieces from her as she was ready to give them up, but that took too much time. What he knew so far only served to confuse and fascinate him.

The photograph told him nothing, really. It was just a face on a piece of cardboard, nothing you could put your hands on and feel and smell the way you could a live human being who was just now in a town called Bastogne, Belgium. There was so much more, and he needed to know it *now*. He was twelve years old, almost thirteen, by gosh, and he wanted to know where he came from. He wanted to know for himself why Daddy Jake refused to talk about Henry, why the very mention of Henry turned him red with anger, why Henry had been banished to some private secret place where only Mama Pastine ever went. Because he sensed that all that business was part and parcel of who Henry Tibbetts was, maybe the most important part.

So, if Henry was a ghost in his own home, where to turn? Henry Tibbetts wasn't a subject you could look up in the library, in the set of *Compton's Pictured Encyclopedia*. There were no photographs of Henry arm in arm with his buddies, like Bugger Brunson had of his daddy. And it sure wasn't something you would dare bring up with Grandaddy Rosh and Grandmamma Ideal Benefield because there was something bad wrong there, too. He had mentioned Henry once at their house and there was a big cold silence that made him squirm with embarrassment, as if he had cut a fart and everybody had smelled it. In fact, he didn't spend much time at Grandaddy Rosh and Grandmamma Ideal's house anymore. It just didn't seem to be the thing to do, for some reason.

Lonnie knew this: He knew his father hadn't just run off and left him. The National Guard had taken him off to the war where (Mama Pastine said) he had become a lieutenant. That counted for something, too. Not just anybody could be a lieutenant. No, Lonnie had no bone to pick with his father. He just wanted to know who the hell Henry Tibbetts was, because if he knew that, he would know where Lonnie Tibbetts came from.

He needed clues, things you could store away in the back of your mind and bring out later to fill in missing parts of a puzzle. That was the thing about figuring. If you had a few clues to start with, you could figure out the rest because, after all, things were pretty logical. Look at the Hardy Boys, how they could take a little bitty thing like a scrap of red bandanna hanging from a nail in a boat house and use it to track down a gang of smugglers bringing in diamonds from Africa. Or a guy like Tom Swift, watching bits of ash floating upward from a camp fire and figuring out how to build his own hot-air balloon with an oil burner that would heat the air while he was aloft. Clues. That's all you had to have. A few clues.

The night after he saw the photograph, he dreamed of Henry on the fire truck. He stood on the corner of the courthouse square downtown, holding Mama Pastine's hand, and the fire truck passed with a man holding onto the back, leaning way out as the truck turned the corner and sped away with its siren wailing and its engine roaring. Lonnie couldn't see the man's face or even tell what kind of clothing he was wearing, but he knew somehow that it was Henry. And he thought. Here's a clue. A big one. So he wiggled away from Mama Pastine's grasp and ran after the truck, down the side street past the newspaper office and then on out Partridge Road, the truck always just beyond him and the lone figure on the rear, holding on with one hand, leaning way out whenever it rounded a curve, always facing away from him. He ran all the way out the road to where it ended at Tunstall Renfroe's house, but the truck and Henry were gone.

He woke, feeling a great ache of disappointment and loss. He stared into the darkness over his bed, but there was nothing there, either, except maybe God. He felt the tears well up in his eyes and roll hot and salty down his cheeks and he turned over and buried his face in the pillow so God wouldn't see him crying and ask him what was wrong, because he didn't want to have to tell God he didn't know where he came from. God wouldn't understand about that. God was Our Father. Everybody's Father. But he wasn't Henry Tibbetts.

Then he heard the baby cry. It irritated him, the raw high-pitched squall, that and the thought of her, mouth gaping, pink toothless gums framing her full-throated bellow, a little pissant stranger in his house. He lay there listening to her for a while, feeling very put out by the whole business of having a baby on the premises, wallowing in resentment. Then suddenly it dawned on him: *There's something else, a big clue, a whopper, right*

here under my nose and I didn't even see it. There's Francine.
Francine, who had shown up on the front porch on Christmas
Eve. Francine, smelling of cold and fright, huge in the belly,
come from Texas in the middle of the night. From Henry Tibbetts.

He had been watching her purely out of curiosity, catching
glimpses around corners, through open doorways, in mirrors;
hearing snatches of conversation, the way she spoke in tight little
chopped-off sentences in a hard nasal accent. Half the time, you
couldn't understand what she was saying. It went by so fast and
sounded so foreign with the words all run together with no space
in between, that you had no time to figure it out before the next
burst caught you. It was like trying to dodge a machine gun.
When Francine said something, Mama Pastine just automati-
cally cocked her head to one side and said, ''I beg your pardon?'' She was from Cleveland, Ohio, which might as well be
Rangoon, Burma, for all you could understand what she said.

She was small and trim and, he thought, pretty young.
Younger than his father, surely. Henry was thirty-four, Mama
Pastine told him. It seemed important to know that, to think of
him as he was *now*, not as he appeared in the photograph in the
bureau drawer. So Henry had a young wife from Cleveland,
Ohio, who spoke like a hedge-clipper, *snip snip snip*. Lonnie
wondered how they had communicated, with her firing off bursts
of run-together words like she did. She moved the same way she
spoke, with quick, economical motions. Lonnie caught glimpses
as she learned to take care of the baby, watching as Mama Pastine tested the temperature of a baby bottle by splashing a few
drops of milk on the underside of her wrist, then as she picked
up the baby by first putting a hand behind her head and then
lifting the baby with one smooth flowing motion that deposited
her gently in the soft curve of her shoulder. Francine watched,
and then she did it, too, exactly the same way, as Mama Pastine
nodded approvingly.

Lonnie watched, but he didn't have much to say. Two days
after the baby came, Francine had appeared suddenly one morning in the kitchen, having walked stiffly and quietly down the
stairs by herself. Mama Pastine had grabbed her by the shoulders and helped her into a chair, fussing all the while about how
a woman was supposed to stay in bed for a week after she had
a baby. Francine was pale and drawn and the old bathrobe she

was wearing hung loosely on her thin shoulders. Mama Pastine hovered over her, clucking, while Francine got her breath. Then Francine looked across the table at Lonnie, who was staring open-mouthed, his plate of half-eaten hotcakes getting cold.

"This is Lonnie," Mama Pastine said.

Francine looked across the table, gave him the once-over. "I'mgladdamecha," she said.

"What?"

She gave him a funny look. "IsaidI'mgladdamecha."

It took a while for his brain to catch up and figure out what she had said, and then he nodded dumbly and said, "Hi."

"Babykeepinyouwake?"

He ran that one through his head a couple of times and after a moment he lied, "No ma'am."

Francine brushed a strand of stringy brown hair away from her face. "Wellshe'skeepinmewake." She gave him a wan smile. Mama Pastine brought her a cup of coffee and she took a sip and set the steaming cup down on the table. "Igottawashmyhair," she said. "It fellslikeratserlivininnut."

Mama Pastine cocked her head to the side and said, "I beg your pardon?"

"Rats," Francine said, tugging at her hair. "Rats."

My God, Lonnie thought to himself, and finished his hotcakes in silence while the baby began to bellow upstairs and Francine rolled her eyes. For God's sake. Rats.

Now it was three weeks later and the baby was still crying, waking them all in the middle of the night, hungry and furious, in the room next to Lonnie's that had once been Great-grandmamma Emma's and then Henry's and then had stood empty for a long time until Francine and the baby came. She slept during the day, but she howled in the middle of the night like somebody had stuck a pin in her rump.

Lonnie had gotten his only good look at the baby one afternoon when Mama Pastine had taken Francine to town to buy a couple of dresses at Hamblin's Mercantile. Mama Pastine gave him strict instructions to sit in the downstairs parlor with the door bolted, and if the house caught fire, to rush up the stairs and grab up the baby. He had no idea in the world how you grabbed up a baby, but he bolted the door behind them and watched through the window as they headed down Partridge Road, and then he went straight upstairs to get a good look for himself at what all the fuss was about. She was quiet and still, just her pink head with its scrunched-up nose and mouth showing from under the blanket. Lonnie stood by the crib and watched her for a long time and saw *that she was not breathing* and with his heart in his throat he knelt down with his head right next to the slats and suddenly she gave out a little burst of sound, not even a cry, and he almost fainted. When he recovered, he watched her up very close and saw the almost invisible flaring of her nostrils as she exhaled and the way her tiny eyelids fluttered every once in a while like leaves trembling in a faint breeze. He decided that the baby didn't look like *anybody*, but that was okay, because she didn't have a name, either. They were waiting for Henry to come home to give her a name, that's what Mama Pastine said. For God's sake. A little old pissant no-name baby that kept them all awake at night.

Like she was doing now. Lonnie lay there listening to her, thinking how this baby and this machine-gun-talking young woman Francine were a link to his father. He listened to her angry wail and thought that this was sort of like the reverse side of a mirror—something that belonged to Henry Tibbetts that Henry couldn't see or feel or hear, the way Lonnie could not see or feel or hear Henry.

He heard Francine moving about and then the baby got quiet and Lonnie heard the rhythmic *creak-cuh-reak* of Great-grand-mamma Emma's old rocking chair. He listened to it for a long time until it became in his mind the sound of a wagon wheel, its axle in need of grease, creaking along the hard frozen clay of a Virginia back road, an undisciplined sound in the dead of night that called out to Captain Finley Tibbetts and the hundred brave and lusty men of the Lighthorse Cavaliers hunkered against the chill in their saddles. Captain Finley turned to Muldoon at his side and whispered, "Fools making music for us to dance by, Muldoon. They take great care to wrap their horses' feet in rags, then forget to grease the axles of their wagons." Captain Finley shifted his weight in the saddle, tilting his head to the side to get an exact fix on the creaking wheel on the road below, raising his arm to signal the Lighthorse Cavaliers to the attack . . .

"Ohshit!" from the next room.

Lonnie threw the covers back and got out of bed.

There was only the light from the small table lamp at Francine's back and it took him a moment to realize the baby was nestled in the shadow cast by the light, nuzzling Francine's bared breast. He stared, face flushing with embarrassment but unable to look away.

"Sallright," Francine said.

"Are you okay?" Lonnie asked after a moment.

"OfcourseI'mokay."

"What?" He strained to hear.

"Isaid'mokay."

He just stood there and looked at her, feeling completely dumb and foolish. Finally, he said, "I can't understand a word you say. You talk like a machine gun."

"Wellyoutalklikesyrup," she said. "Arey'slowersome-thin'?"

He could tell from the way her voice rose at the end that she had asked him a question, and it made him angry that he couldn't understand what the sam-hill she was saying.

"Will you slow down!" he said, exasperated.

She stared at him and he could see, even in the dim light at her back, the way she had little hard lines around her mouth and eyes, even as young as she was. She seemed very self-contained. A tough cookie. It was something James Cagney had said in a gangster movie. One dame in particular he said was a tough cookie, a moll who hung around with a hood named Fingers, as he remembered it. Lonnie imagined Francine clinging to the runningboard of a big long black Packard, speeding from the scene of a bank heist in a roar of squealing tires and flying lead, spitting machine-gun words at the G-men hot on their trail, *ratatatatatatatatat*.

"I can't understand you," he said.

"Wellcomeoninan'closethuhdoor."

"Huh?"

"COME IN."

He closed the door behind him and stood with his back to the wall, watching her, watching the baby at her breast. Francine looked at the baby and then motioned him closer, and he crossed the room to where she sat in the chair with the baby snuggled against her, pink cheek against white breast, small fat arm slung upward, tiny hand clenching and unclenching as if squeezing the breast dry. The baby suckled for a long time, cheeks moving rhythmically, and then she stopped, cheek and hand still until

Francine moved to pull her away. Then the sucking and clenching began again. Lonnie stared, fascinated.

Francine looked up at him. "Ainchaeverseenatitbefore?"

"What?"

"A TIT," she said loudly.

Lonnie could feel his ears and face flame and he thought, My God, what if Mama Pastine hears her and wakes up and comes in here and I'm standing here and she's got her tit hanging out. For God's sake. But if the thought of it bothered Francine, she showed no sign. She let the baby work at it awhile longer until she was still again and then she lifted her to her shoulder and began to pat and rub the tiny hunched back until the baby belched.

"Organ recital," Lonnie said, half to himself.

"What?"

"That's what Daddy Jake calls it when somebody burps. An organ recital."

She left the baby on her shoulder for a few minutes, patting and stroking. Her breast was still exposed, white and blue-veined. Lonnie stared at it. There was a tiny drop of milk on the nipple.

Francine looked down. "I'm leaking," she said, slowly so he could understand it. She covered herself with one hand, pulling her nightgown over the breast, and then she rose and deposited the baby in the crib and covered her with the blanket, tucking in a loose side. The baby gave a deep sigh and stuck a fist in her mouth. Francine sat back down in the rocker and they both watched the baby.

"Why do you put her on her stomach?" Lonnie asked. "And talk slow."

"Pastine says that way, if she spits up, she won't strangle."

The way she said it. Pastine. It was right, what he had told Daddy Jake. They were already thick as thieves. She was as familiar as if she had been living here all the while. She and the little pissant no-name baby. Here he was, been living here most of his life, couldn't get the time of day about his own father, and they just moved in and took over.

"IwishIhadacigarette," she said, almost to herself.

Lonnie caught the word *cigarette*. "I got a cigar," he volunteered. "One of Daddy Jake's."

"A *cigar*?" The way she said it, Lonnie wondered if he had said "cowshit" instead of "cigar." "Wellferchrissake."

He glared at her. "Beggars can't be choosers when they're having a nicotine fit."

A slow grin spread over her thin face and she said, "Well-Ireckon. Sogetthecigar."

So Lonnie went to his room and rummaged in the shoe box he kept in the back of his closet shelf and got out the cigar he had been saving for some special time when he and Bugger Brunson might fire it up on the creek bank and pass it back and forth like tycoons. Francine held it daintily between her thumb and forefinger and lit it with a match she got from the scuffed leather purse on the top of the dresser, puffing lightly to get it started. It flamed up and a cloud of smoke issued from the end.

"I guess it's a little dry." Lonnie said.

"Whew," she said. She took a small drag and coughed, then waved her hand to scatter the smoke and held the cigar out toward him. "Wannapuff?"

Lonnie held the cigar expertly between his forefinger and middle finger, took a big drag, and held the smoke in his mouth for a moment before tilting his head up and sending it in a white stream toward the ceiling, where it dissipated in a widening pall.

"You don't inhale 'em," he said, handing the cigar back to Francine.

"Oh." She nodded. She held it this time like Lonnie had done and stared at it. "Howlong'sit"—then she stopped when Lonnie held up his hand and shook his head. She started over, saying the words one at a time. "How-long-does-it-take-to-smoke-one-of-these-things?"

"Depends," he said.

"On-what?"

"Whatever you take a notion to."

"Take-a-what?"

"Notion."

"Holy cow," she said, shaking her head. "This is like talking with a mud puddle."

"Well, we ain't hicks, if that's what you think."

"Idin'saynothin' . . ." Lonnie held up his hand. "I-didn't-say-nothin'-about-hicks. I-just . . . oh, what the hell. What about the cigar?"

"What about it?"

"HOW LONG DOES IT TAKE TO SMOKE IT, FER-CHRISSAKE?"

"Shhhhhhhhh," he waved his hand at her. "You'll wake Mama Pastine, and she'll come in here and find all this cigar smoking going on and she'll tan my butt."

"Awright, awright."

"Now," he said. "You can make a cigar last a long time. Or if you get wore out with it, you can just stub it out and then come back and finish it later."

"That's a consolation," she said, wrinkling her nose. She tried it again, taking a small quick puff and holding the smoke in for a little while before she let it out. She coughed again. "It's kind of strong."

"Yeah. A cigar ain't like a sissy-stick."

"What?"

"Cigarettes. That's what Daddy Jake calls 'em. Sissy-sticks."

She held the cigar well away from her. "I suppose Daddy Jake just smokes cigars?" The way she said "Daddy Jake" sounded strange and foreign coming from her, in her Cleveland, Ohio, machine-gun accent.

"Yeah," he said. " 'Course, lots of men smoke cigarettes. Hilton Redlinger smokes two packs of Picayunes a day and he's the police chief so he ain't no sissy. But Daddy Jake kids him about it. Daddy Jake will take a big puff on his cigar, and say, 'Hilton, you still smokin' them sissy-sticks?' " He mimicked Daddy Jake, rolling his eyes and batting his eyebrows. And then he thought to himself, What in the hell am I doing this for? This woman's a stranger in *my* house with a little old no-name baby and here I am running off at the mouth like she was Bugger Brunson or somebody. Was it because she had clues? He stopped short and looked down at his bare feet and he could feel the blood rushing to his face, turning his ears hot.

"Well," she said, and he looked up to see her studying him closely, her head tilted slightly to the side as if she might get a better view of him from an angle. "I guess I'll stick to sissy-sticks. You want me to stub out the cigar so you can finish it later?"

He was beginning to get the hang of her talk now. You just had to put your brain in "race" and let it fly along with the words, then digest them for a second. You could get the gist of it, anyway. "Naw," he said, "it's too old. Why don't you just throw it out the window."

She got up from the rocking chair and went to the window and raised it with a rattle, letting a rush of cold air into the room, and tossed the cigar into the darkness and shut the window quickly. Lonnie looked to see if it had waked the baby, the cold air and the cigar smoke, but she was sleeping soundly.

"Thanks anyway," she said, turning back to him. They stood there looking at each other for a long minute and then she said, "I-guess-we-better-get-back-to-bed."

"I 'speck."

"You what?"

" 'Speck."

She gave a little grunt and sat down on the edge of the bed, not in the rocking chair, and Lonnie could tell she wanted to get back to sleep. But he said, "What's it like in Cleveland, Ohio?"

She thought for a moment. "It's big and it snows a lot in the winter and people don't say 'speck.' "

"What's it like in Texas?"

"It's big and ugly and hot and I don't know if people say 'speck' or not because I din'paynodamnattention."

"Do I look like my daddy?"

She stared at him, taken aback, and he looked down at his feet again, stunned that he had just come out with it like that and wanting to turn and run back to his room and get way down under the covers in his bed and not come out for a long time. But he was frozen to the spot by something stronger than his urge to bolt, and no power on earth could have raised his hand to the doorknob not two feet away. Come on, he thought. The clues. The clues.

"Yes," she said after a moment. "Look up at me."

He looked up.

"Yes, I think you do. But different, too." She paused and then said, "You ain't seen him for a long time, have you?"

"No'm."

"Well, I didn't know him but a short time myself."

"But you had a baby."

Francine looked over at the baby and started to say something, then stopped and sat there quietly for a minute or so while Lonnie grew increasingly uncomfortable with the certainty he had said something terribly out of place, like mentioning Henry Tibbetts in front of Grandaddy Rosh and Grandmamma Ideal Benefield.

Then she looked back at him and said, "Yes. We had a baby." The way she said it hit Lonnie with a jolt. This woman and this baby here in this room were not just two people who had turned up on his front porch, they were his father's other life, something he could never, never know anything much about. He didn't know anything about his father, he didn't know where he had come from, and here were this woman and this baby who had a claim on Henry Tibbetts of their own. There weren't any clues here, he thought angrily. Just more puzzle.

"It's funny," Francine said, "you're his kid and I'm his wife and neither one of us knows much about him."

"You don't?"

"No. I just said, I didn't know him very long. We got married in Texas and then a few weeks later he shipped out."

Lonnie tried to imagine her in Texas with his father, wiggling around and making a baby. It made him sick with despair and hurt and lonesomeness.

"You gonna stay here?"

There was a look of surprise in her eyes. "What else?"

"Well, you're from Cleveland."

She laughed, a harsh little laugh. "Huh. Ain't nothin' in Cleveland. I spent too damn much time gettin' out of Cleveland." She looked at him for a moment. "Hell, I'm just tryin' to make out."

"Yeah."

"Look," she said. "He sent me here. He told me to come here and have the baby and wait for him. I'm just tryin' to make out, that's all. He gets home, maybe we'll . . . I dunno, get to know him."

Lonnie nodded dumbly. So much for that. Nothing doing with this tough cookie if he wanted to know who the dickens Henry Tibbetts was and who he his ownself was, because all she had done was wiggle around in Texas and get her belly all pumped up and then send Henry off to Bastogne, Belgium. Maybe during the time Henry had known her he had never understood a goddamn word she said.

He turned and opened the door. "Good night."

Then she said something that surprised him completely. She said, "Gimme a chance, huh?"

He turned back and looked at her and it came to him how hard it might have been for her to say that, how a tough cookie with little hard lines around her mouth and eyes just didn't talk that way. It brought him up short. It took him a long time to say, "Yes'm," and then to wonder what he meant by it.

"Well, g'night."

He could feel her eyes on him as he stepped out into the hall and closed the door behind him, realizing for the first time how cold his feet were on the bare floor.

He got into his own bed and pulled the covers up over his head and rubbed his aching feet to get them warm, and then he wondered where Henry Tibbetts was this very moment. He wondered what Henry ate for supper and whom he spoke to and what he said, whom he thought of just before he went to sleep and whom he dreamed about in Bastogne, Belgium, on a cold January night. He wondered if Henry knew he had a baby with no name and if he thought even for an instant about a twelve-year-old boy (almost thirteen) back home who wanted to know where he came from. He wondered about it until he finally slept.

When he woke in the morning his room was uncommonly bright, even around the edges of the window shades. He got out of bed and pulled back the edge of a shade and saw that it had snowed sometime during the early morning hours, a once-a-year snow, enough of it to blanket the ground and leave a thick topping on the bushes like cake frosting. For God's sake. Snow. And Ollie Whittle hadn't said a thing about it on the radio. It was overcast, but the snow made everything look very bright, very clean, very silent, so that he was almost reluctant to put on his clothes and go tromping around in it, crunching tracks through its perfection.

He released the shade and stood there in the semilight for a moment, then got his clothes off the hook inside the closet door and dressed quietly. He opened the door to the hallway and listened. He was the only one awake. He tiptoed downstairs and stood in the hallway, glancing into the parlor to see if perhaps Captain Finley were sitting there deep in the wing-back chair beside the dying embers of the coal fire. But the parlor was empty. He crossed to the front door and pulled back the lace curtains and looked out and saw Daddy Jake coming down Partridge Road, a small overcoated figure in the great still whiteness, feet making holes in the snow that stretched behind him in a lurching row of black dots and disappeared around the curve by the pasture.

Lonnie watched him as he came and then he stepped back from the front door as Daddy Jake climbed the steps to the porch, shoulders hunched, overcoat drawn tightly about him. He stamped his feet on the porch to shake off the snow, then opened the door and stepped into the hallway and stood there blinking at Lonnie, his great riotous eyebrows batting fiercely. He looked awfully tired, his eyes red-rimmed and puffy, his cheeks sagging. For God's sake, Lonnie thought to himself, he's an old man. It frightened him.

Then Daddy Jake looked up, behind Lonnie, and Lonnie turned and saw Mama Pastine halfway down the stairs, tying the belt on her bathrobe as she came, her hair frizzled from sleep. She stopped, looked at Daddy Jake. ''I thought I smelled cigar smoke last night.''

''I just came,'' Jake said quietly.

There was a great silence and Lonnie looked from one to the other, trying to figure out what was wrong, because there was something awfully, terribly wrong. And then he saw the envelope in Daddy Jake's hand, a small brown envelope, and he knew. Daddy Jake didn't have to say it, but he did, in a voice so small you would have thought it had been lost in the snow.

''Henry's dead.''

Then the great snow-silence rushed back in on top of him and obliterated all sound. Mama Pastine might have howled in anguish behind him, as Daddy Jake's face collapsed and his shoulders heaved with sobs, but Lonnie could hear none of it. There was only the deafening silence, a feeling of lightness. He felt his knees give way, but there was no sensation of falling, just the awesome stillness and the need to be very quiet in a place where he could consider the awful truth that now, he would never, never know where he came from.

FIVE

*T*HE letter arrived on a late April Wednesday and Whit Hennessey brought it around to the *Free Press*. Jake would have picked it up from the post office himself an hour later as he headed home for lunch, but Whit brought it around.

Jake had spent the morning in the back shop laying out the pages of that week's edition of the paper, locking the neat columns of type and the black-bordered advertisements into their forms, ready for the press run that afternoon. There was only the front page to finish. It would have two photographs this week. Its centerpiece would be a two-column picture of Biscuit Brunson receiving a citation from the county war bond chairman for the four hundred dollars' worth of bonds he had bought with nickels and dimes from the Victory Donuts he had sold over the counter of the cafe for three years. Biscuit was donating the bonds themselves to a community fund that would be used to build a war memorial. Jake's front-page column, already set in type, would go on at length about the Victory Donuts. It said that if all the pounds of flesh the community had added from eating them were dropped from an airplane, they would sink a good-sized Japanese battleship. It said nothing about the war memorial.

The front page might also have a one-column photo of Billy Benefield in uniform and dress cap, gold bars on his collar, tie knotted neatly. The caption underneath would tell how Billy had finished advanced flight training, gotten his pilot's wings, and was in Presidio, California, awaiting assignment to the Army Air Corps in the Pacific. What would be left unsaid was what Alsatia Renfroe had done. She had walked out of the bank at midmorning two weeks ago after taking six hundred dollars from her cash drawer, had gone home and packed her suitcase and gotten on the train. She left a note for Tunstall and Marvel on the entrance hall table that read, "I have not been kidnapped. Your loving daughter, Alsatia." They hadn't heard a word from her until two days ago, when she called to say that she and Billy had been married in the base chapel at Presidio. Marvel had taken to her bed and Tunstall, scandalized, had kept to himself at the bank. Ideal Benefield hadn't been out of her house, and Rosh wore a grim look that kept anyone from commenting or questioning. Everyone shook their heads and left them all alone.

Jake looked again now at Billy's photograph and caption and wondered if he should just leave it out. It would be the easiest thing to do. He agonized over it a moment, then told himself he would decide after lunch, the last thing before locking down the front-page form and carrying it to the big Kluge press for the afternoon run. Lonnie would be there straight from school at three to help him fold and label the copies of the paper and tie them into neat bundles to deliver to Whit Hennessey at the post office.

Lonnie. The thought of him troubled Jake. He was quiet, too quiet. Had been, in fact, since the news came almost three months ago. He had fainted there in the hallway when Jake brought the telegram through the snow, and after that, he seemed to withdraw inside himself, making none of them privy to whatever he was thinking about Henry and death. Jake had tried to draw him out several times, but Lonnie gave him a fierce look and refused to talk about it. He was no more responsive with Pastine. But she didn't push. "Be patient," she said. Lonnie showed up faithfully at the newspaper office every afternoon after school. He was catching on quickly in the back shop. His fingers flew over a type box like a seasoned printer's. Before

long, Jake would let him start learning the Linotype machine.
But Jake would catch him frequently, stock-still over what he
was doing, staring blankly at the work, mouth open. Jake worried, but he took Pastine's advice and left the boy to his thoughts,
whatever they were, of the father he had never really known and
now never would.

Jake was standing over the layout table, staring at the skeleton
of the front page, thinking about Lonnie and Billy Benefield,
when Whit Hennessey stuck his head into the back shop. "Jake,"
he called.

Jake jerked his head up and blinked at him. "Hi, Whit."

Whit held up the envelope. "I was coming by this way, so I
thought I'd drop this off. Just came in. Looks pretty official."
In the front office, Jake wiped his hands on his shop apron and
took the envelope, holding it by the edges so he wouldn't soil
it. He held it up to the light from the window. The return said
simply, "The War Department, Washington, D.C." It was addressed to Mrs. Henry F. Tibbetts.

Whit studied him. "About Henry, I imagine."

Jake nodded. "I imagine." He looked at it for a moment.
"Second one in a week," he said. "They wrote Francine the
other day telling her they'd be sending the life insurance. Ten
thousand."

"Well, she's got a baby to raise," Whit said. "Guess it'll
come in handy."

"Yeah. It's a good thing, I suppose."

"A good thing," Whit repeated.

"I guess they've got a policy on every boy in uniform, huh?"

"I'm pretty sure of it."

"I never had a cent of it myself," Jake said. "I guess I'm
getting too old now. Nobody wants to insure a worn-out carcass."

"I've got a little," Whit said. "Lots of folks lost their insurance in the Depression, you know. Couldn't keep up the pay-
ments. I was lucky enough to keep mine."

Jake said, "I always thought Roosevelt should have invented
something called reverse life insurance if he really wanted to
help out the little fellow."

"What's that?" Whit asked.

"That's where a fellow takes out a policy and the insurance

company pays him the full amount right on the spot. Then when he dies, they collect from his relatives.''

Whit laughed. "Sounds like that might make a good front-page column, Jake.''

"It did," Jake said. "About six years ago.'' It was funny, he thought. He could remember the columns from six years ago better than he could the one he wrote last week.

"Well," Whit said after a moment, "I guess I'd better get on . . .''

"How's Arthur, Whit? Did he make lieutenant?''

"Oh, yes.'' Whit brightened. "A shavetail. What they call one of those ninety-day wonders, he says. He's with the Ninety-ninth Infantry.''

"From the look of things, he ought to be coming home before too long.''

Whit shook his head. "I imagine they'll be sending everybody the other way, Jake. Getting ready to invade Japan.''

"Maybe not. Maybe we'll figure something out.''

"Yeah.''

He saw the way Whit looked at him, the way the change registered with people. And there was a change. Henry's death had taken the edge off him. He felt old and tired and he just didn't want to fight with anybody anymore. It was not the way a newspaperman was supposed to be, but it was the way he had become in three months. You couldn't get a rise out of Jake Tibbetts these days—not that anybody tried, considering the circumstances.

"Arthur's a good boy. And not a boy anymore.''

"Yes," Whit said. "They'll all be grown up when they get back. Grown older than us in some ways, I imagine.'' He hesitated for a moment. "I'm sorry . . . I'm sorry Henry didn't get a chance to, ah . . .''

"Come back and make something of himself," Jake finished for him.

"That's right.''

Jake rose from his desk. "Well, I guess I'll get on home and see what's in this," he said, holding up the letter.

Whit reached out and offered his hand and Jake shook it, a good firm handshake, a sign between himself and Whit Hennessey that there was a bond that Jake had been unwilling to admit until now. Sons off at war, one gone for good, the other

in harm's way. Jake could speak of the war now and say "we."
It had become a personal thing, the way it had been all along to
Whit Hennessey and Biscuit Brunson and George Poulos and
Fog Martin and all the rest who had lived through the long
months of dull aching apprehension, dreading the phone call or
telegram that would tell them the war had snatched a piece of
them and devoured it. Jake had had to come to grips with the
war because Henry's death forced it on him. And having done
that, he had to come to grips with Henry, to make peace with
him. Whit understood that, and understanding it, put aside
whatever Jake had said or been before, war memorial and all.

Jake walked home in the warmth of midday with the fullness
of spring exploding around him, engorging the very air he
breathed, and he was a bit winded and sweaty when he mounted
the porch and opened the screen door. Pastine was in the kitchen
fixing dinner, the smell of cooking greens heavy in the room.
Francine was sitting at the table with the baby. Emma Henrietta
they had named her, after Jake's mother and grandmother. Francine had come to them the day after the news of Henry's death,
asked for some Tibbetts family names, and settled on Emma
Henrietta. If she considered anything from her own lineage, she
never mentioned it. She was very matter-of-fact about the whole
business, as she was about everything. Now the baby sat on her
lap, head bobbing unsteadily toward the sound of Jake's entrance, eyes dancing. At four months, she could hold her head
up and make bubbles with her lips.

"You're early," Pastine said, wiping her hands on her apron
and brushing a strand of hair from her face.

"Whit brought this," he said, placing the letter on the table
in front of Francine. They all stared at it for a while.

Francine looked at the envelope, then up at Jake. "You open
it," she said.

Jake and Pastine sat down at the kitchen table, and Jake
opened the envelope carefully and took out the single typed
sheet. He sat there reading it, the tears filling his eyes and spilling over down his cheeks while they stared at him. And then he
folded up the letter and slipped it back into the envelope and set
it down in front of Francine. "They gave Henry a medal," he
said. "The Silver Star. The Army says he died leading his platoon in a fight with the Germans near some little town in Bel-

gium. I can't pronounce it." Jake wiped his face with his hands. "They say he was a hero. They're sending the medal."

They sat there for a long time when he had finished, the baby making gurgling sounds, Tunstall Renfroe's car rumbling past on Partridge Road as he headed home for dinner, a catbird scolding in the pecan tree in the side yard, and here inside, at the table, something of Henry so alive and present you felt you could reach out and touch it. Henry, who had been a ghost at this kitchen table for so very long, was—for a brief moment—back.

A hero. Jake was stunned. He thought Henry incapable of it. But there it was, from the War Department. In the last terrifying moment of his life, Henry Tibbetts had done the one thing he had never done before: He had taken his life in his own hands and shaken it for all it was worth. Poor, lost, wretched Henry—he who had slunk whimpering from every conflict with his own devils and archangels—had this once, faced with death, done mortal combat with his soul and won.

Jake looked over at Pastine, she who had been so incredibly stoical since the first outburst of grief. "Well . . ." he said, and trailed off. There seemed nothing to say. "He did his duty," he said finally.

"You're surprised," Pastine said.

"Yes. I am."

"Perhaps you shouldn't be, Jake."

Jake reached for the envelope, picked it up, toyed with it. "There were just so many times he didn't. This one time, he did."

"And look what it got him," Pastine said. She was completely dryeyed. There was not the slightest break in her voice. It was as if she had steeled herself against it. And maybe that was a good thing, because it took a long time for a soldier to become truly dead to the people he left at home. The government sent letters and medals, meaning well, but every time they did it was a chance to hurt all over again unless you were steeled against it. Pastine had never been an emotional woman, but now, her control was a bit awesome.

"There was another time," Francine said, breaking the silence. It surprised them both—him and Pastine. She didn't have much to say, particularly about Henry. She was a very private, very self-contained young woman, obviously used to making do, making her own way. She occupied a space, as she sat now in the kitchen chair with the gurgling baby in her lap, in a manner that said, "This is mine. For the time being." She revealed little, volunteered almost nothing. They knew little about her past, only that she was from Cleveland and she came from a large family, second-generation immigrants. Polacks, from the sound of her maiden name. And Jake knew that Pastine was afraid she would leave, take the baby with her and leave, now that there was no Henry to tie her here and ten thousand dollars was on its way in the mail. Pastine said nothing about it, but Jake could tell.

"He came to see me when the man I was with got killed in a jeep accident," Francine said. She looked straight at Jake in that strange unblinking way she had, that tough little Cleveland, Ohio, way of hers, spoke in those clipped, harsh sentences that he was just beginning to understand. *The man I was with.* She hit him right between the eyes with it.

"He came to tell me," she went on. "He didn't have to. Nobody had to tell me a thing. I mean, I wasn't married to the guy or anything. But Henry came and told me, and then he came back later to see how I was doing. I was lousy, that's how I was doing. But he took care of me. He didn't have to give me the time of day, but he took care of me. And later on, when he asked me to marry him, I thought to myself, Ain't nobody ever taken care of me before, and what's a better reason to get married to a guy?"

Jake just sat there, not knowing what in the hell to say.

"So now Henry's gone and done his duty again," she finished. She didn't sound bitter about it. Just matter-of-fact. She slid her chair back from the table with a squeak and stood up, hoisting the baby to her shoulder and turning toward the door.

"You can leave her down here with me if you want," Pastine said, perhaps a bit too quickly.

Francine stopped, turned back to them. "You're afraid I'm going to leave," she said. "When the check gets here."

"Yes," Pastine said.

"I guess I can go anytime I want to."

"Yes. Or you can stay."

"Because I owe it to Henry?"

Pastine sat very still in the chair, her voice low and measured. "You don't owe Henry a thing. You can stay or not stay depending on whether you want to. That's all. If it's a matter of going where you're wanted, there shouldn't be any question of that.''

The baby began to whimper in Francine's arms and reached for a fistful of her hair. ''No,'' Francine said, ''there's no question of that.''

''So, will you stay?''

Francine looked at the baby and back at them. ''Yeah,'' she said. ''For now.'' Then she turned and went upstairs, leaving the letter from the War Department on the kitchen table.

Pastine got up and went back to the pot of greens cooking on the stove. Jake sat quietly, thinking that these two women were the people who had a claim on Henry, not he. He had had reason enough to wash his hands of poor, wretched, disgraced Henry who refused to take responsibility for himself. But the fact remained that the hand-washing had been done. Now, about all he could do was to make peace with his lost soul, let bygones be bygones, accord Henry the dignity a dead man deserved and marvel that Henry had died a hero. Other than that, he had no claim. And in this, he was a stranger at his own table. The way Henry had been for so long.

SIX

*I*T was June when they sent the body home, and by then the fighting was over in Europe. There was still the Pacific, but MacArthur had been doing brilliantly with the leftovers from the Big Conflict, and now that the full wrath of the Allies could be turned on the Japs, they wouldn't last long. That's what people said.

George Poulos's boy, with the 82nd Airborne, finished the business in Czechoslovakia as the Americans threw their might at ghosts—the myth of Hitler's secret fortress in Bavaria—while the Russians marveled at their good fortune and raced alone into ruined Berlin. George Poulos, Junior, having fought through the Normandy invasion and the Battle of the Bulge with nothing worse than blisters, was wounded in the arm by flying shrapnel when a burning German Tiger tank exploded in an alleyway in a small Czechoslovakian village. It was a minor wound, but it earned him a Purple Heart to go with the Silver Star with Oak Leaf Cluster and the Distinguished Service Medal he had won in combat. He was recuperating in England.

Biscuit Brunson's boy was frazzled from lack of sleep during the month of June. His Seabee unit was bivouacked next to the huge airfield at Tinian, and the coral and sand shook with the roar of the B-29s lifting tons of bombs from the runway at all hours of the day and night, forming an airborne bridge you could almost walk across to the incendiary hell that Japan was becoming. Iwo Jima had fallen, Okinawa had been stormed on Easter Sunday. Ernie Pyle, the war correspondent, had already headed for the Pacific. Ernie Pyle wrote about men at war, and men were no longer at war in Europe.

But Europe still smelled of death. Allied troops opened the wretched doors of Birkenau and Auschwitz and saw carnage that made even them, battle-hardened men, weak. There was a sickening odor that hovered over the ravaged fields and villages and cities of Europe and haunted the eyes of the survivors. American soldiers wanted to leave it behind, to get home and see if there was any sanity left in the world.

All in good time, the generals said.

But a minor general in Eisenhower's headquarters, with an eye toward public relations, suggested that if live troops could not be shipped home immediately, why not dead ones? A few hundred bodies, he said—to give the signal that things were done with in Europe. Eisenhower liked the idea. So two thousand were chosen, exhumed from battlefields across Europe, men from every corner of the nation. On a day in early June when several thousand Japanese burned to a crisp as eight hundred Superfortresses turned Tokyo's paper houses into a holocaust, a plain gray metal casket bearing the stamp TIBBETTS HENRY F 1LT 02049466 was loaded with hundreds of others onto a transport ship in the port of Cherbourg. In Cherbourg, it was a dark, wet day, the air thick with the cool rains that presage the slipping of spring into summer in northern France. In Tokyo, a globe away, night was day, brighter than sunshine.

It took two weeks for the dumpy little Liberty Ship to make the voyage to Wilmington, North Carolina. From there, the caskets headed homeward, each escorted by a member of the Armed Forces of suitable rank.

They had been expecting the lieutenant. The War Department had telegraphed to say the casket bearing Henry's body would be arriving on the train, accompanied by an escort officer. But still it gave Jake a start, seeing him through the screen door, standing in the shade of the front porch with the late afternoon glare of June behind him. He thought for a brief, stupid moment of Henry. He was tall and bit slope-shouldered, the way Henry had been—tall like the Cahoons. But then he saw it was not Henry, couldn't be, of course. This young man was broader across the shoulders and he had fine sandy hair, close-cropped and matted wetly to his skull in a neat narrow line where his campaign cap had been. The cap was in his hand.

"Mr. Tibbetts?" The young lieutenant squinted into the semi-darkness of the hallway at Jake.

Jake opened the door. "Yes."

"Grover Whalen, sir. From the Army."

"Come in, come in," he said, grabbing the lieutenant's hand, pumping it, pulling him into the hallway. "You've brought Henry home."

There was a little snap to the lieutenant's head, as if it had caught him by surprise to have it put just that way. Jake could see how it must have been, riding the train with the casket back in the baggage compartment, riding down through the hot green countryside with nothing but the monotony of steel clacking on steel, keeping company with a dead stranger whose only kinship was that he, too, had been an officer and a warrior, wondering how the hell it would go with the family, perhaps dreading it. Strange town, strange people, dead soldier.

Jake smiled to reassure him. "You've come a long way, I imagine."

"Yes sir," Grover Whalen said. "Fort Benning." He stood now in the hollow coolness of the entrance hall, cap in hand, silver bar gleaming on one collar point and crossed infantry rifles on the other. Jake noticed the beads of sweat on his forehead, the wet splotches under his armpits. He looked past him at the vacant front yard.

"Did you walk all the way out here?"

"Yes sir. It's not far, really. They gave me directions at the funeral home."

"Not far," Jake repeated. "I walk it twice a day myself, back and forth. But you've got a limp."

"Nothing much," he said, and Jake noticed then the semi-circular RANGER patch on his left shoulder next to the seam.

"Well, come on in," Jake said, pulling him farther into the house. "Have a seat in here"—he directed him toward the parlor—"and I'll get my wife and Henry's wife." Whalen sat down in the wing-backed chair next to the fireplace while Jake went upstairs and fetched Pastine and Francine. Whalen was looking at Captain Finley Tibbetts's sword, hanging above the fireplace in its gleaming silver scabbard, when they entered.

He stood. "Ma'am," he said to both the women.

"Lieutenant Grover Whalen," Jake said. "Come from Fort Benning."

There was a brief bad moment for Pastine, seeing a tall young man in uniform there in her parlor. Jake could see her eyes go soft and he thought for a moment she might let go of her terrible control. But then she squared away her jaw and crossed the parlor to Lieutenant Whalen and gave him her hand. "Thank you for coming," she said. "It means a lot to us." Jake could see, too, the relief in Grover Whalen's eyes as he realized that these people had a handle on themselves, that it would not be a messy business. "And this is Francine," she said. "Henry's wife."

"Ma'am," Whalen said. They appraised each other, the young lieutenant and the young woman, and it occurred to Jake how much the world was given over these day to young people like this, how many young soldiers and young women had made brief lives together, private islands in the midst of chaos and fear and loneliness. "Ranger," Francine said.

Whalen nodded. "Second Battalion."

"Purple Heart." She nodded toward the double row of ribbons above his left shirt pocket. "And a Bronze Star."

"Yes ma'am."

"And hungry," Pastine said.

Whalen grinned, a big easy grin, and Pastine took him by the arm and led him into the kitchen, shooing the rest of them away while she warmed a plate of the dinner leftovers—fried corn, snap beans, ham—and left him alone to eat.

He emerged from the kitchen fifteen minutes later and they were waiting for him in the parlor, all five of them. The baby was up from her nap and Lonnie had come in and Pastine had sent him upstairs to wash his face and hands and slick down his hair so he could meet the young lieutenant who had come from Fort Benning, Georgia.

"This is Emma Henrietta," Jake said, nodding at the baby next to him in Francine's lap. "And this is Lonnie. My grandson."

Whalen crossed the room to where Lonnie sat on the edge of a straight-backed chair and shook hands with him very formally. "Glad to meet ya," Whalen said.

Lonnie gave him a look of unabashed curiosity and stared at the double row of ribbons. "What are all them?" he asked, pointing.

Whalen looked down at the medals and ticked them off with a finger. "Bronze Star, Purple Heart, European Theater medal, Distinguished Unit Citation . . ."

"You get 'em in combat?" Lonnie interrupted.

"Lonnie . . ." Pastine scolded.

"It's okay, ma'am," Whalen said, smiling. "Yeah, I got 'em in combat. But I didn't last long. I got shot the second day."

"Second day of what?" Lonnie demanded.

"The invasion. Normandy."

"Well, now," Pastine said firmly, "that's enough of that. Lieutenant Whalen didn't come all this way to be bothered about his medals. Sit down, Lieutenant."

He sat in the wing-backed chair and looked up again at the sword.

"My grandfather's," Jake said. "He was a Confederate cavalryman."

Whalen nodded and then there was a long silence while they looked at each other. Whalen crossed his legs and then uncrossed them and squirmed a bit in the chair. Finally, Jake said, "The casket. It's here?"

"Yes sir. At the funeral home. Redlinger's."

The baby began to fidget and whimper and Francine got to her feet and put Emma Henrietta on her shoulder. "She's hungry," she said. "Excuse me." Grover Whalen stood as she left the room.

They listened to Francine climb the stairs and Whalen sat down again in the wing-backed chair, and then Pastine said, "We'll receive guests at the funeral home tomorrow night, Lieutenant. And then the services the next day. Saturday. I hope that's satisfactory with the Army."

Whalen spread his hands. "Mrs. Tibbetts, it's up to you. Completely. I'm here to help any way I can. I've got no deadline, ma'am."

Pastine held herself very straight on the green settee next to Jake. "I don't know where you're from, Lieutenant . . ."

"Albuquerque."

"Well, I don't know the custom in Albuquerque, but here, the family receives visitors at the funeral home one day and then has the services the next."

"Fine," he said. "Where will that be?"

"The services? At the Methodist Church," she said. "That's all arranged. Cosmo . . . Mr. Redlinger has taken care of the details."

"And the burial itself?" Whalen flushed. "I'm sorry, I hope I'm not . . . I mean, this is my first time . . ."

"No" she said quickly. "It's all right, Lieutenant. We'll have the procession from the church to the cemetery. It's a mile or two, I suppose. Then something brief at graveside."

Whalen turned to Jake. "There's a local American Legion post, I guess."

Jake nodded. "Some First War fellows, maybe a young man or two who came back early from this one. Fog Martin's the, uh, what do you call it? Commander, I think. Fog runs a service station."

"Do you wish to have a rifle salute?"

"No," Jake said.

"Yes," Pastine said. They looked at each other.

Jake asked, "Is it any trouble?"

"I'm sure not. I'll get Mr. Redlinger to put me in touch with them tomorrow. I imagine they've done it before."

"Fine. All right, then. That would be nice." He looked again at Pastine. "Is there anything I can do?"

"No." Whalen shook his head. "That's part of what I'm here for. Make arrangements like that. I'll get the squad together and make sure they know how to pull it off."

"Will they use bullets?" Lonnie asked. They had quite forgotten about him, sitting still and quiet in the straight-backed chair on the other side of the room, taking it all in.

"Blanks," Whalen said. "I've got some, if they don't."

"Why you got blanks?"

"We . . . ah . . ." Whalen looked at Jake and Pastine. "They issue us a kit . . . for these occasions . . . and, ah, it has blank cartridges in it."

"What else?"

"Lonnie . . ." Pastine said.

"Well, I just asked," he shot back.

"Well, it's not something you need to know anything about," she said firmly. "You go wash up now, I'll have supper in a little while."

Lonnie got up and left and Whalen rose, too, pressing the palm of his hand against his left thigh. "I guess I'll get on back to town and let you folks have a quiet evening," he said.

"We'll be glad to have you stay here," Pastine said.

"Oh, no ma'am. I've got a room at the hotel."

"The Regal?" Jake blurted.

"Yes sir." Whalen gave him a curious look.

"Fine, fine," Jake said hastily. "Commodious. Very commodious. I've stayed there myself."

"Yes sir." Whalen took his campaign cap out of his belt, where he had folded and tucked it, and held it in his hand. "Well . . ."

"I'd take you back to town, but I don't have a car. Never owned one."

"Sure. No problem. It's not far."

Jake stuck out his hand. "Thanks again."

"Yes," Pastine echoed.

"My pleasure," Whalen said, then stopped. "I mean . . ."

"Your honor," Jake said.

"Yes sir. That's right." He hesitated. "I didn't know your son, of course, but they gave me a little information about him. About his Silver Star and all. I, uh, I don't know how you feel about all this, but I would have been proud to serve with him. I think . . . excuse me for putting it this way, ma'am, but I think he was a helluva soldier."

Pastine gave him a long look and then smiled just a bit. "I agree, Lieutenant Whalen. He was a helluva soldier."

They saw Whalen to the door and stood there as he went stiffly down the steps and across the yard and down Partridge Road, keeping to the side where Jake's years of coming and going had worn a smooth bare pathway in the grass, limping slightly but walking very erect with his shoulders thrown back. They watched him until he rounded the curve by the pasture, standing there in the doorway together, not touching, Jake thinking that Henry must have looked something like that in uniform, perhaps on a parade ground in hot dusty Texas a brief year ago.

When Whalen had gone, Jake turned to Pastine, but she cut

him off before he could say anything. "Go away while I fix
supper," she said, and disappeared into the kitchen.

He sat on the edge of the porch for a while, feet on the steps,
thinking that there was still a lot to heal, that it might take a
very long time, perhaps more time than was given to a man who
was almost sixty-five. It would help if Pastine would cry, if she
just needed him a little in a way that let him be the strong one.
But she wouldn't do that. She was taking this in the same quiet,
stoical way she had taken Ideal Benefield's ostracism for almost
fifteen years now. It was, come to think of it, all part of the
baggage that was Henry and the ghost of Henry. Pastine might
have forgiven Henry everything he ever did (Jake imagined that
she had) but she had not been immune. Jake had washed his
hands of Henry. Pastine had refused to. And Jake was hard put
to decide which was worse.

———

He woke in the dead of night thinking the unthinkable. It didn't
come to him in a dream and there was no warning. It was just
suddenly there, full-blown, and it jerked him awake so fiercely
that he almost cried out. And it kept him awake the rest of the
night, lying there in the double bed with Pastine sleeping easily
beside him, unknowing. When dawn began to color the branches
of the pecan tree outside their open window, he got out of bed
and carried the unthinkable down the stairs with him like a beast
of burden, knowing what he must eventually do, and dreading
it terribly.

But he held it inside all that day, avoiding the temptation to
go round to Rosh Benefield's office and unburden himself, perhaps because he sensed that Rosh would recoil at the unthinkable. He wandered muttering about the *Free Press* office all
morning, making futile gestures toward the next week's edition
of the paper. When Lieutenant Grover Whalen came by late in
the morning to tell him he had organized an American Legion
squad for the military salute at graveside, Jake was vague and
distracted. He wanted to blurt out the unthinkable, but something powerful kept him from it, perhaps the dread of knowing
that when he did, things would come unhinged. He kept his
mouth shut at dinner and all through a long afternoon of more
wandering about the press room. He locked up early and walked

home, feeling the unthinkable building in him and knowing that soon it must come out, one way or another.

Twilight grew soft around them as they waited on the front porch for Rosh, who was coming in his car to take them to the funeral home. Jake hunched wan and exhausted on the top step. Pastine sat prim and self-contained in one of the wicker porch rockers, the one in which Emma Tibbetts had rocked her life away after she was done with Albertis's ravings.

Jake looked at his watch. Six-thirty-five. Rosh would get them there early, because that was the way it was done. It was an ironclad understanding that the family arrived first at the funeral home and gave itself a while to make peace with the deceased and compose itself before the community arrived.

Francine, from the other rocker, asked, "Why haven't you ever bought a car?"

Why not, indeed? Maybe it was a self-imposed isolation out here near the end of Partridge Road. The mile and a half that separated them from the center of town might be a path worn smooth from their commerce, but they were a continent away in the utter stillness of their own dark. It suited Jake.

"A car?" Jake said. "Never needed a car. Lots of folks don't have cars."

"They don't live halfway to East Jesus, either," Francine said.

She was a smart-ass woman, Jake had decided. He was getting to where he could understand what she said, and a lot of it was smart-ass. "You can stick a firecracker up a frog's rump, and the frog will jump farther and faster than he ever did before," Jake said, "but when he gets done, he'll figure out he's lost the use of his hind legs."

"Fer chrissake," Francine said. "That's a buncha baloney."

"Hah!" Pastine said from her rocker. "His middle name."

Perhaps it was something about the quality of evening and voices, but a snatch of memory came to him then. His mother's voice, distant and wispy, encased in the rhythm of her creaking chair: "He was," Emma had said, "a sweet man in his youth. He once jumped from the bridge into Whitewater Creek to rescue a child who had fallen from a rowboat. We drove by in the buggy and people were standing up in the boat screaming that they couldn't swim. So he just leaped over the bridge railing and into the water and grabbed the child—a little girl, as I remember—and handed her up to the people in the boat. Then he swam to the bank and collapsed there and started crying, 'She almost drowned. She almost drowned.' As if his heart would break. Then I looked and there was something flopping around in his pocket and it was a minnow and we laughed about that.''

Jake knew he had every word of it perfectly in his memory, just the way she had said it, more to herself than to Jake and Pastine, who had been sitting there, newly married, on the porch with her. He realized, remembering it, that she had been talking about his father, Albertis, in the days before the melancholia had got hold of him. *He was,* she had said, *a sweet man in his youth.*

They heard Rosh's Packard then, rounding the curve in the road, and Pastine got up and went inside to get her crocheted shawl, check on the baby (who was asleep with a Negro woman to stand guard until they returned), and get Lonnie, who came out and stood silently at the edge of the porch as Rosh pulled into the yard under the oak. Rosh hustled them into the car and drove them to Redlinger's, where Cosmo and Grover Whalen were waiting, Cosmo sweating in a dark suit and Whalen crisp and tall in starched khakis, his double row of ribbons making a splash of color above his left breast pocket. They stood about and made quiet small talk in front of the plain gray stainless steel casket, and Jake began to feel the unthinkable welling up in him like a bilious volcano. There were flowers already, several wreaths and a blanket of carnations covering the top of the casket, and the room was thick with the sweet smell of it. There would be more tomorrow, at the service. Jake was a little giddy from fatigue and tension and blossom-smell, but he swallowed hard and let Cosmo arrange them in a little receiving line just to the right of the doorway so that people could speak to them first and then pass on to the closed casket where Grover Whalen stood at ease, and finally into little knots and groups that would ebb and flow like backwater in the small receiving room and out into the hallway, where Rosh would move about, bowing, pressing hands and elbows, keeping things moving.

They began to come promptly at seven-thirty and there was a steady stream for an hour. They all came, the people they had known well from their childhoods and some who were just acquaintances and a few they had seen scarcely at all, because coming here tonight was something you did. It was the proper thing, especially with a soldier come home from war. Everybody came they could have remotely expected to come—except for Ideal Benefield.

Some of it was curiosity, Jake imagined. They would want to get a good look at Henry's young widow from Cleveland, Ohio; or they would want to see how Pastine might have changed in several years of near-seclusion at the other end of Partridge Road (only the Methodists saw her regularly); or they might want to see how Jake Tibbetts was wearing his sackcloth and ashes these days.

There might be some of the morbid in it. Most of the people who streamed through the funeral home had a relative or close friend at war. If Jake Tibbetts's boy had made it home in a stainless steel box, did that improve the chances that theirs would be upright and breathing?

And, too, Henry in death was something of a celebrity because his was one of the first stainless steel boxes to come home. Others had died on foreign battlefields, but most had been buried there and their bodies wouldn't be shipped home until the war was well won. There had been several memorial services in this community, but Henry's was the first sure-enough funeral.

So they came in good numbers, mumbling and touching in the self-conscious way mourners do, not really knowing what to say. Jake had always thought it a ludicrous ritual, but he saw it differently now. They were good people who wanted to forget that Henry Tibbetts had made a godawful muddle of his life, and that Jake Tibbetts had been a burr under this town's saddle with his newspapering, and simply accord a dead man and his family a bit of dignity. So he stood there and pumped and pressed and mumbled for longer than he would have thought possible.

But he never stopped thinking the unthinkable, and after a steady hour of mumbling and pumping, it got the best of him. The crowd had thinned considerably; there were just a few stragglers drifting in from the warm June night. So Jake turned to Pastine and said, "I'm feeling a little faint. I've got to get some air." She looked at him sharply, but didn't say anything. He backed out of the receiving line and headed for the door, and as he passed Lieutenant Grover Whalen, he tapped him on the shoulder and said, "Come with me." He bore through and around the small knots of people in the hallway, nodding and babbling, until he and Whalen burst free of the crowd and headed down the narrow hallway to Cosmo Redlinger's small neat office at the rear of the building. Back here the sharp chemical smell of embalming fluid was strong, the walls and carpet permeated with it. You could probably bury the whole building, he thought, and dig it up only slightly decayed a thousand years from now.

Jake closed the door. "Sit down." He motioned Whalen into a chair and leaned against Cosmo's desk. "Something's on my mind, son, and I want you to level with me."

"Yes sir."

Jake took a deep breath and gave voice, finally, to the unthinkable. "How do you know that's Henry in that box?"

Grover Whalen propped his elbows on the armrests of the chair, clasped his hands in front of him, and stared at them for a moment. "Well, sir, the Army says it is."

"The Army says it is," Jake repeated.

"Yes sir."

"Excuse me for saying so, Lieutenant, but that ain't good enough."

He could see a little flicker of "oh, shit" in Whalen's eyes. "The way I figure it," Jake went on, "is that thousands and thousands of boys have died in the war. So it must be easy for the Army to make a mistake."

Whalen looked a bit relieved. "Just the opposite, Mr. Tibbetts. Because there are so many, the odds against a mistake in any one case are very small, don't you see?"

"But you agree they could make a mistake?"

"Well . . ."

"There are odds, you said. It's not a dead certain . . . excuse me, I didn't mean to make a pun . . . it's not a sure thing."

Whalen thought for a moment. "The Army has a good system," he said. "I saw it myself at Normandy. Every man wears dogtags. Like these." Whalen unbuttoned two of the buttons on his khaki shirt and pulled out his dogtags, two small pieces of metal on a long chain, and held them out so Jake could see his name, rank, serial number, blood type, and religious affiliation stamped on them. Jake nodded and Whalen stuck the tags back and buttoned his shirt. "Even if a man gets killed, the dogtags stay with him. The Graves Registration detail makes sure of it."

"What if the chain gets broken?" Jake asked.

"Well, they . . . ah . . . they wedge one of the dogtags between his teeth. Look, I don't want to upset you . . ."

"No matter. I'm the one who asked."

"So, you see, it's a good system and they're very *very* careful about it."

Jake let it lie there for a moment, and then he said, "How about the ones who are blown to bits?"

Whalen's jaw sagged. "Blown to bits?"

"Sure, Lieutenant. You've got artillery, don't you? And land mines? All sorts of high explosives. Don't some men just get literally blown to bits?"

"Yes sir," Whalen said quietly.

Jake could see the hurt in the boy's eyes and he knew the carnage at Normandy had been horrible. Jake's conscience told him to let this lie, to leave the boy alone; but the unthinkable thing deep inside made him press on.

"So some of 'em are blown to bits," Jake continued. "Nothing left but pieces. This piece, that piece. Who belongs to what? Who's to know? So the Army takes a leg here, an arm there, puts 'em in a metal box, ships 'em home and says, 'Here's so-and-so.' "

"No," Whalen said, suddenly very sure of himself. "That's not the way it happens at all. In a case where there's nothing identifiable, they just list the man as missing in action. They don't send anything home if there's nothing to send home." He hesitated for a moment. "Believe me, Mr. Tibbetts, that's your son's body in there."

Jake took a deep breath and held it in for a moment, then said, "Why don't we open the casket and find out."

"No!" Whalen said sharply.

"Why not?"

"My God, the man's been dead *six months*. He's your son, for God's sake. You don't want to see him like that. Do you?"

"No," Jake said. "No, I don't." And he truly didn't. He would give anything *not* to. It would be like prying into the most intimate secrets of a man's soul, to look upon his long-dead face. That was almost as unthinkable as the need to know that it was indeed Henry Tibbetts they would lay to rest tomorrow with all his baggage, once and for all. Sure, it made no sense. Henry was dead, wherever he lay. But there was something about bringing him back here in death to Jake Tibbetts, who had washed his hands of him. Jake had to be sure. *Not* to be sure, that would be the ultimately unthinkable thing.

"I don't," Jake repeated, "but I have to."

Grover Whalen stared at the floor. "This is crazy," he said.

"Can it be done?" Jake asked.

Whalen didn't answer.

"Can it?" Jake insisted.

Whalen nodded. "It takes an order from a health official. And a special tool."

"A what?"

"Tool. A wrench." Whalen wasn't looking at Jake. "The casket is sealed with special bolts. About forty of 'em. It takes a particular kind of wrench to undo 'em."

"You have one?"

"Yes," he mumbled. "They gave us all a wrench," he said bitterly. "They said, 'You won't have to use it, but just in case . . .' They said nobody's gonna want to open a casket." He looked up at Jake finally. "That's what they told us, Mr. Tibbetts. Nobody's gonna want to open a casket."

"I'm sorry," Jake said.

There was a knock on the door then, and Rosh Benefield stuck his head in, and Lieutenant Grover Whalen looked immensely relieved.

"Jake, you all right?" Rosh asked.

"No," Jake said.

Rosh stepped inside the small office and closed the door behind him, glancing over at Whalen and then back at Jake. "What's the matter?"

"I . . . ah . . ."

"He wants to open the casket," Grover Whalen said.

Rosh Benefield stood there, massive and imponderable, his small, bright eyes sweeping back and forth between Jake and Whalen, blinking slowly. "Why do you want to open the casket, Jake?"

"To make sure it's Henry."

Rosh turned to Whalen, put his hands behind his back, leaned forward in his best courtroom manner. "Is it Henry?"

"Yes sir."

"How do you know it's Henry?"

"The Army says it is," Whalen said.

"What are the odds it's not?"

"A million to one."

Rosh nodded. "Lieutenant, why don't you go on back in yonder and keep the Tibbetts ladies and young Lonnie company, tell 'em Jake and I are having a discussion, and we'll be along in a moment. All right?"

"Yes sir." Whalen got up and left and they could see, as he closed the door behind him, the dark sweat stain soaking the back of his khaki shirt.

"Let's get some air," Rosh said.

There were only two cars in the small parking lot behind the funeral home—Rosh's Packard and Cosmo Redlinger's somber Buick. The snout of Cosmo's Cadillac hearse poked from the small wooden garage next to the open space. A squadron of night bugs and moths flapped and darted around the bare bulb above the back door that bathed the area in a weak puddle of light. The night was warm, but nothing like the sweaty oppressiveness that July and August would bring.

Jake leaned against the back wall of the building as Rosh opened the door of his car and fished a pint jar of Lightnin' Jim's Best from under the front seat. He held it up in the light and watched the amber liquid flash gold, then he unscrewed the lid and passed the jar to Jake. Jake drank and felt nothing. He waited for a moment and took another sip and felt the fire building in his throat as the whiskey broke through the fevered numbness that had encased his brain since early this morning. He passed the jar to Rosh, who took a big swig, closed his eyes, swallowed, and smiled painfully. "We step from the cradle looking for ways to kill ourselves," Rosh said.

He passed the jar back to Jake and they both took another swig, then Rosh put the jar down on the fender of his Packard and leaned against the hood.

"You are about to shit in your own nest, Jake," he said.

Jake hung fire for a moment, and then he said, "You heard him. He doesn't know if that's Henry in that box or not."

"So?"

"So, what if it's *not.*"

"Bury him and be done with it. The dead have no names."

"But I have to *know.*"

"Why?"

Jake shook his head. "I don't know why. I just have to know that it's Henry. I have to put him to rest, Rosh."

"You never seemed to care before," Rosh said quietly.

Jake felt a flush of anger. "That's not so. I cared, but it didn't do a damn bit of good. You know what Henry was. You of all people."

Jake could see it again, as clearly as if it were happening right this moment at the edge of Cosmo Redlinger's parking lot, the searing flash of flame devouring the car wrapped around the pine tree at the bottom of the gully with what was left of Hazel Benefield on the hood, Rosh slumped in the front seat of Hilton Redlinger's patrol car, stupefied with grief. And Henry, cowering in the darkness of his living room.

Now, he could see the pain of remembering flash across Rosh Benefield's massive face.

"You saw it, Rosh. You saw what the bastard did."

"We're all bastards in one way or another, Jake. We spend our lives trying to find a way to live with that."

"Don't tell me you *forgave* him."

"I didn't forgive him or not forgive him," Rosh said. "I just got on with things. And right now, I think you need to get done with burying whomever is in that steel box in yonder and get on with things. I tell you this for sure," Rosh leaned toward him, a mountain moving, "if you persist in this business about opening the casket, you will destroy Pastine."

Jake wanted to turn and walk away, to escape back through the hallway to whatever was left of the mumble-muttering press of curiosity seekers in Cosmo's parlor. But he was rooted to the spot. He could feel the skin of his face tightening around his bones.

Rosh bore in on him. "I don't know where you got this crazy notion, Jake, but I imagine it has more to do with your own devils than it does with Henry. So I'm not going to let you screw things up for Pastine if I can help it. Pastine never gave up. She never let go. Right or wrong, she clung to that boy and it has cost her dearly. Now, she's got to bury him. And so help me God, Jake Tibbetts, I will not let you screw it up. For once in your life, just goddamn well leave things alone!"

They stared at each other for a long, long time before Jake finally spoke.

"You and Pastine," he said.

Rosh's eyes widened with shock and hurt and then he heaved a great body-shaking sigh. He picked up the jar of Lightnin'

Jim's Best from the fender of his car, held it in his hand for a moment, and then poured the whiskey onto the ground between them, splattering their shoes and pants legs with whiskey and dirt. Then he tossed the empty jar into the scruffle of grass next to the building, where it landed with a dull plunk.

"You sonofabitch," he said simply and quietly, and left Jake alone in the night.

SEVEN

AT midmorning it was already oppressively hot with the thick mugginess of June's first heat wave, the promise of unbearable July. Young Scout sat sweltering, grimy, exhausted, in the thicket next to the open field—an expanse of green, freshly mowed, fragrant, alive with the chattering of insects. At the far side, heat phantoms shimmered from the granite and marble of tombstones. Young Scout hunkered behind a bush for a long time in perfect stillness, feeling his legs go numb under him, welcoming the numbness that spread through his body. He didn't know how he had gotten here, or why. He just knew that it had gone badly in the night, that his mind was all fevered, that he was alone here when he should be someplace else, someplace important . . .

And then Captain Finley was there, kneeling at his side, offering his canteen. Young Scout shook his head mutely, avoiding Captain Finley's eyes.

Finally, he spoke. "Where have you been?" Young Scout asked accusingly. "You told me to come. And I came. But I couldn't find you."

Captain Finley didn't answer. He crouched silently, looking

out across the open field, eyes drawn to narrow slits by the blazing sunlight. There was something strange, distant about him. The way he had been last night, upstairs in the house.

He had never been upstairs before. He had always called for Young Scout from the yard, where he and Muldoon and the hundred good and lusty men of the Lighthorse Cavaliers waited in their saddles; or had been waiting in the dead midnight of the parlor, sitting deep in the wing-back chair by the fireplace. But never upstairs.

Young Scout sat bolt upright in bed, wide awake, when he heard the footsteps on the stairs, knowing instantly who it was and why he had come. For the first time, he was afraid.

The door opened, and Captain Finley stood there, drumming his fingers on the stiff leather of his pistol holster.

"You can't come up here," the boy whispered.

"I can go anywhere I want to, boy," Captain Finley said, loud enough to wake the entire house.

Young Scout cringed. "They'll hear you." He couldn't see Captain Finley's face under the brim of the battered campaign hat. There was only shadow there, that and the stub of the cigar jammed between his teeth under the curving slash of his mustache. Captain Finley was not a man who was used to being indoors. He didn't remove his hat. Long months in the saddle robbed a man of the social graces, that's what Captain Finley said.

"Up, boy, there's business to do," he said from around the cigar.

The boy felt his face flush. "But I can't," he said. "They say I have to go with them."

Captain Finley spoke quietly now, his voice like smoke. "Nonsense. The dead got no relatives, boy. Don't you know that? Besides, what do they know? Not a warrior in the whole bunch. Civilians, all of 'em. What do they know about burying a warrior? A warrior's for battle, Young Scout. When he falls, they tote his rotting bones back home for the civilians to fawn over. It's a trifling end for a fighting man."

"But . . ."

"There's fighting to be done tonight, boy. I need you."

There was a long silence between them and Young Scout could feel Captain Finley's profound weariness.

"I need you," he said again, and was gone, vanished from

the doorway, leaving the boy tangled in the bed sheets, a terrible wrenching in his gut. He got up after a moment and padded to the window and looked out into the soft June night, heard the shuffle and stamp of the horses in the yard under the oak tree. He stood there, feeling the dread deep in his gut. Then he heard Captain Finley's voice drifting up to his window from beneath the oak tree. "Are you coming, boy?"

He mustn't. But he dreaded being here, too, dreaded what they must do come morning. Finally, he said, "Yes sir."

Then he could hear them moving off, Captain Finley and Lieutenant Muldoon at the fore, cantering as a single body down the road, their sound fading to nothingness, leaving the great stillness of night. The boy dressed quickly in cotton shirt and britches. He carried his shoes in his hand as he tiptoed past the rooms where the others slept—the others who wouldn't understand a warrior's need to be among warriors this night—down the stairs and out the back door into the darkness of early morning.

But in the darkness, he couldn't find them. They were gone, vanished into air. There was only blackness, night sounds that multiplied until they became a roaring in his ears, and finally nothing. Until now, until he found himself crouched in the thicket at midmorning, dazed and sweating. And now, Captain Finley was back. He put his hand on Young Scout's shoulder, felt the boy flinch. "What's the matter, boy? You hurt?"

Young Scout could feel tears welling up in his eyes and he choked them back and shook his head.

"What is it?" Captain Finley demanded.

"I couldn't find you," he whispered. "I needed you and I couldn't find you."

Captain Finley wiped his gloved hand across his eyes. "I've got my own war to fight," he said, his voice dust-choked and raspy. "And the devil doing it. The war's changed, boy. We're fighting on borrowed time. The Federals, they've got iron in their britches now. There always was more of 'em, but now they've got the iron."

"You ain't quittin', are you?"

He took a long time before he answered. "No. There's the honor of the thing. Honor and duty." He lowered his head then, stared at the ground by his booted feet. "Honor and duty," he said again.

Young Scout stared at him, and then he heard a noise across the broad open field.

He tore his eyes from Captain Finley, squinted into the sunlight, saw the procession snaking its way from the main road through the winding double-rutted trail among the tombstones. They were far enough away that the procession moved like a ghost train through the heat shimmers from the baking earth. Their metal and glass danced in the sunlight. There was Grandaddy Rosh Benefield's black Packard in front, then Redlinger's long black Cadillac hearse right behind, and then the other cars, the muted rumble of their engines an undercurrent on the morning. They took a long time coming, a slow, torturous, shimmering journey through the tombstones.

Lonnie watched as they stopped next to a green open-sided tent and then people began to get out of the cars, black-clad figures—Mama Pastine and Daddy Jake and Francine from the lead car, along with Grandaddy Rosh, who looked like a huge black elephant. They went straight to the tent and stood just inside its shade, and the rest of the people stood back a ways while a group of men got out of the third vehicle and opened the rear door of Cosmo Redlinger's Cadillac hearse and pulled out the dull gray casket with the American flag on top and carried it, three black-clad men on each side, to the little platform under the tent. Then the rest of them clustered around, blocking his view, except for a squad of four men, wearing their American Legion caps and carrying rifles, who stood off to one side in a little ragged row.

Lonnie stood, feeling prickles race through his numb limbs and rump. Over there, that was where he was supposed to be. That was where he belonged, no matter how hard . . .

"Boy," he heard Captain Finley say at his elbow, "I need you."

They were all in place now around the green tent and he heard the voice of the Methodist preacher drifting across the open field.

"Boy . . ."

And then he started running.

Nobody saw him until he was almost upon the crowd. Then somebody called out, "Look a-yonder. There's Lonnie." And the whole blessed crowd of them turned around to stare at him, hotfooting it across the field, and the voice of the preacher stopped in midsentence. The crowd parted, drawing back so that he could see his own kin standing under the tent, looking at him like he was a ghost or something.

"Lonnie!" Mama Pastine cried. He could see the awful wrath in her eyes, even through the thin veil she was wearing over her face. Godalmighty, it would go rough with him.

"You! Young'un!" A different voice this time, a rough, deep man's voice. Lonnie was in the middle of them now and a big strong hand reached out and grabbed his arm and spun him around and he looked with terror into the eyes of Police Chief Hilton Redlinger. "Where the devil you been? Got half the county out searching for you!"

Daddy Jake was there so quick Lonnie thought he must have leaped over the casket in one gigantic bound. But he didn't grab Chief Hilton Redlinger and demand that he let Lonnie Tibbetts loose. No, he stepped back behind Chief Redlinger and slipped the big pistol out of his holster so fast that it suddenly just appeared in his hand. Then he stepped back a couple of paces, holding the pistol pointing down toward the ground, and said, "The whole mess of you. Get away from here."

"Jake!" Mama Pastine screamed.

"Back!" he bellowed, waving the pistol in the air. "Back!" And KER-WHOOM, he fired a shot into the air. People began to scatter wildly, women screaming, men cursing and yelling, the lot of them stampeding across the little double-rutted road, diving for cover behind the cars and tombstones, the American Legionnaires dropping their blank-loaded rifles and racing pell-mell with the rest. They panicked and ran, all except for Chief Hilton Redlinger and Grandaddy Rosh Benefield and Lieutenant Grover Whalen and Mama Pastine and Francine. They stood rooted to the spot, gape-mouthed.

"Jake Tibbetts, you sonofabitch, you're under arrest," Chief Hilton Redlinger cried.

"Bullshit, Hilton," Daddy Jake said. "You ain't gonna arrest nobody without a pistol. Let go of that boy and get over there with the rest of 'em. And take Pastine and Francine with you. Now!" KERWHOOM. He let go with another thunderous shot and Chief Redlinger dropped Lonnie's arm and backed away, a look of rage and mortification on his face.

"I said, you're under arrest."

"Fine. I'll be with you in a minute. Now git."

Hilton Redlinger turned and looked at Mama Pastine and she said, "Hilton, the man's crazy. Don't mess with him." Then she turned to Grandaddy Rosh, standing next to her, and said, "Rosh, do something."

"Jake," Grandaddy Rosh said, "put down the gun."

"No."

"Don't do this, Jake."

"Don't do what?"

"I know what you're about to do, and it's sacrilege."

"You're probably right," Daddy Jake said, "but I'm gonna do it anyway. Lieutenant Whalen, did you bring that special wrench you told me about?"

Lieutenant Grover Whalen looked stricken. "Yes sir."

"Well, come here with it. Lonnie, you go over there with your Mama Pastine and Francine and you take them over yonder across the road a ways." He waved the gun, giving directions. Lonnie stood there and stared at him for a moment. "Move!" Daddy Jake yelped. He moved, and Chief Hilton Redlinger moved, too, because they could all see the crazy look in Daddy Jake's eyes and Lonnie thought for the first time in his life that Daddy Jake had gone stark raving mad and was entirely capable of gunning them down. "Rosh, you and Lieutenant Whalen stay put."

They did what he told them, moving back across the road next to Cosmo Redlinger's hearse, behind which Cosmo himself knelt, ashenfaced. They watched in the unbearable heat as Daddy Jake stood guard with Hilton Redlinger's big pistol and Lieutenant Grover Whalen, the sweat pouring off him and drenching his khaki uniform, removed the American flag from atop the casket and handed it to Grandaddy Rosh, then moved around the casket with a funny-looking wrench in his hand, undoing the bolts one by one. It took a good ten minutes to do it, and by this time, people had begun to edge into their cars and back them out of the cemetery and roar off down the paved road. There were only a handful left when Lieutenant Whalen finished and turned to Daddy Jake.

"That's it," he said.

"Lift it up," Daddy Jake said, motioning with the gun.

"Mr. Tibbetts . . ."

"I said open it."

Lieutenant Grover Whalen pushed up on one side of the casket and the top swung open and he stared inside, then turned his head away. Daddy Jake stepped over to the casket and looked himself, then turned to Grandaddy Rosh. ''Come see, Rosh.''

Grandaddy Rosh walked over and looked inside, and then he put his hand on Lieutenant Grover Whalen's shoulder and said, ''Son, you go tell the United States Government to come get this poor boy, whoever he is.''

Lieutenant Whalen nodded weakly, then closed the casket lid.

Grandaddy Rosh lumbered across the little road to where Lonnie and Mama Pastine and Francine stood, and he looked Mama Pastine in the eye and said, ''It's not Henry. I don't know who it is, but it's not Henry.''

Mama Pastine fainted in a heap on the bare clay next to the road, and as Lonnie knelt over her, he could hear Daddy Jake saying softly, ''That damn Henry has tricked us again.''

BOOK

FOUR

O N E

O*LD* Henry knew who he was before anybody else did, but not by much. He hardly had time to enjoy being somebody else before the jig was up and he had to go back to being Old Henry again.

For a good while, several months in fact, he didn't know who the hell he was and he decided he didn't give a rat's ass. He did know one thing about his past, and that was that he had long been a person who didn't *seem* to give a rat's ass, but really did deep down inside, and now it was a great relief to *actually* not give a rat's ass. A man can know a good deal about himself without knowing exactly who he is, especially when it comes to something like giving a rat's ass.

He knew a few things about how he got where he was. He knew that the very first thing he recalled was hearing voices and remembering that he was a soldier and there had been a battle and that if there were voices, they might shoot his ass. One of the voices even poked its head up under the tank where he was huddled with some dead men. But Henry played possum, even when the voice threw some pieces of metal up under the tank. They went away after a while, and Henry waited a long time before opening his eyes and seeing that the pieces of metal were dogtags. He put one of them around his neck and crawled out from under the tank and that's when he discovered that his left leg hurt like hell. It was encrusted with blood, the pants leg caked and frozen to his flesh. He lay there a moment in the snow, hurting and getting very cold, and then he looked up and saw an old man looking down at him. With that, Henry passed out.

The next time he woke up, he was in a first aid station and his leg still hurt like hell and they were calling him Farquhar. Henry thought about that for a while. Farquhar? It didn't sound right, but it didn't sound especially wrong, either. He told somebody his leg hurt like hell and they stuck him with a hypodermic needle and as he drifted off to sleep again, he thought that Farquhar would do just fine for now, considering the lack of alternatives. As a matter of fact, he thought, he didn't give a rat's ass.

They had been calling him Farquhar for several months as they moved him from aid station to field hospital to the big red brick monstrosity just outside Paris where he was now. It had been a Nazi headquarters during the war and before that a girls' school, and neither group of occupants had been long on amenities. Still, it was a fairly comfortable place and the third-floor ward where Henry mended from his leg wound had a big, airy dayroom at the end of the building where you could sit and stare out the window at Paris in springtime a few miles away and generally not give a rat's ass. A nurse came one day and told him that his family in Idaho had been notified that he was alive and getting along. Did he want to write? Dictate a letter? Well, no, he'd never been much for writing letters. He came close to telling the young nurse that he didn't give a rat's ass about anybody in Idaho, but he decided to let it lie.

It was in the dayroom that he discovered who he was, or at least began to. He was sitting there, legs crossed, hands folded in lap, in a green-upholstered chair, when the major stalked through the room—a cigar-chewing surgeon wearing a white smock over his uniform, a bandy-legged little guy with great bushy eyebrows and gold major's leaves on his collar.

Suddenly, as clearly as if it were there before him, Henry could see a column of type on the left-hand side of the front page of a newspaper:

As anyone knows, the work of the military is done entirely by those of the rank of Captain and below. The decisions are all made and the orders all given by the Colonels and Generals.

This leaves the Majors. The sole job of the Major is to jump through his skin whenever a Colonel or General barks, and to make life miserable for those in the ranks below him.

A Major's sole recompense in life is the hope that he may one day rise to the rank of Colonel.

In any walk of life, there are Majors, whose duty it is to bow and scrape to the gentry and needlessly complicate the lives of common citizens.

One must, in any endeavor, determine who the Majors are, and stay out of their way.

Henry could hear great noises in his head, clangings and bumpings, painful flashes of light, then an overwhelming weakness in his body. There was nothing physically wrong with him. It was just that he recognized the newspaper column, realized that he definitely was not Farquhar, and figured he might have to give up not giving a rat's ass.

Henry sat there a moment and gathered his faculties, then got up from the chair and followed the major down the long corridor until he turned into an office. Henry walked through the door just as the major sat down at his desk and said, "Have you jumped through your skin today?"

"I beg your pardon?"

"Well, I'm not Farquhar."

The major turned him over to a captain, a psychologist who

wore wire-rimmed glasses. They sat across a desk from each other in another office just down the hall.

"So you don't think you're Farquhar?" the captain asked.

"I'm pretty sure of it," Henry said.

"Who do you think you are?"

"I don't know. I just don't believe I'm Farquhar. And I don't give a rat's ass about anybody in Idaho."

The captain went out for a moment and came back with a roster of names, three pages of it, perhaps a list of all the patients in the hospital. He sat down and passed the roster across the desk to Henry.

"Look it over," he said, and watched as Henry scanned the names from A to Z.

"See anything that looks familiar?" the captain asked.

"Well," Henry said, considering it, "I'm quite taken by Lothar."

"Is that your name?"

"I don't think so."

The young captain took off his wire-rimmed glasses, rubbed the bridge of his nose where they had made twin red indentions, then put them back again. "Would you look once more?"

"Ah," Henry said after a moment.

"What is it?"

"Jeremiah."

"Is that your name?"

"I think . . . yes, I believe maybe it is. It has a good sound to it, don't you think?"

"Splendid. Think now, does it suggest anything else to you?"

"Camels?" Henry said tentatively.

"Why camels?"

"Well, it's a biblical name, I believe."

"Yes. Quite. Anything else?"

"No, not a damn thing, Doc."

"But you think Jeremiah may be it? Your name?"

"Yes, I believe so. My first name, anyhow."

He told the captain then about how he had come to under the tank, how he couldn't remember anything about how he had been wounded, how they kept calling him Farquhar all these months. He didn't tell the captain he didn't give a rat's ass, but he did say he was quite confused about the whole thing and had decided to keep his mouth shut until he could figure something out. Just now, he had seen the major stalking through the day-room and it had convinced him that his name was definitely not Farquhar. Jeremiah, maybe. But not Farquhar. How did he get Farquhar's dogtags? Damned if he knew.

Henry was a bit of a hospital celebrity for a week or so. They poked and prodded, ran all sorts of tests, plied him with questions, had him look through geography and history books, magazines and newspapers, trying to recapture the rest of his identity. Some of the things he read tantalized him, but there was nothing he could definitely put his finger on and say, "That's me." Still, bits and pieces began to come to him, little parts of the puzzle. He mulled them and kept his mouth shut. He was in no hurry. No hurry at all.

They put him in a room with another amnesiac, a swarthy-faced young man of twenty-five or so. The doctors called him Joe for lack of anything better. Unlike Henry, Joe was looking high and low for himself.

"I don't know who the fuck I am," he said to Henry. Joe sat propped on his bed, looking at Henry over the top of a recent issue of *Life* magazine, while Henry arranged his toilet articles on the top of a metal washstand. Joe had bright eyes, a lively face. "I mean, ain't that somethin'! Fa'chrissake, I rack my brain, y'know? I mean, it ain't like I ain't tryin'." His brow knitted fiercely and he laid the magazine down across his legs. "And all I draw is a great big fat zero." He made a circle of his thumb and forefinger, then smote himself on the side of his head with the heel of his hand. Then he grinned. "But I'll get it. I'm workin' on it, Jack. I'm beginnin' to get little flashes."

"I'll bet you're from New York," Henry said helpfully.

"Doc says with an accent like mine, prob'ly da Bronx."

"That ought to narrow it down a little."

"Jeez, you know how many sonsabitches there are in this man's army from da Bronx? Prob'ly fifty million."

"That many."

"How da fuck y'figger the Army loses a guy, huh? That's what happened. They just fuckin' lost me, Jack."

Henry finished laying out his toilet articles—shaving mug and brush, soap dish, safety razor, toothbrush, styptic pencil—and stepped back to survey his work. "Have you asked them how that happened? How they lost you?"

"Shoor, I ast 'em. They say you got these millions of dickheads runnin' around, big battle goin' on, lots of guys blown up so's you can't even find a little sliver of 'em, lots of others goin' out of their gourds, y'see? You got some missing, some don't know who the fuck they are. Like me.''

"And me," Henry said.

Joe grinned. "We're sorta like the Lost Tribe, huh?''

"That's one way to put it.''

"I guess they figure you put two of us wackos together, we'll figger somethin' out, huh?''

"Maybe so.''

"I just hope somebody finds me,'' Joe said wistfully. "I just wanna go home.''

But Henry never found out what happened to Joe. Two days later, the captain called him in, offered him a chair and said, "Your name is Henry Tibbetts.''

"Oh, shit,'' Henry said. Because the jig was up. By now, he knew that his name was Henry Tibbetts. He was beginning to add some other big chunks to the puzzle, too, and he wasn't happy with what he was finding. Not one little bit.

"Is that right?'' the doctor asked.

Henry nodded. "Yes. That sounds exactly right. Henry Tibbetts. I'm a first lieutenant.''

"Yes. Anything more?''

"No. Not yet. There's a lot of stuff.'' Henry closed his eyes and tried to shut it out.

"It'll take some time,'' the captain said. "There's no hurry. It'll come to you. We'll help.''

"Oh, boy,'' Henry said.

"You don't sound too excited.''

Henry opened his eyes. "Oh, no. It's not that.''

The captain took off his glasses, played with them a moment, then gave Henry a thin smile. "The way I hear it, they almost buried you. The report from the War Department says the casket was opened for some reason just before the burial. They found out it wasn't you at all. Some kid, I understand. With a stomach wound.''

"Oh, Jesus,'' Henry said. "You got a cigarette?''

The captain pulled a pack of Camels out of his middle desk drawer, pushed it across the desk. Henry took one. The captain leaned across the desk and lit it with his Zippo. Henry inhaled deeply and the smoke rushed into his lungs in a hot flood. He hadn't had a cigarette in months. He felt light-headed. An old habit resumed, an old hand of stench and guilt tightening its grip around his neck, old poisons flooding his mind and body. Old Henry was back.

T W O

THE only thing he could see from the high window of his second story cell was the big pecan tree in the front yard of the county jail, and through a single break in its thick summer foliage, the clock tower of the courthouse a block and a half away. Jake stood there at the window most of the first day he was in the county jail, staring at the greenery and the clock tower and wondering what the hell they were doing with his newspaper.

Hilton Redlinger had taken him first to the little two-cell city jail that everybody called the calaboose in the alleyway behind City Hall. Two tiny cells and a corridor next to the outside wall— damp, filthy, reeking of urine and rot. Jake had gone meekly after he had given Hilton back his huge revolver at the cemetery. Hilton didn't handcuff him. Hilton didn't have any handcuffs. Anybody who balked at going along when Hilton arrested him, Hilton simply knocked out. Jake went meekly, once he had surrendered the pistol. Hilton might be getting old, but he was still a helluva man.

Jake stood quietly in the alleyway while Hilton unlocked the big iron door of the calaboose, followed him down the dark, damp corridor to the second cell, stepped in, sat down on the

302

cot. The mattress smelled like a thousand years of mold and mildew and excrement, but there was no place else to sit.

Hilton stood there filling the doorway of the cell, hands on hips, the big revolver slung low on his right side. Even in the gloom, Jake could see that Hilton's face was still flushed with anger. "I ought to beat the shit out of you, Jake," he said quietly.

Jake felt a sick lurch of fear in his stomach. Hilton could do it here in the dark, quiet, reeking calaboose and nobody would know it, could probably do it in a way that would leave no obvious marks, just a pulverized gut and internal bleeding. He was mad enough, Jake could see that.

"You probably ought to," Jake said.

Hilton took a step inside and Jake flinched, knowing that Hilton was about to lash out with those huge rock-hard hands of his. But Hilton stopped, held his hands at his sides, clenching and unclenching his fists. "You smart-mouth sonofabitch," Hilton said in a strangled voice.

Jake could see then how bad it was between himself and Hilton, how he had humiliated the man by taking his gun away from him in front of everybody, how he had made this man who had been his lifelong friend look like a fool. A doddering old fool.

"I'm sorry, Hilton," Jake said weakly.

"You're goddamn right you are."

Jake didn't say anything else, because he could see that it was beyond words. Hilton stood over him a moment longer and then turned on his heel and walked out, whanging the cell door closed behind him and snapping the big padlock, stomping down the corridor and out into the alleyway, slamming the outer door with another bang, leaving Jake alone, shaking with fear, sick with the smell of piss and doom strong in his nostrils.

As he sat there, Jake remembered the summer evening years ago when Hilton Redlinger had staggered out of a meeting at the Masonic Lodge above the drugstore and got into the back seat of his police car and bellowed for everyone to hear, "Somebody stole my goddamn steering wheel!" A small crowd had piled out the door of the Lodge, roaring with laughter, just as Jake happened by on his way home. They had pulled Hilton Redlinger out of the car and sent somebody to Lightnin' Jim's for another bottle and then all sat on the curb by Hilton's car, passing the bottle and making the soft warm night rich with their voices, to hell with what the Methodists and the Baptists might think.

One of the younger men had asked, "You ain't gonna put this in the paper, are you, Jake?"

"No use overstating the obvious," he had said. "When a trusted public servant makes a fool of himself on the town square, it's better gossiped about than written about."

Hilton, voice thick, had thrown his arm around Jake's shoulder. "Jake, you're a pisser, but you'll do to hunt with. Hooooo, doggies." Then he leaned back and passed out on the sidewalk.

Remembering it now, Jake thought to himself just how much of a pisser he was, how he had pissed into the wind again and gotten it all over himself. And how much damage, too, he had done to an old friendship—damage that might not be undone.

Jake sweltered through the afternoon, the sweat dripping from him until it soaked his clothes and made him light-headed, finally lying prone on the wretched cot and drifting off into a sleep haunted by heat phantoms, chased by grinning corpses that rose from gray metal caskets. He woke finally to see that the afternoon was gone, twilight lingering in the alleyway outside the single window of the calaboose corridor.

He heard a voice, high-pitched and tentative. "Daddy Jake?"

Then Hilton, thundering, "Get the hell out of here, boy! You want me to put you in there, too?"

And small feet running away down the alley.

Hilton unbolted the outside door, brought him a metal plate with two slices of ham and some potato salad and a piece of light bread on it, a metal cup of iced tea, slid it through the open space under the cell door, and stalked out, wordless. Jake ate every morsel and then lay back down in the gathering dark and went back to sleep.

The next time he woke it was morning. He heard bells and saw Rosh Benefield standing in the corridor. He realized it was Sunday and the bells were coming from the two churches—Methodist and Baptist—pealing away at each other like warring artillery from opposite sides of town. Hilton unlocked the cell and Rosh had to turn sideways to get through the narrow doorway. He stood there over Jake, blinking in the gloom. Jake sat up slowly, feeling the raw scratchiness behind his eyelids, smelling the stench of his own sweat. "I was in prison and you visited me," Jake mumbled.

"Do you want to get out of here?" Rosh asked.

Jake nodded.

"All right. We're going over to the courthouse first thing in the morning and you're going to plead Guilty."

"What's the charge?"

Rosh pulled a sheet of paper out of his coat pocket and read from it: "Disturbing the peace, discharging a firearm in public, simple assault, resisting arrest, failure to obey an officer, creating a public nuisance, loitering . . ."

"Loitering?"

"That's what it says here. That's what Chief Redlinger has charged you with."

Hilton stood in the corridor, glaring at Jake through the bars.

"Who am I supposed to plead to?"

"Judge Pettus Rawlins."

"Can I think about it?"

"No. Pettus is leaving town first thing in the morning. He won't be back for two weeks. I'll see him at church in a half hour, and if you want to plead Guilty, I can get him to hold off leaving and see you in his chambers. If you decide to plead Not Guilty, your case will go on the next jury docket. That's August. In the meantime, you'll stay here."

"Here?"

"Here." Rosh took a deep whiff and screwed up his face.

"And if I plead Guilty?"

"I don't know. Depends on what kind of mood Pettus is in tomorrow morning."

Thirty days in the county jail, that's what kind of mood Pettus Rawlins was in at seven-thirty on Monday morning. Jake stood meekly before him, drained from another day and night in the calaboose, with Rosh Benefield at his side and Hilton Redlinger right behind. He answered when asked that he had read the charges lodged against him by a duly sworn officer of the law, and that he pleaded Guilty to the whole lot of them—loitering included.

"One year," Judge Pettus Rawlins said. "Thirty days active in the county jail, eleven months suspended if you behave yourself, another year probation. Pull another stunt like this, Jake, and I'll put you away for so long you'll forget who you are."

Jake ducked his head. Rosh prodded him in the side. "Yes, your honor," he mumbled.

Hilton marched him out of the courthouse, past the pinochle game already going full tilt under the pecan tree on the corner of the courthouse square (the pinochle players paid them no heed; they were old men and had seen every kind of foolishness), on to the county jail a block away on a side street. It was an ugly yellow brick two-story building with a high fence all the way around, topped by two strands of barbed wire. There were two signs attached to the fence. One said COUNTY JAIL and the other said HOLLERING AT PRISONERS PROHIBITED.

So, he thought, I'm a prisoner. And then he thought, *So?* He decided that he wasn't particularly humiliated to be a guest of the county with a criminal record. When a man took his life into his own hands and shook it for all it was worth, he had to be prepared to accept the consequences. That was part of it. If a man couldn't handle the consequences, he wouldn't ever do any shaking in the first place.

Hilton turned him over to the sheriff's wife, who ran the jail, and he took up residence in the tiny second-story cell with the view of the pecan tree and the courthouse clock tower, and spent the rest of the day wondering what the hell they were doing with his newspaper.

The next day, he gave up staring out the window and asked the sheriff's wife for reading material. She brought him a coverless, dog-eared *Look* magazine from 1940 with a lengthy photo section on women's fashions. He read what was left of the magazine twice, every word, wondering all the while what the hell they were doing with his newspaper.

The third day, Wednesday, he decided that they had damned well better be doing *something* with his newspaper, because if it failed to publish, the U.S. Post Office would yank his second-class mailing permit, and there would be the devil trying to get it back. The post office rule was inflexible. Come sleet, snow, sin, sickness, corruption, or catastrophe, you were expected to publish a weekly newspaper weekly. He had heard stories of editors going broke while the post office dilly-dallied over a lapsed second-class mailing permit. Jake fretted and fumed through the day, through the hours when he should have been sitting on the bucket seat at the top of the big Kluge press, feeding sheets of newsprint into its maw while Lonnie ran the printed sheets through the clattering folder nearby. He hardly touched the lunch they brought him at noontime, and by the time sunset flamed the courthouse tower, he was exhausted with the frustration of not knowing. Dusk came quickly and before long he could barely make out the outline of the clock tower against the purpling sky. What the hell was he waiting for, he asked himself, a signal flare? He finally gave up and lay sweating on the narrow bunk until he drifted off into a fitful sleep in which Whit Hennessey chased him across the courthouse square waving an official-looking piece of yellow paper.

In the morning, Rosh Benefield came and brought him a copy of the paper. It was not much of a paper, but it was something. There were eight pages, most of the inside taken up by the usual advertisements (most of them repeated verbatim from the week before) and a lot of filler material, including all the type he had set on Thursday and Friday from the pages of trivia his rural correspondents had brought by. The front page was a curiosity. There was a lengthy account of the sermon given on Sunday by the Methodist preacher. Then there was a rambling and somewhat confused recounting of the Town Council meeting. And under the byline of Lonnie Tibbetts, there was the following:

Mr. Virgil Baker had the Grand Opening of his store today. It is called Baker's Sundries and Mr. Virgil Baker says he has everything from Soup to Nuts. One thing he has is a jawbreaker machine which many people have not seen before. If you have a penny you can put it in the machine and turn the crank and get a jawbreaker which comes in several colors. You can see all the jawbreakers inside because the top of the machine is made of glass. Mr. Virgil Baker says it is the first one in these parts and he got it from St. Louise. Mrs. Biscuit Brunson came in for the Grand Opening and she said she wanted some Luden Cough Drops and Mr. Virgil Baker said they didn't have anything but Smith Brothers but they are awfully good and Mrs. Biscuit Brunson said what kind of drugstore was that anyway that didn't have Ludens Cough Drops and Mr. Virgil Baker said he would have to order some. So they do have everything from Soup to Nuts except Ludens Cough Drops.

"Mother of God," Jake said softly. There was more—an announcement of a new war bond drive from Tunstall Renfroe, apparently written by Tunstall himself; several items about servicemen, a recipe for chicken noodle casserole. But the left-hand column, Jake's column, was blank except for a single paragraph set in boldface and bordered in black.

> The staff of the *Free Press* begs your indulgence for the next four issues while the Editor is indisposed. Correspondents and advertisers are urged to continue their usual discourse with the paper. Personal correspondence to the Editor may be addressed in care of the County Sheriff.

Rosh stood patiently while Jake scanned the paper. It was an abomination, but it was neatly laid out and, most important, it was published.

He looked up at Rosh, "Who did it?"

Rosh clasped his hands behind him. "They, ah, all pretty much pitched in."

"All?"

"Pastine, Francine, Lonnie of course. And they got some fellow from Taylorsville to come over at night and set type and help them make the press run."

"Pastine and Francine?"

"Pastine is responsible for the Methodist sermon. Francine and Lonnie sat through the Town Council meeting and I believe they, ah, got an approximation of it."

Jake looked down at the front page again. "What about Henry? There's nothing here about Henry."

"The War Department is turning Europe upside down, I'm told. It has gotten congressional attention. So far, nothing. And they don't know who the poor boy was in the casket."

So, nothing was settled. All that commotion he had caused, and nothing was settled. Henry, even in death, was up to his old tricks. Henry couldn't even come home in the right casket. Would they never be free of Henry?

"Is, ah . . ." Jake hesitated, "is anybody going to come see me?"

Rosh rocked back and forth on his feet, a mountain swaying. "Well, I'm here."

"And that's it?"

"I think the words Pastine used were, 'Let him rot.' "

"She's still mad."

"I don't think that's quite the word for it, Jake. *Humiliated* comes closer, but that's also inadequate."

"Well, what the hell," Jake exploded. "I was right, wasn't I? That wasn't Henry, was it?"

Rosh let him fume for a moment and then he said, "No, it wasn't Henry."

"Well?" Jake said triumphantly.

"I don't think it's ever occurred to you that you can't just tear around like a wild bull in a china shop and not break things, Jake."

Jake folded the newspaper carefully and put it on the bunk next to him. Then he got up and went to the window and looked out at the pecan tree and the courthouse clock tower. It was cloudy this morning, a thick overcast freighted with the heat and moisture of early summer, ready to unload in a downpour.

He turned back to Rosh, who was watching him. "Why did you come, then?"

"Damned if I know," Rosh said.

Jake ducked his head. "Look, I'm sorry, Rosh."

"All right."

"I didn't mean what I said over there at the funeral home Friday night."

"I accept that."

Remorse swept over Jake. "I'm just what you said I am, Rosh. I'm a sonofabitch. I screw things up a lot. I'm getting old . . ."

"Spare me, Jake."

Jake looked up, surprised at the hard edge in Rosh's voice, something he hadn't noticed until now.

"You can go just so far, Jake," Rosh said. "Folks will take and take and take, as we've all been taking from you all these years, and then finally something tips the balance. It's funny, you know, I think people generally admire what you did out there at the cemetery on Saturday. They're aghast, but they sort of admire you for doing what you thought had to be done, especially since it turned out the way it did. But as for me"—he bit off the words—"I think it was an obscene act."

Jake cringed, feeling the lash of Rosh Benefield's tongue, so civilly brutal, the way so many cowering witnesses and plaintiffs had felt it in the big airy courtroom on the second floor of the courthouse. Rosh never raised his voice in court, but he could use it like a scalpel, peeling away layer after layer of flesh until he left you raw and bleeding, naked and ashamed.

"You couldn't just leave well enough alone," Rosh went on. "It was either be right or be damned, and so now you're a little bit of both. You act like you're the only person in the world, as if the rest of us are supposed to hang on your every exquisite turn of phrase, forgive your every indiscretion, cater to your sense of what will do and what won't. Well, Jake, let me tell you, I've come to the conclusion that you're about nine-tenths horse's ass."

Jake just sat there and took it, gape-mouthed. Then he shut his mouth and swallowed hard, tasting bile, his own wretchedness rising up in his throat. Finally he said, "I never meant to hurt anybody." He put his head down in his hands and shut his eyes and stayed that way for a long time. When he looked up again, Rosh was gone and there was a great yawning space where he had been.

Jake thought a lot about Rosh Benefield the rest of that day and he kept going back to Friday night just past, when Rosh had poured the whiskey on the ground between them in back of Redlinger's Funeral Home. They had wounded each other before, as any friends eventually must. But this time, Rosh had poured out the whiskey. It had been something special between them, more than just the countless jars of Lightnin' Jim's Best they had emptied in the shank of the evening in the newspaper office. For Rosh, it was a small sign of his defiance of the furious and terrible Ideal, who had condemned Jake Tibbetts to perdition and forbade the mention of his name in her house after Hazel had been killed in the wreck. In the face of all that, Rosh had stuck.

He had stuck even when Jake had settled the score with Ideal for the vicious way she had cut Pastine to the quick at Hazel's funeral and then had shut her off from all social intercourse. Jake had bided his time while the rancor built in his gut. And then it happened in 1939 that Ollie Whittle built his radio station in the upstairs over the Farmers Mercantile Bank and, even before he went on the air, arranged for Ideal Benefield to air a weekly Saturday morning news and society program. Ideal was, after all, the town's social arbiter.

Jake wrote in his weekly column:

> This newspaper takes note of a forthcoming competitor in the community. One Oliver Townsend Whittle, until late a resident of the next county, has brought to our midst the marvel of radio.
>
> Henceforth, our sensibilities will be enriched by all manner of intellectual commerce, some of it, according to Mr. Whittle, coming by transcription from such citadels of culture as New York and Chicago. Our community can scarce go unchanged. Surely we unschooled bumpkins of the hinterlands will reap rich rewards. Our ladies will wear mail-order cosmetics, our young will hum the exotic melodies of the Hit Parade instead of good Baptist and Methodist hymns, and our Police Chief will benefit from the exploits of the Lone Ranger.
>
> One would be so bold as to suggest that Mr. Whittle should schedule a periodic program of local happenings, so that we can chronicle the social upheaval in our midst.
>
> Such a program must be undertaken bravely, boldly, incisively. It must be ruthless in its rooting out of the old ways and its heralding of the new.
>
> The key to such an endeavor, obviously, is the host (or hostess). We suggest, in short, that Mr. Whittle engage the services of some local entity who is so unflinchingly mean that her (or his) urine would etch glass. . . .

and then the shit had hit the fan. Everyone knew that Ideal had already been hired, though Jake professed ignorance. A delegation had called on him, he had apologized in print:

> Good souls in our fine community have brought to the attention of the editor their displeasure over the use of the word "urine" in these pages. In using the word "urine," the editor meant to give offense to no one, feeling that "urine" is a natural product of that sublime creation of the Almighty, the human body, and that it is as fit a subject for discourse as the liver or the pancreas or the thyroid. However, in all things, the editor wishes to be

circumspect and ever mindful of the sensibilities of his readers and the prevailing sense of modesty abroad in the community. The word "urine" is henceforth banned from the pages of this newspaper.

But the deed was done. Ideal Benefield banned the *Free Press* from her home and made sure that Pastine's social isolation was complete. Women who depended on Ideal's regard held Pastine at arm's length, like a leper. Marvel Renfroe even suggested to Tunstall that they move, as if the Tibbettses' social disease might steal down Partridge Road in the dark of night and envelop their own house.

But Rosh had stuck. He stayed away until the furor died down, and then he came ambling in one Wednesday evening about dusk carrying a paper sack and they got good and tight and Rosh never mentioned the column.

But now, Rosh had poured the whiskey on the ground. He had called Jake a sonofabitch and now a horse's ass. And he said it with conviction.

"You and Pastine," Jake had said accusingly. And that, he realized now, was what had really ripped it. Not what he had done at the cemetery, but what he had said in Redlinger's back lot. He had said it not knowing exactly what he meant, giving vent in a rush of emotion to something that had been festering inside him for a long, long time.

He knew Pastine had an existence quite outside his own. She had money. Henry Cahoon had left what must have been a sizeable inheritance—the manufacturing business, rich farmland and timberland, perhaps other holdings. Jake would have none of it, of course, and so she had taken her business to a lawyer. Rosh Benefield. Who had once been her suitor. Now he was financial advisor, confidant, intermediary to whom Henry had addressed letters. And what else? Nothing, of course. But Jake Tibbetts, in his perversity, had said, "You and Pastine." And that had ripped it. He had done that most unspeakable of all things a man can do to a friend, especially a friend like Rosh Benefield. Jake had questioned his integrity. So now Rosh was gone and Jake wondered if there was any hope whatever that it could be patched up. Rosh had stuck through everything else. But this . . . Jake was sick with despair and loneliness. The fact of imprisonment, of isolation, of banishment, suddenly struck him full force.

Night came, finally, and he lay awake for a long time in the damp, hot darkness, forlorn in the awakening revelation that a man could take his life in his own hands and shake it for all it was worth and make a goddamn mess of it. He cried into the darkness of his own soul, racked with doubt, before he finally slept, exhausted, near morning.

When he woke, Francine was there to tell him that Henry had been found—wounded, suffering from amnesia, but recovering—in an Army hospital near Paris. And that Billy Benefield was missing in the South Pacific.

THREE

*T*HEY let Jake out of the county jail on a Monday morning in late July, four weeks to the day after he had entered it. He stood for a moment outside the front gate after the sheriff's wife locked it behind him, holding the paper sack containing his clothing and toilet articles under his arm, blinking in the welcome sunshine, feeling the prickle of sweat on the raw tender skin of his freshly shaved face. He felt like a stranger here, back from a long journey. They had left him alone, all of them. It had been three weeks since he saw anyone he knew, anyone he cared about. It could have been three years.

The door of the newspaper office was open and he stood just outside on the sidewalk for a moment, hearing the muffled droning of the big window fan at the back of the print shop, feeling the hot breeze it sucked in the front door. The fan was the only noise inside. Monday morning, a newspaper to get out, and it was quiet. He stepped in, saw Francine sitting at his desk in the front office. She had a leather-bound ledger in her lap, the one Pastine had used all these years to keep the paper's accounts.

"Hi," she said.

His desk was bare except for Captain Finley's photograph,

the old Underwood typewriter, and a neat inch-high stack of clean white paper next to it. All the clutter—bills, flyers, letters, galley proofs, sheafs of copy—gone. There was a new wooden three-drawer filing cabinet next to the desk on the far side. The typewriter itself was scrubbed and shiny.

He looked around the front office. The head-high row of shelves that divided front office from print shop was nearly bare, except for small stacks of newspapers—back issues, he supposed—and the few office supplies he kept for local merchants arranged in small piles and rows, ink blotters, boxes of paper clips. Boxes of old subscription records, worn-out parts for the equipment in back were all gone. A broken chair that had been propped in a corner next to the kerosene stove for years was sitting upright with a new leg. The front windows were clean. And on one shelf—a radio.

He took it all in, and finally he said, "Hello."

"Gladjerback," Francine said.

He set his paper sack down on the chair next to his desk, the chair Rosh Benefield always used. "Where's Pastine?"

"Home. She's expecting you for dinner."

"And what are you doing?" he asked, staring at the ledger.

"Doing the books," she said.

"Pastine does the books," Jake said, his voice rising.

"Not anymore. She quit."

"Then . . ." Jake hung fire, "I'll do my own books."

Francine closed the ledger slowly and sat back in the chair. *His* chair. "Fine. But Pastine told me you once said you were a newspaperman, not a business tycoon. I'm a qualified bookkeeper, and right now you need a bookkeeper, since Pastine has quit."

"Quit," he said.

"That's right. She said she'd rather be a business tycoon than a newspaperwoman. She walked out at the end of last week and she says she isn't coming back. But she showed me what's what before she left." Francine patted the big ledger. "I've got it all organized."

"Organized." Jake spat out the word.

"So you can be a newspaperman and not worry with the tycoon part."

"God knows this place needs a newspaperman," he snapped, feeling the heat rising in him. They had made *his* newspaper a farce in the space of one month. Recipes and sermons on the front page! They had let him sit there and rot in the county jail while they filled the pages of *his* newspaper with chicken noodle casserole and religious homilies! They had not once communicated with him, had not once asked him to contribute a single word to *his* newspaper. And they had cleaned up the goddamn place, to boot.

"You're right about that," Francine said. "I hope I never have to go to another Town Council meeting. I don't know what you find about it that's worth putting in the paper, anyway."

"Well, I'm back," he said stiffly. "And we'll settle this business about the books later."

"Okay," she said, and sat there.

He walked into the back shop, wandered around for several minutes, touching things—the Linotype, the Kluge, makeup tables, type cases—feeling the cool smooth metal, breathing in the smell of ink and glycerin and paper, listening to the hiss and pop of the Linotype as it sat waiting for him. The women had not messed with anything back here, but the printer, the man they had brought in to help them with the paper, had moved a few things about. Nothing major—an ink roller here, a type stick there—but it would take Jake a few days to get things back to normal, back where he could reach blindly and feel every item exactly where he knew it would be. God, he had missed this abominable business.

"Jake . . ."

He turned and saw George Poulos standing there in the opening between front office and shop, a folded paper bag in his hand.

"I brought my copy over," George said, holding up the bag.

Jake blinked at him. "Why'd you do that? I always come get your copy."

"Well, I was over this way."

"Doing what?"

"On business."

Jake motioned him into the back shop. "Well, come on back."

George offered his hand, a bit tentatively, and Jake took it. "Good to see you back, Jake," George said.

"Humph."

"The, ah . . ."—he indicated the front office with a toss of his head—"the ladies took care of me just fine while you were, ah, gone . . ." He paused and the silence hung between them for a moment. "But it's sure good having you back."

Jake heard voices up front and he looked over George's shoulder to see Fog Martin come in, Francine rise to greet him.

"Be with you in a minute," Jake called.

"That's okay, Jake," Fog said. "Miz Francine here can take care of me. Just need to order a rubber stamp. For the filling station. Good to see you, Jake."

"Yeah."

Jake turned back to George and they went over the items and prices George had printed neatly on the paper bag for this week's advertisement, Jake making notes about how each would be set in type and displayed. It took them fifteen minutes, and during that time, two more people came in the front office—a woman with a wedding announcement and an overalled farmer renewing his subscription.

"Stays right busy around here," George Poulos said.

Jake gave him a long look. "What the hell for?"

George blushed. "Well," he said in a low voice, "she's young and good-looking, and folks like to hear her talk."

"Humph."

When George had left, he sat down at the Linotype machine, checked it over, ran his fingers over the keyboard, tapped out a line of type to make sure that everything was all right. The machine wheezed and clattered and popped the slug out of its belly. Jake plucked it from the tray at the side of the machine, held the hot slug gingerly in his hand, examined it, then tossed it in the box of used slugs to be melted down and reused.

He got up, walked to the front office. Francine was still sitting at the desk, leaning over the open ledger. She looked up at him.

"Has anybody done anything about getting out a newspaper this week?"

She opened the middle drawer of the desk, drew out a handful of papers. "Just this stuff. Some things the rural correspondents brought in, mostly. By the way, do you mind if I play the radio?"

"Hell, yes, I mind if you play the goddamn radio!"

"Fine, fine," she said, shoving the papers toward him. "Don't get overheated."

Jake took the papers, thumbed through them. "George Poulos says people like to come in here and look at you and listen to the way you talk.''

Francine considered that. ''Does anybody ever come in here and watch you set type?''

Jake looked at her a moment, then turned on his heel and went back to the Linotype.

At home that night, in the privacy of their room, they settled the business of who would do the books at the newspaper.

''Not me,'' Pastine said firmly. ''I've quit. My boy's coming home, and I've got a new grand-baby to take care of. I've had it with your newspaper.''

''You're just mad at me,'' Jake said.

''Yes, you're right about that,'' she flashed. ''I'm mad at you. I'm furious. I tell you this, Jake, and I want you to understand me. If things had not turned out at the cemetery like they did, I would have left you.''

Jake blanched. ''You wouldn't,'' he whispered.

''I would.''

And he could tell that she meant it, as surely as she had meant to chop his head off with his grandfather's sword when she chased him out of the house on Christmas morning.

''But I'm not *just* mad at you. I'm simply going to do what I *want* to do.''

Jake waited a moment, and then he said, ''I'll do my own books.''

''You'll be out of business in six months,'' she said.

She was right. He would. And that was why Francine stayed on at the newspaper.

———

At two o'clock in the afternoon of Monday, August 6, 1945, Biscuit Brunson stepped out the door of Brunson's Cafe, followed by a small knot of patrons, knelt on the sidewalk, cracked open an egg, and dumped its contents onto the concrete. Then Biscuit stepped back and they all stood in a loose circle, giving the egg plenty of room, watching as it began to turn white around the yolk and the edges began to curl. They watched it for perhaps five minutes, gabbling idly among themselves, until the yolk was glazed over and the white was gnarled and brown at the edges. Then Biscuit knelt again and scooped up the egg with a spatula and they all went back inside. The thermometer in the window at City Hall read ninety-eight degrees, and that was in the shade. But the temperature didn't mean so much as the fact that Biscuit Brunson had fried an egg on the sidewalk.

A man with an appreciation for irony could have made a good deal of the fact that about the same time, an American B-29 was dropping an atomic bomb on Hiroshima, Japan. The plane was piloted by a man named Tibbets.

They didn't hear anything about it, of course, until the next day, and then only a terse announcement from the War Department. Jake heard it first from Francine, who called from home on the telephone.

"Do you know anybody named Paul Tibbets?"

"Who's he?" Jake asked. It was Tuesday morning and he had interrupted a pitched battle with the snorting, clanking Linotype machine to answer the insistent ringing of the telephone in the front office.

"He's a colonel in the Army Air Corps," Francine said.

"Never heard of him."

"Well, you will. He just dropped a big bomb on Japan. An atomic bomb. They just announced it on the radio."

Jake started to turn on the radio on the shelf in the front office, then changed his mind. He shut down the Linotype machine, closed up the newspaper office, and walked around to Brunson's Cafe, where a small crowd was huddled around the Sylvania set on Biscuit's counter, listening to Ollie Whittle repeating over and over the few scant details that were coming over the wires. They could have all trooped up the stairs to Ollie's radio station over the bank and looked at the wire copy for themselves, but the news seemed to carry more weight coming over the airwaves like this. Jake stood at the back of the crowd, chewing on a cold cigar, listening.

". . . what the War Department calls an atomic bomb, with the power of twenty thousand tons of TNT, if you can imagine that, ladies and gentlemen. The early reports speak of terrible destruction in the city of Hiroshima, Japan, and thousands of people killed and injured. Imagine that, ladies and gentlemen, a single bomb of unprecedented power . . ."

Hilton Redlinger, sitting on a stool next to the radio, stood up, hitched up his gun belt, and said, "Well, that ought to just about do 'er."

Jake walked back to the newspaper and found Francine at work in the front office. "It sounds awful," she said.

"It's a big hit with the crowd at Biscuit's. They're all over there listening to Ollie on the radio."

"Do you think it will end the war?"

"I imagine," he said. "As Hilton Redlinger said, 'This ought to just about do 'er.' "

"I guess we're all ready."

"Yes, I think we all are."

Jake cranked up the Linotype again, but he sat for a long time at the keyboard, thinking about the bomb. He decided it was a little bit of a cheap shot. He thought about all of the millions of square feet of bloody geography all over the globe, fought for bitterly, inch by inch, all the great desperate battles and private individual horrors. And now to have it end with one big cheap bang.

Then he felt ashamed for having thought that way. If the bomb ended the war, it would end the horrors, great and small. It was obscene for Jake Tibbetts to contemplate the death of one more boy. They should all, friend and foe, lay down their arms and go home. Enough had been done in the name of honor.

He thought about Billy Benefield, lost in the vastness of the Pacific, his entire flight vanished in a huge storm that nobody had known was there. Weeks, and no word. Rosh had not come around. He kept to himself, waiting.

And he thought about Henry, coming home tomorrow, lost and then found.

———————

After dinner, they left Francine at home to tend to the baby and Jake and Lonnie walked back to the newspaper office together, Jake keeping a brisk pace, arms swinging, legs pumping, Lonnie trudging along beside him, slump-shouldered and terribly quiet, the way he had been ever since Jake had gotten out of the county jail. It had been a month, and Lonnie had scarcely said a hundred words to him, or to anybody else for that matter.

"I would have to say that was first-rate okra," Jake said as they rounded the big curve on Partridge Road, trying to make conversation.

Lonnie grunted.

"Not everybody knows how to cook okra, you know. Your

Mama Pastine, she's a marvel as an okra cooker. Some women try to stew their okra, and I had just as soon be forced to eat a rutabaga as to have to eat stewed okra floating around in a puddle of potlikker.'' He cut his eyes over at Lonnie. "But your Mama Pastine, she *fries* okra. The way it's supposed to be done.''

Another grunt.

"Do you have any particular thoughts on okra?''

"Nosir," Lonnie mumbled.

They walked a little ways and then Jake said, "Boy, if your bottom lip sticks out any further, you're gonna trip over it.''

That didn't even elicit a grunt. They marched on in silence through the blasting heat that made the sweat pop out on Jake's brow and course down the sides of his face. His shirt was wringing wet by the time they had gotten halfway to the paper and his underwear clung uncomfortably around his crotch.

"How long you gonna keep sulking?'' Jake demanded finally, breaking the awkward silence.

"I reckon 'til I get finished," Lonnie said fiercely, eyes glued to the ground.

Jake stopped dead in his tracks and whirled on him. "Boy, don't you sass me!''

"Yessir," Lonnie said quietly, drawing all up inside himself. My God, Jake thought, Henry again. Just like him, just like the way he used to curl up into a ball like a roly-poly so that you couldn't penetrate the tight, hard crust.

"Damn!'' he said. The silence, the sullen, insular silence was beginning to nettle Jake like a heat rash. Lonnie had simply stopped talking to them. Just the way Henry had done. It was maddening. He wanted to seize Lonnie by the shoulders and shake him violently and yell at him to wake up before it was too late, before he indeed became Henry made over. But he didn't do that. Instead, Jake stomped off and left Lonnie standing there.

Inside the print shop, it was sweltering. Jake turned on the huge fan in the back window of the press room and left the front door open, but all it did was stir the hot air. Lonnie came in after a few minutes and went straight to the type cabinet, where he was setting copy for George Poulos's advertisement. Jake watched him, but Lonnie didn't even look his way.

Jake sat down at the Linotype machine and mopped his brow with a handkerchief. And then the spell of dizziness hit him. It was very quick, a sudden roaring in his ears and the objects in front of him seemed to turn shades of black and gray and fall away from him, beyond his reach. All he could do was to lean forward and grip the edge of the Linotype keyboard and steady himself. He sucked in great gulps of air while the roaring got louder and louder and his vision dimmed to almost nothing. Then after a moment, as quickly as it came, it passed, leaving him cold and clammy and a bit sick at his stomach.

It was the second time it had happened in a week. The first had been in the front parlor after he had walked home late one evening. The heat had been oppressive and he had put in a hard day, and when he stepped up on the porch after the walk home, he felt weak-kneed and short of breath. He got through the front door and into the parlor before the reeling blackness hit him. He staggered to the sofa and slumped onto it, lying half-on, half-off until the dizziness passed. Then he raised himself to a sitting position and sat there very still and very quiet for a few moments until he got himself back together.

Nobody had seen him. They had all been upstairs. He heard Pastine coming down the stairs and then she poked her head into the parlor and gave him a curious look. He sat up very straight. "What are you doing in here?"

"Oh, nothing." His voice sounded hollow and distant.

"Is anything wrong?"

"Just the heat."

"Well, I don't wonder," Pastine said. "You insist on parading in it four times a day."

Next, he thought, she'll say for the umpteenth time, "Why don't you get an automobile?" But she didn't. It was just as well. He was too old for an automobile.

Now it had happened again, and as Jake sat at the Linotype machine trying to get his head cleared, he wondered if he ought to stop trying to go home for dinner in the middle of the day when it was so hot. But then he thought that he was *not* old enough to start pampering himself. What would the young men think if they got home from war and saw a bunch of doddering old fools lurching around town and hiding from the noonday sun? They would be eager enough to run things as it was. They would take a look at men like Hilton Redlinger and decide it was time for some fresh blood. Hilton was a doddering old fool. The heat made him cantankerous. He forgot things. He shuffled when he walked. Something had seemed to go out of him just over the summer. There were one or two who were bold enough to say (though not around anybody who might carry it back to Hilton) that he hadn't been the same since Jake Tibbetts had taken his gun away from him at the cemetery. It was there for everybody to see. And when the young bucks came home from war, the Town Council would take a look at some quick-footed youngster, maybe with military police experience, and gently suggest to Hilton Redlinger that it was time to retire. Well, that was okay for Hilton Redlinger. But not Jake Tibbetts. Nobody had taken Jake Tibbetts's gun away from him and he wasn't about to stop walking home in the heat.

Jake sat back in his chair and looked over at Lonnie. He was standing in front of the type cabinet, back to Jake, head down. *Click-click.* His fingers moved deftly, setting type. He seemed not to have noticed.

Jake sat awhile longer until he was sure the spell had passed and then he stood up, steadied himself, walked over and leaned against the layout table next to the type case where Lonnie was working. Jake felt drained and lifeless and old, both from the spell of dizziness and from the mystery that Lonnie had become. It left him baffled and miserable. Not like Henry, he pleaded. For God's sake, not like Henry. There was still time. Or was there? Lonnie was still a boy. He would be thirteen years old next month, September, but he was still small and wiry. There was no break in his voice, no fuzz on his upper lip. But there was one enormous change. He had stopped trusting in the way a child can trust.

"How's it going?"

"Almost done," Lonnie mumbled.

"Did you check everything?"

Lonnie looked up at him. "Sure."

"George is awfully particular about his prices."

Lonnie finished the line of type he was setting, then turned to the layout table and placed it neatly in the corner of the page form where the Jitney Jungle ad would run.

Jake peered over at the line Lonnie had just set.

"It's *f-i-e-l-d*, not *f-e-i-l-d*." He pointed at the word. "Field peas. You misspelled *field*."

Lonnie stared at the type and Jake could see his shoulders hunch up, his arms tremble with some deep, hidden rage. They

stood there, both of them looking at the type, and finally Jake
reached over and reversed the two errant letters.

"I've been thinking about something," Jake said. "I've been
thinking it's time you learned the Linotype. You've got this"—
his hand swept over the cabinet of type—"down pat. You think
you can handle the Linotype?"

Lonnie shrugged.

"It's a cantankerous old sonofabitch. But I think you can do
it."

"All right."

"We'll start Thursday morning. After we get this week's edition out. Okay?"

Lonnie nodded.

"Turn around here and look at me," Jake said.

Lonnie turned slowly and stood facing Jake, arms at his sides.

"Why don't you talk to anybody anymore?"

Silence.

"Are you mad at me?"

Still nothing.

"Well, for God's sakes, boy, what in the goddamn blue blazes
is wrong with you?" Jake exploded.

Lonnie just stared at him.

Jake took a deep breath and waited for a moment until he
calmed down and then he said, "What do you think about your
daddy coming home tomorrow?"

Lonnie shrugged.

Jake threw up his hands. "Well, to hell with it." He turned
to go and then Lonnie's voice spun him back around.

"What do *you* think about it?"

Jake studied him for a long time, trying to find something of
himself in Lonnie's face, wondering how he would answer this
most simple of questions.

"I don't know," he said finally. "I'm not mad anymore."

"What were you mad about?"

"Because . . ." Jake hung fire. How to say it? Mad because
Henry wouldn't *do right*? Mad because he clammed up? Mad
because of what happened with Hazel?

"I never thought your father took much responsibility for
himself," Jake said. "That's all I ever wanted him to do, really.
I was tough on him about a lot of little things, I suppose, but all
I ever wanted him to do was just take responsibility for him-

self." It was strange, standing here and saying these things to his grandson, talking to a boy about the father he had never really known and now would have to come to grips with.

"I reckon the war changed that," Jake went on. "It seems your daddy finally did take things on himself, and I . . ." he hesitated, "I admire that. I don't know how it will be between us, but that really doesn't matter. What matters is how it is between you and him. I'm an old man. I've had my chance. Now it's your chance and his. Depends on what you want to do with it. Depends as much on you as on him."

They stood there and looked at each other across the open space between the type cabinet and the layout table, boy and old man, and Jake wanted to reach out and touch him. But then he thought, No, this is not the time for that.

"What are you going to do?" Jake asked.

Lonnie ducked his head, but not before Jake saw the tears fill his eyes. "I don't know what you're talking about," Lonnie said.

"Yes, you do. Your daddy's coming home tomorrow and he and Francine are going to want to have a place of their own and they'll want you with 'em."

"No!" Lonnie jerked with a convulsion that shook his small body.

"That's what it's all about, isn't it?" Jake demanded. "All this sulking around with your bowels in an uproar."

"No!"

"You just don't want to make a choice. You don't want to take responsibility for yourself. Time's come you have to grow up a little, and you just can't stand it."

"No!" he screamed. "You don't know a goddamn thing!"

Jake slapped him. The blow stunned them both. It snapped Lonnie's head around and left a broad red welt on his cheek. Jake stood there, gape-mouthed, staring at him.

"Lonnie . . ."

But it was too late. Lonnie bolted. He was past Jake and through the print shop and out the door before Jake could turn around.

"Lonnie!" he yelled, following. By the time he got to the sidewalk, Lonnie was nearly a block away.

"Go on, then!" Jake bellowed after him. "Quit! Turn tail! Run away from it!"

Lonnie stopped, spun around, yelled back at him. "Just like you! You wouldn't even fight over the war memorial!" His eyes bulged with rage. "You quitter!"

And he was gone.

A woman came to the door of the house across the street, peered out through the screen. "What's going on out yonder?" she called.

"Mind your own business," Jake thundered, and went back inside and closed the door.

———

He telephoned and said he would not be home for supper. There was too much to do. He wanted to finish the layout of the paper tonight and get the forms on the press because there was other business tomorrow.

He also wanted some time to sit quietly at his desk with his feet propped up as the front office mellowed with dusk and think about how much he missed Rosh Benefield.

He opened the bottom left-hand drawer and got out the pint jar of Lightnin' Jim Haskell's Best and one of the glass tumblers and poured three fingers. The other glass was there, but it had been unused for two months, since the business at the funeral home, since Rosh had poured the whiskey at his feet.

Jake had gone to Rosh's office the day after they had let him out of the county jail. He had begged Rosh's forgiveness, grieved with him over Billy. And Rosh had said that it was all right between them. But Rosh had not been back around to the newspaper office. True, he had his hands full at home. Ideal Benefield was paralyzed by grief, as isolated in her own home as Pastine Tibbetts was in the house out Partridge Road. Jake wanted to comfort his old friend, but Rosh didn't come around. So Jake drank by himself in the shank of the evening while the heat gradually gave up its terrible grip and left the air close and lifeless.

What he would have told Rosh Benefield, had Rosh filled the enormous void in the chair next to the desk, was that he had come to question his most basic and cherished belief—that a man could indeed take his life in his own hands and shake it for all it was worth. It was a terrible question for a man to have to ask himself, after sixty-four years of believing. But the question itself was the consequence of all that had happened these past few months when things seemed to take on a life of their own, Jake Tibbetts be damned.

He had always assumed that what a man did in this life, if there was anything to him, was to try to come to grips with his imperfect self in an imperfect world. He started, stumbled, farted, and fell—and then picked himself up and tried again. In the process, he came to decide what was important and what was not. He came to some conclusions and sometimes he threw them out and started over. But through it all, he made no excuses and accepted the consequences of what he did and thought.

That was what he, Jake Tibbetts, had done for sixty-four years. What was different now was the dawning suspicion that no matter how much a man took responsibility for himself, he might not, at the bottom of things, have much say. He might, like Jake, be whipsawed by a sequence of events and circumstances that took away any sense of control over his own destiny. Or he might, like the hundred thousand poor bastards of Hiroshima, Japan, be here one second and gone the next. Grab your ankles, Jap, some fat-assed general in Washington, D.C., has decided to turn you into vapor. In either case, could or would God hold a man to account? And, faced with what a man like Jake was beginning to suspect, how should he act? Could he, indeed, take responsibility for himself? And was his life his own, to take in his hands and shake for all it was worth?

Sitting right here in this newspaper office, a few months ago, Rosh Benefield had agreed that Jake Tibbetts's cherished belief held true, indeed had said that it had saved his own life at a moment of personal anguish. Rosh had said then that Jake himself didn't really believe it, because he wouldn't give Henry the right to his own consequences. He said that Jake had been toting Henry's guilt around all these years.

So, what was it? Was the premise true and Jake's practice of it bankrupt? Or was the premise itself rotten at the core? He would like to ask Rosh Benefield that right now. If he were here.

And where was God in all this business? Jake might not be a religious man in the strict sense of the word, but he had always assumed there was an Almighty and that the Almighty had plenty to keep himself busy. What He expected of a man like Jake Tibbetts was that he would make his own way without a lot of whining and in the process bring no harm to man nor beast. He assumed that the Lord operated on common sense, and it made common sense that if a man toted his share of the load, the Lord would not meddle in his affairs. He considered it his own compact with the Almighty, a form of religion quite privately his own.

But recent events, including the big bang at Hiroshima, made him wonder: Was God a meddler after all? Did a man in truth really have no say? Was there something basically wrong with the notion that God operated on common sense and could enter into a reasonable compact with a man? Irony of ironies, had *Henry* been closest to the truth all this time? Henry expected nothing, ventured nothing, judged not at all. As far as Jake could tell, he absolutely refused to take responsibility for himself. He simply survived. They had sent another man home in Henry's casket, while Henry, incredibly, had survived. Was Henry proof that ultimately there was no such thing as responsibility—only survival?

Or was it just the opposite? Was the fact that Henry survived, was the fact that Hiroshima happened, proof positive that God specifically did *not* meddle? That rather than manipulating fate He instead just stood back and let 'er rip, allowed men to fart and fall and take others with them into perdition, if that's what they had a mind to do?

The questions swirled in Jake's head and doubled back on themselves and banged against each other. But what it all came back to, after due consideration of the great cataclysmic tides that swept mankind, was what went on in the piddly-ass life of one aging small-town newspaper editor. How was he, Jake Tibbetts, to act, in the face of all that had befallen him these past few months? Was he to throw up his hands? Or did the compact still hold? Must a man take responsibility for himself *no matter what?*

He and Rosh Benefield could have had a fine time with all that. Rosh would sit there, hands clasped across his great belly, small bright eyes blinking slowly, and argue all sides of the question and invent some new ones. The two of them would chew the great question like lions worrying the carcass of a water buffalo, and then Rosh would sigh a great sigh and take another sip of Lightnin' Jim's Best and say, "Well, at bottom, it appears to me . . ." and there you would have it.

But Rosh Benefield did not come around anymore to drink his whiskey. Rosh had his private grief and his private sense of honor. Jake had violated one and thus could not share in the other. And there you had it.

Jake was so lost in thought that he had no idea Francine was standing there until she placed the plate of food on the table in front of him, covered with a cloth napkin. He looked up, focusing slowly on her, and realized that he had drunk a good deal of the whiskey. His eyebrows were a little numb. He smiled, thinking of Captain Finley, setting type by hand with a fruit jar of whiskey at his elbow.

"What's so funny?" she asked.

"My grandfather," he said. "He was a pisser. 'Scuse me."

"You're a bit of a pisser yourself," she said.

He squinted at her in the dim light of the bare bulb hanging from the ceiling in the front office. She was indeed young and sort of pretty, and yes, she did talk funny.

"Yes, I am," he said finally. "A bit of a pisser."

She stood there for a moment with her arms clasped across her bosom and then she said, "Aren't you going to offer me a drink?"

"Yes, I guess I am," he said, motioning to the chair. "Sit down. Right there. It's a helluva big chair, but you can sit in it, I suppose."

She sat, and he got the other tumbler out of the desk drawer and poured a little splash of whiskey in the bottom. He looked at her, but she didn't say anything, and he poured another splash.

"That's fine," she said, and when he put the fruit jar down, she picked up the glass and took a good healthy swig. It made her eyes water a little. "Sheeez . . ."

"You may be the first cultured lady who ever had a drink of that," he said.

"You mean Lightnin' Jim doesn't sell to ladies?"

"What do you know about Lightnin' Jim?"

"Enough," she said, and shoved her glass over to him. He poured another splash. "I know he sells whiskey and he lives in what they call Haskell's Quarter and he knows more about white folks than they know about themselves." She smiled. "Have you ever thought about getting him to write a column?"

"Lightnin' Jim has no truck with newspapers," Jake said. "His place is piled high with magazines, but he has no truck with newspapers. He says they are triflin' things. And do you know what?''

"No, what?''

"The sonofabitch has real estate in Buffalo, New York.''

They let that hang there for a moment and drank a little more of the whiskey, and then Jake said, "What about tomorrow?''

"What about it?''

"Are you ready?''

"What's to be ready for?''

"Henry.''

She shrugged.

Jake gazed into the depths of his glass, where the whiskey gave off swirls of light. "Are you up to it?''

"I guess we'll see, huh?''

"He's no bargain,'' Jake said.

She laughed. "I never had a bargain in my life.'' Then she brushed back her hair with her right hand and she looked very, very young for a moment. You could see a girl there. Not a young woman. Not a tough little cookie. Then, as if she could tell what he was thinking, she said, "You want to know about me?''

Now it was Jake's turn to shrug. "I didn't ask.''

"Well, there's not much. There's eleven kids in my family. My old man was a timekeeper for the Cleveland Electric and Gas Company. Made sure everybody punched in and punched out, kept the time cards, made out the sheets for the payroll office. He wore a starched collar to work every day. He was very proud of that. A white-collar man. At Christmas, they gave him a bottle of whiskey and a big ham. None of the working stiffs got it, but he did because he was white-collar. He did okay. Kept his job when they were laying off people right and left. He used to say, 'Yer best defense against the vagaries of this world is a good occ-yer-pation.' '' She mimicked the hard twang.

"Good man,'' Jake said.

"The trouble was, they kept having kids. We coulda done fine, except the place was run over with kids. They couldn't ever own their own place, always rented. Never could get ahead.'' She stopped, took a big drink of the whiskey, gasped for breath, and went on. "But you're right, he was a good man. A big, jolly, red-faced man. God, he'd come in at night and he'd just go crazy hugging and kissing everybody. Mama always big in the belly, whining, and he'd just grab her up and say, 'Now don't you worry yer little head, darlin', there's always room for one more. Always room.' "

"Catholic?" Jake asked.

"How'd you guess? Anyway, they'd go right on making babies. I was the fifth in line, and by the time the hand-me-downs got that far, they were in pretty bad shape. Never anything new, just hand-me-downs. The whole parish helped. I think they were in awe of us. All of 'em good Catholics, but they'd look at Mama and Papa and shake their heads and say, 'Bless his Holiness, but *eleven*?' "

She stopped abruptly, emptied her glass, looked around the office as if trying to find something. She set her glass down and Jake poured two fingers. There was a flush of color in her cheeks. She sat there for a long moment before she went on. "So as soon as I could, I got out. I finished high school and then I got a job and went to night school and learned bookkeeping. And then I left."

"And that's it?" Jake asked.

"That's just about it." She nodded.

"And what about your family?"

"They're still there. All of 'em. All still in Cleveland. I'm the only one that got out."

"What about Texas?"

She took a small sip of her whiskey this time and watched him over the rim of her glass. "That's where I met Henry."

"I know."

"And that's just about it. I could tell you all about Henry and me, I guess, but that's just between us. I'll tell you this, he was very kind, very gentle. Like I said before. He's a gentle man, your Henry. I knew him for a few weeks before he shipped out, but he was very gentle to me. I don't know what the Army is sending home tomorrow, but I know what he was like in Texas."

It was strange, hearing her talk about Henry like this. He tried to imagine them there in Texas, in the heat, Henry being kind and gentle. But nothing came of it. It was impossible for him to think of Henry in just that way.

"He made a helluva mess of himself before you knew him," Jake said finally. He wondered how much Henry had told her—if he had told her about Hazel, about Lonnie, about all the lost jobs and drunken binges.

"Yes," she said. And there was just the tiniest note of accusation in her voice. Was it that, or was it the whiskey working on Jake's imagination?

She rose then and polished off the whiskey in her glass and set the glass down on his desk. "Eat your supper," she said. "I'm going home before I get stink-faced."

Home. That's what she had called it. Home. And then again, as if she were reading his mind, she said, "We'll get a place of our own."

"You can stay as long as you like," Jake said.

"The sooner we get settled, the better. We'll all have a lot of adjusting to do."

Jake nodded. "Everybody. Especially Lonnie."

"Yeah. This is all tough on him. I've asked him to try it with us, but I don't know what he's gonna do."

"He'll do whatever he's told to do." Jake started to tell her about the blowup they had had this afternoon, but he kept his mouth shut.

"Don't force it," she said. "He'll work it out. We'll all work it out. With a little luck."

"You'll need it," Jake said. "You'll have your hands full. This ain't Texas."

"I know," she said softly, and he could tell that she was a little frightened. But then she stuck out her chin. "We'll see, huh?"

"Yeah."

Jake sat there for a long time after she was gone, staring into the night outside his window, hearing an occasional car pass on the street and once, the drone of an airplane high overhead. He wondered for a moment if it was some lone, frightened Jap passing over on his way to exact atomic revenge on Washington, D.C. But then he thought, Of course not. The war's over. What happened at Hiroshima, as Hilton Redlinger said, that'll just about do 'er.

He ate a little of the okra and field peas and sliced ham on the plate Francine had brought him, trying to soak up some of the whiskey puddled in his stomach, and he was just about to get up to go to the Linotype machine when the phone rang.

"Hello, Jake."

"Rosh."

There was a moment's pause and then Rosh said, "I know

Henry's coming in tomorrow, and I want the town to be represented officially. He's a decorated war veteran and we ought to do something. What I'd like to do is . . . ah . . . present his Silver Star to him when he gets here. Maybe have a little ceremony. Something brief.''

Jake wanted to cry. Maybe it was the whiskey and the sound of his oldest, dearest friend's voice on the telephone, maybe the gesture itself and all that it meant among old, dear friends. "I'd be honored," he said. His voice was strangled. "If it's all right with Pastine."

"She said it's up to you."

"Fine, fine."

"Good. I'll be there."

"Rosh. Any word?"

"No."

"I'm sorry."

"Well, maybe something soon. I'll see you in the morning."

Rosh hung up and Jake sat there with the receiver in his hand for a moment before he set it back in its cradle, thinking of Billy Benefield lost in the blackness of the Pacific and Henry, plucked from the blackness of death.

It rang again almost as soon as he had hung it up.

It was Pastine. "Is Lonnie there with you?"

"No. I haven't seen him since early this afternoon."

"He hasn't been home. It's almost nine o'clock, Jake."

"We had a row," he said. "He's off someplace licking his wounds. He'll be there before long."

"And what if he's not?" she demanded.

"Then let him sleep in the woods all night."

She hung up on him. Things are not getting any easier, he thought. By God, Henry better be straight as an arrow tomorrow. Or Jake Tibbetts would kick his butt all the way back to Germany.

FOUR

*I*T was awesomely quiet out in the field. Even the sound of his own breathing was lost in the great silence. It was as if the soft night had swallowed up every evidence of life and left only ghosts there in the pasture.

There should be men here, a hundred good and lusty men on horseback, and a bantam-legged captain with a sumptuous black moustache and a great curving saber at his side, astride a powerful black horse.

But in the dread silence they might as well be dead as living; as well imagined as real. There might be a hundred poised for battle, or ten thousand. They might be Spartans or Roman legions or warriors of some yet-to-be conflict. They might be great machines instead of flesh and blood—tanks, troop carriers, landing craft. At any moment a radio might crackle to life with static and voices from miles and centuries away. Instead of a stumpy cavalry captain, their ghost-leader might well be MacArthur standing on the command bridge of the *Nashville* watching waves of Higgins boats making streaks of silver through the dappled waters of Leyte Gulf. Or Patton, the mud ankle-deep on his mirror-polished cavalry boots, standing beside a battle-churned road inside the breached walls of the Reich, waving his tanks on toward Berlin.

Or there might be nothing. Just the quiet, the dark, the boy.

This time, the captain had not called. There had been no muffled sound of men and horses out in the yard under the big oak tree, no weary voice deep in the wing-backed chair next to the fireplace. The captain had his own war to fight, he said. He had not come for a long time, had not needed Young Scout. But now the boy needed him, needed desperately to ride with him to the secret places where only warriors could go, to where things were as simple as danger, courage, honor. Back there, there was only confusion and hurt, angry words, dread of the unknown. So he had set out in the night to find his captain.

There was not much time left, now. Only a few hours until dawn, and an early morning fog was beginning to drift in over the open field, dimming the meager light of the half-moon. He strained his eyes to see. Nothing. Nothing to do now but wait and see if the captain would come.

Just then a crow flew from the tree line across the far side of the pasture and headed straight for him, his raucous caws splitting the night, startling the boy. He stifled a cry as the crow circled overhead, cawing irreverently, then flew on, leaving his echo and a thrill of foreboding in the boy's chest. It came to him again how near it was to the end, how little time was left. He sucked in air in a great gasp and tried to calm himself. What was about to happen? Would Captain Finley die in battle this night? No, of course not. He would finish the war and go home to his wife and son and begin a newspaper called the *Free Press* and leave the mark of his mind on yellowed pages of newsprint for a young boy to find. Captain Finley would survive. Then what was about to happen?

"Is it me?" the boy asked softly into the night, and got no answer.

The fog was thickening now and he was trapped there, waiting. Trapped, and unsure of who he was or where he came from. Young Scout? Lonnie Tibbetts? If he couldn't find Captain Finley this night, who had the answers? Tomorrow was something he couldn't think about. The dread was palpable, something he could almost hold in his hand. He wanted to cry out now for Captain Finley, to plead for him in the dark and fog. But it was not something a man would do, no matter how young. So Young

Scout waited silently, despairing, and at length he lowered his head against his breast and closed his eyes.

He stayed that way for a long while, and then he realized that he was on the chestnut horse, felt its great bulk move ever so slightly between his legs, a shudder ripple down the sinews of its flanks. His breath caught. He could smell the horse. And others.

He lifted his head. And the captain was there. Young Scout could see him plainly, sitting on the great black horse, the reins loose in his fingers, eyes hooded by the brim of the campaign hat. Silent. Watching him. Young Scout started to speak, and then he heard the commotion behind Captain Finley, back there lost in the fog somewhere—horses, many of them, at gallop, shaking the earth with their hoofbeats; the cries of men; a crackling burst of shots. Captain Finley jerked his head toward the noise, back to Young Scout. His face was grim, his mouth a tight line across the stump of his cigar. There were splatters of blood across the front of his tunic: bright red splotches, and older, rust-colored stains.

Then Captain Finley suddenly stood in his stirrups, unsheathed the great saber with a clatter from its scabbard in a single rippling motion, waved it over his head. "Charge the skulking bastards!" he roared. "Take no prisoners!"

"Captain Finley . . ." the boy cried.

"Fight, or be damned!"

And then . . .

LONNNNNNNNNEEEEEEEEEEE . . . HOOOOOO, LONNIE!

Back across the pasture yonder, the high clear voice beckoning him . . .

He rose in his own saddle, confused, caught between time and space. Time was running out. The light was coming fast. Beyond them, in the other direction, the Lighthorse Cavaliers were drawing away. Captain Finley wheeled the great black horse to go after them.

"Captain Finley!" he called.

LONNNNNNNNNEEEEEEEEEEE . . . HOOOOOOOO, LONNIE!

Captain Finley reined to a stop and the black horse reared on his hind legs, pawing the air, spun again to face Young Scout. There were just the two of them in the fog, perhaps twenty yards apart. Captain Finley raised his sword again.

"I can't!" the boy screamed.

"I know," Captain Finley answered. His face was suddenly gray and old. "Do your duty, boy. You hear me?"

"No!"

They trotted toward him, black horse and gray rider, and stopped a whisper away. Captain Finley pointed the gleaming curved blade of the saber toward him and the boy reached out and touched the very tip. There was blood there. There was just a moment, suspended magically above all others, when he touched the metal and knew it was real and marveled at its smooth power. The thunder of horses was gone and there was a great deathly silence there in the open field.

"Do your duty," Captain Finley said quietly.

Lonnie drew in a deep breath. "Yes sir."

And then he wheeled and was gone, leaving the boy alone in the breaking day. There was only the feel of the sword tip tingling the ends of his fingers and the echo of the three words.

DO YOUR DUTY.

FIVE

*I*T was the first automobile a Tibbetts had ever owned.

Jake heard the honking out front at late morning and dismissed it at first. But when it persisted, he walked to the front office and looked out through the open doorway. "For God's sake," he said to himself.

It was a gray 1937 Ford coupe, one headlight smashed, huge rust spots along the fenders front and rear, the whole business listing badly to port like a battered warship. Francine was behind the wheel, Lonnie beside her on the front seat holding the baby in his lap. He had a Band-Aid on his forehead. Pastine sat prim and dignified behind Lonnie in the back.

Jake stepped out onto the sidewalk and looked the car over, front to back. He chewed on the stump of the cigar in his mouth, took it out, spat onto the sidewalk, put the cigar back.

"Let me guess," he said. "It fell out of its nest and you found it in the yard this morning."

Francine gave him a cool look. "Fog Martin got it for me."

"Well," he said, "so much for that friendship."

"Fog says it may be two or three years before you'll be able to buy a new car," Francine said. "He found this one at a

338

widow's house out on Taylorsville Road. It's been sitting up for a while, but Fog got it running again.''

Jake gave the car another once-over. Cord showed through the cracked rubber of the tires. ''First motorcar ever owned by a Tibbetts,'' he said.

''And high time,'' Pastine said from the back seat.

''Lonnie,'' Jake said, ''have you checked under the back seat? There may be some Confederate bullion hidden under there. Or maybe even the bones of a Reb general.''

Lonnie gave him a curious look.

''What did you do to your head?'' Jake asked.

''I reckon I ran into a limb.''

''Where?''

''Out in the woods, I reckon.''

''That's what you get for running around in the woods in the dead of night,'' Pastine said. ''Like a crazy person.''

''Yes'm.''

Jake could tell a couple of things about Lonnie this morning: He wasn't consumed with rage anymore; and there was a firm set to his jaw that hadn't been there before—not yesterday's mule-stubborn, defiant look, but something else, something altogether different. Jake wondered what the hell had gone on out there in the woods during the night. He had come home near midnight himself, exhausted, to find his bed and Lonnie's empty. He had collapsed into a fatigued sleep, only to be wakened in the early morning hours by Pastine and Lonnie clomping up the stairs, Pastine's voice lashing at the boy, rising and falling like a whip until the door to Lonnie's room closed. Then she snapped on the light in their room and stood there in the doorway, hair askew, eyes flashing, dressed in nightgown and robe, while Jake turned over and squinted blearily at her. ''Crazy,'' was all she said. They had all been asleep when he slipped out of the house early in the morning and headed to Biscuit Brunson's for breakfast and then to the paper to make the final preparations for his press run.

''Well, are you all right?'' Jake asked.

''Yes sir,'' Lonnie said. He stuck his index finger out and let the baby grasp it with her tiny hand.

''Get in the car, Jake,'' Francine said. ''The train will be here in a few minutes.''

''I'd rather . . .''

"A mule," Francine said, turning to look at Pastine in the back seat. "I never knew anything about mules until I came South."

Pastine nodded. "Get in the car, Jake. Act civilized for once."

So Jake went back inside the newspaper office and turned off all the lights, latched the back door, turned the sign in the front window to the GONE side, and locked the front door. He reached for the back door of the car on the driver's side. It wouldn't open. He yanked hard on it, but it was frozen shut.

"It doesn't work," Francine said. "Go around."

He went around to the other side and Pastine slid across the seat and let him in. The interior of the car was rich with the smell of decaying upholstery. He slammed the door and Francine mashed down on the starter and the engine groaned in protest for several seconds before it caught with a roar. Billows of gray smoke poured from the rear and acrid fumes came up through the floorboard.

Lonnie turned around in his seat and looked at Jake and Jake slapped his knee and said, "God, a smoke screen for the landing craft. What won't these crafty Americans think of next!"

Lonnie grinned and turned back to the front. "It's got a great horn," he said. "Do the horn, Francine."

"Not now," she said. Francine eased the gearshift into reverse and backed slowly out into the street. Then she hauled down on the lever, trying to get it into first, and the gears clattered and ground like a jackhammer. She tried it again. "I think the clutch needs a little work," she said, then jerked fiercely on the gearshift. It slipped into first and the car bucked twice and moved forward. She steered it into the street, gripping the wheel hard, then as it moved on at a stately pace, she settled back into the seat and pushed the horn button in the middle of the wheel. It bleated like a frightened goat.

"By God!" Jake cried. "Gabriel cometh."

Lonnie turned to him again. "You gonna learn to drive it, Daddy Jake?"

"Lord, no. I expect to be chauffeured about like royalty in my old age. Pastine, do you plan to learn the art of the motorcar?"

"It's Francine's car," Pastine said stiffly. "Francine and Henry's car." *She is on edge,* Jake thought to himself, *and I had better watch my smart mouth.* He vowed not to cross her, not in the slightest way, because by God he loved the woman and he would get back into her good graces and her sweet loins if the Lord let him live long enough and gave him the wisdom to keep his mouth shut.

"Well, I'm gonna learn to drive it," Lonnie said. "Francine said she'd teach me. It's got three forward gears and one reverse, I know that already."

"I think maybe only one of the forward gears works," Francine said. "We'll have to see Fog about that."

They turned the corner at the courthouse square and rolled down the south block, past Biscuit Brunson's cafe and the bank building with the radio station upstairs.

"Give 'er another honk, Francine," Jake said, and she mashed down on the horn again. BLEEAAAT. Biscuit came to the big front window of the cafe, drying his hands on a dish towel. Jake stuck his head out the window and waved, and he could see Biscuit turn and say something to the stool sitters at the counter. Francine turned the corner at the end of the block and headed along the east side of the square just as Herschel Martin came out the door of the Jitney Jungle Super Saver, carrying two bags of groceries, headed for his three-wheeled delivery cycle parked at the curve. Jake leaned out again and gave Herschel a grand wave and Herschel stopped and stared over the tops of the grocery bags and cut loose a huge grin. "Howdy, Jake!" he called. "That Tojo, he sure is some sonofabitch!" Jake sat back in the seat, pulled the cigar stub out of his mouth and held it up like Churchill. "Ah," he intoned, "give me a good ship and a few stout-hearted men . . ."

"Shut up, Jake," Pastine said without turning her head.

Jake jammed the cigar back in his mouth and took note of what a fine day it was. Hot as blazes already, here at late morning, the way August was supposed to be. But very fine, the sky perfectly clear and blue. Things seemed infinitely more possible this fine August morning than they had just twelve hours ago when he had sat, drunk and racked with doubt, at his desk. The man coming on the train might change all that, but for the moment, things did indeed look possible. He knew this: He indeed meant what he had said to Lonnie yesterday; he was not mad at Henry Tibbetts anymore.

"Why does Winston Churchill smoke cigars?" Lonnie asked from the front seat.

"Because he's a Navy man," Jake said. "A good cigar is the mark of a sailor. Sailors smoke cigars to ward off beriberi and pellagra. It's like an asafetida bag, only it doesn't smell as bad."

"Humph," Pastine grunted.

Lonnie turned around to Pastine. "Is he telling the truth?"

"Lord knows," she said. "Fact and fancy dribble off his tongue in such torrents nobody can tell the difference."

"Nonsense," Jake said, waving his cigar. "You can tell the difference, can't you, Lonnie?"

"Yes sir," Lonnie said. "When you're lying, your ears and your eyebrows twitch."

"Lying!" Jake cried, "why, you cut me grievously. I've never told a lie in my life. I admit I've indulged my fancy at times. But I've never told a lie. There's a great difference."

He looked over at Pastine, but she wasn't paying him any attention at all. She was somewhere deep inside herself, gathering strength.

"Lies are an abomination, told by blackguards and rogues," Jake went on. "Fancy is . . . well, fancy is harmless embellishment."

"Like pretending?" Lonnie asked.

"That's part of it," Jake said.

"Or magic?"

Ah yes, there it was. Fancy, distilled. And reserved for young boys, who lost it by bits and pieces until they had only the haunting memory of fancy. As long as they lived, they would know bittersweet, fragmentary reminders of the fancy that had been—the soughing of wind through a pine thicket, the smell of a smoldering leaf pile, the ripple of a clear creek over half-buried stones, the high lonesome call of a crow over a winter-hardened field of corn stubble. Magic, too soon gone, leaving only its ghosts and a vague yearning that even an old man could know now and again.

"Yes, magic. That especially," Jake said quietly.

But Lonnie was looking out the window now, lost in his own thoughts, lips slightly parted as if in silent conversation with someone or something out there in the fine August midday.

The platform at the train station was nearly empty. There were two cardboard boxes, tied with twine, waiting for shipping; an old brown-and-black dog belly-flopped in sleep under a bench;

and Whit Hennessey, leaning on the handle of the two-wheeled dray cart he would use to tote the mail bag the half-block to the post office. Rosh Benefield was not there yet.

Jake shepherded his little crowd into the shade of the covered platform, shooed the dog away and seated Francine and Pastine on the wooden bench. Francine held the baby, Pastine held her pocketbook. Why, Jake marveled, would a woman come to the train station to meet her son coming home from war and bring a pocketbook? Because when a woman went to town, she took a pocketbook. Just as when she went to church, she wore a hat. Jake made a mental note of it—a good front-page column.

Lonnie wandered down to the end of the platform where he could see the train when it rounded the curve after crossing the trestle over Whitewater Creek. Jake walked over to where Whit Hennessey stood with his mail cart. "Morning, Whit," Jake said.

"Morning or afternoon, I can't decide which," Whit said. "Never could decide whether noontime was morning or afternoon. You meeting somebody?"

"Henry," he nodded. "Henry's coming in."

Of course Whit Hennessey knew that Henry was coming in, everybody in town knew it. The question had been, Go down and meet him, or stay away? There was reason enough to go. Henry Tibbetts was a curiosity. He had won the Silver Star, hadn't he? Been wounded in action, given up for dead? But there was more reason to stay away. So folks were staying away. Maybe even Rosh Benefield had decided at the last minute to stay away.

"How's Arthur?" Jake asked Whit.

"Fine. His outfit's heading for the Pacific, now that it's all over in Europe."

"I don't believe they'll ever send 'em."

"The bomb?"

"Yeah, the bomb."

"They say it killed a million Japs," Whit said.

"Well, the Japs can't hold out like that very long. Maybe Arthur'll be coming home before long."

"Sure hope so," Whit said. "Henry. He's all right?"

"Fine, as far as we know. He got a leg wound at the Bulge, but I think that's pretty well healed. And he had amnesia for a while. Didn't know who he was or where he was. But he's over that, too. We got a letter from the hospital in France a few weeks ago. He sounded fine.''

"Haven't seen Henry in a long time,'' Whit said.

"It was the fall of 'forty-one the Guard got called up,'' Jake said. "That's the last we've seen of him.''

"He hasn't been back at all?''

"No.''

They heard the train for the first time then, the faint distant whistle as it approached from the north. Jake looked down the platform at Lonnie, standing at the edge with his arms folded across his chest, sun-browned arms and legs growing like strong ropy vines from the neatly pressed shorts and shirt. Henry would hardly know him. Henry had missed the magic years.

Whit took out his pocket watch, snapped open the cover. "She's a mite late today.'' There was a touch of irritation in his voice. "It puts a crimp in things when you get a late start. Just you watch, there'll be a lot of mail today. A big sackful. Always happens. When the train is late, there's always more mail than usual.'' Whit put the watch away, took a rumpled handkerchief from his back pocket, pulled off his wire-rimmed glasses and wiped them vigorously. His eyes were large and pale, strained by years behind the window of the post office, squinting in the dim light at the barely legible scrawl of other people's names and addresses. Jake wondered for a moment how a man did that, how he labored for years in the small, circumscribed world of postal regulations, tucking his life's work into pigeonholes, nettled by the tardiness of trains. There was that essential thing in Jake himself that abhorred order, made him a man whose eyebrows and thoughts ran riot, doomed to loose ends and shifting convictions, sentenced to wander eternity saying, "Yes, but . . .''

He heard the train whistle again, closer now, and felt the hand on his arm. He turned, startled from his reverie. It was Rosh.

"I'm getting old, Rosh,'' he said. "I stand around daydreaming all the time. I'm glad you came.''

Rosh nodded, then waved to Whit. "How's it going, Whit?''

Whit took his watch out of his pocket again. "Ten minutes late,'' he said irritably. He shoved the watch back into his pocket and pushed his dray cart down to the end of the platform where the baggage car would stop.

The train was rounding the curve now—hulking black engine

slowing for the station with jets of steam spurting from its sides, three passenger cars, a baggage-and-mail car bringing up the rear. It lumbered slowly up to the platform and screeched to a halt with a spinning of wheels, clattering of couplings, and one last belch of black smoke. The baby bellowed with fright and Pastine and Francine got up from the bench and came to stand with Jake and Rosh at the platform's edge, Francine holding the baby and jiggling her up and down. Jake looked around for Lonnie. He was down at the end of the platform with Whit Hennessey.

"Lonnie," Jake called, waving him back. He walked toward them, peering up into the windows of the passenger cars.

"What's the matter with Emma?" Lonnie asked.

"The train scared her," Francine said.

Lonnie poked his fingers in his ears. The baby's angry screams split the air and Pastine reached over and patted her on the back.

Two people got off the train, a large puffing man with a bulging brown leather sample case—a drummer—and a young woman with a small child collapsed in sleep on her shoulder. They blinked in the bright sunlight. The woman sat down on the bench and the man disappeared around the corner of the station house, lugging the sample case with both hands.

They waited another minute or so. The conductor swung down from the doorway of the last passenger car, fanned himself with his round blue cap, and walked over to the ticket window to talk with the agent. At the end of the platform, a man in the baggage-and-mail car hoisted two sacks down to Whit Hennessey, who stacked them on the dray cart. Whit pushed the cart back toward where Jake and his group waited.

"See, I told ya," he said. "Train's late and there's two sacks today. Never fails. Is Henry here?"

"He hasn't gotten off the train yet," Jake said.

"Maybe he missed the train. Coming on another one, huh?"

"That's possible."

"No," Pastine said firmly. "We got a telegram. He's on this one." Jake looked up, scanned the windows of the cars, There were only a few faces, none of them Henry's. In the second car, a young sailor slept, head pressed against the glass. "Wait here," Jake said, and clambered up the steps of the first passenger car. It was almost empty—a man reading a newspaper, a boy about Lonnie's age sitting with his suitcase beside him on the seat.

Jake walked down the aisle, looking into the seats, went through the rear door and into the second car. It was sweltering in here. The handful of people looked wilted: collars open, hair matted with perspiration, fanning themselves. They paid him no attention. He walked the length of that car and into the third.

Henry was sitting at the back, in the last seat on the side opposite the platform. He was staring out the window. Jake walked to the back of the car and stood in the aisle at the edge of the seat.

"Henry," he said.

Henry turned to look at him. "Who, me?"

Jake was stunned to see how Henry had aged. He was very thin, the flesh of his face tight around the bones, his jaw gray with a stubble of beard. His khaki uniform shirt looked two sizes too big in the collar. His hair was salt-and-pepper. But it was his eyes that made him look so terribly ancient—deep-set, framed by a network of crow's-feet, unseeing. Henry turned, gave him a blank stare.

"Henry," Jake said again.

Henry shook his head as if to clear it, then he craned his neck back, looking up at the ceiling. Then his eyes softened and he sighed. "Sometimes," he said, "I don't know exactly where I am. I've been sitting here thinking I might see something I recognize." His voice was dull, lifeless.

Jake sat down beside him. "Well, you're home now."

Henry looked out the window again. "Yes, I can see that. I see the clock tower on the courthouse beyond the trees. And over there. That's the back lot of the feed-and-seed store." He turned to Jake. "Is that right? Have I got the right place?"

"Yes." He hesitated a moment. "The family's here. They're all waiting for you."

"Who?"

"Your mama, and Lonnie, Francine and the baby. And Rosh Benefield. He wants to pin your medal on."

"Medal? What medal?"

"Your Silver Star," Jake said. "Didn't they tell you you won the Silver Star?"

Henry shook his head. "I don't know. Maybe they did." He looked at his hands. "I haven't done anything to win a medal."

"Well, we've got the citation at home. You can read it."

"Okay." He didn't seem very interested. He seemed far away

somewhere, maybe still in Europe or back in Texas, or maybe even up in that big elm tree in Bugger Brunson's front yard where they had dropped cowshit on passing cars. Henry had always been wherever he wanted to be, not where you wanted or maybe needed him. That much, Jake thought, hadn't changed.

"Your wife and baby are here," Jake said.

Henry nodded. Then he sat very still for a long time before he said, "I want you to know I haven't had a drink in a long time."

"That's good," Jake said. "You never did handle it very well."

They sat there for a moment, and then Jake said, "You ready to go now?"

Henry shook his head. "Not just yet. I've come a long way, you know." He seemed very fragile. Jake wondered if the Army doctors should have told them something before they sent Henry home, or if they should have sent him at all.

"You've been through a lot, Henry," Jake said. "But you're home now and you can just take it easy for a while. It's going to take some getting used to. Nobody's gonna rush you."

"I hardly remember . . ." Henry said.

"Just take it one step at a time. But you've got to start somewhere." He had indeed come from a very far place, Jake could see. Henry had been dead and gone in ways that only he could truly understand. Now he had to cross back over the great gulf that lay between the living and the dead. That was a tall order to ask of any man, maybe impossible for a man like Henry. But then, there had been that exquisite moment of truth in the snow of Belgium. Perhaps again . . .

Jake stood up. "You've got a bag?"

Henry nodded. "A duffel bag and a suitcase. Back in the baggage car."

Jake stood over him, waiting, not knowing quite what to do or say.

"I want to tell you this, Henry, before you get off the train." Henry looked up. "I ain't mad at you anymore, Henry. Never mind what's gone before. That's all been and done. I'm proud of what you did."

"Proud?"

"Yes."

"Hell," Henry said, showing a spark of life for the first time, "I almost got my ass killed, and you're proud?"

"You finally hitched up your britches and did something, Henry," Jake said evenly. "That's what I'm proud of. Maybe that means you'll do something else. Maybe you're ready to take care of your family now. Anyhow, I ain't mad anymore."

Henry's face went blank again. "Okay. Okay."

Rosh and the conductor appeared at the front of the car then, Rosh peering over the conductor's shoulder. "Jake," he called. "Everything all right?"

"Train's leaving," the conductor said, marching down the aisle toward them. "You gotta get off or get a ticket to ride."

Jake turned to the conductor. "My son's got a couple of bags."

"Well, he better get 'em off in the next forty-five seconds, or they're heading for the next stop," the conductor said officiously. "We're running late as it is."

Jake stared at him. "Kiss my ass," he said.

"Jake . . ." Rosh started.

"Now, just lissen here, mister . . ." the conductor said.

Jake pushed up close to him. "Look, lardbutt, you pull out of here with my son's bags in that baggage car, and I will beat the be-jeezus out of you and sue the be-jeezus out of your scumbag railroad."

"Jake, THAT WILL BE ENOUGH!" Rosh Benefield said, pushing his massive form between them. The conductor backed away, redfaced and sputtering. Rosh turned to him. "Just go get the bags, will you?"

The conductor stormed back up the aisle. "Jake, for goodness' sake," Rosh said, passing a hand through his thinning hair. He looked down at Henry then and Jake could see the shock in Rosh's eyes. "Henry, welcome home." He stuck out his hand and Henry shook it silently. "I guess you can see your father hasn't changed much."

"I didn't expect he would," Henry said.

The conductor was tossing Henry's two bags out the open door of the baggage car when they emerged from the train— Rosh first, then Jake, Henry standing for a moment in the open doorway as if he were afraid to take the last step onto the platform. But then he straightened, tilted his chin up, gave them a thin haunted smile, and stepped down into their arms.

Pastine enveloped him with tears streaming down her face, whispering, "Oh, Henry! Oh, Henry!" But she held him for only a moment and then passed him on to Francine, who stood a little way back holding the baby, who was quiet now, sucking on her fist. They stood there for a moment, staring at each other, time suspended. There was a flash of panic in Henry's eyes. Francine reached for him and gave him a quick awkward hug. "This is Emma Henrietta," Francine said. Henry touched the baby's cheek tentatively and she gave him a wide-eyed look. "Ah," he said quietly. And finally he turned to Lonnie, reached out and put his hands on Lonnie's shoulders, looked down into his face. "Lonnie," he said. His hands shook and Jake thought for a moment that Henry was going to cry. But then he dropped his hands and stood there while they all looked at him and saw how marked and changed he was. And how frightened he looked. There was a long awkward moment before Rosh Benefield stepped up and broke the silence.

"Henry, I'm here to represent the townsfolk. You're our first returning war hero." Henry flinched at that. "I've asked your mama and daddy to let me pin on your medal and tell you how proud"—another flinch—"we are of you. Pastine, do you have the medal?"

Pastine opened her pocketbook and took out the small rectangular box with the medal in it, and a handkerchief. She handed the box to Rosh and dabbed at her eyes with the handkerchief while Rosh opened the box, took out the medal, and handed the box back to her. Then he stepped forward and pinned the medal on Henry's chest just above the left pocket of his khaki shirt, smoothed the bit of bright ribbon with his finger, and stepped back. "Welcome home," he said.

Henry looked down at the medal and then he looked up and gave Rosh a salute and said, "Thank you, sir. It's good to be back." Then he asked, "How's Billy doing?"

There was a long terrible silence. Jake felt a rush of despair, an agony for all of them—for Rosh, whose son and heir was lost in the vastness of the Pacific; and for Jake and all his kin. The United States Army had taken a drunk off their hands and sent them back a ghost, a thirty-five-year-old man who wasn't even sure of where he was and who looked as if he might bolt and run like a frightened horse. And all the baggage that Henry had taken off to war—all of what he had done and been—he had brought back home. And more. *Goddammit all!* he wanted to cry out.

It was breath-sucking hot on the platform and they all just stood there looking stricken.

"Billy is . . ." Rosh started to say, and his voice sounded far away, as if it came from the other end of a great empty room. Jake strained to hear. The sun was excruciatingly bright. It hurt his eyes terribly and made a bitter, vile taste rise up in his throat, something foul and polluted. He opened his mouth, wanting to say something, to explain, to make amends. But nothing would come out. He stood there with his mouth open, his tongue huge and swollen, blocking the sound from his throat. And then he summoned all his strength and forced out a strangled, anguished sound—"aaarrrrrggghhhh"—and they all turned and stared at him as his knees buckled and everything went black.

When he came to, he was sitting spraddle-legged on the platform, head forward between his knees, the rest of them hovering anxiously over him, Rosh's huge shadow blocking out the awful sun. " 'Mawright," he mumbled. His head throbbed. He could feel the blood pounding through every nook and cranny of his brain.

"It's the heat," Henry said. "It sneaks up on you. I saw a lot of it in Texas."

"Yeah," Jake said. Then he looked up into Henry's eyes and saw the unspoken words: *Keep your shirt on, old man. I've been dead and it's not so bad.*

"Well, I ain't ready yet," Jake said out loud. He damn well wasn't ready. Not now, not when things seemed so inside out, not with him sixty-four years old and nothing tied up neatly like it was supposed to be when a man cashed in his chips. Besides, he had a newspaper to put out this afternoon.

"No rush," Rosh said. "You just tell us when you're ready." But Henry knew what he meant. Henry nodded.

After a moment they helped him up and got him steady on his feet. And then they all went home in the first automobile a Tibbetts had ever owned.

SIX

LONNIE sat for a long time in the shade of the open-sided lean-to behind the toolshed, feeling the clammy coolness of the bare earth beneath him, gusts of August afternoon heat on his face and arms like fingers of fire licking in from the sunshine outside. It was hot, awful hot, here in the shade—but nothing like it was out in the open, where the heat would suck the breath right out of your lungs and the blinding light made your eyes hurt.

It was the time of day when nothing moved. The only thing in motion downtown would be the rhythmic waving of the cardboard church fans held by the old men who played pinochle in the shade of the big pecan tree on the east side of the courthouse square across from the Jitney Jungle Super Saver. The pinochle players were there regardless of the heat. They were dried up like prunes anyway. The only thing that drove them inside was a thunderstorm. If you were almost thirteen years old you knew enough to stay away from the old men and their pinochle game. If you stopped to watch, even from twenty or thirty feet away, they would put down their cards and turn and stare at you like a gaggle of old pointy-beaked mud turtles until you went away.

Early one morning, before the courthouse square had begun to stir, Lonnie and Bugger Brunson had climbed up in the pecan tree and waited, as still as Indians, until the old men shuffled up and sat down to their game. They hadn't been there five minutes, sitting at the little rickety wooden table in their cane-bottom chairs, when one of the players, Old Man Fillingim, had put down his cards with a slap and said, "I think there's a couple of little pissants up in the tree." Lonnie and Little Bugger clung there, frozen in discovery, until they mustered enough courage to shinny down the tree, blushing under the glares of the old men, and slink off. Bugger said that Old Man Fillingim must have eyes in the top of his head, but Lonnie guessed it was a tiny mirror fixed somehow to the old fart's eyeglasses, perhaps a trick he had learned as a spy in the Spanish-American War, a trick for fighting Cubans hiding in palm trees.

Thinking about it, he blushed again with the embarrassment of discovery. It was like being caught down by the creek with your pants down, rubbing yourself. Embarrassing and unfair. Folks ought not to know your secrets—words or deeds. God, now, He knew everything. But you just had to accept that and say, "God, listen up, I'm fixing to . . ." whatever, and go on about your business and settle up later. God was just one Big Secret, and you had to figure out for yourself what He was like. They talked a lot at Sunday School about "knowing God" and "taking Jesus into your heart," but if you asked them what He looked like, they just gave you a funny look as if you had just cut a fart.

What he wished for sometimes was that he could be God for just about five minutes and look down and see what kind of secrets people were carrying around with them. If he could do that, he could figure out some things. Like why people said one thing and did another. Or, just now, what Henry Tibbetts had in his heart.

He had tried not to stare at his father as they all sat at the table eating the huge dinner Mama Pastine had fixed. Henry had been ill at ease, eyes darting, squirming in his chair like his under-wear was bunched up, fingers picking at little bits of food around the edge of his plate. He didn't eat much and he didn't have much to say. Mama Pastine kept piling stuff on his plate—okra, squash, congealed fruit salad, fried chicken, biscuits—and keeping up a steady stream of chatter. But Henry just sat there in agony, smoking cigarette after cigarette, filling the room with smoke, stubbing out the butts on the edge of his plate until he finally ran out of cigarettes and crumpled up the red-and-white Lucky Strike package and dropped it in the middle of his squash. The baby was fussy, Francine distracted, Daddy Jake withdrawn, still looking a little peaked after he had passed out on the train platform. Lonnie just ate and watched, wondering what the rest of them were thinking, especially Henry. They had struggled through the meal and then Daddy Jake had gotten up and said he had to finish getting the paper out and Henry had gone upstairs to take a nap, leaving the rest of them sitting there exhausted.

Lonnie would have gone to the newspaper office, but there was nothing left for him to do. Daddy Jake had done the press run and the folding this morning while Lonnie was sleeping off his night in the woods. So there was nothing to do on this incredibly long and empty August afternoon but come out here and sit in the shade of the lean-to with his back to the rough wall of the toolshed and his fanny and legs on the cool black dirt and think.

There was not much left to the lean-to. It was ancient, used once upon a time, he had been told, to store stovewood. That was back in the days when Daddy Jake's mama, Emma Tibbetts, had cooked on a wood stove. Now, one of the corner posts had rotted clean through so that the tin roof sagged like a drooping eyelid. Wild hedge had grown up around the lean-to until it was all but hidden. From inside the dark nest, he could see the path that led from the backyard down toward the pine thicket, but he could not be seen from the outside unless somebody got right up close and poked his head through the hedge. The place was not a hideout, not in the way you would stock a hideout with a favorite book and a half-box of saltine crackers snitched from the kitchen and an old apple crate to keep stuff in. It was just a place where he came when he wanted no intrusion on his thoughts, the kind of place he didn't even tell Bugger Brunson about. Bugger wouldn't understand about the need to be absolutely still inside a secret place on a boiling afternoon so that the bubbling pot inside his head could simmer down.

So when Bugger came by in the early afternoon, Lonnie stayed quiet. Bugger and Mama Pastine called him from the back porch. "Hoooooo, Lonnie, Lee Mason's here. Hooooo, Lonnie . . ."

But he kept quiet. "He's probably back yonder in the woods,
Lee Mason," he heard Mama Pastine say. "You go on back and
find him. And you boys be careful back there, you hear? Y'all
watch for snakes."

"Yes'm."

He heard Bugger scrambling down the back steps, then in a
moment the crunch of parched grass underfoot as Bugger
rounded the corner of the toolshed and stopped on the path.
"Hey, Lonnie! It's me. You down yonder?" He looked in the
direction of the ruined lean-to, took a step over, stared at the
thick covering of wild hedge for a moment. Lonnie looked Bugger straight in the eye but Bugger couldn't see him. It gave Lonnie a funny feeling of invisibility. He could leap up and yell and
scare the piss out of Bugger Brunson, and on any other afternoon
he might have done it. But not today. So he kept quiet and stared
Bugger down and after awhile Bugger stepped back onto the
path and started down toward the pine thicket. Lonnie heard
him calling down there for several minutes and then he trudged
back, head down, kicking at rocks on the path, moving slowly
in the heat.

After he was gone, Lonnie had a pang of remorse. But he
would see Bugger later. He would go over there tonight and
Bugger would climb out his window and they would do something. Maybe they would sneak downtown, skirting the edge of
the square, darting in and out of the shadows like commandos,
and then making a dash across the street in front of the Jitney
Jungle to the great spreading pecan tree on the courthouse lawn
to examine the old men's rickety pinochle table. Maybe they
would find the secret of how Old Man Fillingim had discovered
them hiding in the pecan tree.

But that was tonight. Right now, Lonnie Tibbetts needed some
time to think, to puzzle over the Big Secret of his father, who
had been a mystery, and then a dead man, and now was alive
and home and just as big a mystery as ever. Lonnie had looked
him over good. He had watched and waited and listened since
Henry had stepped off the train. But there was nothing there to
tell him who Henry was or what he had been. And so Lonnie
Tibbetts was still in the dark about who *he* was and *where he
had come from*.

There had been a brief time a few months ago when he was
actually relieved to think his father was dead. That meant the

Big Mystery of Henry Tibbetts was unsolvable and Lonnie might as well get on with other things. But then Daddy Jake had opened the casket and Henry Tibbetts had, in a way, leaped out alive. So now it was writ in the Great Book of Sin that Lonnie Tibbetts had been relieved to think his father dead, and Henry was home, and Lonnie was just as puzzled as ever. Caught between sin and bafflement, he felt like Peter Rabbit, impaled on a thornbush in Mr. MacGregor's garden while the angry farmer bore down on him. In the story, Peter Rabbit got loose at the last possible instant and suffered nothing more than a dose of camomile tea and the loss of his new jacket. In real life, Mr. MacGregor would reach down and clamp his gnarled hand over Peter Rabbit and pop his neck like you would crack a whip and then have him for dinner.

Lonnie squirmed with shame and fear under the lean-to in the scorching hours of August afternoon while his brain rolled and tumbled and wrestled with itself until he felt faint with all the thinking. It put him in a kind of daze in which the scorched yellow world outside and the green dappled latticework of the wild hedge and the semigloom of the lean-to's shade melted together and inflamed his mind like a fever.

He woke with a hand on his shoulder, the touch light but insistent, and looked into his father's face, the face of his dreams and night sweats. He drew in his breath in a rush.

"You all right?" Henry asked.

Lonnie tried to speak but nothing would come out. He nodded.

Henry released his grip on Lonnie's shoulder and sat next to him on the bare earth, back to the toolshed wall. He seemed more relaxed now. His eyes didn't dart about like a bird's. He was wearing only an undershirt and his khaki pants and there was the powerful gamy man-smell of travel and sweat about him. "Hoo, boy," he said with a whistle. "It's hot as blue blazes out there. It ain't as hot as Texas, but it's plenty hot." He rubbed his hand over his face. "There ain't nothing as hot as Texas." Henry looked up at the sagging roof of the lean-to. "I'd have thought this thing would have tumbled down by now. I think Great-grandaddy Finley must have put it up when they built the toolshed."

"Were you alive then?" Lonnie blurted.

Henry laughed. "No, old Finley was a little before my time.

I didn't even know my own grandfather, Albertis. He died before I was born.''

Lonnie felt a pang of disappointment. Henry had no connection with the past, it seemed—at least, not the rich dark past that was peopled by gray men on fast horses.

"You come out here much?" Henry asked.

"Some," Lonnie said.

"It's a good place to think."

Lonnie looked up at him. There were gray streaks in his hair, lots of wrinkles around his eyes, the eyes looking in your direction, but not looking *at* you. The boy in the photograph, grown old, still revealing nothing.

"I used to come out here a lot," Henry said.

"What did you think about?" Lonnie asked.

He laughed again, a quick dry laugh with no humor in it. "I used to think about crazy people. I used to think about Albertis. My grandfather. They said he was as crazy as a bedbug. He used to stay in his room for weeks at a time while Grandma Emma and Pa and Uncle Isaac put out the paper." It took Lonnie a moment to realize that when Henry said "Pa" he was speaking of Daddy Jake. "When Albertis died, Pa had to come home from college and take over the paper."

"He did?"

"Yeah."

"What did Albertis die of?"

"They called it melancholia. Depression. He just wasted away." He paused for a moment, stared up at the sagging roof of the lean-to. "Anyhow, I used to come out here and think about Albertis."

"Why?"

But Henry didn't answer that. He fell silent and Lonnie could hear only the echo of his words. Henry had a rich whiskey voice with a bit of a rasp in it and something sad about it. It made Lonnie think of the big bend in Whitewater Creek where the current etched into the limestone face of the bank and the water flowed swift and dark under the overhang of the trees with a low insistent murmur.

Lonnie was struck suddenly by the realization that he was sitting here, actually sitting here, talking with the Great Mystery called Henry Tibbetts. Not only that, but in the space of a few short moments they had spoken of things that connected them—

people and places, even if Henry didn't know his own ancestors. Lonnie was stunned by it.

"There's a curse on us, you know," Henry said, breaking into his thoughts.

"A *what*?"

"A curse. It started with Captain Finley. He was a pisser. He dropped dead in the front parlor with that old sword in his hand. He hacked the sofa near in half, then dropped dead. The curse was after him."

"He did not!" Lonnie said hotly.

"Ask Mama," Henry said calmly. "We're all certifiable loonies."

Lonnie stared at him and he could see then the starved, haunted look in Henry's eyes. It came and went, but it was there if you watched and waited. Oh, my God, Lonnie thought, he's crazy! For God's sake, he has been gone so long and now he comes here and starts talking about curses. Lonnie was suddenly frightened, afraid to be here under the lean-to with this stranger who had not only existed for him as the Great Mystery, but moreover was so deeply locked inside himself that he might well be unknowable. The thought of it lay curdling in his stomach.

Then Henry smiled and the look in his eyes was gone and Lonnie wondered if he had been just seeing things. "Anyway, you don't want to be bothered with that kind of stuff. Tell me what you been doing."

"You mean here?"

"No," Henry waved his arm. "I mean everything."

"Well," Lonnie swallowed his fear, "I been working at the paper. I can set type and make up ads and run the folding machine and stuff like that. And tomorrow Daddy Jake's gonna start teaching me the Linotype."

"You like it—the paper?"

"It's okay. I like to write."

Henry nodded. "So did I."

"You did? Why didn't you become a newspaperman?"

"I guess I never got the chance," Henry said. "I hated the print shop. I hated standing there all day setting type and getting my hands dirty and smelling the ink and the machinery. I wasn't very good at it. One day Pa just came over and took the type stick away from me and sent me home. I never got to the writing part."

"You and Daddy Jake didn't get along, did you," Lonnie said.

"No," Henry said, and then there was the look in his eyes again and he fell silent and once again Lonnie was frightened. Henry could change so quickly. The silence grew and grew until it filled the space underneath the lean-to and pounded in Lonnie's ears.

Then Henry sighed a great, sad sigh, as if he had surrendered to something. And he said, "Hooo, it's gonna be a bitch."

Lonnie stared at him.

"It's gonna be a bitch and I'm not sure . . . ." His voice trailed off and he closed his eyes and leaned his head back against the worn gray boards of the toolshed. He sat that way for a moment and then he struggled to his knees.

"Where you going?" Lonnie asked in a small voice.

Henry looked confused. "I'm . . . I'm going to see what I can do about it."

"About what?"

Henry didn't answer.

"Can I come?" Lonnie asked.

Henry looked at him. "I'll be back in a minute," he said finally. "You wait for me, okay? You stay right here and wait for me."

"Yessir."

Lonnie sat for a long time, waiting, as the afternoon sweltered through its zenith. When he gave in to the realization that Henry wasn't coming back, he remembered what Captain Finley had told him last night, there in the fog-shrouded pasture, about doing his duty. He knew what it meant now, at least part of it.

So Lonnie got up and went to find his father.

S E V E N

*H*ENRY walked slowly down Partridge Road in the midafternoon heat, skirted the edge of town on the levee that bordered Whitewater Creek, then cut across the pasture where once upon a very long time ago a huge Santa Gertrudis bull had chased him. He stopped, feeling even now the memory of terror pounding in his ears and the bull bellowing at his back, closer and closer, until he lunged and cleared the fence with a great leap, leaving most of his pants hanging on the barbed wire and a deep blood-gushing gash along the inside of his leg and the bull raging and pawing the ground on the other side. The pasture was empty now. He realized that it was the first time he had set foot in it since that day more than twenty years before. The path, this back way to Haskell's Quarter, was worn smooth in his memory. But he had always detoured around the pasture. Until today. Why today? He stopped at the fence, just about at the place where he had leaped across. He stood looking back at the field, grown rank with weeds. He waited, but nothing spoke to him. There was only the heat, sweat trickling from his hairline down the sides of his face, the field empty and withering. He went on.

Haskell's Quarter was a single dirt road that hugged the lee of the levee with a row of ramshackle houses on either side, weather-warped gray boards and tar paper, glassless windows open to the heat like unseeing eyes, the yards bare red clay that turned to muck when it rained, each with a small plot of vegetables in the back. Everything was coated with dust. Except for Lightnin' Jim's house. Dust seemed to avoid Lightnin' Jim's house.

Henry could feel all the small twinkling black eyes of Haskell's Quarter watching him as he walked up the front steps and rapped on the frame of the screen door. Across the porch, the front door of the house was closed, even against the heat. Henry knocked again, but there was no sign of life.

"Hoooo, Jim."

Nothing. He could hear the buzz of an insect in the grass behind him, the squeal of a child in a yard down at the end of the street.

"Hoooo, Jim. Y'all got so rich and uppity you stopped doin' business in the daylight? Folks got to sneak around here in the dark now?"

He waited, feeling the sweat puddle in the small of his back. Finally, a hand pulled back the curtain on one of the front windows a couple of inches, held it a second, then dropped it back into place. Another long moment and the front door opened a few inches. He couldn't see anybody inside.

"Hey, yonder," Henry said. "Anybody seen an old whiskey nigger name of Lightnin' Jim Haskell that used to live here?"

"Which white sonofabitch wants to know?" The voice was rich and deep like thunderheads piling up black and powerful on a sweltering afternoon.

Henry bowed from the waist. "Henry Finley Tibbetts," he said.

The door opened another few inches and back in the shadows he could see the stooped form of the old man.

"Henry?"

"Yep. I'm back. Back at the old stand, Jim. Come to do some business."

"I heard you was coming," Lightnin' Jim said. "Come on the train this noon."

"I come all the way from the war to see you," Henry said. "I thought about you all the time I was at the war, Jim. I lay there in the snow in Belgium with my ass turning blue and I thought, 'Boy, if I could just have a little taste of Lightnin' Jim's Best, just a little something to ward off the evil spirits, I could last through this thing.' And you know what? I lasted. Just the thought of your old rotgut whiskey pulled me through."

"Horseshit," Lightnin' Jim said.

"I thought to myself," Henry went on, "there ain't but two things in the world worth doing. That's riding on the fire truck and drinking Lightnin' Jim Haskell's Best. I wish I had had a tankerload of it in Europe, Jim. It will burn the lining right out of your stomach and make your bowels tremble with terror, but if I had had a tankerload of it in Europe, I could have made us both rich men."

Lightnin' Jim stepped out to the edge of the porch and held onto the doorjamb with one gnarled hand and Henry could see how thin and bent with age he was. But the voice. It hadn't changed. "You been home since noon and already you're over here wantin' whiskey."

"Yes sir, Mr. Lightnin' Jim. Just a little something to ward off the evil spirits." Henry shuffled a little bit, shifting his sweat-soaked fanny around. "Hooo, boy. It's gonna be a bitch, Jim. I got . . . ah . . . I got lots to take care of. Lots of folks looking at me. I got a new wife and a new baby and all the old stuff to boot. I just need a little something to tide me over 'til I get straight and figure out what to do." He could feel the thirst powerful in his throat and his gut. "Sometimes I don't know exactly where I am or what I'm doing, but I'm gonna get it all straightened out. I just need . . ." He blushed, felt like a fool standing here in front of this old whiskey nigger like some penitent. He pulled a wad of bills out of his pocket. "I got money," he said.

"You didn't always have money, Henry," Lightnin' Jim said. "Lots of times you came and you didn't have money. You just had a craving, but no money."

"No, and you never sold me any on credit, either," Henry said. He waved the bills. "But the United States Army gave me a wad of money to go away and leave 'em alone. Now you gonna sell me some whiskey or not?" He reached for the handle on the screen door.

"Don't you come up here on that porch 'til I say you can," Lightnin' Jim said.

Henry dropped his hand. He was breathing heavily. "You gone out of the whiskey business?" he asked after a moment.

"I never was in the whiskey bidness," Lightnin' Jim said. "I always been in the foolishness bidness. White folks' foolishness. Goddamn white folks."

"Niggers drink too," Henry said.

"Niggers get drunk and go on about they bidness," Jim said. "White folks sneak around and buy my whiskey and go back behind the shed and get drunk and act like fools and pretend they don't. Goddamn white folks, put a bad name on whiskey."

He turned and went back inside and slammed the door behind him, leaving Henry standing there on the front steps with all the twinkling black eyes watching him and the sweat coursing from every pore of his body. Several minutes went by. Well, piss on it, he thought. He turned, started to go, and then the door opened again and Lightnin' Jim stepped out onto the porch, holding a pint jar in one hand and balancing himself on his walking stick with the other. He clumped slowly across the porch, stopped, stared at Henry through the screen. A fly buzzed at his head and Lightnin' Jim reached up with the hand holding the jar and waved at the fly impatiently. The amber liquid inside the jar sloshed about, shimmering with refracted color. The old yellow eyes were sunk deep in Lightnin' Jim's head. He was dying, Henry thought, but he had probably been dying for years. It might take him another hundred years to die. Unless he started drinking his own whiskey.

"You got a new wife and a new baby," Lightnin' Jim said.

"That's right."

"And one boy half-grown."

"Lonnie. Yep, he's about half-grown all right."

"Does he act like you?"

"No," Henry said. "He doesn't act like me."

"You tell that boy . . . Lonnie," Lightnin' Jim said, "when he gets growed up so big that he thinks he's about to bust his britches, don't come around here wantin' to buy no whiskey. You tell him Lightnin' Jim Haskell ain't got no whiskey to sell to Lonnie Tibbetts. You tell him to pay attention to what his Grandmamma says. You hear that?"

"You're a nosy old bastard," Henry said.

Lightnin' Jim smiled then, showing a mouthful of very nice,

very even, very white teeth. "Thass right. But I got the whiskey."

Henry pushed open the screen door and Lightnin' Jim handed him the pint jar. Henry turned it, held it up to the sunlight, watched it ripple and swirl and give off flashes of blues and pinks like a prism. "The quality don't appear to have changed," Henry said. "Same old rotgut as always. I believe . . . I believe it will put my mind at ease." He looked up at Lightnin' Jim. "How much?"

"Same as always," Jim said.

"You gonna need a price increase," Henry said, peeling two dollar bills off the wad. "All the boys coming home from the war gonna have a fistful of money. Prices gonna go sky-high."

"What I charge ain't none of your bidness," Jim said. "You drink the whiskey, I do the bidness." He took the money and pushed the screen door closed. "Henry, you remember what I said for you to tell that young'un. No whiskey for Lonnie Tibbetts. And mind what his Grandmamma says."

What in the hell is he going on about it for? Henry wondered. What does he know? What is in that ancient wrinkled black woolly head, behind those old yellowed eyes?

"You tell him that, you hear?"

"All right," Henry said.

"Now you go on. I ain't got time to stand out here in the heat and jaw with you. You got what you want. Go on, now."

He went back inside and left Henry standing on the steps, holding what he came for—a little something to ward off the evil spirits. Just 'til I get it all straightened out, he thought. Just 'til I figure out what I'm doing.

———

In the early evening the heat still clung to the earth like flypaper. Henry could feel it on his face as he peeked over the parapet of the flat roof of the fire station at the courthouse square two stories below. The pavement of the sidewalk and street held the heat stubbornly. Long after dark it would be warm to the touch. Henry remembered, as a boy, sneaking out of the house in the middle of a summer night, walking barefoot downtown, feeling the last of the day's heat on the toughened soles of his feet.

Up here on the roof it would be so horribly hot in the middle of the day that it would burn the skin off a man's body. The tar would absorb the heat until it turned to a bubbly black liquid in places. It was still warm, still spongy underfoot, here near twilight.

Henry didn't know how long he had been there. His mind seemed to fester and bubble like hot tar. Awareness was a narrow slice of time, bounded by the last few minutes and the next several. There was just now, just here. Just Henry and the fruit jar and the sword.

The courthouse square was deserted. To the north of his position, the hulking red shape of the courthouse blocked his view. Beyond it were the bank building, with the radio station upstairs, and Biscuit Brunson's cafe. If anybody was about at this dusky hour, it would be there—a few people having a bite of supper at Biscuit's or maybe Ollie Whittle putting the radio station to bed. But perhaps Ollie had already gone home and left the airwaves to the clear-channel giants from Cincinnati and Chicago and New Orleans.

To his left, on the west side of the square, Henry could see lights on in the City Hall building—downstairs, where Hilton Redlinger would be puttering around in the cubbyhole of a police station, tidying up; and upstairs, in the telephone exchange. In a few minutes Hilton would turn off the downstairs light and lock up and go home, and if anybody needed the strong arm of the law during the night, they would call him on the telephone. Upstairs, Em Nesbitt would be at the switchboard until eight, when her relief came.

Everybody else had already gone home. They had, as local people used to joke, rolled up the sidewalks. On the east side of the square, the Jitney Jungle Super Saver and Hamblin's Mercantile were shut tight. The green window shades of the barbershop were pulled. The four cane-bottom chairs at the pinochle table beneath the pecan tree on the courthouse lawn were empty. People were at supper, at rest.

Henry gave the square a long careful look, then settled back into a half-crouch, his back to the brick parapet. He patted the pockets of his pants, searching for his cigarettes, remembered that he was out, felt the dry tickle of anticipation in his throat. He reached for the pint jar beside him, lifted it, saw that it was empty, set it back down. He didn't know how long it had been empty, but he thought that the fact that it *was* empty might have something to do with why he couldn't remember back very far.

And he didn't know when or how he had gotten Captain Finley Tibbetts's sword, but it was there, too, propped against the wall beside him. Just the sword, not the scabbard. The thin polished blade gave off a soft gleam in the dimming light. The thin point made a small precise indentation in the soft tar of the roof. He looked at it for a long time, studied the intricate engraved scrollwork on the blade, read the inscription: *Aide toi et Dieu t'aidera.* French, he guessed. *Toi.* That sounded French. Ooh-la-la. He didn't know what it meant, but that really didn't matter. What mattered was that he was here and he had a job to do.

Henry stood again, rising to his full height, the upper half of him exposed over the top of the parapet in full view of anybody who might be below in the courthouse square. Dangerous. A sniper upstairs in the courthouse or on the roof of the Jitney Jungle could pick him off with one clean shot. Right through the head. BAM!

"Hey, you sonsabitches!" he yelled.

His voice rose and then died immediately on the soft warm cushion of the evening. And nothing happened. Nobody came running out into the square to see what the hell was going on and who the hell was up on the roof of the firehouse yelling, not even Hilton Redlinger, who was—given the soft gleam of light in the ground-floor window at City Hall—still in the police station.

Henry unbuttoned his khaki pants, leaned over the edge of the parapet, and peed. The dark yellow stream arced out and fell splattering on the sidewalk below. Henry waggled the stream from side to side, hosing a dark pattern onto the concrete. Then he looked around the square again. Nothing. Nobody. No sign that anyone had seen a man pissing off the roof of the firehouse.

Henry tucked himself away and buttoned his britches, and just as he did so, Hilton Redlinger stepped out the front door of City Hall, locked the door, rattled it to make sure it was secure, and then headed down the sidewalk. Hilton was stooped, the hair on top of his head thin and white, showing the soft pink of his scalp. The leather holster with its huge pistol hung loosely from his waist and Hilton listed slightly gunward. He shuffled slowly in a sort of loose-jointed gait, head down, feet barely clearing the concrete. He crossed the street at the end of the block, turned left, and headed down the south side of the square along the sidewalk in front of the fire station. He walked directly under Henry, straight through the dark splashes on the concrete, kept going. At the end of the block he turned right, disappeared toward home.

So, Henry would have to do it by himself. Hilton Redlinger could have been a lot of help. At any instant, Hilton could have looked up, seen Henry standing there on the roof of the fire-house, could have called up to ask what the hell he was doing. Henry would have told him. He could have turned the whole thing over to Hilton. But no, Hilton Redlinger had shuffled on droopy-drawered toward home and his supper, leaving the whole thing on Henry.

Henry turned, sat down again on the roof of the firehouse with his back to the still-warm brick of the parapet. He felt fine, just fine. But he had always felt pretty fine, hadn't he? Well, maybe not. But over the past few minutes, which were all he could remember just now, he had felt just fine.

But it began to worry him a little, as he sat there, that he couldn't remember anything past the last few minutes. He knew who he was, by God, he was Henry Tibbetts back from the war. And he knew what he had to do. But here he was up here on the roof of the fire station with an empty pint jar and his great-grandfather's sword. Now how the hell had he gotten his ass in this particular position?

Henry thought it would help if he could remember just one thing beyond a few minutes ago. So he strained very hard until the blood pounded in his head and after a few minutes he thought of the captain, the psychologist, in the Army hospital outside Paris.

He was a young man, younger than Henry. He wore wire-rimmed glasses and he liked to lean back in his swivel chair and put the tips of his fingers together like a tent and look at Henry over the top of his fingers.

"So you're not Farquhar," the young captain said.

"No, I'm not Farquhar."

"But you thought you were Farquhar."

"No," Henry said, "I never thought I was Farquhar."

"Who did you think you were?" the captain asked.

"I didn't know who I was," Henry answered.

"Then why did you keep answering to Farquhar?"

"Well, I didn't know I *wasn't* Farquhar, either."

The captain sat up in his chair, leaned toward Henry, propped his elbows on the desk. "What was it like, being Farquhar?"

"I don't know," Henry said.

"What do you mean?"

"Well, I never was Farquhar, so I don't know what it was like being Farquhar."

So it went, on and on. The young captain played word games with him day after day. Until finally they found out that he was Henry Finley Tibbetts.

"I think I liked it better being Farquhar," Henry said wearily one day after the captain had been picking at his mind, the way gnats do an open sore, for almost two hours.

The captain smiled. "But you never were Farquhar."

"Yes, but I could have been. If I hadn't said something about not being Farquhar, you would never have known."

"Would you rather be Farquhar?"

"I don't know."

"Farquhar's dead, you know."

"So was I until you dug me up."

The young captain stared at him across the top of the finger tent. "Lieutenant, you're a chronic escapist, that's what you are. You have a great capacity for separating yourself from pain and pleasure. That's why you suffered amnesia after you were wounded. That's why you still refuse to deal honestly with who you are. You just won't face reality, Lieutenant."

"Well, that's just damn well not true," Henry said mildly. "That's not the case at all."

And it wasn't. They missed the point. It wasn't that Henry was trying to hide from reality. It was that he simply wasn't paying attention. And he wasn't paying attention because he wasn't interested.

"Is it that you don't give a damn?" the captain asked.

"That could be," Henry said. But that was not quite the whole truth. You had to have a little touch of hostility in you to really and truly not give a damn. But Henry Tibbetts wasn't mad at anybody or anything. He felt very sad sometimes in a way he couldn't explain. But mad? No sirree. He just wasn't paying attention. He had not paid attention to the young captain in the Army hospital outside Paris for a whole month, and finally the guy had looked at him one day in exasperation and said, "All right." That was it. The guy had tried everything he knew to

get Henry to pay attention, but he had finally just given up because he had other fish to fry.

And that's where Henry's memory stopped. He could remember the young captain saying, ''All right.'' But there was nothing between then and right now, sitting here on the roof of the
fire station in the warm twilight with an empty pint jar and
Captain Finley Tibbetts's sword and feeling fine, just fine.

Henry picked up the sword, laid it across his outstretched
legs, studied it for a moment. The blade was magnificent, the
intricate engraved scrollwork free of tarnish, the fine silver softly
gleaming in the late afternoon light. He pointed it up, away from
him, felt the solid heft of it, sighted down the long curving
blade. Then he remembered another soft summer evening,
peeking around the corner into the parlor, seeing his father sitting in the wing-backed chair with the sword in his lap, polishing
and polishing, the soft cloth moving back and forth along the
thin blade, Jake lost in thought. The memory of it was fleeting,
here for an instant and gone. Henry sighed. It was time to stop
trying to remember and get up off his ass and go do what had
to be done.

He rose, holding the sword in one hand, clutching the top of
the parapet with the other to steady himself. He weaved a little,
but he stood for a moment and breathed deeply a few times.
Just fine, he thought. He felt just fine.

He crossed the roof and opened the trapdoor that led from
the roof to the attic of the firehouse. He let himself down, taking
care not to bang the gleaming sword against anything, closing
the trapdoor behind him. The only light was from a small window at the front of the building, overlooking the street, but it
was enough to let him pick his way back as he had come, through
the dust-covered rubbish that littered the attic floor, to the open
stairway that led down into the bay where the fire truck sat
expectantly.

There was a bit more light down here from the row of high
windows that formed part of the big garage door. Henry walked
around to the front of the truck and stood for a moment looking
at it. It was a fine piece of machinery, an American LaFrance
pumper purchased not long before the war to replace an aging
balloon-tired truck with a hand-operated pump that took the
heaving effort of four strong men to get a feeble gush of water
through a single hose. This one had an on-board hydraulic pump

operated off the truck's engine, the very latest. No town within several counties had a fire truck so modern, so efficient, so beautiful. Most of the money for it had come from the Messrs. Harsole and Bingham, whose bolt factory was the most valuable piece of property in town.

Henry remembered something else now. His first ride on this fire truck, a few months before the National Guard unit got called to active duty—the flush of Lightnin' Jim's Best coursing through his veins, the rush of wind against his body. God, it was fast. It had taken two other men to hold Henry onto the truck. When they rounded curves or corners, he wanted to let go of his handhold and simply fly off into space, laughing. But they held him on, drunk as he was. When they got to the fire, a two-room frame house already half-consumed, Henry grabbed the nozzle and ran lurching toward the blaze, pulling hose behind him. When he got so close he could feel the flames curling the hair on his arms, he shouted, "Turn 'er on!" and the powerful force of the water bursting from the end of the nozzle smacked him flat on his ass. He writhed there, laughing and yelling, the hose thrashing him about on the ground like a giant snake, water shooting everywhere, until the others ran and got it under control. God, that was fine.

Henry touched the side of the truck, felt the smooth cool red metal, ran his hand over the chrome and glass of the valves and gauges, then walked around to the back and looked at the neat folds of hose. Everything was clean, orderly, polished. It was a good volunteer fire company. It had been a very fine thing back before the war when they went clanging off into the night on the old pumper—Hilton Redlinger, Fog Martin, Big Bugger Brunson, George Poulos, the others. The flames made their faces glow as if they wore red masks.

Now he needed the fire truck. They wouldn't mind. They would understand, as they always had.

Henry walked around to the other side of the truck and climbed up in the open driver's seat. He had not driven the fire truck before—not this one or the old one—because he kept showing up drunk and they wouldn't let him drive. Fog Martin drove the fire truck. But now Henry would have to drive. He reached for the ignition switch on the dashboard just to the right of the steering column, turned it, heard it click. He checked the gears and hand brake. Gearshift in neutral, hand brake on. Then with his left foot he pushed down hard on the starter pedal and the engine turned over heavily once, twice, three times, grinding loudly in the firehouse bay. Nothing. Henry stared at the dash, then he remembered the choke. He pulled on the handle, pulled it all the way out, then pumped the gas pedal twice with his right foot. He mashed down on the starter again and it ground in protest, trying to coax the big engine to life. Come on, come on, come on. Still nothing. He pumped again lightly on the gas pedal. Then he smelled gasoline fumes and felt a rush of panic, fearing he had flooded the engine. If that happened, there would be nothing to do but shut it off and sit here and wait until the carburetor drained. And by then the last of daylight would be gone. He mashed the starter again and it ground angrily. Push in the choke, stupid. He pushed it in halfway and then the engine coughed and caught and roared to life. Hot damn! He gave it a little gas, goosing the engine, then let it sit and idle for a moment, warming up.

Henry felt the truck vibrate happily under him, the big engine running smoothly now. It was Fog Martin's engine and he kept it finely tuned. Fog lived a couple of blocks away and he got the first alarm from Em Nesbitt when a fire call came in at the phone office. Fog would pull on his pants and rush to the firehouse and climb quickly up on the roof and crank like hell on the hand-operated siren, sending a wail across the town to signal the others. Then he would scramble down and crank up the truck so that by the time the volunteers came running from wherever they were, Fog had the door open and the truck halfway out into the street. When he had three or four other men, he would take off, and anybody who arrived late had to get to the fire the best way he could. There were two dozen volunteers in all, and when they all got there, they milled around getting in each other's way while Hilton Redlinger tried to keep order. And when it was over, somebody would bring out a jar of Lightnin' Jim's Best and they would pass it around and re-fight the fire. It was all very fine.

Henry sat thinking of them while the truck warmed up and then he climbed down from the seat, went to the front of the bay, hauled down on the big counterweight and sent the huge hinged door rattling up into the ceiling, opening the bay to the evening. He blinked, looking out at the still-empty square, the courthouse hulking like a brooding red beast in the middle.

Then he turned and saw Lonnie, standing on the sidewalk next to the firehouse, staring at him.

"Whatcha doing with the fire truck?" Lonnie asked.

Henry turned, looked into the bay at the truck idling throatily. "Just warming her up," Henry said.

"I ain't heard the siren," Lonnie said.

"No," Henry shook his head.

"Is there a fire? Where's the rest of the men?"

"No, there ain't exactly a fire. I'm just warming her up, that's all."

"Does Chief Redlinger know you're warming her up?" Lonnie asked.

"He was by here just a little while ago," Henry said, not wanting to lie about it.

Lonnie crossed his arms over his chest. "You gonna take the fire truck out?"

"Maybe," Henry said. "Look, ain't you supposed to be home eating supper?"

"I ain't hungry," Lonnie said. "What if there's a real fire and you've got the fire truck out tootin' around town?"

"I didn't say I'm going tootin' around town," Henry said.

"But you got the motor running and the door open," Lonnie insisted.

"That's so the fumes don't get so bad in the bay while I'm warming her up."

Lonnie gave him the fish eye, the same don't-give-me-any-nonsense look he remembered from the Pastine Tibbetts of his ancient youth. Lonnie looked inside the bay, checked the truck over carefully, then stepped inside and looked up in the front seat of the truck. "Naw," he said finally. "You're getting ready to take her out."

"Don't sass me, boy," Henry said.

"I ain't sassing. I'm just saying what I see. You got the motor running and the door open. And you've got Captain Finley's sword up there on the front seat. What you got the sword for?"

"Protection," Henry said. He felt a rush of panic, a powerful need for drink. He wanted to pull down the big bay door and shut off the engine of the fire truck and make a beeline for Lightnin' Jim Haskell's place. But he fought down the urge. Not now. He knew what needed to be done and time was wasting. The light was fading fast.

"All right," he said. "Come on."

He turned to go back into the open bay, but Lonnie stood rooted to his spot on the sidewalk.

"What you gonna do?" Lonnie asked.

"I can't tell you," Henry said. "Not yet."

"You afraid I might squeal?"

"No, but it's a secret. Look," he said, the urgency rising in his voice, "I've gotta get moving or it's all over."

"What's all over?"

"Dammit!" Henry shouted. "Get in the truck or go home!"

"Okay, okay. You don't have to yell. I'm coming."

They climbed up into the high seat. Lonnie's legs dangled over the edge. He pushed the sword against the backrest behind him. Henry revved the motor a couple of times, then shoved in the clutch and eased the gearshift lever into first. He let out on the clutch and mashed the gas, but the truck lurched forward a few inches and died. "Shit!" Henry cried. He cranked it again, geared up, eased the clutch out, gave it some gas, and it lurched again, coughed and expired. He banged the heel of his hand angrily against the steering wheel.

"Why don't you let out the hand brake," Lonnie said.

Henry stared at the brake lever sticking up through the floorboard between them. He shook his head, grabbed the lever with his right hand, squeezed the hand release, heard the click as the brake disengaged. He cranked the engine again, gunned it, slipped the truck into gear, and eased it out of the gaping door of the bay and into the street. He was halfway across the street before he turned the steering wheel hard to the left. It wasn't enough. The truck rolled across the street in a broad arc and the right front wheel whumped against the curb and bounced up onto the lawn of the courthouse.

"Shit!" Henry yelled. He jammed on the foot brake and Lonnie flailed the air beside him, fighting for balance. Lonnie threw out his arm and jammed it against the dashboard. "Ow!"

"Goddammit, hold on," Henry shouted at him.

"Awright, awright. Can't you drive?"

Henry glared at him. The little bugger had a big mouth. Just like Jake Tibbetts. Jake Tibbetts could jaw and jaw and jaw at you until you felt like he had stripped off all your flesh with his tongue. Jake Tibbetts could make you weary with his jawing. He could make you not want to pay attention at all.

"You all right?" Henry asked.

Lonnie squeezed his wrist. "I think it's broke."

"No, it ain't broke. You just jammed it. Now hold on."

"I ain't got nothing to hold onto," Lonnie said. The hand-hold on the dashboard was beyond his reach.

Henry felt a little crazy. They were sitting there in the fire truck with one wheel hiked up on the courthouse lawn and the ass-end of the truck blocking the street and he had a job that needed to be done and they were farting away the shank of the day jawing.

"Put your feet up against the dashboard," Henry said. "You got on sneakers. It won't scratch anything."

Lonnie scrunched down in the seat and braced himself against the dash with his feet. "Now I can't see out the windshield," he complained.

"Goddammit, you ain't got to see out the windshield. I'm driving."

"Well, you ain't doing too good."

Henry balled up his fist and jammed it under Lonnie's nose. "You shut up, you hear! Shut up or get out!"

"Awright, awright. You don't have to be so mean," Lonnie snuffled, tears welling in his eyes.

"Okay. I'm sorry," Henry said. "You okay now?"

Lonnie stared straight ahead at his feet, lips tight. Damn, Henry thought. Fresh-mouthed little kid. Scrawny neck and arms, thin features stretched tight with growing, spattering of freckles across the bridge of his nose, unruly hair, a semicircle of dirt behind his ear. Henry could feel a tingle behind his own ears, the rough scrubbing of a long-ago washcloth, Pastine saying, "You could farm behind here."

Henry shifted the fire truck into reverse, grinding the gears loudly. "Look," he said. "It's gonna be all right. You just hang on, okay?"

Lonnie nodded.

Henry eased out the clutch and backed the truck off the court-house curb, straightening it out in the street. He stopped, looked around the square. Still nobody in sight. Damn wonder with all the racket going on. It was getting late now. The sun was only a trace of violent orange over the roof of the City Hall building and the light in the upstairs window of the telephone exchange was a square of bold yellow against the darkening face of the building.

Henry shifted the truck into first gear and headed down the street, turned right at the corner, then veered left across the center line and pulled up in front of City Hall. The front door of the city office was padlocked, the big plate-glass window giving only a faint reflection of the square and the red fire truck and the gaunt man and scrawny kid sitting on the high seat.

Henry put the truck in neutral, pulled up on the hand brake, left the engine idling.

"You stay here," he said to Lonnie.

"Where you going?"

"To the phone exchange," Henry said.

"What for?"

"Business. Now you sit right here and don't you budge. I mean it." Lonnie gave him a defiant look. "I'm telling you now," Henry threatened, "if you get off the seat of this truck I'm sending you home. I got serious business and I want you to sit here and behave yourself."

Lonnie shrugged. "Okay."

Henry reached behind Lonnie and got the sword. Lonnie's eyes widened. "You ain't gonna hurt anybody, are you?"

"No. I don't want to hurt anybody," Henry said. He didn't want that. He didn't want anybody to get in his way, just let him do what had to be done. Then he could go home and go to sleep. He felt weary now. He wasn't just fine anymore, he needed some rest.

Henry climbed down from the truck and stepped up the high curb to the sidewalk and then started up the narrow open staircase that led from the sidewalk to the upstairs phone exchange. He carried the sword in front of him, point out, careful not to bang it against the wall. He didn't want to hurt the sword. At the top of the stairs he stopped and looked back to see if Lonnie had followed him. The staircase was empty.

He paused there on the second-floor landing and listened for a moment. He could hear the soft murmur of Em Nesbitt's voice inside, the click of wires on her console as she rang up a connection. He waited a moment, knowing she would be absorbed in the conversation on the line. Em listened in, everybody knew that. Especially this time of night, when the calls came spasmodically. Jake Tibbetts had once suggested in his front-page column that the entire town government be turned over to Em Nesbitt because she was the only person in town who knew everything that was going on. At Sunday School the following Sunday, Em Nesbitt—Henry's teacher—had fixed him with such a withering stare that he wanted to sink through the bottom of his chair and disappear. It was not easy having a father who laughed at people on the front page of the newspaper.

Henry turned the knob and pushed open the door. Em was hunched over the console, back to him, arms folded, headset on, absorbed in somebody's trivia. She was smaller than he remembered, shrunken and stoop-shouldered with age, a tiny old woman with thinning white hair, a small pink bald spot at the back of her skull from years of wearing the headset.

"Miss Em," Henry called softly. He didn't want to scare her. "Miss Em," he said again, a little louder, and this time she spun around in the chair and stared at him.

"Henry Tibbetts," she said without hesitation. She still had the same hard gray eyes.

Henry squirmed a little. "Yes'm. It's me."

"What do you want?" she demanded. "You know you're not allowed in the exchange. What am I going to have to do, lock the door?"

"Look, Miss Em—"

"And if I do that, and fire breaks out up here in this old rattletrap office, I'll burn to a crisp before I can get the door unlocked. Is that what you want?"

"No'm . . ."

The console buzzed and Em turned back to it. She flicked a switch. "Exchange," she said, then listened for a moment. "She wasn't home a half hour ago. Marvel Renfroe tried to call her, but I didn't get any answer. I'll try again if you want. Maybe she's back now, unless she's gone over to Taylorsville to see the new grand-baby." Em pulled a wire from the bank in front of her and plugged it into one of the holes on the face of the console, then cranked jerkily on the ringing device. She waited, then cranked again. "No, she's still not there. All right, then."

Em pulled the plug, then turned back to Henry. "Now what do you want?" she demanded.

"Miss Em," Henry said, "I've got to shut you down."

"You've what?" She raised the earpiece on her headset to hear him better.

"I said, I've got to shut you down. So they won't get hold of the phone system."

"So who won't get hold of the phone system?"

"The Germans." There. It was out. Having said it, Henry felt incredibly stupid. She would laugh.

But she didn't. "Henry, there aren't any Germans around here."

"Not yet," he said, "but they're coming."

"Coming from where?"

"The prison camp. Over near Taylorsville. They've all escaped and they're coming here. If they get hold of the phone system . . ." his voice trailed off.

"What makes you think that?"

How to explain? He just knew, that's all. He didn't know how or why he knew, but he knew. And a man had to hold on to what he knew, especially when he sometimes couldn't remember who he was or where he was. When you're in that kind of shape, you hold on to those things you know for sure—like the fact that the Germans had escaped and were headed this way. And he, Henry Finley Tibbetts, had to do something about it. Rosh Benefield had said it, he was the first war hero to come home. You couldn't expect these old geezers to do anything, shuffling old fart-knockers like Hilton Redlinger, who didn't even know when he was walking through a puddle of piss. Hilton had had his chance.

"Henry," Em Nesbitt said, "they sent the Germans home a long time ago."

"No," Henry said, "that's not so."

"You're drunk, Henry."

"No ma'am," he shook his head firmly. "I definitely am not drunk, Miss Em. I may be a little shaky, but I have fortified myself, and I am in complete command of my faculties and as a matter of fact I am also in command of the fire truck." He was calm—very tired, but calm. The palms of his hands were dry. "Anyway, I don't have time to talk about it. I've got to do what needs to be done."

"Henry!" Em Nesbitt half rose from her chair as Henry raised the sword. Her headset clattered to the floor. "You put that thing down, Henry!"

"You think I'm crazy, don't you!" Henry shouted.

"You bet your boots I do!"

"Well, I'm not. For once, I'm not. I know what the hell—'scuse me—I'm doing."

He took a step toward her and she froze, terror-stricken. Henry strode quickly behind the console, stood in the space between the console and the wall, raised the sword over his head with both hands, and brought it down on the big trunk line that ran from the console into the conduit on the wall. The sword was sharp, the blow powerful. THUNNNNNNK! It severed the big wire completely and the blade of the sword whacked into the floor beneath it and Henry pitched forward with the force of his swing, sprawling on the floor, his forehead smacking into the wall. He crumpled, stunned, the wind knocked out of him, still holding the sword.

Henry lay there gasping for breath, eyes glazed. His chest heaved and a horrible rasping sound came from his throat as he clawed for air. Oh, my God, he thought, I'm going to suffocate here on the floor. He closed his eyes and waited for death and as he did he remembered—for the first time in a long, long time—the ache of the bone-chilling hours under the blasted tank on the hillside in the Ardennes with Bobby Ashcraft dying beside him, weighing his own life and finally giving it up. He had died once. Now again.

But he didn't. He opened his eyes, blinked, saw Lonnie standing over him. Lonnie's fists were clenched, his eyes accusing. "What did you do to Miz Em?" he demanded.

Henry opened his mouth, but only the rasping noise would come out. He turned his head and saw Em Nesbitt sprawled on the floor in front of the console. Oh, God! Not again! Lonnie knelt over her. "She's still breathing," he said.

"Aaaagh. Aaaaagh," Henry croaked. He gulped a fistful of air.

Lonnie stood up and looked behind the console where Henry lay. The severed trunk cable dangled from the console and there was a deep slash mark on the wooden floor.

"You cut it," Lonnie said.

Henry nodded.

"Why?"

"Germans," Henry gasped. Lonnie stared at him. Henry inhaled again with great effort. "Germans. On the way. Got out of the prison camp." He stopped, chest heaving. "If they'd got hold of the phone system, it'd be all over."

Lonnie gawked at him, speechless. Henry struggled to get up and Lonnie backed away. He made it finally, one hand pressed against the wall to steady himself, the other making a crutch of the sword, digging the point into the floor. He stood, weaving, his head throbbing, eyes glazed. I'll stop now, he thought. This is enough. Somebody else will have to do the rest of it.

But who? This scrawny kid? He can't even drive the fire truck. And somebody's got to warn them.

Henry looked over at Em Nesbitt crumpled in a heap on the floor. He knelt beside her, pulled one of her eyelids back with his thumb. There was nothing but white. He touched the side of her neck, felt for the jugular under the soft folds of skin. The pulse was weak but regular. A soft snore escaped from her mouth.

Henry looked up at Lonnie. "She just passed out, that's all. Just fainted." He looked back down at Em Nesbitt. "You didn't think I'd hurt her, did you?"

Lonnie didn't answer.

"I didn't mean to hurt anybody. I didn't start out to touch a hair on anybody's head. See?" Henry laid the sword down on the floor, held his hands out for Lonnie to see. They both saw how badly his hands shook, how rawboned and grimy and shaky they were.

Henry stared at his hands. "I never meant . . ." he started, then choked. The tears washed down his face and he let his hands fall into his lap and squeezed his eyes shut, but the tears wouldn't stop. He felt miserably ashamed, crying in front of his son, but he was powerless to stop. The sobs racked his body like silent explosions and he rocked back and forth on his knees, digging them into the hard floor. Stop! Stop! But there was no stopping. Henry cried for his own wretchedness and weakness, because he had screwed up so many times and had stumbled drunkenly through his life with a burden of guilt and shame that weighed him down like a sodden greatcoat. He cried because he had killed his wife—that's what Jake Tibbetts said, he had killed Hazel—and he had abandoned his son and he had lost the one chance he might have to die honorably. And he cried because now, when this job was half-done, he wanted to quit and go home and go to sleep.

Finally, after a long while, he stopped crying and then he opened his eyes and Lonnie wasn't there. There was only Em

Nesbitt, unconscious on the floor, snoring peacefully with her thin wrinkled lips slightly parted. It was dark outside. The harsh light of the single bulb hanging from its cord made him think suddenly of a barracks, of the bleak, sparse, hot existence of Texas, of a woman, of a few blessed hours of sanity.

He got up then, brushed off his clothes, picked up the sword. It was time to finish things.

Down on the street the fire truck was still parked at the curb where he had left it, motor idling. Lonnie was sitting up on the high seat behind the steering wheel. Henry stood next to the truck with one foot on the running board. "I can't leave it like this," he said. "I've got to warn 'em. About the Germans."

"I ought to go tell Chief Redlinger what you done," Lonnie said.

"Okay," Henry said. "Go ahead if you want. That ain't gonna stop me. Not you or him. You don't believe me, do you."

"I reckon not."

"Well, I know what I know," Henry said. And he did. He might not know who he was or what he was doing sometimes; but he knew this. And he clung to it as he had clung once before to life itself, even when he told himself he was ready to die. "So," he said to Lonnie, "you can get your ass out and run tell Hilton Redlinger, or you can go home and let Mama blow your nose, or you can help me get my business done."

Lonnie looked at him a long time. Then he moved over on the seat to let Henry in.

Henry laid the sword down on the floorboard of the truck and climbed up, gripping the steering wheel. He pressed down on the accelerator a couple of times and the engine roared with life. He eased down the hand brake, shifted into gear, and pulled away from the curb. Then he glanced over the dashboard, found the siren switch, and clicked it on.

It started slowly, a deep throaty whine, and then rose in pitch and volume until it cried out like a banshee across the empty expanse of the courthouse square. Damn, what a siren!

Henry shifted into second and took a hard right at the corner. The siren wailed, bouncing back at them off the buildings, as they rumbled past Biscuit Brunson's cafe and the bank building with the radio station, darkened now, upstairs. He saw Biscuit come to the corner of the counter inside the cafe and stare out the window at them. He switched on the truck's headlights and the revolving red beacon mounted just behind the driver's seat. It sent a throbbing flash of red against the side of the buildings. He took another right at the corner and looked over at Lonnie, who was standing up now, feet wide apart on the floorboard, holding onto the hand rest on the dashboard to steady himself, peering out over the top of the windshield. He took the next corner, swung by the fire station with the bay gaping and empty, then another right. As they passed City Hall, he looked up and saw Em Nesbitt at the open upstairs window of the phone exchange, watching them, mouth agape. Henry felt a surge of excitement. The siren wailed powerfully, the headlights cut a swath of white on the pavement ahead of them, the red beacon throbbed.

"We gotta wake 'em up!" he shouted to Lonnie.

"Where we goin'?" Lonnie yelled back.

Right. Where the hell *are* we going? What's the plan, Lieutenant? "Around the square a few more times," Henry said. No sweat.

By the time they passed Biscuit's cafe again, Biscuit was standing out on the sidewalk with two other men, wiping his hands on his apron. Biscuit yelled something, but Henry couldn't hear him over the siren and the roar of the engine. Henry waved and the truck rolled on. One of the men standing with Biscuit dashed across the street as the truck passed and headed across the courthouse lawn.

Henry felt better now. There was a little breeze on his face and the noise of the truck and siren got his blood up. He felt a surge of energy. It was a fine evening, still warm but soft like summer twilights are supposed to be. He felt fine now, just fine. And he was paying attention. He was, by God, taking things in his own hands. He turned right at the next corner and thought how good it would be to keep doing this for a long, long time— maybe the rest of his life—making right turns in a soft evening atop a powerful machine that ran on time itself. It might not get any better than this. It never had before.

"Lonnie," he called over the noise.

Lonnie's eyes were bright with excitement. "Yeah."

"You okay, boy?"

"Yeah, I'm okay." He looked at his father. "You okay?"

"Fine. Just *fine*."

And he was. He didn't even, for just this moment, want anything to drink—and he couldn't remember a time like that, ever. He didn't want a cigarette, either. He didn't want a damn thing except just what he had here and now. He felt a sense of equilibrium, of delicately balanced time and place, so tenuous he must take small shallow breaths so as not to scare it away. Right turn, right turn, right turn, with the throaty roar and the banshee wail bearing him on. A man had to hold fast to the one thing he knew for sure and find some boundaries to put it in. A simple thing like a square, bounded by four right turns and enveloped in a summer night.

He almost ran over Hilton Redlinger. He felt Lonnie jerking on his arm and then he heard the boy hollering and he looked ahead in the street and saw Hilton standing there, caught like prey in the stabbing beam of the headlights, waving his huge pistol, eyes wild and thin white hair falling down over his forehead. Shit! Henry slammed on the brakes and Lonnie lurched against the dashboard. Henry reached out and grabbed him, hauled him back against the seat, jammed in the clutch with his other foot. The truck screeched to a halt a couple of yards from Hilton.

"Stop!" Hilton bellowed. "Stop or I'll shoot hell out of ya!"

Henry could just hear him over the dying wail of the siren. He could hear shouts off to his right on the courthouse lawn, had a quick vague sense of people running toward him. He turned to look and his foot slipped from the clutch and the truck lurched forward, leaping half the distance toward Hilton, and the old man jerked his pistol down and fired. A huge roar, the *whang* of bullet on metal, the shattering of glass, a dull sickening *whumpf* as it hit something else. It all happened very fast, the sounds mashed together. Then Lonnie turned slowly toward him, mouth open, a quizzical look on his thin face. There was blood everywhere, bright red, spreading. Lonnie rose up and then his knees buckled and he began to topple sideways out of the truck. Henry clawed frantically for him, clutched only air, watched Lonnie fall away from him, down into the waiting arms of Jake Tibbetts, who caught him roughly around the chest and stood there for a frozen second before Jake's face contorted horribly and his own legs gave way and he went first to his knees and then fell onto his side with Lonnie on top of him. There was blood on both of them. Jake's face was riven and twisted with something that went far beyond grief and rage. His mouth opened and the muscles and sinews along his jawline stood out like ropes and a terrible growling cry wrenched itself from his throat. Henry stared into the gaping mouth of the beast, transfixed. And somewhere out beyond it all he could hear Hilton Redlinger, screaming and sobbing. "Ain't no Tibbetts gonna get the best of me! I'll shoot you all! Sonsabitches! Sonsabitches!"

Then Henry laid his head down on the leather seat of the fire truck and went quietly away.

EIGHT

For a long time he was a prisoner of his own mind. He was unaware of his body, suspended in a state of pure consciousness in which each thought was perfectly defined, like small birds perched on a high-voltage line, seen against a bright sky. He marveled at the sweet clarity of it, an initiate in the first flush of religious grace.

At first there was only memory, scenes of such exquisite detail that he became a passenger on a time transport, not so much remembering the past as re-entering it. Only now the scenes were even more real than the original, vivid in color and dimension, purified through the filter of age.

He saw things he had missed before—tiny droplets of water on the leaves of an azalea bush just beyond his mother's elbow as they sat on the front steps of the house right after a rain; a splash of rouge on the cheeks of the woman in the long bustled dress and plumed hat in the lithographed calendar that hung behind the cash register in the mercantile store; the pungent smell of decay when he kicked aside a certain small pile of leaves beneath a particular poplar tree on a singular day. He studied them intently, intrigued by the knowledge that they had been there all this time, waiting to be discovered if only one were quiet and still enough. A man need not have eyes to see such things—only time and patience.

Later, there were richly evoked scenes full of life and movement, smell and color.

He stood for a long time on the top step of the eastern entrance to the courthouse, looking out across the lawn at the row of store buildings that bounded that side of the square. At the corner, four old men played pinochle at the small table under the pecan tree, their movements slow, their bent forms dappled by sunlight filtering through the leaves above them. He knew their names, the precise route each had taken from home to the pinochle table earlier in the morning (it was morning because the buildings across the street cast a long shadow across the courthouse lawn, the grass dark green/light green along the razor edge of the roofline's shadow). He watched the old men for a long time as they played at their game, gnarled hands clutching the cards, their gestures ancient and crotchety. They seldom spoke. Old men had said everything already, it seemed.

Across the way, the door was ajar at the Jitney Jungle grocery store as a woman with a shopping basket on her arm stopped on her way out, letting the flies in, talking with someone inside.

Next door was the barbershop with its single wide window and the red-and-white candy-striped pole on its fixture next to the door, a bright light hanging above the first chair, which was occupied now by the barber, who smoked a cigar and waited for a customer. He took the cigar out of his mouth, waggled it between his second and third fingers, said something to one of the other men in the shop, laughed, stuck the cigar back in his mouth. He imagined himself inside the barbershop, sitting in the first chair with a pinstriped sheet draped over him, pinned at the back of his neck, watching time and space disappear in a succession of receding images in the big mirrors that faced each other on opposite walls of the shop. Was there a place on the other side of one wall or the other where they ended? Or did the images reverse themselves somewhere and come echoing back? And when they did, would your hair be parted on the other side?

At the end of the block, a man came out of the hardware store carrying a brown-wrapped package under his left arm, crossed the street and lawn to the courthouse steps, paused on the top step towering above him, spoke to his father.

"Trial still going?"

"Yes, it is."

The man with the package under his arm passed them, disappeared into the dark cool hallway of the courthouse. Above them now, from the open window of the second-floor courtroom, he could hear the singsong drone of a lawyer questioning a witness, the answers faint and halting, all of it a dull buzz that floated softly on the cushion of morning and sunlight.

He felt his small hand in his father's hand, turned, looked up into his father's face. There was nothing there. It was the only missing detail.

Other than that, his recall was total. They were perfect crystals suspended in his mind, powerfully evoked—place and time, sight and sound, touch and emotion—and uncluttered by the baggage of all that had happened since. He remembered them just as they *were*. They came unbidden, some of them more than once, and there were long silences between when he waited for another re-creation from memory. They came without warning, emerging full-blown, so sharp and real they were almost painful, like stepping from a dark room into blazing sunlight. And they came without rhyme or reason, without chronology. One moment from his childhood might be followed by another in which he sat at the keyboard of the Linotype machine, pecking out the words of a story or column that could only have been recent.

Through it all, though, there was a sense of a moment anticipated but unrealized. "No," he said to himself after each had passed, "that wasn't it." It was as if his mind, floating in the great silence, worked itself slowly toward some event so cataclysmic that it had to be approached cautiously, from downwind, as you would approach a beast.

Suddenly, there it was. The beast leaped. It was the clear, terrifying memory of the fire truck sitting in the middle of the street, the flash of orange and deafening roar from Hilton Redlinger's big pistol, Jake running, blood everywhere, Jake reaching to catch Lonnie as he fell. Then a searing flash tore through his own head. Jake thought he had been shot. His legs crumpled under him and the weight of Lonnie's body carried them both to the ground. Then blackness, out of which grew the great silence and the re-creation of his past.

When it finally came, Jake recognized it for what it was. He had had a stroke. What's more, he had been waiting for it a long time without realizing it. Something deep and secret inside him had known of the microscopic weakness in that certain blood vessel buried deep in his brain. It had whispered to him in a breath so small and fleeting it had seemed a wisp of smoke. But it was there. That was the beast, his beast, a small silent beast. He wondered how it had subtly altered his life. Had he held back from anything in fear? Had there been a trace of dread at the edge of all he did and thought? Probably.

Then he remembered Captain Finley Tibbetts, how they had found him sprawled on the parlor floor with a twisted snarl on his lips, the silver sword in his hand, a deep slash across the flowered brocade of the sofa. They had wondered. But Jake knew, at least now he did. Back then, he had seen only the twisted face, the death mask, as his grandfather lay in his casket in the parlor. He remembered the hushed surprise of the people who streamed in to see Captain Finley. Why, they asked in shocked mutters, had they opened the casket with the old man looking like that? His widow, Henrietta, had looked at him and shuddered.

Jake had waited until long after midnight when they were all gone, had slipped down the stairs past the dozing uncle who slumped in a chair at the parlor entrance, then stood on tiptoe and peered into the open casket in wonder. Captain Finley's face was waxen, colorless, the eyebrows and lashes starkly black against the pallor, the features molded of putty. Except for the snarl. Captain Finley's lips were twisted around to the left, the muscle along that side of his jaw bunched like a fist, the yellow-stained teeth showing. Jake stared at him, fascinated, until he felt something cold and hairy crawling up his back. He turned quickly, but there was nothing there, only the sleeping uncle in the chair and the soft emptiness of the death room. He went quietly back to bed. Remembering it, he knew that the cold hairy thing crawling up his back had been his own beast, burrowing itself into his skull to hibernate for a long, long time until it was Jake Tibbetts's turn. And his turn had come, as had Captain Finley's. The beast inside the old man's head had broken loose and Captain Finley had fought it with one last desperate slash of the sword that had laid low the Yankees at Cemetery Ridge. Too late. Beasts weren't as easy to kill as Yankees.

So Captain Finley had had a beast. Well, so had Albertis, his son. Only it was not the kind that suddenly leaped forth, clawing and slashing. Instead, it slowly ate away at Albertis's mind, a small sneaky beast that nibbled and nibbled until there was nothing but melancholia, driving Albertis to the locked room upstairs where he alternately paced and slept in the horror of his own inner sanctum. In the end, the beast had won, but by then there was nothing left for it to exist on. Albertis, defeated, simply gave up and the beast went away, leaving a carcass.

There must be, he realized now, something of the same quiet devious beast in Henry. He saw again and again in his vivid memories the small boy with the sadly sardonic grin, the young man aging before his time with wrinkles spreading beneath his eyes like tiny roots, the air of wry resignation.

And he, Jake Tibbetts, victim of a beast that leaped suddenly from hiding, tore at the flesh of his brain, felled him as it had felled his grandfather, Captain Finley. Only this beast hadn't done its job as completely as it had on the old man.

So. There seemed to be two species of the Tibbetts beast, existing in alternate generations. He and Captain Finley. Albertis and Henry. Had Lonnie, then, inherited the vicious one? Would he someday crumple with a searing flash of white heat across his brain? Then Jake remembered Lonnie falling from the high seat of the fire truck, the blood. Oh, Lonnie! Oh, Lonnie! Deep in the prison of his own mind, Jake Tibbetts cried out in grief and anguish. But of course there were no real tears because he had no real body. Thy beast had torn it apart. And of course no one could hear him when he cried.

After that, the memories ceased.

There was a long period of blank silence. A month? A year? Was he dead? There were no devils or angels lurking about. Purgatory, perhaps, but not heaven or hell. Just silence, colorless and odorless. No, he decided, he wasn't dead yet. It was just a period of waiting, after which he would either get better or he would die.

Then Albertis came to see him.

The sad, raspy voice broke the silence like the crumpling of parchment paper. "So, what is it you want to know, Jacob?"

Jake didn't answer right away. He studied the voice, recognized it.

"Open your eyes, Jacob."

He did. Albertis sat in a straight-backed chair next to the bed, close enough for Jake to touch if he could reach out. But nothing moved except his eyelids and his mouth. He blinked, ran his tongue across cracked lips. It took great effort.

It must be late afternoon because the light at the window behind Albertis was waning. September, he guessed from the certain quality of the light. A man didn't live sixty-four years (almost sixty-five) without learning how light betrayed seasons. September. He had been held prisoner in his inner sanctum for a month.

"I took over the paper, you know."

"Yes," Albertis said. His legs were crossed, one thin limb hitched across the other, bony knees outlined by the thin fabric of his pants.

"I was wondering, does every man have a beast?"

The trace of a smile passed Albertis's face and then was gone. Albertis answered with a question of his own. "It wasn't as easy as you thought, was it, Jacob?"

"What do you mean?"

"Your trouble was, you always made up your mind."

"What's wrong with that?" Jake asked.

"Things change. People change. And then there's always the 'beast,' as you call it. You never learned that you can't make up your mind about too many things."

Jake studied the gaunt face for a moment. Albertis was an unkempt man. His hair was matted and tousled, his face rough with unshaven black stubble. He remembered that Albertis would go for days without shaving when the melancholia hit him, that the rank odor of his unwashed body would fill the hallway outside his room, that he would allow nobody to touch him until the spell had passed. Then there would be a great airing-out with Albertis splashing in the tub and the windows of the room thrown wide and sour bedclothes piled on the back porch, gray with dinge, Albertis emerging pale-eyed and frail in freshly starched clothes with little blood specks on his face where he had shaved off the stubble. He looked now, sitting by Jake's bed, as if a spell were just beginning. He would be quite lucid for a while, but soon the door to the room would close and the pacing would start and then even that would end and Albertis would take to his bed.

"You were always so sure that you knew what you knew," Albertis said, breaking the silence. "You made up your mind too much. You judged."

"Yes," Jake said. "Maybe I did." He would have nodded, but only his lips and eyelids moved and he realized how crippled a man can be without his gestures. "But," he went on, "a man has to take his life in his own hands and shake it for all it's worth."

Albertis dismissed him with a snort.

"A man has to take control of his life . . ." Jake started.

"Hah! Control, you say! Just look at you, Jacob. You can't even control your own bowels. Can you?"

"No," he admitted. "But that doesn't mean . . ."

"Every man does what he can with what the Lord doles out," Albertis said.

Now it was Jake's turn to snort with derision. "You think the Lord does it, eh? Well, you're wrong! The Lord doesn't meddle."

Albertis gave him a long, slow smile. "And who do you think invented the beast?" he said quietly. He uncrossed his legs, crossed them the other way. There was such an air of futility and resignation about the act that it made Jake furious. That was the way it had been all along. Albertis had given in to the beast and let it gnaw and gnaw and gnaw.

"You just ran away. You just ran under a rock and hid," Jake said accusingly.

Albertis wouldn't argue. "You don't run away from a beast, Jacob. It's always with you. Look at Henry. Did he escape?"

"Henry!" Jake spat, disgusted.

"And what about you, Jacob?" Albertis leaned forward against the bed. "Did you escape? Look at you. And you were always so certain of what you knew. Always so sure of your opinions."

"Based on fact!"

Albertis gave a short, mirthless laugh. "Give us less fact and more possibilities. What's a fact, anyway, but what you want it to be?"

"Henry disgraced himself, that's a fact."

"Were you there? Do you know what happened?"

"I could see. I could see what a mess he left," Jake said hotly. "I saw what a bloody mess he left on the front of that car, what was left of Hazel when he got done. I could see that. You should have been there to see the blood and the gore! She wasn't a saint, but my God!"

Albertis sat back in his chair, stared at Jake for a long time. Jake felt weak with anger. Albertis shouldn't be here, getting him riled up like this. Albertis showed up when you didn't need him. And when you did need him, he was up there in his room, pacing the floor with his own little beast gnawing, gnawing at his mind.

"Pastine never gave up on him," Albertis said quietly.

"Pastine's a woman," Jake said. "All Pastine ever did was wrap her skirt around Henry and tell him everything was going to be all right. She wiped his snotty little nose and let him keep screwing up. She did it even when he disgraced himself. What does a woman know about a man's honor and dignity?"

"Maybe more than you think, Jacob," Albertis said quietly.

"Hah!"

Albertis hung fire for a moment, and then said, "I could tell you something."

Then it was Jake's turn to give pause, because he could see in his father's face, could feel palpably in the room, some secret that, once told, would make everything irreversible. Be careful, he told himself. He wanted Albertis to go away now.

"Well, Jacob?" Albertis insisted. "You're a man of fact, as you say. Opinion based on carefully considered fact, eh? You can't decide, not really, unless you know."

The hell with him, Jake thought. "All right. Tell me."

"Pastine kept the paper afloat all these years. It hasn't made money since you took it over, Jacob. You were such a stickler for your almighty fact and so proud of your precious opinion. But a disaster as a businessman. A disaster, that's all you can call it."

He stopped for a moment, gave it time to wrench like a knife in Jake's gut.

"You were so busy making great journalism you didn't have time to keep up the subscription files or sell advertising. Look at it, if you ever get up, Jacob. Go back and look at the paper when I had it and compare the advertising space with what you have now. A third, perhaps. And you never raised the rates.

And the bills? They just kept piling up on your desk the way
they did on mine, until Pastine would finally come and get them
and pay them. Not out of what the paper brought in, Jacob. Out
of her money. Pastine is a wealthy woman. It wasn't much,
really, not to her. She paid the bills and kept the paper going.
And you say she doesn't know anything about a man's honor
and dignity? Bullshit, Jacob. Bullshit. She kept it from you, the
fact that you were a godalmighty failure.''

"No!"

"Oh, yes." There was a hard, insistent edge to Albertis's
voice, something Jake had never heard there before. Albertis
had no backbone, no gumption, no pride. Did he? What right
did he have after all these years to use that tone of voice?
Albertis was a weakling, a man who ran away and hid in dark
rooms when others needed him. A Judas. A betrayer. He had
no right . . .

"So, Jacob. You make up your mind about so much. When
you know so little."

"Go away!" Jake squeezed his eyes shut, pressed the lids
together so hard it was like two fists jammed against his face.
But he could hear Albertis moving from the chair, rising, bending toward him.

"No! No!"

And then he could feel the hands on him, on his shoulders,
sliding up toward his neck. But they were strong hands, big
beefy hands and now they were shaking him and the voice above
him wasn't sad and raspy at all, but a big booming voice that
yelled, "Pastine! Pastine! Come here, he's opened his eyes!"

And Jake jerked his eyes open again to see Rosh Benefield
towering over his bed, big fat Rosh with his face all flushed and
his eyes bright, and then steps in the hall, Pastine running toward the bed and then bending over him, pushing Rosh out of
the way.

"Oh, my God, my God," she moaned, clutching him in her
strong arms, choking back a sob.

Jake looked wildly about the room, eyes dancing from one
spot to the other, and then to the window where the waning light
said that it was indeed September and that he was back from a
far country. A deep, sad ache floated up out of the dark well of
his existence. If only he could have stayed away.

NINE

J_{UNE} 28, 1945. Dawn exploded on the gray wings of Billy Benefield's P-50 like napalm and seared the cockpit with a blinding whiteness. Billy threw one arm up in front of his eyes and kicked the plane sharply to the left in a tight circle until the sun was at his back. Then he lowered his arm and let his eyes adjust to the intense orange glow that bathed the instrument panel, marveling again at how the sun could just pop up out of the Pacific as if it had spent the night in the cool depths, husbanding its energy for the great leap.

He was utterly lost. The storm had done that—the storm and Muehler, the pig-headed squadron leader who had led the little formation into a boiling mass of thunderheads so huge it stretched for miles, so fast-moving that once they were into it, there was no escaping in any direction. God, he thought, they will fry Muehler's ass for this one (unless Muehler was shark food by now, which was a good possibility). Of course it wasn't all Muehler's fault. Nobody had known the storm was there. Nothing on the weather charts in the ops shack had hinted of it. But it waited out there for them in the dark, the great yawning Pacific dark, like the gaping mouth of a dragon.

It had leaped on them after they had turned loose the B-29s they were escorting halfway to Tokyo and had turned back toward Okinawa. There was just the turbulence at first, buffeting the wings of their planes, and then, sweet Jesus, they were into the thick of it with lightning exploding like ack-ack around them, sending the dials of their instruments spinning wildly, the horrible winds tearing at their wings and wrenching controls from their hands, the blast of rain like fifty-caliber bullets on the thin metal of their planes. The P-50 was a swift, powerful, deadly piece of machinery; but in the face of such a storm, it was a toy. The storm blew their tiny formation to pieces.

Billy, at the height of his terror, had reached for the radio mike, had screamed, "Muehler, you faggot! You asshole motherfuckin' sonofabitch!" and then realized that he held only air in his hand, that the microphone was flopping around somewhere down by his feet at the end of its cord. The great grip of the storm took the plane from him and tossed it about the tortured sky like a Ping-Pong ball while Billy gripped the controls in raw terror. And then, as if it had toyed with him enough, it seared his plane with a single blinding flash of light that swallowed all existence and pitched plane and pilot into a great roaring well that went down and down and down until the blackness reached up and enveloped him.

Suddenly, Billy felt himself outside the plane, suspended in air, watching the P-50 spin and lurch just below him, a figure still inside slumped over the controls. He thought, It's all right. He watched for a moment, then knowing how it would end, with the plane exploding into the water, he turned to go. But something stopped him. He was ready, but there was something back there, something he needed. He hesitated, torn between the powerful feeling that he must go on and the pull of whatever was there in the plane below him. He sighed, a great sad sigh, and then he went back.

The storm spat him out like a scuppernong seed and he came to his senses in the cockpit. It took him a long minute to realize it, but then he felt the controls stiffen in his hands and became aware he was flying the plane again. He sensed, though, that something was very near and very dangerous and he sat very still with the stick at dead center until a flash of lightning off to his left showed him that he was only a few feet above the wave tops, rocketing along at 350 miles an hour, a hairbreadth away from instant death in water that would be as hard as concrete. His heart leaped into his throat and he stifled a scream, then carefully, very slowly, he eased back on the stick and brought the nose up. He climbed until he was out of danger and then he threw up all over the floor of the cockpit.

The stillness was awesome. Even the great throbbing drone of the plane's engine was a whisper. The storm had tossed him into a vacuum of sound and sight in which he floated, suspended, not sure if he were really alive or not. But as he slowly came to his wits he took stock and found that he truly lived and so did his airplane. He had been at the doorway of death. But now he lived, and he was utterly shaken by it.

"I can't hear anything," he said out loud, and the voice was strange and weak and small in the vastness of the cockpit, but it was his voice. He reached out and touched the instrument panel, moving his fingers along from dial to dial, watching with fascination how the needles jiggled in their lighted glass cages. Then he touched himself, his legs, his torso, his head. There was little feeling in his hands and body, but enough to tell there was flesh there, flesh and muscle and bone and sinew. He existed where all natural law told him he had no right to exist. He began to cry and he cried for a long time, great tears of fear and awe and relief flooding down his cheeks and wetting the front of his flight jacket.

Finally, he got a grip on himself. "I'm in shock," he said into the stillness, remembering how they had described it to him in flight training in one of the first aid classes, how a man might be badly injured and think he was okay and then find that he was bleeding to death and didn't know it. He checked himself again for blood, but there was none. Just numbness, a protective film over his consciousness that the shock had put there.

But he flew on through the calm night and the shock gradually wore off and he began to get control of his surroundings and think about where he was and where he was going. His plane was intact, but his instruments didn't work. They jiggled about in their cages, but they made no sense. The lightning bolt had knocked them cockeyed. The fuel gauge and the compass, the altimeter and the artificial horizon were gone completely, the rest of the dials registering numbers that were ludicrous fiction. He could only guess at how much fuel he might have left, and he had absolutely no notion of where he was located in the vast openness of the Pacific or in which direction he was headed.

He realized, then, that the radio was still on. There was the familiar hiss and crackle in the tiny speakers of his leather helmet. He found the microphone dangling on its cable at his feet, picked it up, pressed the button. "Cobra Four to . . ." he hesitated. To whom? "Cobra Four to any traffic." Nothing. Just the empty sizzling sound that said space, space, space. "Cobra Four to all traffic. Mayday, mayday." Nothing. He was completely alone.

He glanced at his watch and saw that the face of it was smashed. He felt his wrist and discovered the dull pain of the bruise beneath the watch where his arm had been flung about in the wild catapulting of the plane and the watch face had smacked against something in the cockpit.

So, where the hell was he and what to do?

They had taken off around two in the morning, linked up with the B-29s over Saipan, and sped on through the star-sprinkled night toward Japan, shepherding the sleek silver ghosts of the bombers as they passed over the pitiful little outpost islands the Japs still held, the scraggle of bomb-pocked airfields carved out of jungle and coral that occasionally still mothered a Zero or two. Nothing had risen to threaten them this night, though, and when the P-50s reached the limit of their range, they waggled their wings at the bombers and peeled back toward Okinawa and flew fat, dumb, and happy across the empty expanse of ocean until the storm boiled in from nowhere and kicked their butts up around their ears. Billy Benefield imagined that he might be the only one of the flight to have survived it, and by all rights he, too, should be dead.

Odds were he soon would be, because unless he lucked onto a piece of land, he would run out of fuel. Then he could ride the plane down, or he could parachute out and take his chances.

"Shit," he said to himself. Another piece of asshole luck, the kind that had been dogging him since he put on a uniform. The war was finished, and so was he. Billy Benefield was going to end up with the seabirds pecking the dead eyes from his shriveled head in a life raft. After he had gotten to the war six months too late, and then decided he no longer wanted to be a hero.

That had happened when he had shot down a Jap plane two

weeks before. The evidence was painted on the side of his fuselage just below the canopy of his cockpit, a single white stenciled Rising Sun. A coonskin. It had happened while they were flying air cover for the big and growing flotilla anchored off Okinawa, watching for the kamikazes that had started peppering the fleet with their frenzied, suicidal assaults, setting off panic on the ships.

Muehler spotted them first, three Zeros arcing in out of the east. Green pilots. They could tell by the way the Japs started their approach much too far out, dropping down out of a cloud bank and aiming for a line of fat little transports.

"Bogeys! Bogeys!" Muehler yelped. "Two o'clock, about a thousand feet. Two of 'em. No, three." The Japs were below and to the right of them, slanting directly across their course toward the ships, and there was nothing to do but keep going, keep their tight echelon formation, reach forward and unlock the safety switches on their guns. Then the Zeros spotted them and one plane panicked and pulled out of the long steady dive and climbed up and away.

"Cobra Four. Cobra Five. Get 'im!" Muehler barked. "Everybody else. Keep it in tight. Paste the bastards."

Billy slammed the throttle to the wall and kicked his P-50 out of the formation before his wingmate, Schlosser, had time to blink. He headed for the lone scrambling Jap, climbing with the fierce morning sun behind them, gaining quickly on the Zero, which had once been the scourge of the Pacific but was now no match for the powerful, nimble P-50. The Jap jerked his Zero back and forth across the sky, but Billy just kept boring in on him. He looked back and saw Schlosser just behind and to the right of him as they closed into range. Then the Jap dived off to the right, directly into Schlosser's sights. "I got him! I got him!" Schlosser screamed. Over the crackle of the radio, Billy could hear his fifty-calibers thundering, spraying tracers all over the sky, missing everything in his excitement.

"Dumb ass," Billy muttered to himself. "Hold still, Schlosser, for Christ's sake. You got him, just hold fucking still!" The Jap was going wild out there. Then suddenly he whipped the Zero around to the left and seemed to stop in midair dead in Billy's sights, turning in a sharp rolling curve that presented a fat topside view of the plane. He could see the pilot inside, the top of his head and his arms on the controls. "Asshole," Billy said softly, and pulled the trigger. There was nothing to it. He banked his own plane to the left, following the gentle curve of the Jap's course. The P-50 bucked with the recoil of the fifties, but it was nothing. The Jap sat there frozen while Billy poured a thousand rounds into the Zero and it came to pieces in front of him. The cockpit dissolved in a shattered mass of plexiglass and metal and exploding flesh and then the bullets ate through the fuselage and the engine cowling, raking the plane from front to back. Huge chunks of it flew off and finally it simply disintegrated. Billy flew through the empty space where the Zero had been a split second before, still firing. He released the trigger and eased back in the seat and let his breath out. The air was clean, empty, filled with nothing but the sun and the perfect hurtling machine that was his own plane, while below him the million tiny pieces of the Zero rained into the Pacific. He heard then the excited babble on the radio—Muehler and the others below and behind him, shooting down the two Japs that had dived on the ships. And Schlosser was yelling like an idiot, telling them that Billy had shot down the third one.

He felt nothing. It had been too easy. The Jap—a kid, no doubt, maybe even a very little kid—had cheated him. He had sat there frozen in Billy's sights, petrified, while Billy simply pressed the trigger and chewed him to pieces. That was not the way he wanted it. Then, suddenly, he just wanted to go home, to be done with it.

That had been Billy Benefield's war, and now it was about to end stupidly, with a whimper. Storm-tossed and lost.

Then dawn came, and he at least had some idea of how long he had to live. Dawn meant that he had been in the air three hours, and there was about an hour's fuel left in his tanks. An hour to find land.

The sun spread its glow quickly over the face of the water and Billy banked his plane in a broad arc, scanning the horizon in all directions. Nothing. No ship, no island, nothing but water. He knew which direction the sun came from, but there was no fixed point from which to get his bearings. He could fly east toward the sun, but east from what—and to what? Any course could as easily take him away from land as toward it. He throttled back as far as he could without stalling the plane and turned west. It was simply a direction, and he had to go somewhere.

As he flew on, he thought about his odds should he run out

of fuel without spotting land. He tried to think of everything
they had taught him at Presidio in the special briefings. And he
decided the best thing to do would be to stay with the plane and
ditch it in the ocean. Bailing out would be less risky in the
beginning, but then he might end up in the water with nothing
but his life vest and then the sharks would get him. He was
terrified at the thought of sharks. His legs drew up involuntarily
as he imagined them slashing at his limbs, ripping away his
groin. God, not that! No, he would stay with the plane. You
could bash yourself up riding a plane into the ocean, but if you
made it down in one piece, you could get out with the life raft
and survival kit with its matches and flares, a little water and C-
rations, fishhooks and a knife. You could live perhaps a couple
of weeks on a raft, parceling out your water and sucking the
juices of fish. And if nobody found you, you would eventually
lapse into delirium and then a coma and death wouldn't hurt
much.

The sun was well above the horizon now, clean and warm,
bronzing the surface of the Pacific. He thought briefly of Alsatia—asleep in the tiny walk-up room in Presidio, hair splayed
across the pillow, wakening eventually to the same sun that fired
his ocean, rising naked—oh, God! (Billy squeezed his knees
together)—to stand lithe and tawny in the sun-exploded room.
There had been only a few days for them, barely enough time
and just enough luck to find the tiny room. Then he had seen
her once more at the gate to the air base in a crowd of other
wives and girlfriends just before the squadron left. A few nights
and a fistful of letters. And now this. He would never know if
he could have handled her.

Then he thought of his father, who had told him to get out of
the Army Air Corps, who wanted so badly for him to come
home from the war and go to law school and become mayor,
the way Rosh and his own father had done. He had decided
before he took off from Partridge Road on Christmas Eve Day
that he would not quit flying, and over the past six months he
had decided he probably couldn't do the rest of it, either. He
had traveled too far and seen too much to go back, at least not
for long. It would be a great disappointment to Rosh Benefield,
who loved him but said he lacked judgment. Or it would have
been. Billy would never know if he could have handled that,
either.

Then he saw the island.

It was nothing, a small green-brown bump all by itself on the gray-green elephant's hide of the Pacific. It would have been easy to miss, but it popped up there in front of him like a Zero in his sights. He would soon be out of fuel. And there was the island.

He closed the distance, and as he drew nearer, he could see that the island was not the perfect round hump he first thought, but rather an oval, stretching out away from him with a small indentation at the near end, a lagoon, and a slash of gray showing through the canopy of trees, running lengthways along the island. An airstrip. Nearer, and he could make out a seaplane tethered in the quiet water of the lagoon. The airstrip itself was empty. Japs, he thought. One of the tiny forgotten islands in the vastness between Okinawa and Japan, a pitiful chunk of coral and sand that might sink back into the sea at any time, unmourned. The Japs would have stripped it of everything valuable. Except the lone seaplane. But if there was a seaplane, there was gasoline. And if he could get to it, he could refuel.

What to do? If he landed, the Japs would probably kill him then and there. If he didn't, he would die in the water. The only thing to do, he decided quickly, was try to take it away from them.

Billy dropped down to five hundred feet and bore in on the island, knowing he had the sun at his back and a light wind in his face and he was almost sure of surprise. The island grew big in his windshield and he eased down a bit more, a hundred feet off the wave tops, heading straight for the lagoon. He flipped the safety lever on his guns, arming them, cursing himself for not having tested the fifty-calibers before now. His eyes strained toward the lagoon with its thin stretch of tan beach, toward the seaplane rocking gently at its mooring with the Rising Sun emblem on the fuselage.

There was no time to think about anything. The island was on him and he squeezed the gun switch. The plane jerked with the recoil of the fifties hammering away and he held it steady, nose pointing directly at the seaplane riding helplessly in the water. The bullets began churning the water well ahead of the seaplane, every fifth round a tracer marking the progress of his fire as it crept toward the plane and then simply ate it alive. The plane exploded as the shells chewed through the wing tanks and ignited the fuel and pulverized the cabin. It blew, showering pieces of debris over the lagoon. Then there was another explosion behind the plane, up on the beach, and Billy realized he had set off a fuel dump. There wasn't a lot of it, but it went with a big *whump* and a ball of flame shot skyward. Shit! The gasoline! Then he was on the island, roaring above the splintered smoking shell of the seaplane and seeing, just before he heeled the plane over to the left, the little gaggle of huts back away from the beach under the trees. He pulled a tight circle and gained altitude, then swung back over the island and by this time the Japs were stumbling from the huts, firing at him with their rifles.

The Japs struck the next blow and it stunned him. As he banked and started back over the island, a sudden puff of black appeared off his wingtip and then a concussion rocked the plane. Sonofabitch! The little bastards had ack-ack. He jerked the plane back to the right and headed for the deck while another wicked black puff and then another and another danced around him, peppering his plane with bits of shrapnel. He could see several holes in his left wing. He slammed the P-50 right down to wave level and then he made a low swing out over the ocean and headed back toward the island, below the gun's angle of compression. He could see it there at the edge of the beach under the trees, pumping away, firing ineffectually over his head. A single gun in a sandbag emplacement. He bore in again and the Japs realized what he was doing and he could see a couple of them scrambling out of the gun emplacement. The muzzle of the untended gun swung skyward. He squeezed the trigger and the bullets hit first in the trees, arcing in from the wings of his plane. He pushed the nose of the plane down just a hair and the shells seemed to settle in on the gun emplacement like rain. They tore it apart. Sandbags, pieces of the gun flew everywhere and some of the ammo exploded. He saw a Jap running behind the gun and then the fifties tore him in half and the torso just disappeared.

Billy hauled back on the stick and released the gun switch as he roared over the beach and the smashed gun and then he felt bullets hitting his plane. Small-arms fire. Something caught in the engine, a small shudder, and he felt the plane suddenly lose power. Goddamn. He looked over the nose of the plane, through the whining propeller, and saw the airstrip—neat, gray, hacked out of coral—and at the edge of it, the Japs. Two rows of them, a tiny formation. The front rank kneeling, the back standing, perfectly disciplined, blazing away at his plane. A bullet smashed through the plexiglass of the canopy near his head, ricocheted off something, and smacked into the instrument panel. Sparks flew. Billy screamed, felt his face. No blood. He was past the Japs now and he could hear and feel the bullets whanging into the fuselage and tail of the plane. They were riddling him. Then he saw, as he passed over the end of the runway, what they were protecting. There, under the trees, wrapped in camouflage netting, a lone Zero. A small ragged piece of the once-mighty Japanese air force, stranded here in the backwash of the war. Maybe not even operative, grounded because there were no parts, nobody to come fix the damn thing so it could kamikaze into an American ship. Or maybe that's what the seaplane was doing here. Whatever, it was fiercely defended by a pitiful little garrison of small funny men. And maybe there was more gasoline.

Billy turned far out over the water, cursing them. His engine sputtered and coughed. Either the bullets had crippled it, or he was running out of fuel. Then he saw the thin wisp of smoke trailing from the engine cowling. A bullet had severed the oil line and the oil, hitting the superheated engine, vaporized into evil black smoke that said the plane was mortally wounded. Without oil, the engine would soon freeze, fuel or no fuel.

He swung the plane back around to the right, back toward the island. It was limping badly now, coughing black blood from the wounds deep in its gut. Billy was at five hundred feet. He could see the airstrip as he approached and the small knot of men—perhaps ten in all—massing their firepower. They started popping away at him when he was well out from the beach, heading straight in at them, losing altitude, the plane's engine squalling now in protest. He presented a fat wounded target. As he came, he could hear the slugs beginning to hit the plane, ripping into the metal. Two bullets hit the windshield and shattered it and he felt a searing pain in his shoulder and the sharp pinpricks of plexiglass cutting his face. He couldn't squeeze his hand, couldn't pull the trigger, because the arm was frozen from the bullet in his shoulder.

"No!" he sobbed. Through the fractured windshield he could see the formation of Japs getting bigger. They were winning.

Finishing off his airplane. And he thought, This is how it's supposed to be. An even fight. Then there was another eruption of
oil from the engine—not smoke this time, but liquid oil, hot and
black, spraying back over the engine cowling and splattering the
blasted windshield. He bellowed with rage and somehow he
forced his frozen hand to squeeze the gun switch and he heard
the guns buck and roar in awesome noise, drowning out his own
frenzied battle screams. Then the guns quit and the plane itself
became a hurtling projectile. He pulled back on the stick at the
last possible instant and the plane pancaked onto the runway
and into what was left of the Jap formation, spraying bodies in
all directions. The last thing Billy remembered was the P-50
screeching on its belly, headed straight for the Zero under the
trees, in an incredible crescendo of noise that was bigger than
creation itself.

———————

Billy came to with flames all around him, and he thought, This
is it. But he reached up with his good hand and found the canopy
latch and gave it a mighty shove and the canopy slid back and
the fierce heat of the flames licked at him. He unbuckled his
harness and scrambled up out of the cockpit, onto the stub of
jagged metal that was all that was left of the wing, and sprawled
onto the sand. He picked himself up and started to run, whimpering with fright, and then the two planes—his own and the
Zero it had skidded into—blew with a mighty roar behind him,
slamming him onto the runway.

He lay there for a long time, semiconscious, and then realized
that he was alive and that nobody had walked up and shot him.
He had made it. He staggered, exhausted, to a shallow trench
on the other side of the runway, collapsed into it, and passed
out. When he awoke, it was late in the day. The wreckage of the
two planes was still smoldering. On the runway, bodies and
pieces of bodies. He had killed the entire Jap garrison. He in-
spected his own wounds. A slug had passed through the meaty
flesh of his right shoulder and there was a small piece of shrapnel
in his left foot. Other than that, and some singed hair from the
fire, he was all right.

He found two small huts at the end of the runway. One of
them was the Japs' living quarters, with bamboo and thatch
pallets on the floor, each under a canopy of mosquito netting.

The other was an operations building. In one corner was a stack of foodstuffs, a large bag of rice, canned fish, tins of hard crackers, some items he couldn't identify. In another corner was a small table with what was left of the Japs' radio. It was in a thousand pieces, obviously unusable. There were maps on the wall, a pile of yellowing newspapers and magazines on the floor, and in another corner, incongruously, an old windup Victrola and a stack of Nelson Eddy records. Outside, behind the building, were a rain barrel half-full of brackish water and a small lean-to where Billy found a shovel. Using it as a crutch, he hobbled back to the center of the runway and managed to drag the Japs' bodies over to the shallow trench and cover them with sand. Utterly spent, he returned to the huts, ate some canned fish and drank some water from the rain barrel, threw up, and went to sleep for two days.

He awoke feverish and light-headed, and wandered about the island, half-delirious, for several days. Then he stumbled onto a bunker dug into the sand back under the trees, covered with sturdy palm logs except for a small padlocked door. He busted off the lock, opened the door, and found the Japs' booze cache—several cases of a powerful rice wine in brown corked bottles. He lifted out one bottle, uncorked it, sniffed the strong tart odor of the wine, poured part of it on the festering wound in his shoulder and drank the rest. Within days, the wound had begun to heal. He took stock of his provisions, figured that he had enough food to last a year and ample fresh water from the frequent rainstorms. He hauled rocks and logs to the beach, constructed a sign large enough to be seen from several thousand feet up. He supplemented the Japs' food with fresh fish and coconuts, swam in the small lagoon, listened to Nelson Eddy, drank rice wine, and waited.

He had been there for two months, completely out of touch with the world, when a Navy PBY circled over the island one afternoon and its crew noticed the big block letters in the sand on the beach that read FUCK TOJO.

"There's got to be an American down there," said the pilot to the copilot, so they circled the island and landed the PBY in the bright green water of the small lagoon on the island's east side. They rowed ashore in a rubber dinghy and found Billy Benefield, dressed in a Japanese loincloth, quite drunk, lying in a makeshift hammock stretched between two palm trees at the edge of the island's small runway. Billy watched them cross the runway toward him, and when they reached the hammock, he swung his legs over the side and gave a lurching salute.

"Glad to see you sonsabitches," he said, "I was about to run out of wine and I'm bored with whacking off." Then he passed out.

So Billy Benefield came home the hero he no longer wanted to be.

The war was long over. Hitler and Roosevelt were dead, Churchill was deposed, Hiroshima and Nagasaki had been reduced to ashes and MacArthur had become de facto emperor of Japan, and American soldiers were rioting in Manila and Paris, demanding to be sent home. Several million had already gone, streaming back into civilian life in a country that wanted to forget places like Tunis and Tarawa.

But Billy Benefield was too good to pass up. The Army Air Corps brass figured the country could handle one last hero. So they dried Billy out in a hospital in Hawaii and sent him home with decorations—the Distinguished Flying Cross with Oak Leaf Cluster, the Silver Star, and the Purple Heart—and two escort officers, one of them a former Hollywood press agent.

Billy stepped off the C-47 at Presidio and told a waiting crowd of reporters, photographers, and newsreel cameramen how he had single-handedly captured an entire Japanese island and held it until Uncle Sam came to find him. On instructions from the Air Corps brass, he left out the role of the Navy and the Japanese rice wine.

That done, the Air Corps unleashed Alsatia and she dashed wailing across the tarmac, holding her hat on her head with one hand, and threw herself into Billy's waiting arms while the bulbs popped and the cameras whirred. Then the Air Corps handed Billy his mustering-out papers, and after a wild night in a San Francisco hotel, Billy and Alsatia boarded a TWA flight for Chicago.

Tunstall Renfroe, like the Army Air Corps, also knew a good thing when he saw it. Once news of Billy's rescue hit the papers, Tunstall wired Alsatia, forgiving all. Then Tunstall took it upon himself, as the town's wartime air raid warden, to organize a welcome-home celebration for the hero and his bride.

There was another press contingent waiting at Midway Airport in Chicago, along with Tunstall and Marvel Renfroe and Rosh and Ideal Benefield. The Benefields and Renfroes carried bundles of newspapers that featured front-page pictures of Billy and Alsatia's passionate kiss on the tarmac at Presidio and accounts of Billy's heroics. There was a tearful and somewhat awkward reunion and Billy recounted his exploits to the Chicago press; then they all took a taxi across town where they caught the train. They changed trains in Cincinnati and headed south toward home, into a land ablaze with autumn.

They wired ahead to let the town know of their arrival time, and when the train pulled into the station just after noon, there was a crowd at the platform including the high school band, members of the Town Council, a colonel from the upstate air base where Billy had done his flight training, and an honor guard from the American Legion post, whose ranks had been swelled by returning veterans.

Inside, as the train slowed, they all stood and began gathering up their parcels and coats (it had been cold in Chicago, but not so much that it prevented Marvel and Ideal from doing some shopping while they waited for Billy and Alsatia to arrive from the coast). They all stood, all, that is, except Billy. Rosh Benefield looked back and saw him sitting there in his seat on the opposite side of the car from the platform, looking glumly out the window toward the middle of town where the courthouse clock tower rose above the brown-leaved trees.

Rosh pulled on his heavy gray overcoat and eased his big bulk past the others back to Billy's seat, where Alsatia stood, bent over Billy, talking softly to him.

She turned to Rosh and shrugged. "He says he doesn't want to get off."

"Let me talk to him," Rosh said. "Let us be alone for a minute."

She gathered her things and moved past him, stopped to whisper to Tunstall and Marvel and Ideal. Then the four of them went to the front of the car, leaving Rosh and Billy alone. Rosh lowered himself heavily into the seat next to Billy and looked for a long moment at the back of his son's head.

"Billy," he said. Billy turned to look at him and he saw again how much Billy had changed. His face was deeply browned from the Pacific sun, the skin taut over the bones like a drumhead, small crow's-feet under his eyes from squinting. That would change. The tan would fade, the flesh would fill out, most of the wrinkles would go away for a while because Billy was still young. What would not change was the look in his eyes. The boy was gone, and with him the last flicker of Rosh Benefield's own youth. Rosh understood it as the look of a man who had been places and seen things he could never express to you because you were incapable of understanding, things that became part of his own fabric as surely as those you had drilled into him as a boy. Rosh had seen the look in the eyes of the others who came back from war. There was something of horror in some of them, the ones who had seen the worst of it. But beyond that was the common experience of having been away, having been scared and homesick and sometimes near death, and then having come to grips with it. A whole generation of young men, Rosh thought, would carry the same secrets in their hearts for a lifetime and be irreversibly altered by them. Even in the quiet and private hours of midnight in their own bedrooms, even in the most intimate moments of sharing, they could not share this. It was beyond comprehending. He wondered for a moment how it would change them and how it would change the country.

"I want to just keep going," Billy said to him. There was still a strange, hesitant quality in Billy's voice, that of a man who had been alone for a long time with no one to share his thoughts.

Ideal called to them from the front of the car. "Rosh, Billy, they're waiting for us."

Rosh gave her a hard stare and turned back to Billy. "So you want to keep going."

"I just don't want to talk to them. Can you understand that?"

Rosh could hear the off-key blatting of the high school band out on the platform, playing "When the Red Red Robin Comes Bob-Bob-Bobbin' Along." He looked out the opposite window at them for a moment. Twenty or so kids, mostly boys, in white shirts, dark pants, and white buck shoes. They looked unmercifully young and pimpled, but he thought that if the war had lasted another year, half of them would have gone.

He turned back to Billy. "I understand, son." He paused for a moment and looked down at his big hands, folded in his lap over the broad gray expanse of his overcoat. "What will you do if you stay on the train?"

"I don't know," Billy said quietly. "I just want to sit here until it gets to the end of the line, wherever that is, and then get off where nobody knows me and nobody expects anything."

"And what do you think they expect here?" Rosh asked.

"I guess it's you I'm talking about," he said.

Rosh grunted. "Okay. What do you think I expect of you, Billy?"

"You want me to go to college and then to law school and then come back here and settle down and become mayor. It's all you've ever talked about. And now, with my war record and my ribbons and all this hoopla, I guess I can see it happening, just like you want."

"Rosh!" Ideal called back again, "everybody's waiting. The conductor says they have to get the train moving, and all those people are standing out there . . ."

"Dammit, Ideal, will you shut up a minute!" Rosh snapped, and she stood there stunned, as if he had hit her with a wet dishrag. Tunstall Renfroe cleared his throat and said, "Well, we'll be waiting outside, Ideal," and he took Marvel by the arm and left. Rosh could see him through the window, waving and smiling outside where the crowd was thick on the platform around the band. Ideal stood her ground inside the railroad car, arms full of packages, glaring at them, Alsatia beside her with a bemused look on her face.

Rosh turned to Billy again. "Son, you don't have to decide right this minute what you're going to do with the rest of your life. Look, you've been away and become your own man. You can do anything you damned well please. Yes, if you want to go to law school and become mayor, it's there for the taking. Maybe even more than that. Congress, if you wanted it. But if you want to get off the train here and say hello to all the folks and then go home and prop your feet up and wait for some sort of inspiration to hit you, that's all right, too. You have to be your own man now. You can't do what I want, or what you think people expect, unless it's what you want."

Billy studied him for a moment. "You mean that, don't you."

Rosh nodded. "Of course. That's all a man should ever want from a son. As Jake Tibbetts likes to say, a fellow has to take his life in his own hands and shake it for all it's worth. Do that, and I'll be satisfied."

"But if I get off," Billy said stubbornly, "that's taking the first step."

"Have you talked with Alsatia about this?"

"No. All we ever do is"—he stopped and blushed.

Rosh smiled. "Well, don't you think she's got some say in the matter?"

Billy shrugged. "I guess."

"That's one thing about having a wife. You can't do anything without her putting her two cents' worth in."

They sat there for a moment, Rosh looking at Billy, Billy staring at the back of the seat in front of him. The conductor swung inside the car and called out, " 'Board! Got to get moving, folks. We're behind schedule!"

Rosh got heavily to his feet. "Billy, I don't think the Army Air Corps has taught you a damned thing about judgment. But you're not going to learn any by sitting here on this train until it runs out of track. Now if you don't want to get off, fine. I'll step out there and give your regards to the folks and tell them you've got business elsewhere."

Billy waited awhile, deep in thought, and then looked up at him. "Aw, what the hell," he said.

"Yeah," Rosh nodded. "What the hell. You've been through a lot, son. Come on home and take time to sort it out."

Billy sat there a moment longer, pondering it, and then got to his feet with a jerk, reaching for his uniform cap in the overhead rack and jamming it on his head. He managed a grin, almost the kind he used to have when he was a kid full of mischief, Rosh thought. At the front of the car, Billy kissed Ideal on the cheek to let her know everything was okay, gave Alsatia his arm, and stepped out onto the platform. There was a moment of silence and then the applause started and the band struck up "Red Red Robin" again.

Rosh held back, watching as the crowd pressed in around Billy and Alsatia, and Billy reached out to touch them, grinning and squeezing their flesh with both hands. He looked very handsome in his uniform, the winter tans resting easily on his shoulders, the cap cocked back on his head a bit, the way fly-boys wore them. He must look very dashing and a little exotic to them. Rosh could feel the tears welling up behind his eyes, very close to the surface, tears he had carefully held back all those long months when there had no longer been any reason to hope

Billy was alive. What an amazing thing it was for God to return a man's son to him. And if a man could see the miracle in that, was it unreasonable for him to want much for such a son? Maybe it was a sin, even a great one, but the kind that would surely be forgiven.

There was a brief ceremony. Cosmo Redlinger gave a little speech on behalf of the Town Council and presented Billy with a large brass key to the city, handmade at the Harsole Bingham plant. A young girl from the First Baptist Church gave Alsatia a big bouquet of flowers, a significant thing because it meant her peccadillo was officially forgiven and that Ideal Benefield, who ran the First Baptist Church, had put her blessing on the business.

Then Tunstall called on the colonel from Billy's air base and the colonel, a decorated bomber pilot himself, stepped forward and read the citations for Billy's Distinguished Flying Cross with Oak Leaf Cluster, Silver Star, and Purple Heart. He handed the boxes containing Billy's ribbons to Rosh, Ideal, and Alsatia, and they took turns pinning them on the front of his tunic. Alsatia was last and when she was finished, she gave Billy a long kiss while the crowd hooted and cheered and the high school band played "There's No Place Like Home for the Holidays," and that was when Rosh Benefield cried. He stood there with tears streaming down his cheeks and Billy, seeing him, walked back to where he stood and gave him a big hug. There wasn't a dry eye in the crowd except for Cosmo Redlinger, who had trained himself as an undertaker to keep careful check on his emotions.

The band stopped and then started immediately into "Red Red Robin" again and Francine Tibbetts shouldered her way to the front of the crowd with Henry in tow. Henry was holding Jake Tibbetts's big Speed Graphic camera as if it were a time bomb. "Let's get a picture, folks," Francine called out.

Billy stared at Henry for a long moment. "Mr. Jake?"

The mistake was natural. Henry looked ancient and frail, his complexion sallow and mottled, hair thinning. Then, too, he had Jake Tibbetts's bushy, riotous eyebrows and his stubborn jaw. Rosh could feel Ideal bristle beside him. After all these years, she still had the great hate inside her.

"No, Billy, this is Henry," Rosh said, stepping forward. "Henry Tibbetts. And his wife Francine."

"Henry, my God," Billy said, reaching out, pulling Henry's

hand into his own. "Gee, it's good to see you. And Francine, is it? Well, my God." He pumped Henry's hand, and Henry just stood there, looking as if he didn't know what to do.

"Okay," Francine interrupted, "let's get everybody in here. All the Benefields and the Renfroes, and Mr. Redlinger of course. And you, Colonel." She took charge, arranging the group while Henry stood back holding the camera gingerly. When she had them set, Henry fumbled with the camera for a long awkward moment while the smiles froze on their faces, then raised it to his eye and mashed the shutter release. It clicked and Henry lowered the camera, looked at the flash attachment, mumbled, pulled a flash bulb from his pocket and inserted it, then changed the plate in the back of the camera and took another shot. This time the flash popped, leaving a small bright spot in front of their eyes. Francine stood to the side, silent, watching patiently until Henry got it done.

"Where's Mr. Jake?" Billy asked when they were finished.

Henry blanched and it was suddenly very quiet. Rosh moved quickly, grabbing arms, moving the crowd down the platform. "Well, time to get on to the house and get these young folks some rest," he boomed. "Where's the car? Oh, yes. Over here." He pointed and just kept shoving them ahead of him toward the end of the train station where he had left the Packard when they boarded the northbound train three days ago. Billy gave him a funny look, but Rosh shook his head. He kept himself between Billy and Ideal because he just knew Ideal was dying to say something, say it loudly right there so everybody could hear it. By the time they got to the car, she was fuming.

"Damn you, Rosh," she hissed in his ear when they reached the car, "don't you ever curse at me again, you hear me!"

"What?" he said in surprise. "I haven't said a word, hon."

"Yes, you did. On the train. You uttered a curse word at me. Don't tell me you didn't."

"Sorry, hon," he mumbled.

"And just now . . ."

"Okay, hon, later. Okay?" And he opened the rear door of the car and shoved her in. He would pay for that, he thought to himself.

They drove home in stony silence, Ideal sitting ramrod straight and red-faced in the front beside him, Billy and Alsatia in the back. There was another big crowd waiting for them, people milling through the house (Rosh wondered how they had gotten in), huge piles of food in the kitchen, the dining room table set for dinner. The women of the First Methodist Church had organized it, had brought whole hams and turkeys and roasts, casseroles, plates and bowls of vegetables, big urns of sweetened tea, enough to feed them for weeks. They hugged and kissed and shook hands for a long time and then sat down, exhausted, to eat while the churchwomen hovered over them. It was midafternoon before they got the house cleared and Ideal retired upstairs with a headache and Alsatia went not long after to take a nap in the spare bedroom, leaving Rosh and Billy alone in the living room with all the unanswered questions.

Billy slumped into an overstuffed chair, coat off, collar undone, tie loose. Rosh sat across from him on the sofa and, since the ladies were gone, undid the top button on his trousers and let his stomach take ease.

"Tired?" he asked Billy.

"Not especially. I've had a long time to rest up."

"You want to talk about it?"

"Not yet," Billy said. "I'm not sure why. There's really not much to tell about it. I just sat around for two months waiting for somebody to find me. Nothing very glorious or heroic about that."

Rosh grunted. The room was warm, he was full of food. He could feel sleep coming on.

Billy took off his shoes and placed them neatly beside his chair and began massaging his left foot, the one the shrapnel had pierced. "The Army says I have a drinking problem," Billy said. "I stayed drunk most of the time, I guess. I found some Jap wine."

Rosh opened his eyes and blinked. "You don't look like an alcoholic to me," he said.

"What does an alcoholic look like?" Billy asked. "Henry Tibbetts?"

Rosh knew it was time then to tell him everything. And he did. How Henry came home and got drunk and stole the fire truck and wrecked the telephone office and scared Em Nesbitt half out of her wits. How Hilton Redlinger stopped him in the middle of the street and fired his pistol and the shot ricocheted and hit Lonnie. How Jake came running up and saw it all and had a stroke on the spot and spent a month in a coma. Rosh told it all, organizing the story as he would a presentation to a jury, and Billy sat there rubbing his foot and listening. One part of Rosh's mind told the story and another part listened to it, analyzing, thinking how the lives of Jake Tibbetts and his kin had dissolved into utter chaos.

"And Lonnie?" Billy asked when Rosh was through.

"He wasn't too badly hurt. The bullet must have hit him a glancing blow. It went in up here"—Rosh tapped his chest just above the breastbone—"and went out here"—he pointed to his left side below the rib cage—"and broke a couple of ribs along the way, but it didn't hit anything vital. He's back in school now."

"What about Mr. Jake?"

"Ah, Jake," Rosh said with a long sigh. "He lives but he doesn't. He's recovering from the stroke pretty well. It's downright remarkable, in fact. He's beginning to get up and around. But I think with the weeks he was just lying there unconscious, his body came out of it in better shape than his mind. At first, he was just plain nasty. Now, he just sits there for hours and says nothing. I don't know," Rosh threw up his hands, "he's just waiting for something. Maybe to die."

Billy lowered his foot, wiggled the toes inside the tan sock. "You and Mr. Jake have always been pretty close, haven't you? Even . . ."

"Yes," Rosh nodded. "Even with *that*." It loomed large before him now, the always-unspoken thing that had hovered over Jake Tibbetts and himself.

"Jake always blamed Henry for Hazel's death," Rosh said.

"Well . . ."

Rosh shook his head. "It's not as easy as that. Hazel"—he took a deep breath—"was difficult."

"What do you mean?"

Rosh searched his soul for the right words. How did a man deal with a truth so painful and so hidden that it festered like a wound deep inside him? How did he pass judgment on his own flesh? He thought about it for a long time, feeling Billy's eyes on him. Finally he said, "They were just terrible for each other. Hazel picked at Henry until he bled. And Henry just cowered down and took it and took it until you wanted to pick him up and shake him. Then he'd go off and get drunk and stay that way for days at a time. I don't know what happened in the car that night on the way back from Taylorsville, but something awful had been building for a long time.''

"But Mother . . .'' Billy started to say.

"I know,'' Rosh interrupted him gently. "Your mother won't ever get over the hurt, and the only person she's got to blame is Henry. She deals with it as she has to.''

"And you blame Hazel,'' Billy said.

"No, I don't blame anybody,'' Rosh said, suddenly feeling very tired. "Blame is a difficult thing, Billy. I think only God can assign blame. Maybe it's that I'm too much the lawyer, but I'm condemned to deal with what passes for fact. I can't assess blame, not even here.''

Billy stared at him, then looked down at his hands clenched in his lap.

"It's not fair to say all this to you, when you're just home,'' Rosh said.

"No,'' Billy shook his head. "It's not. It's not something I need to deal with.''

"But one day, you'll have to,'' Rosh said.

"Yes.'' He paused. "And Henry? What happened to Henry?''

Rosh told him how Henry spent two months in the county jail for stealing the fire truck and wrecking the phone exchange. It would have been more, but Henry had come back from the war with a Silver Star. How his feisty little wife had taken hold of him after he got out of jail, put him to work at the *Free Press*.

"They're running the paper now,'' Rosh said. "I think Lonnie goes down there after school. They hired a printer to run the Linotype machine and put the paper together. The paper is pretty awful, but they manage to get it out. They haven't missed an issue.''

And, he told him about how Francine and Henry had married in Texas, and about how she had shown up in the middle of the night on Jake and Pastine's front porch.

"Where was Lonnie today?'' Billy asked. "You said he's okay now.''

"He may have been there, back in the crowd someplace. He's a funny little fellow. Quiet, mind going all the time. Too much, I think. I know Pastine's worried about him. Since the, ah, incident he's kept pretty much to himself. We don't see much of him anymore.''

"What a mess," Billy said.

"I suppose it is," Rosh said, "but they manage to muddle through, all of them. We all, I suppose, manage to muddle through."

He thought again how strange it was to be sitting here like this, talking to Billy this way, talking of things he would never have thought of discussing with him before. There had been no call to. Billy had gone off to war a boy, but he had come back with the look of the world on his tanned face. Rosh felt a pang. There was something here forever lost, and it wasn't just Billy's youth and innocence. He grieved a bit for himself, for all men who must grow old and face the certainty of their own mortality, knowing that for all their age and wisdom, they go naked and blind into the dark night.

"Billy," the velvet voice floated down to them from the top of the stairs. "Billy, don't you want to come up and take a nap with me, darling. I know you must be worn out." There was in the voice alone, Rosh thought, enough to make a man's blood run hot.

Billy flushed. "Geez," he said quietly so that only Rosh could hear. He rolled his eyes toward the ceiling, then rose from his chair, looked down at his father.

"Don't worry, son," Rosh said. "An old country doctor told me one time that it's impossible to wear it out."

Billy grinned and then he left Rosh alone there in the living room with his vast belly hanging out of his trousers and the clock in the front hall ticking away the afternoon.

Rosh thought suddenly of Lightnin' Jim, of clear fiery liquid in mason jars, and of Buffalo, New York. He smiled to himself, thinking that no one in this small Southern town would guess that its wealthiest man and its wealthiest woman—Lightnin' Jim and Pastine Tibbetts, one black, one white—jointly owned a goodly share of Buffalo's real estate. There was something perfectly delicious about that, something a lawyer who had managed their affairs could enjoy in the most confidential moments. Each client knew there was another, silent partner. But neither knew the identity of the other. Both, he thought, would take a particular delight in it. But it would not do to tell, here or in Buffalo, New York. And it was time for him, their lawyer and confidant, to advise them to sell out. The postwar boom meant that the value of their property was already skyrocketing. Take it and run and let no one be the wiser. There was another reason, too. The sharp pains in his chest that took his breath were coming more often now. If he was careful, if he got his rest and kept agitation at a minimum and took a daily dose of Lightnin' Jim's Best for medicinal purposes, he could last another year or so. Time enough to set things in order. Time enough, perhaps, to see what happened to that old ornery sonofabitch Jake Tibbetts. God save a man from having such a friend.

Rosh Benefield went to sleep on the sofa thinking of Jake and his dreams were full of devilment.

TEN

JAKE TIBBETTS awakened from his long sleep in mid-September, about the time the PBY discovered Billy Benefield on the Pacific island.

He woke to the knowledge that he had crossed an enormous expanse of time and space since August, and that he had washed up on the near shore in wretched shape, a shadow of the man he had been a few weeks before. He woke because his father appeared at his bedside and spoke vile things that altered all he had ever been and done in unspeakable ways.

A week later, Jake spoke himself. No one could understand him—it came out as a strangled, guttural, animal noise—but he knew damned well what he meant to say. He meant to say, "Goddamn you all, leave me alone." Pastine and Francine and Charlie Ainsworth and Rosh Benefield were all hovering over him, clucking and prodding and farting about, and all he wanted them to do was go away. He wanted to die, but they would not let him go in peace.

In fact, he kept getting better. In another week, he got some control of his mouth and vocal cords so that he could cuss them and they knew they had been cussed. By this time, they had him sitting up on the side of the bed, a person on each side to prop him up. And then, as October came and Billy Benefield came home on the train, the feeling returned to him in a rush. The broken connections in his brain somehow fused again, as Ainsworth said they might. Jake was, essentially, over the stroke, except for some lingering numbness on his left side and a bit of a droop on that side of his face. But what the stroke had left was a shell. He had lain flat on his ass longer than a sixty-four-year-old man can afford to do. Muscles had atrophied, coordination was gone, he had even lost his sense of up and down, right and left. Still, he would not die, at least not yet.

Since he could not die, he could make the rest of them wish he had. He lashed at them with his tongue, the only thing that worked right, until he drove them all away. Except for Pastine. She stuck, even when the vilest things spewed from the poisoned recesses of his brain—stuck, suffering silently through his abuse. She cleaned him when he fouled himself, kneaded his ruined flesh for hours, while all the time, he raged at her for his own humiliated helplessness.

But she could only take so much at a time, so she left him alone for long periods. With no one to rail at, his anger spent itself and he was forced to consider what made him unable to act like anything but an unreconstituted sonofabitch. He began to understand that one reason he railed was so he wouldn't have to face other things—for one, the unspeakable thing that Albertis told him Pastine had done; and the other, what had happened at dusk on the courthouse square on August 7. So one evening in early October, he faced it. She had brought him his supper, propped him up in bed with a towel under his chin to catch the pieces of food that spilled from his mouth when he tried to feed himself. He mumbled a thank-you and otherwise held his wicked tongue in check. She gave him a curious look, and after she had left him with the tray, she came back with a bowl of bread dough and sat in the rocker by the window as dusk fell, kneading the dough, concentrating on the work.

Finally, he asked, "What happened?"

She never stopped kneading. Her strong hands, white with the flour, worked the dough, pressing, pulling. She looked up at him for an instant, then down again at her work. "I wondered if you would ever ask," she said.

"I was afraid," he croaked.

"Well, they're all right," she said. And she told him then how Charlie Ainsworth had happened to be heading home from a house call out in the country when he saw the commotion on the courthouse square, stopped his car, and grabbed the spurting artery that was gushing blood out of Lonnie's chest, holding it all the way to Taylorsville until they got Lonnie to the hospital and sewed him up. She began to cry, telling it, but she sat there and kept pulling and tugging with her tears dropping into the bowl and mixing with the yellow dough. And Jake began to cry, too, great sobs racking his wretched body as he remembered the blood, all the terrible blood, and the searing flash of pain and heat and light that tore through his own head. Now, the tears seemed to flood through those same passages in his brain, cleansing, washing out some of the rancid poisons. They cried, both of them, for a long time—she in the chair, he on the bed, never touching. Finally, they composed themselves.

"How is he?" Jake asked.

"He's mended," she said. "He's in school now."

"Why hasn't he come to see me?"

"He hears how you are," she said simply. "And I think he blames himself in some way for all that's happened. I don't know why, but he does."

There was a long, empty silence. "And Henry?"

"They put him in the county jail. He's out now, helping Francine run the newspaper."

"Francine and Henry?"

"Yes," she said. "They hired a printer and they're getting it out. They haven't missed an issue."

Jake didn't ask any more about the newspaper. He just didn't want to know, not now. In fact, he didn't ask any more questions about anything for a long time. And he stopped abusing people with his vile tongue.

It was his voice. It haunted him. It was the dry raspy whisper of Albertis Tibbetts, and it echoed maddeningly through his brain whenever he tried to speak. It floated through this very upstairs room, the one where Albertis had paced and lain abed years before during the awful periods when the melancholia got him. Now it had become Jake's own voice. Albertis's beast possessed him and he could hear its grating rasp in his throat and feel the leaden weight of its sadness filling his breast. It was not fair that a man should have to put up with two beasts. But then, he thought, he had been cleaning up his father's mess all his life. Albertis had left a newspaper in shambles, and Jake had made something of it. Or had he? Albertis had sat in this same room, in that straight-backed chair there, and told him that he was a failure, that it had been Pastine's money all these years that kept the *Free Press* going. What right had he to do that? Goddamn his wretched soul, he had no right. And Pastine. She had no right to do what she had done. She had no RIGHT!

But wait. Who had sat in that chair and told him these things? Albertis Tibbetts was dead, and even if his ghost came back to haunt his son, there was no way he could know what he seemed to know. Had it been Rosh Benefield sitting there? Had Rosh told him something he had hinted at before, sitting in the *Free Press* office on a summer evening, recounting how he had helped a woman deceive her husband? Or was it something Jake himself had somehow known all these years—the accumulation of a thousand small clues tucked away in some secret place in his mind? But no matter. It was done and it cut deeply. They had betrayed him, all of them—Albertis, Rosh, Pastine, all of them. They had let him go on this way for a lifetime, thinking he was a newspaperman, while they sneaked around behind his back and propped him up. What pity they must have felt. Goddamn them all! Tears of frustration filled his eyes as he sat through the unbearably long hours and pondered it all and the bile of his own bitterness filled his throat.

So he walked. He had to do something with the great rage that built like an overheated boiler inside him. He could no longer cuss them because Albertis Tibbetts haunted his voice. He wasn't strong enough to break things. So he walked. At first, he just got unsteadily to his feet with Pastine holding him up and stood there, feeling faint as the blood rushed from his head, right hand gripping the walking stick she had got for him. Then after a few days of doing that, he took the first halting step. He stood by the bed, steadier now, commanding his left foot to slide forward an inch or two, beads of sweat popping out on his forehead, teeth grinding with frustration because the damned foot wouldn't go. He strained every muscle and nerve until the tears coursed down his cheeks, and then, finally, by God, it moved. "Enough," he croaked, and lay back on the bed, exhausted. Pastine cried and hugged him, patting his cheek until he drifted off to sleep, totally spent. The next day he did it again—once in the morning and again in the late afternoon. And by the end of the week he was rasping at Pastine every hour or so, Albertis's voice be damned, to come and help him. She came, brushing the loose strands of hair away from her face, wiping her hands on her apron, while he fretted impatiently. She stood there, silent, gripping the waistband of his trousers, as he took each step.

By the middle of October he was ready to navigate on his own. One morning, Jake turned to her and said, "Let go."

"Jake . . ." she protested.

"Let go my goddamn pants," he insisted.

She let go and he took one step and fell in a heap on the floor and lay there, cussing and crying while she hovered anxiously over him.

"I'm all right," he said finally. "Help me up."

It was a terrible strain for both of them, but somehow they got him upright. "Now let go," he said again.

She started to say something, but she could see the awful, trembling rage in him and she released her grip. He took a shuffling step, wobbled, steadied himself, took another. He kept moving, one foot after the other, head down watching his slippered feet slide agonizingly along the floor, an inch with this one, an inch with that one, like some creaking ancient machine. He moved, kept moving, put every ounce of his concentration and energy into what he told himself was the hardest thing he had done in his life. Then his forehead bumped against the far wall and he stopped, unable to go any farther, unable to turn around because the only movement he could make was straight ahead. He coughed and sputtered with anger. The raspy voice of Albertis Tibbetts rattled in his throat. Then Pastine's gentle hand touched him on the elbow and she took hold and guided him so that he could turn slowly to the left, an inch at a time, until he was headed back toward the bed. Once there, he collapsed and slept the rest of the day.

But it had been a start, and once started he went at it fiercely. He flung himself against the stubborn barrier of his own physical incompetence, every move agonizingly slow and graceless. He shuffled the length of the room, back and forth, back and forth, realizing as he did so that he was retracing the haunted steps of Albertis Tibbetts, who had paced this room so unremittingly that he had worn a threadbare path in the carpet. Jake trod the same path now because it was the only place in the room that was wide enough and long enough for him to traverse. He studied each tattered thread in the carpet until the path was etched in his mind, hating it, hating Albertis, hating himself. But he walked until he exhausted himself and then sleep came mercifully to wipe his mind clean and restore his body enough to try it again.

Pastine finally left him alone, inventing excuses to come back upstairs every few minutes to check on him, but he glared at her when he caught her watching him.

"Stop that," he said.

"Are you all right?"

"No, I'm crippled," he snarled.

She shrugged it off. "Don't you want to stop and rest awhile?"

"No. Now go away. I'll either walk or I'll fall and bust my ass."

"Your foul mouth is an abomination, Jake Tibbetts," she told him, angry now.

But she went away and gave him a few moments' peace to lose himself in his struggle.

Before long, he got up enough strength to pass through the doorway of the room and out into the upstairs hall, where there was another space of several feet open to him. And from there, it was a matter of days until he tried the stairs.

"Jake!" she screamed up at him from the downstairs hallway as he teetered on the third step from the top, left hand gripping the banister, right hand pressing the walking stick hard into the smoothworn pine of the stair.

She started up the steps toward him, but he stopped her with an angry bellow. "Stay back," he yelled, "or I'll jump!" Jump, he thought, what a joke. He couldn't jump two inches. "I'll topple," he said, correcting himself.

She stepped back, gave him a disgusted look, and wiped her hands on her apron. "All right, topple," she said, and turned on her heel and marched back into the kitchen, leaving him there on the stairs. He mumbled under his breath for a moment and then panic began to set in. He couldn't do it. He would, indeed, either topple forward and kill himself or he would have to sit down here on the staircase and stew in his juice until he swallowed his pride and yelled for help. To hell with them all. He took a deep breath, got his bowels under control, and after a few minutes he took another step and then another until he made it down to the bottom.

"Pastine," he rasped.

She took her time, but after a moment she poked her head around the doorway from the kitchen.

"I made it," he said.

"I see you did. How are you going to get back up?"

He stared at her dumbly for an instant, mouth agape, and finally said, "I don't know."

It took them half the afternoon to hoist him back up the stairs, Jake straining to raise each foot the few inches to the next step, Pastine next to him hauling on the seat of his pants. When they finally made it, they both sat, exhausted, on the top step, eyes glazed with fatigue.

"You're a stubborn old fool," she said.

He nodded, unable to speak, and then he collapsed against her, put his head in her lap while she stroked his forehead with her firm, gentle fingers.

"When are you going to stop being so angry?" she asked after a moment.

"When I stop being a sick, wasted, washed-up old man," he growled.

"Maybe if you didn't act like one, you wouldn't feel like one."

"Hah! That's easy for you to say. You're only sixty-one and you don't have to have anybody haul you up the steps by the seat of your britches." He tried to raise his head, but she forced it back down in her lap and kept kneading his forehead.

"Well, I will haul you, Jake, despite your rottenness," she said.

He waited for a long time, poised on the edge, feeling the beast gnawing, gnawing in his gut, before he finally asked, "Why did you do it?"

Her fingers didn't stop. "Do what?"

"Take my newspaper away from me."

Then it was her turn to hang fire and he thought, She's going to deny it, and if she does I'll never know for sure because she's the only one I can ask. But then Pastine sighed deeply, sadly. "Ahhhhh. I didn't take your newspaper away from you, Jake." She paused. "What do you think I did?"

"I know you paid the bills."

"How do you know that?"

"My father came . . . while I was sick . . . he told me."

There was another long silence before she spoke. "Your father's dead, Jake. He's been dead a long time," she said gently.

"I know. But he came and sat in the chair next to my bed and told me how you paid the bills."

"You always said you weren't a business tycoon, you were a newspaperman. And that's what you are. A fine newspaperman. An ornery newspaperman who makes people mad and makes them think. So, why does the rest of it matter?"

But he didn't answer that. She knew why it mattered, why it would matter to him of all people.

"Well," he said finally, his voice still the hoarse rattle of Albertis Tibbetts, "it's over."

"What do you mean?"

"The paper. It's finished."

Her fingers stopped abruptly. "No, it's not, Jake. It's still there when you're ready to go back to it. And there's Francine and Henry. And Lonnie."

Jake wanted to cry out in anguish. Henry. Goddamn him, he wouldn't go away. He was everywhere, the ghost of nightmares past and present, a specter that no jail cell or even casket could hold. Henry. Always there was Henry—confounding him, maddening him. Why couldn't Henry have had the decency to just blow himself away after what he had done, or at least quietly disappear and never be heard from again? No, he clung fiercely to life, a shipwrecked survivor, forever muddling and haunting and always *there*. Jake wanted to cry out with the rage and frustration that had always been Henry. Goddamn him! Goddamn him!

And Lonnie. God, he thought, the baggage that boy carries around with him. There's Henry and all his craziness and beyond that, Jake's own craziness, and even before that the assorted lunacy of Albertis and Captain Finley, all of it echoing back and forth like thunder through their mad generations and coming to rest on the frail shoulders of a twelve-year-old boy. No, thirteen now. Lonnie would have had a birthday in September. How they must mock him at school—the grandson of the loony old newspaper editor, son of the idiot who stole the fire truck. The thought of it brought back the sting of his own youth, how cruelly they aped his mind-sick father, how their laughter followed him as they yelled down the street, "Hey, Jake, did your daddy come out today?" The curse of the Tibbetts men lay on all of them, the burden growing heavier as father passed it on to son.

"The curse," he said out loud.

"The what?"

"Never mind," he said. "I'm tired. I want to go to bed." But he lay there a while longer with his head in her lap, only the soft sounds of the house around them and the downstairs hallway darkening with evening. After a while he heard the rumble of Tunstall Renfroe's car passing on Partridge Road, going home from a day at the bank. Finally Pastine rose and helped pull him to his feet so he could take the last stair step to the second-floor landing. Fatigue covered him like a blanket now, shutting out everything except Pastine's tug on his arm when he started to turn right in the hallway and shuffle toward the spare bedroom.

"No," she said gently. "You're coming home tonight."

He felt a great uncontrollable shudder go through his body then, as if something that had possessed him were leaving. The beast? Having done its foul work? Or maybe something as simple as surrender? He couldn't answer, because he was already asleep before she ever got him onto the bed and pulled a quilt over his tired old bones.

He began, in the days that followed, to make a certain peace with himself. Certain things were irrevocably gone. All the days of his youth, for instance. A man of sixty-five had no claim at all on the days of his youth. Certain pretensions, too. A man of sixty-five could no longer put off considering the things he had not done, because if he had reached this age without doing them, there was precious little chance he ever would. Jake Tibbetts began, as Henry had begun under the blasted tank in the Ardennes eleven months before, to tick off the items of his life and put them to rest. Scenes of his past returned to him, almost as vividly as they had done in the weeks when he had been a prisoner of his own mind. He stood again with his father on the steps of the courthouse; knelt sobbing at the top of the embankment as Rosh Benefield's shattered car burned like an inferno below him; held Hilton Redlinger's huge pistol as Lieutenant Grover Whalen loosened the bolts of the casket with the strange boy inside.

He did it all with a strange, stark honesty. This was good, he said, and this was not. I succeeded here, I failed utterly there. In this instance I sinned and fell short; in that, I acted with dignity and grace. In many things, I was inadequate: I did not try hard enough, or have charity or grace or wit enough. What he could not forgive in himself, he tried to reconcile.

Long hours passed for Jake Tibbetts, long hours alone with his soul. Slowly, methodically, he made a kind of peace. But one puzzle from the past remained.

He woke with it in the middle of the night.

"Pastine," he said. She didn't answer. He listened for a moment to her soft even breathing, then nudged her shoulder. "Pastine," he said again, "wake up. I've got to ask you something."

She moaned and turned to him in the bed. "What's the matter?" she murmured.

"Did you . . . ." he started, then swallowed hard. "Did you and Rosh Benefield . . . did you ever . . . ."

There was a long, awful silence and Jake could feel the dark chill of the night deep in his soul as he prayed that she would tell him the truth, no matter how bad it was, so that he could make peace even with this.

Pastine took a deep breath and then she said softly, "No." And then, after a moment, "You're a fool, Jake Tibbetts, but you're the only fool I ever wanted."

He started to cry then, and after a moment Pastine began to cry, too. They clung to each other like orphans in the middle of the night, as only a man and woman can cling to each other after they have passed through a long journey and have known the perils of traveling together, each burdened by private agonies and hopes. When finally they slept, Jake Tibbetts was ready to be at peace. The war was over and all the boys were coming home.

On November 17, 1945, Jake Tibbetts observed his sixty-fifth birthday. It was the Saturday before Thanksgiving and he sat alone in his upstairs room at midafternoon and contemplated being sixty-five and wished they would all let him suffer through the indignity in peace. He hated being fussed over, and they were making a fuss over him today. The telephone had been

ringing downstairs all morning and half the afternoon. People
were calling to wish him well, Pastine said, to congratulate him.
More people than had ever called the Jake Tibbetts residence in
one day. Francine and Henry had put it in the damned newspaper, for God's sake.

He sat on the side of the bed and stared out the window for a
long time, heard a couple of cars drive up and park in the front
yard, heard the mutter of voices in the downstairs hallway, too
distant and soft to recognize. Jake hoped that would be the end
of it. He didn't need a caravan tooting out here from town to
help him be sixty-five.

He felt, rather than heard, something at the doorway of his
room and he turned from the window and saw Lonnie standing
there. A bit taller now, but thin and drawn, the skin on his face
pinched, neck and arms scrawny, sleeves and collar too big for
him. He stood back, hesitant, waiting.

Jake stared at him. "Ha!" he finally snorted. "You look a
little peaked, boy."

"Yessir," Lonnie said. Then he blurted out, "You don't look
so great yourself."

Jake stared at him. "I've been a little sick."

"Yessir."

"God save a man from doctors. They'll make you old before
your time," Jake said. Then, "You haven't been around to see
me."

Lonnie ducked his head. "Well, I've been sick, too."

"Yeah, I heard," Jake said, and then he choked, the tears
rising up. "I thought . . ." He turned his face away and stared
out the window until he got himself under control again. "Well,"
he said, "I missed the hell out of you, boy."

"I missed you, too," Lonnie said softly.

"We're just a couple of old lame ducks, eh?"

"I guess so," Lonnie said.

There was a long silence while they looked at each other and
then Lonnie cut his eyes away to the window, where the Saturday
afternoon was pale with thin washed-out November sunshine.

"How's school?"

"Okay, I guess. They sent my books home while I was in the
bed. I stayed caught up, mostly. Bugger Brunson come around
and helped me about every afternoon."

"*Came* around," Jake corrected.

"Yessir. Well, he came around and helped me, especially with arithmetic. I ain't much on decimals."

"I'm *not* much on decimals."

"Nosir, I know that. You always said you weren't much on figuring."

God, what a truth, Jake thought to himself. I thought I had it all figured out, but it turned out there was so much I didn't figure on, so much that hit me blindsided. And thereby hangs the great question: Can a man truly take his life into his own hands and shake it for all it's worth when there is so much he can't figure on?

"Lonnie . . ." he said.

"Yessir."

"Nobody's to blame, I want you to understand that. Things just happen and nobody has any control over them. Sometimes a fellow gets run over just because he's standing in the way. At the wrong place, the wrong time. You see?"

Lonnie nodded, but Jake could tell he didn't see, and why should he? Talk to a thirteen-year-old boy about cause and effect? And what of any sense could come from a lame old man who didn't know what he believed himself anymore?

"So," Jake said, "how are things at the paper?"

"Okay, I guess," Lonnie said.

"You gettin' it out every week?"

"Yessir. Pa's learning how to run the Linotype machine. He's getting so he don't make so many mistakes. Francine is doing the ads and most of the writing and keeping the books."

"And you?"

Lonnie shuffled his feet. "I'm just helping out. They've got a printer. His name's Holladay. He's kind of fussy, don't like nobody messing with the type cases, but I showed him I could hand-set and he's letting me do some of that now. And I run the folder on Wednesday afternoons. I guess I'm not much help, really."

"And Francine's doing the writing."

"Yessir. And Pa, too. He covered the Town Council meeting this week."

"My God," Jake said softly.

"When are you coming back?" Lonnie asked.

Jake waited a long time before he said, "I don't rightly know that I am."

"What?"

"Sounds like you-all have got things under control down there," Jake said, and when he said it, he thought for a moment that he didn't give a damn about it anymore. He had put forty-six years of his life into that goddamn newspaper, tried to speak a little truth, tried to do what a good newspaper was supposed to do—keep things stirred up enough so that fools would have to stop and think for a moment before they went on being fools. But now he was old and worn out. And they didn't need him.

'Yes sir," he went on, "sounds like you've got things covered just fine. If you can write a newspaper and print a newspaper, then that's about all there is to be done. That's pretty much the be-all and end-all of putting out a newspaper. You don't have to get fancy about it. Just write it and print it. Sell some ads, cover some meetings, throw in a little society claptrap and some births and deaths, then print it and take it to the post office. That's newspapering, all right."

Lonnie stared at him, mouth open. "But that's what *you* do."

"*Did*," Jake corrected. "I haven't *done* that for three months, and like you said, you-all are still getting out the newspaper."

"But it's your newspaper," Lonnie protested.

"Hah!" Jake laughed. "Don't seem like it."

"But don't you *care*?"

Jake waited awhile and caught his breath and calmed down before he answered. "It's not that," he said. "It's just that a man has to know when it's time to let go of things."

A moment of time hung suspended between them before Lonnie said softly, "Quitter."

"What?"

"You're a quitter. You're quitting on me now, just like you quit on me when the thing about the war memorial got hot and heavy. I wanted you to *fight* but you just quit."

"Now, you just wait a goddamn minute . . ." Jake exploded.

"Quitter!" Lonnie hissed it again. "I ain't been to see you these past weeks because I thought you were mad at me for messing things up and riding around with Pa on the fire truck and getting shot and getting you sick. I didn't come over here because I was afraid if I came you'd *die*!" His voice rose and tears sprung from his eyes and his fists clenched. "But I ain't coming to see you anymore because you're just a quitter! I counted on you!"

And he fled, leaving Jake stunned and speechless.

He was still sitting there with his jaw open when Pastine came in a few minutes later. "Ready?" she asked.

He looked stupidly at her. "For what?"

"The party," she said.

"What party?"

"Your birthday party, for goodness' sake." She looked him over for a moment. "Are you all right, Jake?"

"No," he shook his head, "I'm a worn-out old man."

"Did Lonnie come up here to see you?"

"Yes."

"Well? You look like you've seen a ghost."

"Maybe I have," he said.

"Did everything go all right?"

"No, it didn't."

"What happened?"

"He called me a quitter," Jake said.

"Ummmm," she said. That was all. Then she picked up his walking stick, resting against the wall next to the dresser, and handed it to him. "We'll be waiting for you downstairs," she said, and left him sitting there.

After a moment, he heaved himself to his feet, using the cane for leverage, and stood there by the bed. I won't go, he said to himself. I'll just stay here. I'll just get back into the bed . . .

But then he heard the rustle of bed covers beside him and he looked and saw Albertis Tibbetts there in the bed between the sheets, his face ashen behind the week-old stubble of beard, paper-thin eyelids closed. Jake's heart leaped into his throat and he moved, one shuffling foot in front of the other, panic-driven, until he was out of the room and in the hallway. He stopped at the head of the stairs, chest heaving with exertion and fright. He could see feet down at the bottom of the stairs, people waiting for him. I can't go any farther, he thought, and then he heard the shuffle of ancient footsteps behind him and he lurched forward and started down the stairs, holding onto the railing with his good hand and propping himself on the walking stick with the other. One step at a time. Shuffle, clomp. Shuffle, clomp. He could feel Albertis's eyes on his back, looking down at him from the top of the stairs, waiting for him to topple forward and spill his brains on the landing below. Halfway down, he teetered for a terrible second, then steadied himself, feeling his bowels lurch and praying fervently he would not lose control and shame himself with the foul excretion of his ruined body running down his legs. Shuffle, clomp. Shuffle, clomp. The noise of his laboring breath wild and thunderous in his ears, crowding out all sound. He feared for his heart, his bowels, his legs, his soul. He must stop, rest. But he couldn't, not with Albertis's dead eyes boring into his back. Sweet Jesus, sweet Jesus, sweet Jesus, he thought over and over, knowing as the cadence of it echoed through his brain how stupid it was for him, of all people, to call out "Sweet Jesus."

Then, suddenly, he was at the bottom and there was a great empty silence around him, the kind that had been his place of abode in those first unmeasurable days after his stroke. He turned slowly, shifting the walking stick to his good hand, and looked back up the stairs. Albertis was gone. Albertis had never been there, had he. No, Albertis had always been there, always would be.

Jake straightened himself, smoothed the front of his shirt, and looked at them. Pastine, Rosh, Henry, Francine holding the baby. Lonnie, standing off to the side. All of them watching him. Then they applauded, all except Lonnie. "That was great, Jake," Francine said.

"Well, here's the birthday boy," Rosh said. "Many happy returns, Jake."

"The birthday boy," Jake mumbled. "Yeah, I'm the birthday boy." And then they all went into the parlor, where there was a coal fire going in the fireplace and in front of the fireplace a small table with the birthday cake on it—white with big red letters on the top that said HAPPY BIRTHDAY JAKE and a scattering of candles. There was a stack of small plates and napkins and forks next to the cake. Jake shuffled over to the wing-backed chair next to the table and sat down heavily, leaning his cane against the arm of the chair. The rest of them sat down, all except for Lonnie, who stood behind the couch where Francine and Henry sat.

Jake caught his breath and then he looked around at the rest of them and said, "Well, this is very nice. Very nice of all of you to come and help an old man celebrate his birthday." My God, he thought, this is incredibly awkward. He avoided looking at Henry. He had not seen Henry since . . .

"You're only as old as you think you are," Rosh said.

"Well," Jake said with a laugh, "I think I'm pretty dad-gummed old."

"But looking better all the time," Francine said. The baby gurgled on her lap, reaching up to grab at Francine's hair.

There was a long silence and then Jake said, "Lonnie tells me things are going well at the paper."

Nobody said anything for a moment and then Francine said, "We're getting it out."

Another long silence. "Ahem. And how's Billy doing, Rosh?" Jake asked.

"Just fine. He'll start school after Christmas. He's going to State. To study aeronautical engineering."

"What kind?"

"Aeronautical. Airplanes. He's going to design airplanes."

"Ah. Yes. I wanted to be an engineer one time, but that didn't work out." He nodded. "I think that was before we had airplanes."

The silence was even longer and deeper this time, a great cocoon of quiet that held them suspended inside. Finally, Rosh said, "How about a little something to toast the occasion?" He looked over at Pastine, who sat primly, hands in lap, in a stiff-backed chair near the sofa.

"Fine," Pastine said, and she and Rosh got up and went to the kitchen, leaving Jake and Francine and Henry and Lonnie and the baby there in the parlor. Nobody even attempted to make conversation. They all just stared at the floor, all except Lonnie, who stared at Jake until Jake could feel the top of his head burning. It seemed like an eternity before Rosh and Pastine came back, Pastine bearing a tray with crystal cups of red punch, Rosh carrying two cups that had a slightly different color. He handed Jake one of the cups while Pastine served the rest and sat down. Rosh towered over them, his great body filling the room, hand outstretched.

"I propose a toast," he said. "To my friend and fellow sufferer Jake Tibbetts, who on this day marks a milestone worthy of any good man. He has cut a wide path, and sometimes he has cut a fine figure. I salute him."

They all took a sip of their punch and Jake could taste the beautiful sweet tang of Lightnin' Jim's Best. Ah, sweet Jesus. Now that was something to say "Sweet Jesus" about. His first drink in three months. It burned all the way down. Godalmighty, it was good. He turned the cup and drained it completely, set the cup down on the table next to him, and smacked his lips, feeling the warmth of it flood his belly.

"Ahhhhhh . . . ," he said. "God bless you, Rosh."

"And now," Pastine said, "it's time to cut the cake." She rose from her chair and reached for the knife that lay next to the cake on the table.

"No," Jake said suddenly. "Let me."

She stopped, stared at him.

"It's my birthday," he said. "Let me cut the cake."

"Well, all right." She sat back down.

Jake pushed himself up with one hand on the arm of the wing-backed chair and stood wobbling for a moment until he got his balance.

"I . . . ahem . . . ," he cleared his throat. "I . . . ahem . . . have taken great pride all my life in being a stubborn fool and keeper of my own conscience, and now I am reaping the benefits. I have reached the age of great wisdom, surrounded by my friends and family," he swept the room with his arm, taking them all in, "and I bask today in your great warmth. Speaking of warmth, would someone care to light the candles?" He looked around at them, looked directly at Henry for the first time. Henry. Gaunt, hollow-eyed, a ghost. But clean-shaven, hair neatly trimmed, wearing a coat and tie today. Jake could not remember ever having seen Henry Finley Tibbetts in a coat and tie. He sat next to Francine on the sofa, looking terribly uncomfortable with the whole thing. But there, nevertheless. Next to Francine. And wearing a coat and tie, by God.

"Henry, would you light the candles?"

Henry jerked his head up. They looked into each other's eyes for a long time. Then he said, "Sure," and got up from the sofa, fished his Zippo lighter out of his pants pocket, and lit the candles one by one. His hand trembled a bit, but he got it done. There were ten of them. Then Henry closed the lighter with a snap, put it back in his pocket, and sat down.

Jake took a deep breath, leaned over and blew as hard as he could at the top of the cake. One of the candles went out, but the rest of them barely fluttered. He tried again and got one more candle.

"Lonnie," he said, looking up, "come over here and help this old windbag blow out the candles."

Lonnie gave him a sharp look, hesitated a moment, but then came around and stood next to the table.

"Now let's do it together," Jake said, and they both blew on the cake at once and all the candles went out, leaving little fingers of smoke curling up.

"Now you stand here and help me serve," Jake said. He picked up the knife from the table next to the cake, stared at it for a moment, put it back down.

Then in a twinkling, before any of them realized what he was doing, he reached up above the fireplace mantel to his right and lifted Captain Finley Tibbetts's sword off its hooks. He stuck the scabbard between his left arm and his rib cage, and using his body as a vise, he unsheathed the gleaming blade and let the scabbard fall with a clatter to the floor. He did it with a swift grace he would have thought impossible only a few seconds before. He thought fleetingly of Tunstall Renfroe, dashing to defend his women the day Billy Benefield's airplane landed on Partridge Road, a moment of pure truth and beauty.

And then, while they sat transfixed by the suddenness of it, he raised the blade and brought the sword down squarely on the top of the birthday cake. THHHH-WHOK! It exploded under the blow, sending fragments of cake and icing flying in all directions.

"Ta-DAH!" he bellowed, and then he raised the sword and brought it down again, this time at a slight angle—THHHH-WHOK!—launching a big chunk of the cake zooming off toward the doorway, where it landed with a splat on the hardwood floor. The plates on the table next to the cake fell smashing to the carpet and forks and napkins scattered everywhere.

"Sixty-five and not a gray hair on my ass!" he yelled.

"Holy shit," Lonnie said softly, leaping back from the table out of the reach of Jake's sword.

Pastine started to rise from her chair, but Jake brandished the sword in her direction. "SIT DOWN!" he commanded. "I'm the birthday boy, and by God, I'm running the birthday party!" She sat. "And," he thundered, turning to where Henry and Francine sat on the couch, staring open-mouthed at him, "I'm still the goddamned editor of the goddamned newspaper!" Emma Henrietta, sitting in Francine's lap, howled with fright and Francine clutched her against her chest.

He brought the sword up and whacked at the cake again.

THHHH-WHOK! "We'll all have a little cake"—THHHH-WHOK!—"and celebrate the return of the editor." He looked over at Rosh, who was sitting speechless for once, eyes wide. "And you can tell those fools on the Town Council"—THHHH-WHOK!—"that if they think I'm through fighting over the war memorial, they can think again!" Pieces of cake and icing filled the air like the first snow of winter.

Then he stopped. The fire went out of him as quickly and magically as it had come and the sword felt incredibly heavy in his hands. He stared bug-eyed at each of them in turn, at the ruined cake, the deep slashes on the wooden top of the table, broken plates on the floor, napkins and forks scattered about. He thought then of old Captain Finley, standing here in this very parlor a millennium ago, slashing with this very sword at the brocade of the sofa, the same sofa where Henry and Francine now sat, dispatching whatever beast had leaped and grabbed him by the throat. There was one big difference, though. Captain Finley Tibbetts had died fighting. Jake Tibbetts—what was left of him—had to stay and face the music.

Jake breathed a great sigh and then he collapsed backward into the chair, holding the sword limply between his legs. The rest of them just sat there and stared, unable to take their eyes off him. Oh my, he thought to himself, I have pissed into the wind again.

It was Henry, finally, who got up and came to him. He knelt by the wing-backed chair, and took the sword gently from Jake's grasp. He took a handkerchief out of his coat pocket, carefully wiped the cake crumbs and icing off the sword, and laid it across Jake's lap.

"Henry," Jake rasped, "I don't know what the hell I'm going to do with you."

"You never did," Henry said. Henry had tiny flecks of cake icing on his face, and Jake thought of ice, of the snows deep in the forests of Belgium, of Henry lying there for days under the shattered tank, freezing to death, with dead and dying men all around him.

"I'm an old sonofabitch," Jake said.

Henry nodded. "That's true."

"And you are what you are."

"Yes," Henry said, "that too."

"I suppose we're both too old to change."

"Probably."

Jake looked at Lonnie then, standing back from them, frightened by what he had seen. "Come here, boy," Jake said.

Lonnie hesitated, then he stepped around the table and stood next to Henry by Jake's chair, frail boy and two frail men. It seemed for an instant that only the three of them were in the room—he and Henry and Lonnie—and that the rest had left, scared away by the beast or beasts that stalked the souls of the Tibbetts men. The sword was leaden in his hands, but he lifted it up and held it out to Lonnie. "Here," he said, "you take it."

And he did, grasping it by the handle, reaching down to pick up the scabbard from the floor, sheathing the sword again and holding it, looking at his grandfather without speaking.

Jake looked at Pastine then and saw what was in her eyes. *Don't try to fool yourself or us, Jake. The question is, Have you learned anything?*

And then to Rosh, great gentle Rosh, who wore a bemused expression, and also spoke with his eyes. *Do you yet believe what you say?*

Jake wanted to say to them both, "I don't know." And he wanted to speak to them both of all there was to be mended. But there would be time enough for that, if he could keep his devils at bay for a little while longer. Instead, he said, "I think I'd like to go to the newspaper now."

"Can I give you a ride?" Rosh asked.

"Yes, that would be nice."

The newspaper. And once there, perhaps Rosh would fetch a pint jar of Lightnin' Jim's Best and they would sit in their old familiar places while the dusk fell and ponder all the questions, spinning them out like silken threads to shimmer in the last glow of day. Perhaps in good time Rosh would fold his hands across his belly and say, "And at the bottom of it . . ." And there you would have it. Or perhaps there was no bottom, only the questions, like echoes.

Ah, Jake Tibbetts thought, we are all pilgrim souls here, all ragged-ass wayfarers, stopping to huddle against the cold and dark around what we call our home fires.

Does a man indeed learn anything? Only that his home is his own heart, and there he must abide.

About the Author

ROBERT INMAN, an Alabama native and University of Alabama graduate, now lives in Charlotte, North Carolina, where he works as a newscaster.

TA-141